Fa

Chapter 1

Amy put her Kindle down, sat back against her headboard and let out a breath.

"Oh my God," she said to the empty room. "That was *awesome!*"

That was Jillian Ashley's latest lesfic novel, *Rego Park Romance*, book four of her best-selling *Gotham Lesbians* series, a collection of wlw romances about the intersecting lives of a group of New York City lesbians. Each book takes place primarily in one of New York's five boroughs and this one took place in Queens. It featured two rival softball players whose teams meet for the city championship, played at a local ballfield in the titular neighborhood. It was one of Amy's favorite tropes: enemies to lovers, and it delivered big-time. All of Jillian's books delivered, quite frankly. Jillian Ashley was Amy's favorite lesfic author—hell, Jillian Ashley was practically every gay woman's favorite lesfic author—and each new release filled Amy with excitement and anticipation. *Rego Park Romance* was close to her best work yet, topped only by *Fordham Road Fling*, the series' Bronx-based novel. Not only were the characters well-developed and the pacing good, but the sex scenes were out-of-this-world hot. In fact, Amy's center was still reacting to the last sex scene in the book, about ten pages from the end. Amy was certain she hadn't blinked once while reading it and she knew she'd have to take care of the throbbing between her legs if she wanted any hope of getting to sleep tonight. Such was the danger of reading a Jillian Ashley novel this close to bedtime.

However, that could wait—though not for long, she knew.

Managing to ignore her arousal, she reached over and picked up her MacBook from the nightstand, placing it on her lap. She took a brief glance at her bedside clock. It was only just past nine p.m.; still early. Her alarm would wake her up for work at seven the next morning. As long as she was asleep by ten, no later than eleven, she'd be fine. Midnight tops.

She opened her website in edit mode and began editing her blog, *Lesbeing*, first, hammering out a glowing review of *Rego Park Romance*, being sure to also link the review to a written interview Jillian had agreed to do for Amy last year after the third book in the

Gotham series was released. For that interview, Amy had emailed Jillian the questions and Jillian had sent back her written responses.

Naturally, Amy had wanted to conduct that interview over the phone but Jillian had begged off, writing that she was painfully shy and would probably come off sounding like an idiot or something. Disappointed, Amy had nonetheless understood. She knew that a lot of writers were introverted and shy and she certainly didn't want to ask Jillian to do anything that would make the author uncomfortable.

But since the release of that book and this one, Amy had branched out into podcasting. *Lesbeing—the Podcast,* had just released its twenty-fourth episode, a discussion with a professor of Lesbian Studies at UCLA about the changing representations of women in contemporary cinema. Previous episodes had included topics ranging from lesbian sex tips to real-life examples of common lesfic tropes. She had also produced several episodes featuring interviews with some of the top lesfic authors in the world, women who were always more than happy to discuss their work and the world of lesfic in general.

Except Jillian Ashley.

"Jillian's the holy grail, apparently," Susan Lyons-Dell, another popular lesfic author, had told Amy just before their podcast interview began several months ago. "You're not the only one with a podcast who's tried to get her on their show, but Jillian turns them all down. Don't know why. I mean, any publicity is good publicity, right?"

Susan had even added that perhaps *not* appearing on podcasts was part of Jillian's marketing strategy. After all, the reclusiveness of Jillian Ashley was actually a popular topic in the lesfic community, Susan had pointed out.

Sitting on her bed now, Amy sucked her bottom lip between her teeth and thought for a moment.

She wanted to do something special for the twenty-fifth episode of *Lesbeing—the Podcast.* It was a milestone—a quarter of the way to one-hundred!—and should be celebrated by having a truly special guest on. Jillian Ashley would be such a special guest, and, damn it, Amy was going to have her even if she had to beg.

She picked up her Kindle again and paged ahead to the *About the Author* page at the end of *Rego Park Romance.*

Her eyes went first to the photo, which, unlike a typical author's photo, did not show the smiling face of the woman whose book you just finished. Instead, it showed a taken-from-behind shot of a shapely brunette woman on the beach, looking out at the sea. Even from behind, the woman seemed young and she was certainly very fit. But completely anonymous.

Amy already had Jillian's bio memorized—an easy task given how it only contained one line and that she used the same bio for all of her books.

Jillian Ashley lives in sunny Oceanside, California.

Oceanside.

The next town north from Carlsbad.

A town so close to Amy's apartment that she could actually walk to it.

That fact had always somewhat excited Amy. One of her favorite daydreams was imagining encountering Jillian in a meet-cute fashion somewhere and the author falling madly in lust with her. They'd end up back at Jillian's place, not able to get their clothes off fast enough; then, in the bedroom, Amy would push Jillian down on the bed, totally top her, look into her eyes and say, "Chapter 25 in *The Fordham Road Fling*. Do that to me!"

Putting the Kindle down again, Amy opened her Gmail account. Tomorrow was Friday and should be an easy day. The North County Women's Rights Group, the non-profit Amy was assistant director of, usually wasn't terribly busy on Fridays; ergo, Amy felt like she could do with less sleep tonight. Which was good, because she planned on spending however long it took crafting the most perfect email to Jillian Ashley, trying to convince the author to be a guest on her podcast. As long as she was asleep by midnight. One o'clock, tops.

After that, seriously, she really needed to take care of what was happening between her legs.

Chapter 2

Sally put her Kindle down and stretched out on her sofa, easing the muscles in her long legs because she had been sitting still for a while.

"Awesome!" she exclaimed to the ceiling of her one-bedroom condo.

She had just finished Jillian Ashley's newest lesfic book, *Rego Park Romance* and, as usual, she absolutely wanted more. Seriously, why couldn't the woman write faster? Sally knew of lesfic authors who practically churned out a new book every month. Granted, they weren't very good and the writing proficiency was somewhere around the grade-school level, but still...

No, no...Jillian Ashley was an artist, Sally reminded herself now, and artists take time to craft quality work. Sally would have to be fine with waiting the few months it might take Jillian to put out the final book in the *Gotham Lesbians* series.

But, seriously, Jillian couldn't write just a *little* faster? She made a note to ask her that—jokingly—on Twitter. Jillian was one of several lesfic authors Sally followed on that platform and Sally wasn't above doing a little fangirling every time she finished one of Jillian's books, sending Jillian a DM to say how much she enjoyed it. Sometimes, Jillian even responded, just to say thanks for her kind words, which always made Sally super excited.

Sitting up, she poured herself another glass of wine and then pulled her black hair into a ponytail. It was Friday night and so a little wine headache tomorrow wouldn't matter.

Just as she was about to take a sip, her phone rang. It was her bestie, Lisa.

"Did you finish it?" Lisa asked in lieu of hello.

"I did! Did you?"

"I did!"

Both women then squealed.

Whenever a new Jillian Ashley was released, Sally and Lisa always read it together, calling or texting each other along the journey with comments about the book.

"Oh my god! That last sex scene!" Lisa exclaimed.

"I know, right!" Sally agreed. "Like, thanks for making me need to change my underwear, Jillian!"

Both women broke into fits of laughter. Lisa and her had known each other since the fifth-grade and had been best friends ever since, that's why she felt fine admitting how aroused she had gotten reading the book's final hot passages.

"And I know Jillian always delivers with the happy endings," Lisa said, "but fuck she had me thinking they were really going to break up."

"She's so good at that!" Sally added. "But she also knows if she doesn't give us an HEA, her fans will hunt her down and slay her."

"God, I can't believe she lives in Oceanside," Lisa said after a moment. "Like, literally, the next town over."

"I know! Like, can we stalk her somehow?"

"Probably if we knew her real name," Lisa mused. "But you just know that Jillian Ashley is a pen name. I mean, it totally sounds made up."

"Totally," Sally agreed.

"Unless…"

"Unless what?"

"Unless her name really *is* Jillian Ashley and she knows how made up that sounds and so she just assumes people will think it's a pen name and so would never bother trying to look for her under her real name which sounds like a pen name."

That made sense to Sally.

"Yes, it's genius!"

"So, how do we find out, like, where she lives and where she hangs out?"

Sally laughed.

"Wow! You want to do, like, *real* stalking!"

"Not creeper stalking! Just, you know, *accidentally* bump into her at her favorite coffeeshop or something. We can systematically visit each and every café in Oceanside! How many can there be?"

"Stand in line behind her at Starbucks," Sally suggested, picking up the thread, "and when she gives her name to the cashier, say something like, 'Oh my God, what a coincidence! Our favorite writer is named Jillian! Jillian Ashley!'"

"Right! And then she'll say, 'But I'm Jillian Ashley.'"

"Right! And then we'll say, 'No way! Oh my God, we're huge fans!'"

"Right! And then she'll say, 'Thank you! That means so much! And you two are super cute!"

"Right! And then we'll all sit and have our coffees together and then end up back at her place for a threesome!"

"Exactly!" Lisa exclaimed. "I mean, I'd rather just have her to myself but you're my BFF, so I can share."

The two of them broke into fits of laughter again.

"So, what kind of coffee do you think Jillian orders?" Lisa asked.

Sally thought a moment.

"Hmm…I think she's a caramel latte girl," she decided.

"I get the caramel," Lisa said, "but I think she's a mocha chick. Like with whipped cream with the caramel drizzled on top."

"And chocolate shavings."

"Yes, good one! And I bet she adds a shot of espresso."

Sally nodded.

"Ooh, yeah! She needs that extra caffeine for all those late-night writing sessions. And I bet her sex life is off the charts! I mean, she's the woman who wrote Chapter 25."

"God, yes," Lisa groaned. "Anyway, her sex life *has* to be better than mine. I've never had a dry spell like this, Sal!"

"Preaching to the choir," Sally replied with a deep sigh. When *was* the last time she had sex? It would have been Orla, which means…*before Thanksgiving?* It was April now!

"I'm doing the same thing," Lisa said after Sally had been quiet for a few moments. "Figuring out how long it's been."

Sally laughed.

"I don't understand," she then whined. "We're hot! Why are we not having sex, like, every night?"

It really did confuse her. Sally knew she was a desirable woman: lithe and long-legged, she had a runway model's height of five-ten, with the physique and looks to match. Growing up, she had even been encouraged by many to explore modeling as a career but her natural shyness made the idea of showing up for cattle call auditions nauseating. She was much happier as a graphic designer.

And Lisa was flat-out gorgeous as well. Not nearly as tall as Sally, she was curvier and had an exotic beauty created by a Chinese mother and a Native-American father.

How they both didn't have girlfriends now was a mystery.

"Anyway, I'm not going to dwell on it," Lisa sighed. "Otherwise, I'll reach for the tequila and you know that never leads to good things. Listen, I gotta go…I promised Mom I'd come over to watch the new season of *American Horror Story* with her."

"Fun," Sally said, though it sounded anything but. She had never taken to that show personally. She and Lisa promised to speak tomorrow and ended the call.

No sooner had she put her phone back down on the sofa cushion when it rang again. This time, it was her best *male* friend, Max.

"Hey, babe!" she greeted enthusiastically. She always loved hearing from Max.

She heard him sigh deeply.

"How many times do I have to tell you?" he said. "Having a lesbian call me 'babe' is weird. Cut it out."

"Sorry, babe!" Sally replied, knowing he could hear the huge smile on her face in her voice.

Max sighed again.

"God, you are such a child sometimes," he murmured.

"Well, compared to you, I am," she rejoined before adding, "Babe."

Last month she had helped Max celebrate his fifty-first birthday. That had been three weeks after he had helped her celebrate her twenty-eighth.

"So, what's up?" she asked.

"What are you doing tomorrow?" Max inquired.

"Um…nothing. Which means I'm all yours."

"Excellent. I'd like to buy you lunch, talk about something."

Sally felt alarmed. The last time someone Max's age had told her that he needed to talk to her about something, it was her Dad because her grandmother had died.

"Is everything okay?" she asked.

"Everything is fine. No one died and I just had a physical last week during which my doctor declared me immortal. So, stop panicking."

"Okay, okay. So, are you going to give me a hint what this is about…?"

Max paused. Finally, he said, "Look, I'd rather just do it tomorrow, alright? Much simpler."

Max then told her he had to leave to run some errands and that he would text her tomorrow morning and they could decide on lunch plans.

After the call ended, Sally tried to figure out how to spend the rest of her girlfriend-less night.

Chapter 3

On Saturday morning, Amy was with her best friend Rachel, waiting in line at their favorite coffeeshop, La Vida Mocha. It was a chilly morning and so Amy, born and bred in Southern California, was dressed in her winter jacket, a slouchy beanie hat and black fleece-lined leggings covering legs that would normally be bare because of the casual flare dress she was wearing. Rachel, on the other hand, a transplant from New England who had met Amy freshman year at UCLA, was dressed as if it was the middle of summer in a fitted tee and nothing warmer than skinny jeans on her legs.

"Hey, Amy!" Vanessa, the owner of La Vida Mocha greeted her when it was their turn to order.

Amy smiled wide behind her mask.

"Hi, Vanessa," she gushed like a teenager. She always gushed like a teenager when she got to speak to Vanessa. Vanessa was every lesbian's dream. Even straight women went weak at the knees looking at Vanessa, Amy was sure. How could they not? For the longest time, Amy had harbored fantasies of somehow ending up with the stunning coffeeshop owner but those never came to pass and now Vanessa was engaged to Megan, some bigshot I.T. exec who also owned the art gallery next door to La Vida Mocha.

"My usual, please, and also a caramel latte," Amy ordered for her and Rachel. Whenever they went out for coffee together they took turns buying and today was her turn.

"Coming up," Vanessa said, punching in the order on the POS and taking Amy's debit card. She then turned to Chloë, one of her assistants, behind her. "A caramel latte, please, Chloë, and Amy's usual." Turning back to Amy, she asked, "Are you staying to work on your blog?"

"No, not today," Amy answered her. "We're just going for a walk."

"Hey, I meant to tell you," Vanessa began after handing Amy back the card, "I really enjoyed that podcast episode you did with Patty Conroy; I think two episodes back? She's one of my favorite writers."

Amy smiled again behind her mask.

"Oh, thank you! Yeah, I love her. And she was so super nice!" She paused a second. "Have you ever read anything by Jillian Ashley?"

Vanessa gave her an *Are you kidding?* look.

"She's amazing!" she said. "Like, my *favorite* writer. No offense to Patty. I know Jillian just released a new book but I haven't gotten around to reading it yet."

"It'll blow your mind," Amy insisted. "I just finished it and—" Amy used her hands to indicate the apparent explosiveness her mind underwent. "I'm hoping to get her on the show."

"God, I hope you do! You're so good at interviewing!"

Amy looked down, blushing. She couldn't help it. Vanessa had that effect on her. Praise from her was like praise from a goddess.

In a few minutes, Amy and Rachel had their coffees in hand and left La Vida Mocha, heading west on Grand Avenue, towards the beach.

Rachel nudged Amy as they walked.

"Like I always say," she began, "Vanessa really likes talking to you."

Amy nudged her friend back.

"Quit! She's just super friendly with all the regulars."

"And yet she barely glanced in my direction," Rachel said, taking a sip of her coffee.

"That's probably because you put off this incredibly strong 'I'm straight and only like dick' vibe. Anyway, Vanessa is happily engaged to Megan."

"Oh, come on, bestie," Rachel said. "Like if Vanessa threw herself at you, you wouldn't take her up on that?"

Amy's mouth dropped open in indignation.

"I happen to have scruples, Rach! Give me some credit!"

The two women walked on for a few more steps.

"God, who am I kidding?" Amy suddenly exclaimed. "I would totally do Vanessa! And I would let Vanessa do *anything* she wanted with me! Even if she was married to Megan. Even if she and Megan were the poster women for lesbian marriage!" She took a somewhat frustrated sip of her coffee. "Fuck, I need a girlfriend!"

"No luck online, then?"

Amy sighed. Luck? She had no idea what that was anymore when it came to women. Twenty-seven-years-old and the last time she had a girlfriend for more than six months was two years ago. Okay, fine…she *was* something of a workaholic. But being assistant director of an organization whose purpose for existing is to help vulnerable women meant that Amy often worked long hours and sometimes even took work home. She was simply that committed to the cause. And, okay, fine…the blog and the podcast both sucked up a lot of time as well. Nonetheless, Amy never felt as if she had made herself so busy as to completely wall off any possibility of romance.

"I mean, I'm an attractive woman, right?" she asked Rachel.

"Well, speaking from the I'm-straight-and-I-only-like-dick perspective, yeah, you're super pretty."

"Then why am I single?" Amy exclaimed, throwing up her hands, careful not to splash her coffee from its to-go cup. "And why do only crazy women hit me up on Zoosk?" Amy inquired. They had reached the corner of Grand and Carlsbad Boulevard, waiting for the light to change, and while they did, Amy regaled Rachel with the story of the woman she had been chatting with on Zoosk. Everything seemed fine, until they met for drinks this past Tuesday.

"At least ten years older than all her profile pictures," Amy said. "Which, okay, I was willing to let slide because A: it was obviously still her, and B: she's still attractive. But then she spent the whole date talking about cute *guys*."

Amy made a face but then a thought came to her.

Podcast idea: fake lesbians on dating sites.

"I take it talking about cute guys is something lesbians don't do much?" Rachel asked.

"Um, hardly *ever*!" Amy muttered.

"Don't worry, Aims," Rachel said. "There's somebody out there for you. Somebody who actually likes women and will spend the entire date talking about how cute *you* are."

The light changed and they crossed the wide expanse of Carlsbad Boulevard, one of the main thoroughfares of the town. On the other side, they continued west. They were now only a couple of blocks from the stairs that would lead them down to the beach and they could hear the ocean's surf getting louder with each step.

"So, who is this writer you and Vanessa were chatting about getting on your podcast?" Rachel asked.

Amy smiled reflexively. Last night, she had re-read that final sex scene in *Rego Park Romance* almost out of compulsion, it was that good; and the memory of the orgasms she then gave herself afterwards were still fresh in her mind. Not that she would tell Rachel that.

"Jillian Ashley," she began instead. "No shit, my favorite writer. Problem is, she's this super reclusive person. She doesn't post pictures of herself or her personal life on Twitter and she refuses to do interviews except by email." Amy raised her right arm in a gesture of defiance as she walked. "But she will be mine! I am determined to convince her to come on my show!"

Amy thought about the email she had written on Thursday night. It had kept her up well past her normal bedtime but she hadn't cared. The email *had* to be perfect and, in the end, after numerous drafts, she felt she had finally sent off a message that was an appropriate mix of fawning admiration for Jillian's amazing talents and down-on-her-knees fangirl begging.

As of yet, Amy still had not heard back from Jillian. Earlier today, her phone had chimed with an email notification and Amy had almost dropped the device on the Mexican tile floor of her kitchen in her haste to pick it up, praying it was a response from Jillian. No luck. It was only her grandmother in Wichita sharing pictures of gingersnap cookies she had just baked.

That's what Instagram is for, grandma, Amy had thought.

"Maybe I'll read one of her books, then," Rachel said. "I just finished a good mystery and could use something new."

By now, they had reached the stairs which led down from Ocean Street to the beach and were walking down them. Amy laughed at Rachel's statement.

"What?" Rachel asked.

"It's lesfic, Rach," Amy said.

"So? Are straight women not allowed to read lesfic? Is there a permission setting on my Kindle which will block me from downloading books about gay women?"

"Have you ever read any lesfic, Rach?"

Rachel rolled her eyes.

"No, but how much different can they be from any other books?" she asked. "Instead of boy meets girl, it's girl meets girl.

Instead of two male cops solving crimes, it's two female cops solving crimes. I get it…the books all have women."

Amy smirked.

"You know what? Go for it! Find Jillian's books on Amazon. You might as well start with the best of the lesfic writers. I will be *so* interested in learning what you think."

Chapter 4

Sally arrived at The Fisherman, a seafood restaurant in Carlsbad close to the beach, to find Max already waiting for her. That wasn't a surprise; Max was never late for anything. It was his superpower. He had once told her it was a product of his New York City upbringing and since he had become a big part of her life, Sally had discovered that his influence had rubbed off on her, making her more time-conscious and less prone to what used to be a habit of always running late.

Sally had first met Max back when she was still in college. Back then he was the director of a division of one of Southern California's biggest graphic design firms and Sally had been hired as an intern during her senior year, working as his apprentice and assistant. Max was someone she had quickly developed a strong admiration for upon joining the firm because his skills and talent as an artist amazed her. However, it always seemed to her that Max merely tolerated her presence, never actually wanting her around. In fact, she was certain that he hadn't bothered learning her name until three months into her tenure there when she overheard someone remind him discreetly that her name was Sally, not Samantha. When the internship ended, Max hadn't even come to the going-away party the rest of the division threw for her.

So, it came as a huge surprise to her when, two days before she graduated from San Diego State, Max himself called her to offer her a job with his team, telling her that he saw such talent and potential in her that he'd be a fool to let her go work somewhere else.

When Max eventually became president of a new division of the firm that was to handle more high-profile projects for big multinational brands, Sally was one of the few people he handpicked to join him, promoting her to lead artist in the process.

Somehow, they became close friends: The middle-aged guy from New York City; and the millennial lesbian from Carlsbad. Sally had known then that if Max had had his way, he probably would happily not be bothered with her outside of the office and would still be calling her Samantha; but Sally had felt he needed her in his life, and wormed her way in until now, they saw each other at least twice a week, even with the pandemic.

A year ago, Max abruptly retired from the firm. He had told Sally that he had enough of a retirement nest egg accrued and that he had also recently come into some money. And that was that, he was gone from the office, leaving Sally feeling like a piece was missing from her daily life.

"Hey, babe!" Sally greeted Max when she arrived at the booth he had secured for them. California was pretty much open again now that everyone was eligible for vaccinations and getting them. She herself had just gotten her second shot last week. Sitting down, Sally noticed how Max discreetly checked his watch.

"I'm three minutes early," she told him, sticking out her tongue at him.

Max merely grunted. He was a slender man who always dressed well. Today, he was wearing jeans and a black fitted blazer over a white tee shirt. He had this silver fox thing going on, which Sally knew a lot of straight women—even straight women her age—found attractive. This was proven when their waitress, a pretty young thing who looked like she could be just starting college, materialized when Sally sat down. After taking Sally's order for coffee and refilling the cup Max already had, the waitress had looked at him, shyly hoping to catch his eye.

Damn, why do all the cute ones have to be straight?

When the waitress left to get Sally a mug of coffee, Sally leaned over the table a bit and whispered, "She wants you!"

Max, a perplexed frown on his face, asked, "What are you talking about? Who wants what?"

"The waitress," Sally continued in a whisper. "She's totally into you!"

Max looked over his shoulder at the waitress, who was several yards away at a coffee station. He then looked back at Sally like she was completely insane.

"God, she's, like, fourteen-years-old!" he hissed. "What kind of person do you think I am?"

Sally sat back in the booth and crossed her arms.

"I doubt she's fourteen-years-old, Max. Child labor laws and all that. She keeps looking over here at you! Besides, she's gorgeous and I hate that you're alone." She pouted for good effect, knowing it would irk him.

"Okay, fine, I'll ask her parents later if it's alright if she comes out to play," Max sniped. "Now, would you stop trying to fix me up with felonies?"

The waitress—her name tag read "Tiffany"—returned with a mug of coffee for Sally and asked if they were ready to order food. As Max gave his order, Sally had to stifle a laugh at how Tiffany was so clearly flirting with him. For his part, Max was either oblivious to it or choosing to ignore it. After ordering a salmon burger for herself, Sally said to Tiffany, "Excuse me, but you look *soooooo* super young! Do you mind if I ask how old you are?"

Tiffany smiled at the compliment.

"I'm twenty-three," she answered, stealing another glance at Max, who was glaring at Sally.

"Wow!" Sally exclaimed. "I have to start using whatever skin cream you use!"

Tiffany giggled.

"Stop! You look amazing! You're super pretty! And I wish I was as tall as you! You could be a model!"

"Aww, thanks!"

With a final smile at Max—not that he noticed because he was still glaring at Sally—Tiffany left the table to get their food order in.

"See?" Sally said. "Older than fourteen."

"Why am I friends with you again?" he asked.

"Because I'm adorable and I make you happy?"

"I'll give you adorable," Max began. "The happy bit has always been up for debate. Now, if you're done being silly, I need to talk to you about something important."

Sally rubbed her hands together.

"Ooh, finally I get to learn the great mystery of why we're here!"

Max pursed his lips and looked out the window. Sally knew from having worked closely with him that something big was on his mind and once again she felt a little afraid, certain that the big thing was medical related, despite what he had told her on the phone last night.

"I know you like reading," Max began. "Do you read any lesfic?"

What the fuck? Curveball!

Sally chuckled.

"Lesfic, Max? I'm, like, totally surprised you even know that term!" She took a sip of her coffee. "Next you'll be telling me you know what 'wlw' stands for."

Max sighed.

"Women-loving-women, every idiot knows that."

"Yeah, every *lesbian* idiot," Sally countered. "I can't imagine it's that common a term in your heteronormative world."

"Just answer the damn question. Do you read any lesfic books or not?"

Sally nodded.

"Almost exclusively," she told him.

"Fine. I need your help with something," Max stated.

Sally nodded to indicate he should go on.

"Have you ever heard of a lesfic writer named Jillian Ashley?"

Sally's eyebrows shot up. Heard of her? That was like asking a baseball fan if they had ever heard of Babe Ruth.

"I just finished her latest book! It was amazing!" Sally stared at Max for several seconds. "Seriously, how do you know all of this? Lesfic? Jillian Ashley…?"

Max went back to looking out the window for a moment before eventually turning back to her, holding Sally's green eyes with his grey ones.

"I'm Jillian Ashley," he said.

Sally blinked.

It sounded like Max had spoken to her in English yet the words he had just said made absolutely no sense to her. Seriously, what was he talking about?

"What are you talking about?" Sally asked aloud. She felt as if her question should have been more profound, somehow. But the shock of what he had just said rendered her unable to come up with anything close to profound.

"I'm Jillian Ashley," Max repeated. "I wrote those books."

Sally squeezed her eyes shut and briskly shook her head.

This makes zero sense!

After taking a deep breath and then a fortifying sip of her coffee, Sally said, "Jillian Ashley is a woman. She lives in

Oceanside. She's a lesbian. She writes books for lesbians. Really, really good books."

"No, Jillian Ashley is a man—me, who, yes, does live in Oceanside. I'm not a lesbian but I do write books for lesbians and I'm glad you find them enjoyable." Turning to his left, Max reached into his familiar brown leather messenger bag, which Sally hadn't noticed was next to him on the seat. "Here, I'll prove it to you," he said, extracting his iPad Pro from the bag. After tapping the screen a few times, he held out the device towards her so she could read the screen.

Sally didn't quite know what she was looking at; there was a lot of information on the screen, but it seemed to be an Amazon-related site.

"What is this?" she asked.

"It's my KDP account," Max told her. "Kindle Direct Publishing," he added when it was clear Sally had no clue what KDP meant. "Every Kindle author has one. Now, look…" he pointed at the screen "…there's my name."

Sure enough, Sally saw "Max Tremont" where he indicated.

"And, look…" he pointed to another portion of the screen "…here are all the books I've published."

Sally saw a list of about eight books, all with Max's name as their author. But there were four additional books listed. All four written by an author Sally was very familiar with: Jillian Ashley.

"Jillian is just a pen name," Max explained. "She's made up."

Sally was feeling a little lightheaded. First, there was the fact that, by the evidence being shown her on Max's iPad, her favorite lesfic author, Jillian Ashley, didn't exist. Second, there was the fact that, wait a minute, Jillian Ashley actually *did* exist, just in the form of one of her best friends. Third, there was the fact that Max—a man she thought she knew at least fairly well—had a secret life as a writer.

Before she had a chance to construct further questions in her mind, Max tapped the screen again. Suddenly, Sally was seeing charts and dollar amounts.

Holy fuck!

The dollar amounts were impressive.

"And, see," Max continued, "the money from all of Jillian's books belongs to my KDP account. In fact, Jillian's books are really the only ones that actually earn me any money." He actually sounded a little sad about that. "I tried writing mysteries but those barely sold. Then I tried sci-fi and those also barely sold. I didn't hit it big until I became Jillian." He put the iPad down. "So, are you convinced?"

Sally had to take a moment before answering. Those dollar amounts were still swirling around in her head. Max was making *a lot* of money from Jillian Ashley books. In fact, if she had interpreted the chart that Max had just shown her briefly a few moments ago, even though Jillian's latest novel had come out only this past Tuesday, Max had already earned enough from it to not only pay Sally's rent but also her car payment.

"Why?" Sally finally asked. A one-word question that sounded childish to her ears but, really, what else was there to ask at this point?

The waitress brought their lunch. Fortunately, this time she didn't linger because another table needed her attention.

"I mean, did you do this to meet women?" Sally whispered.

Max leveled his best boss-glare at her.

"Yes, Sally, I became a best-selling lesfic author to meet *gay* women. This was all part of a brilliant but diabolical dating strategy I came up with."

Sally blushed. When he put it like that, it was a silly question.

"But why lesfic?" Sally asked, quite happy with herself because it sounded like a better question than her most recent one. "I mean, you're a man and, therefore—as you pointed out—not a lesbian."

Max sighed and took a bite of his kale salad with trout.

"You know how Amazon sends those emails each month with a list of free books you can read on Kindle?"

Sally nodded. She got the same emails and every now and then she'd find a new book to try from that list.

Max went on.

"Well, a while ago, one of the books listed was a lesbian romance—I forget which one. None of the other books interested me and so I downloaded that one and read it out of curiosity. Halfway through it, I started thinking, 'Hell, I could write a better book than this!' And so I did. When I was done, I published it on Kindle. I figured nothing would come of it. But the next thing I know, that stupid lesfic book I wrote was outselling all my other books combined."

"Stupid?" Sally asked indignantly. How dare Max call any of Jillian Ashley's books stupid! Where did he get off disparaging—

She gasped as she realized her mistake.

Son of a bitch!

"Anyway," Max went on, "I figured since that book sold so well, I'd write another one."

The Queens from Kings County, Sally considered. The second book in the series.

Max went on.

"Lo and behold, that one also sold really well and so then I wrote another one. The rest is history. Now I'm Jillian Ashley, one of the top lesfic writers in the universe."

Max sat back with his left arm on the back of the seat, looking patiently but expectantly at Sally, indicating he was done with his tale.

This was all so surreal to Sally. Jillian Ashley was important to her. During the depths of the Covid pandemic, reading and sometimes re-reading Jillian Ashley books had helped her deal with the enforced isolation because of the quarantine in California. Even now, with the quarantine long over and most Covid restrictions relaxed because of the distribution of the vaccine, Sally still often pulled up a Jillian Ashley novel to read even though by now she practically had the first three books memorized.

But that's what Jillian Ashley meant to her. Jillian Ashley was like comfort food to Sally—something she returned to when she just needed to feel centered and cozy and safe. The women in a Jillian Ashley novel were just like her. They weren't fabulously wealthy celebrities or ice-queen CEOs. They were gay women who had jobs and bills and cars which occasionally needed new fan belts and parents that drove them crazy. And because they were just like her, Sally always connected with them.

Now, she suddenly found herself sitting across from the woman who had created those characters. And the woman was a man.

"So, I don't get it," Sally began after taking a moment to compose her thoughts. "What do you need my help with?"

"Ah, yes," Max said, leaning forward again, holding Sally's eyes with his own. "The crux of the matter." He took a sip of coffee. "I need you to pretend to be Jillian Ashley."

Sally, who had just taken her own sip of coffee, nearly choked to death on it and spent a few embarrassing moments hacking like a cat about to upchuck a hairball. When she finally gained control again, red-faced, with tears streaming out of her eyes, she dabbed at her eyes with a napkin and said, "What are you talking about?"

"I got an email the other day from one of those pod people…"

"Pod people?" Sally interrupted.

"Yeah, you know, the ones with the podcasts. I don't know what the people who host those are called."

"Podcasters. Just podcasters."

"Alright, fine. Anyway, this *podcaster* contacted me—well, she contacted *Jillian*—begging Jillian to come on her show. Now, normally I'd say no—Jillian always says no to things like that, for obvious reasons—but now I feel she can't do that anymore. This whole Jillian Ashley thing has just gotten so big. I mean, do you have any idea how popular she is?"

"Yeah, Max, I do! I'm a lesbian!"

"Anyway, if Jillian doesn't start doing things like podcasts or YouTube interviews, people are going to start getting suspicious and might do some digging around, and so I need someone to pretend to be her."

Sally's eyebrows shot up.

"Max, I'm not an actress!"

"I know, that's perfect! If you were, you might come off as a fake."

"I *will* be a fake!"

"You don't have to worry about anything. During any interview you do, I will be there next to you telling you exactly what to say."

"How many will I have to do?" she asked.

Max shrugged.

"Who knows? Not a lot. I don't want to overexpose her. The reclusiveness thing works for her. I just need you to do enough of these interviews to get Jillian some face-time, show all her fans that there's a flesh and blood woman behind the books and then I can get her back to being a shadowy figure again."

Sally sat back and took a deep breath. She needed time to wrap her mind around all this.

"God, Max, it just sounds so deceitful…"

"I'll give you twenty percent of the royalties I earn from Jillian's books," Max stated.

Sally's mouth dropped open.

Whoa!

Sally busied herself with stirring more sugar into her already sweetened coffee while she attempted to appear cool, calm and collected.

"Um…well, I suppose that, um, a twenty percent cut sounds about right," she said, hoping her voice sounded normal.

Max nodded.

"Especially considering that I'm about three-quarters of the way through the next book in the series and you doing all of these Jillian interviews will go a long way towards drumming up the sales numbers once I release it…"

That was a good point, Sally considered. A good twenty-percent point.

"Um…yeah, I see the logic behind that," she said.

"So, we have a deal?" Max asked.

"Fine, we have a deal. Wait! On one condition!"

Max quirked an eyebrow, waiting.

"You let me get Tiffany's phone number for you and you call her for a date!"

Max stared at her.

"Who's Tiffany?" he asked.

Sally sighed.

"Our waitress."

Max winced.

"Oh, for fuck's sake, Sally! You're determined to send me to jail, aren't you?"

"She's twenty-three, you goof! Anyway, that's the offer. Deal?"

Sally held out her hand expectantly. A moment later, Max took it and shook.

"Deal," he grumbled.

Chapter 5

Later that afternoon, Amy was at home in her living room, sitting on her super comfy, incredibly-expensive-but-so-worth-it Italian leather sofa she bought last year, typing with her laptop on her lap. Even though it was only three p.m., she was already dressed in a favorite pair of flannel pajama pants and a cami top which clung to her small, round breasts. She had no plans to go out for the rest of the day. Her and Rachel had spent the morning walking the beach as far as the Oceanside pier and back—an easy 10,000-plus steps—and then had eaten lunch together at their favorite pizza spot. Now, she wanted to just be comfy and get some work done.

Amy was currently blogging about a lesfic novella she had started reading the day before and had just finished about an hour ago. It was not going to be a good review. She didn't normally like to tear down the works of lesfic authors, but this one had been particularly bad. One of the risks of the ease with which writers could get their books published on Amazon's Kindle was that a lot of really bad fiction was out there. And *At Lynette's Place* was terrible.

Putting aside the plot holes, one-dimensional characters and sex scenes that were damn near impossible—Scissoring on an exercise bike? Really? What were they, acrobats?—the writing was awful! Amy was certain her seven-year-old niece had a better grasp of writing the English language. The writer had also managed to hit virtually all of Amy's pet peeves, like using "of" when she meant "have"; "you're" instead of "your" and using the non-word *irregardless*. What's more, the author had trouble remembering that in some passages, there were two characters! During one sex scene, for instance, Lynette had not only kissed herself hungrily with lips tasting of strawberries but she had also sucked her own clit to a toe-curling orgasm.

If I could do that, I wouldn't be looking for a girlfriend.

So, Amy was now feeling like it was her duty to the lesbian community to make sure no gay woman ever read *At Lynette's Place*.

Her laptop pinged and a little notification window popped up. A new email had arrived. Clicking the notification, her Gmail account opened and when she saw who the email was from, Amy gasped and hurriedly took the laptop off her lap and placed it down on the coffee table as if the computer had suddenly become too hot to touch.

She sat super still on the sofa, her legs crossed, staring at the machine with wide eyes, hardly daring to breath.

The email was from Jillian Ashley.

The subject line read "Re: An Invitation."

Amy was too afraid to open the message. She got up, went to her kitchen, opened the fridge and pulled out a chilled bottle of white wine that she had first opened a couple of nights ago. Pouring herself a glassful, she went back in the living room and started drinking the wine while pacing in front of the laptop, occasionally looking at the screen where the email seemed to mock her, taunting her.

Jillian Ashley had replied to her message.

The Jillian Ashley had replied to her message.

The only question now was, what was the reply? Yes or no? All Amy had to do was click open the email to find out.

Instead, she called Rachel.

"What's up?" Rachel asked by way of greeting.

"She wrote back," Amy replied.

"Who wrote back?"

"Jillian Ashley! That writer I told you about! The one I want on my podcast!"

"Oh, yeah." Rachel paused. "Well, what did she say?"

"I don't know, I'm too afraid to open the email."

Amy heard Rachel sigh over the phone.

"Aims, just open the message!"

"What if she said no?"

"Tell you what, if she said no, I will hunt her down and kick her ass for you."

Amy sucked her teeth.

"Stop being silly!"

"Silly? I'm not the grown woman afraid to open an email! Now, go on...open the damn thing."

Amy knew Rachel was right. This was silly. After taking another fortifying sip of wine, she sat back down on the sofa. She put Rachel on speakerphone and then rested the device on the coffee table next to the laptop.

"Okay," she slowly told Rachel, "I am opening the message…"

"Okay," Rachel replied. "Be careful. Do not cut the green wire!"

Amy blinked.

"What?"

Rachel laughed.

"It just sounds like you're trying to defuse a bomb."

"Shut up! Okay, I'm opening it now."

Using her forefinger on the trackpad, Amy guided the cursor to the message and clicked it open, wincing as she did so, prepared to see bad news.

Hello, Amy!

Thank you so much for reaching out to me! I am super happy that you liked my latest book! Fans like you are so important to me!
Regarding your invitation to be on your podcast, I would love to!

The message continued but Amy didn't care.

"Oh my god, she said yes!" she squealed. "She fucking said yes!"

"Yay!" Rachel cheered from the phone.

"Holy fuck, I'm going to be interviewing Jillian Ashley! This is…This is un-fucking-believable!"

"Congratulations," Rachel said. "Can I go now? My Saturday just won't be complete without a nap."

After saying goodbye, Amy hung up and then sat back on the couch and let out a relieved breath.

Wow!

Now that the initial exuberance of Jillian's acceptance was out of her system, Amy read the rest of the email. It was mainly Jillian asking for details about the day and time for the interview, stipulating that it had to be in the late afternoon or evening because she was always busy during the early part of the day. She also asked about the technical requirements for participating in the podcast.

Amy pulled up her calendar. If it were up to her, this interview would be happening *today*, but she knew that was impossible. She thought about suggesting tomorrow, Sunday, but many people were often uptight about being disturbed on Sundays. Sunday was a family day. But wait...Did Jillian have a family? Was she married? Did she have kids? There was so much Amy didn't know about her favorite author. So, Sunday was out. But would Jillian also think that Monday was too soon? Amy didn't want to appear overeager even though she was, in fact, very overeager.

Tuesday?

Tuesday sounded right. It was far enough away that Jillian wouldn't feel hounded by Amy. It also gave the impression that Amy was a cool customer; like, "Oh, well, thanks for agreeing to be on my podcast but I think we can wait until Tuesday to get this done."

So, Tuesday.

But what time?

Jillian's email was frustratingly vague in this regard. "Late afternoon or evening" covered a lot of hours. Not only that, both of them were open to interpretation. What did Jillian consider *late* afternoon? Three o'clock? Four? And would Jillian prefer early evening or late evening? And when did early evening *become* late evening? Five o'clock? Six? And speaking of evening...when did Jillian usually have her dinner?

Shit!

Amy wanted at least an hour of actual interview time with Jillian. But before the actual interview could begin, there would need to be checks done to make sure Jillian had no trouble connecting to the podcast software; then of course they'd spend a few minutes introducing themselves and just chatting a bit before Amy hit *Record*. All told, she'd need about ninety minutes of Jillian's time.

After a quarter of an hour deliberating with herself, Amy finally settled on suggesting 4 p.m. to Jillian. She then spent another quarter of an hour composing the perfect reply to Jillian, one that was appropriately grateful but also *chill*, like, *Hey, this is no big deal, really.*

When she finally hit *Send*, Amy then sat back and looked at the screen, waiting anxiously for a reply before rolling her eyes at her own silliness. She was acting like a lovestruck teenage girl waiting for the girl she had a crush on to text her back. Besides, *the* Jillian Ashley probably received a bazillion email messages every day. Not only that, but Jillian was probably way too busy to be sitting around anxiously awaiting Amy's response.

Just as she was about to get up and refill her wine glass, though, the laptop pinged and Jillian's reply magically appeared in her Inbox. Amy didn't hesitate opening this one.

Tuesday at four is perfect!

Chapter 6

On Tuesday afternoon, after work, Sally took a deep breath before shutting off the engine of her BMW in Max's driveway. She wondered if what she was feeling now was how an actress feels when about to walk into an audition. Only, this wasn't an audition, she reminded herself. She *had* the part! All she had to do now was perform it.

She gave herself another look in the rearview mirror because for some reason Max had promised this Amy Whatever-her-name-is that this could be a *video* podcast episode.

"I really need Jillian to start being *seen*," Max had explained last night over the phone. "I've been keeping her hidden for too long. Any longer and my readers are gonna start rebelling."

Sally had understood. She had been following Jillian Ashley on Twitter since Jillian's first book was released. Frustratingly, Jillian had never tweeted a photo of herself. Her profile picture on Twitter was the same one used as her author photo in her books: an image of a dark-haired woman, seen from behind, looking out to sea. The various Jillian Ashley Twitter topics which Sally followed often contained tweets by others wondering what Jillian Ashley looked like and why she only consented to written interviews.

Max let her into his large, two-level house in Oceanside which was just a two-minute walk from the beach and which offered fantastic panoramic views of the Pacific Ocean from the upstairs picture windows. Upon entering, Sally immediately made for the floor-to-ceiling mirror Max had in the foyer and once again examined her appearance.

"Come on, you look fine," Max said, gently taking her elbow and leading her away from the mirror and deeper into his house. "We only have twenty minutes before Jillian is supposed to dial in and I need to explain the set-up."

After crossing his sunken living room, Max led Sally to his den, a room decorated in the art-deco style. Sally had always admired Max's sense of style. His entire house was tastefully decorated with artworks and stylish contemporary furnishings that were cosmopolitan but not overly masculine. There wasn't a sports poster or a picture of bikini-clad bimbo holding a bottle of Miller Lite to be found.

In the den, Sally saw that Max had added a large folding picnic table, the kind people use when they're hosting a backyard barbecue, and one folding chair. On the table were two Apple laptops. One of the laptops had a small external LED lighting rig attached to it.

"Okay," Max began, "Here's the deal." He pointed at one of the laptops. "I've got this computer talking to that one via Zoom." He pointed at the second machine, the one sitting in front of the folding chair. "*That* computer will be connected to Amy via some podcasting software we'll connect to when the time comes."

He went on.

During the podcast, every time Amy asked a question, Max would type the response he expected Sally to give, which she would read using the Zoom chat window.

"I've got the Zoom window perfectly positioned on the screen so that as you read from it, it will still look like you're speaking to the camera. So, whatever you do, don't fiddle around with it."

"Got it," Sally said, feeling her nervousness increase.

"I'll be sitting over here," Max said, indicating a leather club chair that had no chance of being seen by the webcam of the laptop Sally would be using. "Questions?"

Sally thought a moment.

"No," she said. "It seems pretty straightforward."

"Good. We got about fifteen minutes left. Wine?"

Sally nodded and then Max left. While he was gone, Sally sat down in front of the laptop. The webcam's preview window was open and she could see herself on the screen. She smiled because she looked rather good. The lighting thingamajig Max had installed filled in the shadows on her face and really brought out the color of her eyes as well.

"Hey, can I have this when we're done?" she asked when Max returned with two glasses of white wine. She pointed at the lighting device. "I want to use it at home for meetings at work."

Handing Sally her glass, Max shrugged.

"Take it," he said.

He sat down in the club chair. Sally turned to face him.

"So, I wanted to ask you something," she declared after sipping the wine, which was very good.

"Shoot."

"I follow Jillian Ashley on Twitter…"

Max raised his glass to her.

"And Jillian thanks you for that," he said.

"Anyway, how do you—a man—make her seem so like a real woman? I mean, I was so convinced that an actual woman writes her tweets."

Max scoffed.

"It's really not that hard. All I have to do is use a lot of OMGs and LOLs and stupid fucking heart-eyes emojis and, boom, everyone assumes you have a vagina."

Sally's mouth dropped open.

"Fuck you, that is so not true!"

But Max just looked at her for a moment and then picked up his iPhone. He tapped the screen a few times and then held the device out to her. Sally took it from him.

The screen showed their most recent text exchange, from this morning, when they were ironing out the details for her coming to his house to do the podcast. Sally's indignant anger from a moment ago turned into embarrassment when she realized that every single message of hers to him included at least one OMG or LOL—sometimes both, sometimes multiple instances—and that when she replied to his text telling her he'd buy her dinner after the podcast, she had done so with two—two!—heart-eyes emojis.

"Fuck you," she muttered, handing the phone back, just as an alarm on the phone started chiming.

Max got up, gathered his laptop and returned to the club chair.

"Show time in three minutes," he said, and suddenly Sally had to take a couple of deep breaths.

"Okay, OMG, what do I do, what do I do, what do I do?" Sally asked, flustered, but not flustered enough to not realize that she had said *OMG* instead of *Oh my God,* proving Max right.

"When I tell you, just click the green button on the bottom window."

"Green button, bottom window. Got it."

"And relax. You'll do fine. Just keep repeating to yourself, 'Twenty percent.' 'Twenty percent.'"

Right. Twenty percent. I got this. Twenty percent.

A few moments later, Max told her to click the green button.

***

The bottom window on the Apple's screen flashed a message: *Please wait while we connect you.* And then: *Connecting...*

Sally wished she had done another obsessive check on her appearance but it was too late now.

The window on the screen went dark for a brief second and was suddenly replaced by a live video image that made Sally's breath catch and her heart beat faster.

On the screen was an incredibly beautiful woman. She had milk-chocolate brown hair with honey-colored highlights, brown eyes and inviting lips glossed with pink. Sally thought that she looked to be about her own age.

This was the woman who was going to be interviewing her?
Fuck, how am I supposed to concentrate?

The woman, Amy, stared back at Sally for several moments, and Sally felt a twinge of anticipation. The look she was getting from the podcaster was doing very little to hide the desire in Amy's eyes.

Oh, God...

Finally, Amy cleared her throat.

"Um…Hi!" she greeted Sally. "Jillian, I'm Amy!"

Jillian? What? Oh, yeah...

"Hi, Amy!" Sally replied. "Jillian Ashley. Yep, that's me! So pleased to meet you."

"Oh my god, I cannot tell you how super excited I am that you agreed to be on my show! Thank you so much!"

Sally saw that Max had typed a reply in the Zoom window. Trying not to be obvious about it, she read it aloud.

"Well, I figured it was time to start really introducing myself to the lesfic community. They've been so supportive of my work! And you're the perfect person to help me do that because I'm a big fan of your blog."

I am? Blog? What blog?

Sally noticed Amy blushing and it was so fucking adorable.

Amy seemed at a loss for words for a bit.

"I...I am so honored that you've read my blog," she managed to get out. "I really had no idea someone as accomplished as you even knew about it."

Max provided the answer to that as well.

"I love it!" Sally recited. "You really have a lot of good insights into the whole being-a-lesbian-in-the-twenty-first-century thing, and your reviews of my books are amazing." Sally smiled widely then because it seemed that's what the situation called for.

Another blush appeared on Amy. The woman was just too adorable!

"Okay, well..." Amy said. "It looks like we're all set up with our...*connection*." As she said this, she stared at Sally with nothing less than fuck-me eyes. Sally sucked her bottom lip between her teeth and somehow managed to stop herself from groaning as this time she actually felt her clit pulse. "So, we can start whenever you're ready."

"Um..." Sally hesitated, pretending to scratch her ear so she could turn her head and steal a look at Max who gave her a nod. "Yeah, sure; let's do this!" she told Amy.

"Great! I'll start recording now."

Sally saw Amy self-consciously fluff her brown locks and then heard her clear her throat. She must have then clicked something because the podcast window on Sally's screen suddenly started flashing the word *Recording* in red, in the upper right-hand corner.

"Hi, everyone!" Amy started. "Welcome to another episode of Lesbeing—the Podcast! Yay! I'm your host, Amy Broadnax. Thank you for joining me! Today, for my twenty-fifth episode I am super excited because I have as my guest my favorite writer of lesbian romances, Jillian Ashley! And I know that she is a favorite of many of you as well! Jillian, welcome!"

Sally thought Amy was really good at this. She had a great voice, like a professional newscaster—trustworthy but not without sexiness—and even though the video only showed her from her sternum and up, she exuded an infectious energy and enthusiasm. So captivated was she by Amy that it took her a moment to remember that she was supposed to respond to Amy's official on-air greeting.

"Oh! Hi, Amy! Um…" Sally tried to remember what guests on things like this said at this point. Then it hit her. "Thanks for having me!"

"Thank you for coming," Amy replied, and Sally had to stifle a laugh as her mind went directly to imagining Amy, naked in Sally's bed, peering up at her from between Sally's legs, Sally's center still convulsing from a recently-induced orgasm, and Amy purring, "Thank you for coming."

"So, let's get started," Amy said. "You are a hard person to get an interview with, Jillian! I know many others have tried and failed so I don't mind admitting to feeling rather excited that you chose to finally come out into the open, as it were, on my show."

The Max-sanctioned response appeared almost immediately and Sally read it.

"Well, I'm just naturally shy, is all. Even as a little girl I hated school plays or recitals—anything where I'd be the center of attention. It's why I like writing. I can just keep to myself and not have to feel like there's a spotlight on me."

"I totally understand that," Amy said. "So, let's start off with some basics first. For example, when did you discover you had a talent for writing?"

"Oh, when I was in high school, actually," Sally read. "One of my English teachers had everyone in the class write a short story and so I did. When we got our stories back, the teacher had given mine top marks and just couldn't stop gushing about it. She then encouraged me to take an advanced writing class she taught and that's when I knew."

Sally wondered if Max had just related his own experience. She made a mental note to ask him about that later.

"And what made you start writing lesfic?" Amy then asked.

"Um…" she hesitated, buying time until Max transmitted the first sentences of her allowed response. "I have been a fan of lesfic novels for years! I can't even imagine my life without them! They have brought me so much joy and entertainment, and one day I thought to myself, 'Why not write one of your own?' And so I did and that's how the *Gotham* series was born."

"Let's talk about that for a moment," Amy said. "You live in Oceanside, California…"

No, I live in Carlsbad. Oh, she means Jillian!

"Right," Sally said.

"And I don't detect an accent of any kind…Are you originally from California?"

"Um…yeah; born and bred."

"But all of your books take place in New York City. What's the connection?"

Yeah, Max, what's the connection?

But she shouldn't have doubted her friend. Before Amy had even finished her question, Max must have known what she was leading up to because his fingers had started flying over his keyboard as Amy was still talking. The result was that Sally had Jillian's answer ready instantly.

"My Dad is from New York," Sally read. "The Bronx, in fact. And my family used to vacation there a lot when I was growing up. I love New York; it's such a great city! And when it came time to decide where I would set my lesfic story, I decided on New York because the city itself kind of becomes a character, you know? And I wanted the women in my story to be products of and reflections of all the urban drama and complications of the Big Apple."

"Awesome!" Amy replied, and Sally thought that, yes, it was awesome. Max's answer made Jillian Ashley, as played by Sally Lassiter, seem full of depth and insight.

She had to admit: She was having fun.

Chapter 7

Amy was now about forty-five minutes into her interview with *the* Jillian Ashley. It was hard for her to remain focused at times because no matter how much she paid attention to Jillian's answers; no matter how much she thought about what her next question to the writer should be or how to appropriately respond to something Jillian said, part of Amy's mind simply kept repeating the same thing over and over again.

Fuck, she's hot!

Because Jillian Ashley *was* hot!

The woman talking to Amy over the internet from Oceanside was every fantasy Amy ever had about Jillian come true! She thought about that favorite daydream of her, meeting Jillian serendipitously and then topping her in bed, saying, "Chapter 25 in *Fordham Road Fling.* Do that to me!" This time, it made Amy cross her legs because now that she could put a face to the daydream, the thought of acting out Chapter 25 with this woman was enough to make her center feel molten.

Earlier, when the podcast software had created the video link between her and Jillian and Jillian's face appeared on Amy's monitor, Amy's mouth had dropped open and all she could do was stare like an idiot at the gorgeous woman in Oceanside while her heart thudded in her chest. Fortunately, she had recovered quickly, but it still made her feel like a silly twelve-year-old girl spotting her celebrity crush in a restaurant.

But she had known from the bemused look on Jillian's face that she hadn't recovered quickly enough and had, in fact, conveyed her attraction to the writer. That had caused some momentary embarrassment, sure; however, Jillian hadn't seemed bothered. It wasn't as if she suddenly canceled the interview out of fear that Amy would be some kind of creepy stalker chick.

In fact…Amy was sure Jillian was attracted to her as well. A possibility that made Amy feel a little lightheaded and want to do her happy dance.

Checking the clock on her computer monitor, Amy knew she should start wrapping this interview up. Maybe two more questions. Three tops.

"So, how does it feel knowing about all the attention your novels garner? And what do you think about all the Jillian Ashley topics on Twitter and Facebook? Do you follow any of them?"

Jillian smiled.

"I do follow them! But not, like, obsessively or anything. I just like to take a peek every now and then to see what people are saying. Any writer who tells you differently is lying to you, by the way. The truth is, every writer wants to know that he—damn! I mean, *she*—has reached a certain group of people and is creating works that make those individuals happy. So, when I see positive things about my books, it's very humbling."

God, can this woman stop being so damn perfect?

Throughout the interview, Jillian had proven to Amy that she was smart, well-spoken, well-read, funny and insightful. Now she was displaying an appropriate dash of humility as well.

"Excellent answer," Amy complimented Jillian. And now Amy wanted to turn the conversation to a steamier topic. In her brief podcasting career, Amy had learned that lesfic authors loved to discuss the sex scenes in their books.

"So…" she began, "I know for a fact that there are countless women out there who want to learn the magic behind how your amazing sex scenes develop! So…how do you come up with those ideas? What's the Jillian Ashley process for approaching a steamy scene and then actually writing it?"

"Ah! Um…"

Amy was surprised that her guest seemed a little flustered, but it was also super cute.

"So, the sex scenes," Jillian started again. "They are a mixture of fantasy and real life, actually. Some of the scenes contain elements of things I've done with women—I'm not going to tell you which ones," she added with a laugh, "and others are simply made up. Let's face it, us humans think about sex *a lot,* and I don't mind admitting that I come up with my fair share of fun sexual scenarios on a daily basis. Some of them end up being so good I decide to write them in a novel."

I have some fun sexual scenarios in my head now that I'd like you to write about, Jillian…

Jillian. Amy thought of another question to ask.

"Do you mind telling us if Jillian Ashley is a pen name? Trust me, I won't ask your real name if it is."

Amy saw Jillian doing that scratching thing with her ear again. She wondered if it was a nervous tic or if the writer should schedule an appointment with her doctor.

"It is a pen name, yes," Jillian answered, but didn't elaborate.

Amy wrapped up the interview by getting Jillian to tell viewers that the next novel in the *Gotham* series takes place in Manhattan and that, with luck, it should be finished and released sometime before Independence Day.

Damn! Two or three months?

Amy then launched into her sign-off.

"And that concludes this episode of 'Lesbeing—the Podcast.' I would like to thank the fabulous Jillian Ashley for joining us today! Jillian, thanks so much!"

"It was a pleasure, Amy!" Jillian responded, that unbelievable smile of hers making Amy's center react.

"Until next time, everyone, this is Amy Broadnax reminding you to be safe, respect your fellow humans and for god's sake, get the vaccine or get a mask!"

She clicked the Stop button on her laptop, feeling incredibly excited.

Scoop!

She had just scored the first live interview with Jillian Ashley! And it was a video interview too! Double scoop! All the other lesfic podcasts out there could suck it!

She looked back to Jillian. She really, really did not want to say goodbye yet.

"So, really, Jillian, thank you so much!"

"I had fun. This was interesting."

"I'm glad you think so."

"So, what now?"

"Well, now I edit our recording. Don't worry, I won't edit it into making you look like a pro-Trump asshole."

"That would definitely put a crimp in my book sales."

Amy laughed.

"Right. Anyway, once I edit it, I'll release it. Would you like me to send you an email when I do that?"

"Please!"

Amy's mind was working furiously. They were at a natural stopping point now. She was sure Jillian was incredibly busy and as a good host, she should just let Jillian get back to her evening. But damn, she really didn't want to do that!

Just ask her already!

"Hey, listen," she started, "I'd really like to buy you coffee one day. Or a drink. As a thank you for appearing on my show. I'm live right next door in Carlsbad."

"Oh my God, I'd love that!" Jillian responded instantly, making Amy's heart soar. Amy thought she heard something fall in the background on Jillian's end. Jillian looked off to her side in surprise and then returned her focus to Amy. "Just the cat," Jillian said.

"Aww, I love cats! Anyway, um…coffee one day soon? I know the perfect place. How does Friday evening sound? I have a day job, so…"

Jillian laughed.

"I have a day job too, so I get it."

"Really? And here I was thinking your legions of Jillian Ashley fans supported you entirely."

"They do a good job of it, but my day job has a 401(k)," Jillian retorted.

"Ah, yes. So important to plan for the future," Amy said.

They agreed on a time for Friday and then, reluctantly, Amy said goodbye and terminated the connection. When Jillian's face disappeared from her monitor, Amy let out a deep breath.

"Oh my God!" she said aloud to no one. "Gorgeous!"

Chapter 8

"Coffee, Sally? Seriously?" Max was pacing in the den now. "You *had* to agree to meet for coffee?"

"What was I supposed to say when she asked?" Sally wondered, still feeling a buzz from Amy's obvious attraction to her and the subtle flirting with each other they had done during the interview.

"Oh, I don't know," Max began. "You're super busy, perhaps. You have a girlfriend. You're one of those bubble people who can't step outside. *Anything!*"

"Relax. It's only coffee; it's not going to turn into a TMZ exposé."

"A what?"

"Never mind. Anyway, how could you expect me to *not* have coffee with her? She's amazingly beautiful!"

She got up from her seat and approached her friend, grabbing hold of both his arms and making him stand still to look at her.

"I know this freaks you out," she told him. "But be cool, alright? I won't screw anything up, I promise! I rather like pretending to be Jillian Ashley, bestselling author. Besides, it's only coffee. Who knows? Her and I might meet in person and not be able to stand each other's company."

But Sally hoped not.

"Anyway, you promised me dinner," she reminded Max.

They ordered Chinese food and when it arrived, they ate in the dining room. Max put on some jazz music. Sally loved jazz, it was one of the many things she and Max had in common which cemented their friendship.

"So, how did you come up with Jillian Ashley as a pen name?" Sally asked.

"You met my parents, right? Two incredibly loud old people who don't want to acknowledge that they're both deaf and who save used wrapping paper?"

Sally laughed and nodded.

"What's my mother's name?"

"Jill," Sally answered.

"Right. Short for Jillian."

"Ah!" Sally speared a shrimp from off Max's plate.

"And you met my sister, right? Incredibly large woman with three annoying kids, one of whom had to repeat kindergarten? What's her name?"

Ash.

"Short for Ashley," Sally said before Max could. "Got it."

"So, I have a question for you, young lady," Max said.

Sally looked at him expectantly.

"How come you don't do much dating, Sally? I'm beginning to worry about you."

Sally laughed again.

"Worry?"

"Yeah. I mean, you're talented, smart, funny, somewhat good-looking…"

"Somewhat?" Sally asked with a smirk, knowing he was just kidding.

She shrugged.

"I don't know what to tell you about that," she said. She honestly didn't. On paper, Sally knew she was a catch: pretty, intelligent, good job and a fun personality. But her luck with women lately was non-existent. It didn't help that the pandemic kept most crowded venues like lesbian bars closed for over a year. In fact, her and Lisa's favorite lesbian spot in Vista had shut down for good thanks to Covid, never to reopen.

"The few dates I've been on lately just haven't been with anyone I felt really connected to, you know? Despite my mother's best efforts at fixing me up with every unattached lesbian she deems worthy," she added. "I mean, look…I know I can get laid anytime I want, okay? And, fine, I'm not a prude and will definitely hook up with a woman for that. But I want more already. Maybe it's because I'm almost thirty. Maybe it's because I'm just tired of going from girlfriend to girlfriend. I don't know."

She wondered what Amy would turn out to be. It was obvious that Friday evening was going to be a date. But what kind? A hook-up? A night of hopefully great sex followed by vague promises to keep in touch and see each other again soon? Or will it be a proper date—an evening to lay down the foundations for something bigger?

"It's sweet that you care so much, though," she said to Max.

He shrugged.

"I do care. I mean, you talk too much but I like you."

"Whatever," Sally said. "Anyway, maybe I'll really hit off with Amy."

Max groaned.

"I'm still not happy about that, by the way," he growled, glaring at her and putting down his fork. "I rather like the extra money coming in from my books, Sally. Not only that but I have fun writing them. So, what *is* your game plan with Amy?"

Sally did have to concede that Max had a point and that his concerns were justified. In retrospect, she *should* have turned Amy down, or at least thought through meeting up with her more. But Amy was…Sally took a deep breath now. Amy was yummy! And when the coffee invite happened, Sally's brain—and certain other parts of her—had reacted on autopilot.

But she loved Max and didn't want to do anything to jeopardize something which was obviously very important to him.

"She thinks I'm a writer," she said. "I can pretend to do that. I mean, it's not like she's going to test me by having me write a short story while we're having coffee."

Max scoffed.

"Yeah, well, my experiences on Twitter as Jillian have taught me never to put anything past lesbians."

"Shut up. Anyway, it's just coffee."

***

Sally's phone started trilling almost as soon as she walked into her condo later that night.

"Hi Mom," she answered, knowing from the ringtone who it was. She put her bag down and toed off the Skechers she had worn to Max's.

"You're going to thank me," Leslie Lassiter greeted.

"I doubt it," Sally mumbled.

"What was that, honey?"

"Nothing, Mom. I was saying hello to Lena." And on cue, Sally's super fluffy Maine coon sashayed into the room, spared Sally a look and then leapt up on the sofa to claim her favorite spot.

"Oh," Leslie said. "Well, anyway. You are going to thank me! Turns out, Dr. Janowicz's daughter is a lesbian and single and…wait for it…also a doctor!"

Sally rolled her eyes.

This again!

The woman never stopped! Her mother, a surgeon at Scripps Memorial in Encinitas was forever trying to fix Sally up with the daughters, granddaughters, nieces, cousins or best friends of her work colleagues. Moreover, Leslie also would scan each year's crop of new interns and residents to see if any of the attractive, young and newly minted lady doctors were gay, single and looking; all in her never-ending quest to see her daughter married off to a Doctor Somebody or at least to a close relation of a Doctor Somebody.

"Mom, seriously?"

So far, Leslie's efforts had yielded little. It wasn't that Sally had anything against doctors; it was more that Sally knew from being the daughter of one the demands on a doctor's time, especially a young doctor. And Sally really did not want to envision a future of lonely evenings at home or date nights interrupted by somebody's exploding gallbladder or whatever.

Sally wanted a woman to build a life with, not build a life *for*.

Then there was the fact that most doctors—even lesbian doctors—had permanent chips on their shoulders and behaved like they had deigned to visit Earth from Mount Olympus.

"Look, I've met Ainsley…" Leslie continued.

Ainsley? Good lord!

"…and she's absolutely charming!" Leslie gushed. "And gorgeous! She's a surgical resident in San Diego and I just think you two would get along so well!"

Sally doubted she could do anything well with someone named Ainsley.

She had to nip this latest attempt of her mother's in the bud.

"Mom, first of all, I've told you I can find my own dates…"

Dates, yes. Actual girlfriends, no.

"Secondly, I'll have you know that I just met someone and we are going to meet up for a date on Friday."

"Huh!" Leslie chuffed. "Who is she?"

"Her name is Amy."

"Amy," Leslie repeated, as if trying out the name. "And what does she do?"

Shit!

Sally realized now that she actually knew next to nothing about Amy. For all she knew, Amy *was* a doctor. But she doubted it. Amy didn't give off that Mount Olympus vibe.

"Um…she a blogger," Sally answered.

"A blogger."

"Yeah, well, I mean…that's *one* thing she does; I'm sure she does something else! Like, a real job."

"Huh!" Leslie chuffed again. "You mean, you've met this woman and you have no idea what she does? It hardly sounds serious, then; certainly no reason for you not to meet Ainsley."

The name Ainsley is reason not to meet Ainsley!

"Mom…"

"One drink!" Leslie pressed. "See what happens! Besides…"

Sally's Mom Warning System started flashing red.

"What?" she asked brusquely.

"IalreadygaveAinsleyyournumberandshesaidshe'dcallyoutomorrow," Leslie blurted out.

"Mom!"

Sally knew she was stuck now. She respected her mother and her mother's career too much to risk doing anything that would create any kind of awkwardness between her mother and this Dr. Janowicz, like, say, *not* taking Ainsley's phone call or *not* meeting Ainsley for at least one drink.

"Fine," she told Leslie, an edge to her voice. "I will meet Ainsley for one drink. One! Understand? Don't expect any miracles, though! And *do not* start sending out wedding invites!"

A few moments later, the call ended and Sally plopped down on the sofa next to Lena. She picked up the cat and held its face close to her own.

"Mothers!" Sally muttered.

Chapter 9

Amy had her interview with Jillian Ashley edited and ready for posting just an hour after disconnecting the video call with the author. Once she was sure that it was ready for the world to see, she stopped, made herself a Cosmo and then clicked the *Upload* button on her website as she took the first sip of her cocktail.

She had then spent the better part of an hour posting links to this latest edition of *Lesbeing: the Podcast* on her various social media accounts, starting with Twitter.

Hey, everybody! Just posted my awesome and exclusive interview with the amazing Jillian Ashley @ashleylesfic on Lesbeing—the Podcast! Click here to check it out!

When she checked all her accounts the next morning, particularly Twitter, her jaw dropped. Her tweet already had over 500 likes and had been retweeted more than eighty times. Over two-hundred people—all women, by the looks of it—had commented on it, as well.

OMG, she's my favorite writer! And you got to speak to her???

Just watched the podcast! Amazing job!

Such an insightful discussion with one of the best! I'm going to reread her books now after hearing her explain things like that!

She is GORGEOUS! I don't think I'll ever read a Jillian Ashley book quite the same way again!!!

Her inboxes on Twitter and Facebook, not to mention the email inbox for the Lesbeing website were stuffed with messages, so many in fact that she knew she didn't have time to read more than a handful of them before she had to leave for work. She really had scored the lesfic scoop of the century!

But one email *did* catch her eye. The one from Jillian.

> *Hey, Amy! Thanks for sending me the link to our interview last night! I so enjoyed watching it that I actually watched it twice, LOL! Seriously, though, it was such a fun experience and you were an amazing interviewer! Talk to you soon!*

And she signed off with a heart-eyes emoji.

Amy reread the email.

Huh! No mention of their date on Friday.

She knew it was only just past eight a.m. but she also remembered Jillian telling her that she always got up early in the mornings. She decided to fire off a quick text.

> *Hey, Jillian! I just read your email! So glad you liked the interview! I'm really looking forward to buying you that coffee on Friday!*

There! Nothing weird about that. It sounded casual, breezy even. Not at all like a text from a woman who was currently panicking that maybe an incredibly gorgeous and talented woman like Jillian Ashley had changed her mind about meeting her in a few days.

She tapped *Send*. And then tried to not obsess about when—or if—Jillian would answer.

Fortunately, Jillian's reply came almost instantly.

> *I am soooooo looking forward to Friday! I hope you have a great day today!*

Amy slowly let out a relieved breath. Their date was still on!

Finally tearing her eyes away from her smartphone, she was just about to toast a bagel for breakfast when the device rang. She smirked when she saw the name of the person calling her.

"Bitch! How did you get Jillian Ashley?" Rhonda Kessing screamed in lieu of a normal greeting. Like *Hello*, for instance.

Amy couldn't help the self-satisfied laughter which now bubbled up out of her.

Rhonda Kessing was another lesbian blogger and podcaster, based in Chicago, who mainly covered lesbians in pop culture:

movies, TV, even comic books. She also had a very popular lesfic review site which many readers of the genre relied on.

Before Covid altered the world, Amy and Rhonda had been guest panelists at a symposium in Miami on lesbianism in the internet age and for some reason, Rhonda had begun considering Amy something of a rival in the relatively tiny sphere of lesbians-blogging-about-lesbians. Amy knew that her scoring an interview with Jillian Ashley would keep Rhonda up for a few nights.

Imagine telling her I scored a date with her!

But Amy wasn't going to do that. Superstitious by nature, she had never encountered a ladder she refused to walk under. Somehow, telling Rhonda Kessing about her date with Jillian felt like it might jinx it. Rachel, however, was another story; jinxes didn't work when it came to best friends and Amy planned on telling her later today.

"What can I say, Rhonda?" Amy said. "I guess I just knew how to appeal to Jillian's good nature."

Rhonda scoffed.

"What do you have? You got something on her? Was it a blackmail thing? Or did you send naked pictures of yourself?"

Amy gave a faux gasp of horror.

"Rhonda! I'm shocked! I will have you know I run a clean operation here!"

"Yeah, yeah, yeah. Lucky bitch! It was a good interview, though. Congratulations."

"Why, thank you, Rhonda!"

"I mean, there *were* one or two things I would have done differently, but…"

"Like offering Jillian your firstborn if she revealed the plot of her next book?" Amy asked.

"Bite me."

***

After work that evening, Rachel came over to Amy's apartment. They ordered Chinese food to be delivered and while waiting for it to arrive sat together on the sofa, each with a glass of white wine.

"Do you think I have time to get my boobs done before I meet her?" she asked her best friend while they waited, peeking down her own shirt at her small breasts which were currently without a bra.

Rachel looked at Amy.

"By Friday night? Probably, but I'm not sure you'll like how they turn out."

"Aargh!"

"Sweetie, calm down," Rachel said.

"Calm down? You haven't seen this woman!" Amy exclaimed.

"I have too!" Rachel retorted. "I watched your interview with her! In fact, I've seen her in the exact same way you've seen her: on a laptop screen, from the shoulders up!"

Amy had to concede that was true.

"Isn't she pretty?" she asked, smiling secretly to herself.

"She's gorgeous!" Rachel affirmed. "Like, I'd be gay for her."

"Well, too bad because I'm going to be gay for her."

"She seems nice, too."

"Doesn't she?" Amy then had an alarming thought. "I hope she isn't, like, an ogre in real life, though. Like, I hope her niceness wasn't an act just because she was being interviewed."

What if that were true? Amy wondered now. What if the sweet, polite, somewhat shy woman she talked to yesterday and who had made her insides feel liquid, turned out to be a Grade-A ice queen? It would ruin reading Jillian Ashley books for Amy forever!

What was it that somebody once said?

Never meet your heroes.

Tapping Amy's knee comfortingly, Rachel assured her that she was certain Jillian would be just as nice in person.

"I'm also sure she'll like your boobs," she added.

All day long, Amy had been on a high. Not only did she have an upcoming date with Jillian Ashley, who had to be the most beautiful lesfic author on the planet, but thanks to her interview with Jillian, *Lesbeing—the Podcast* was even more popular than ever. Subscriber numbers had been climbing all day and the hits on her website had been astronomical. What's more, other lesbian podcast hosts—with the exception of Rhonda Sour Grapes Kessing—had written to Amy, asking her to appear on *their* podcasts to relate the story of how she managed to get Jillian to come out of her shell.

Work had even gone well today. One of the San Diego County supervisors had agreed to a meeting with Amy and Makeda, the director of the North County Women's Rights Group, to discuss upcoming debates on proposed legislation that would write equal rights for women into the County's constitution. All in all, it had been a great day.

Their Chinese food arrived and while they ate, Rachel lamented about her own dating woes with men. The last guy she had gone on a date with had not been seated for five minutes in the outdoor bar Rachel had met him at before he started talking about how the 2020 election had been rigged and stolen from the Republicans. Before a server had even approached their table to take their drinks order, Rachel had got up and left.

"You should come over to our side," Amy said around a mouthful of kung pao chicken.

"I'm sure there are some stupid lesbians, too," Rachel reproached.

"Oh, lots of them! But at least they have boobs!"

Chapter 10

On Wednesday evening, Sally finally felt human enough to leave her darkened bedroom at a little past five. She was famished but otherwise feeling terrific.

Thank God!

This morning, she had taken a sick day from work because she had woken up with a terrible migraine. As she typed out the *There's no way in hell I'm working today* email to the team of designers she managed, Sally had had to wince in agony at the brightness of the small screen and how it made her feel like broken glass was inside her skull.

The email sent, she had set her phone to silent mode and then started the business of ridding herself of the migraine.

She had gotten up once during the morning, around eight a.m., to use the bathroom. Though the migraine was still with her, she had taken the opportunity to check her emails to make sure no one on her team of graphic designers was completely lost without her leadership. She had also noticed that Lisa had sent her three texts, but she hadn't wanted to be bothered reading them and so she ignored those. But Amy had also sent a text! That one she did read, though the brightness of the phone's screen was not helping her head. Amy's text had said something about an email and then how she was looking forward to Friday.

Sally had had no idea what email Amy was talking about but she did send a reply telling her that she too was excited about Friday. Then she had put the phone back down and hoped she would die.

Death didn't come but sleep apparently did, thanks to the prescription migraine pills she had popped upon waking up.

Her bedside clock told her that she had pretty much slept all day: all morning, through lunch and into the evening. Now, her migraine was gone, she was starving and she was looking forward to an evening on the sofa continuing to binge-watch *The Great Pottery Throw Down* because who knew that watching British people making pottery could be fun?

She was trying to decide between ordering a pizza or ordering Thai food when her doorbell rang. Not expecting anybody, she warily looked through the peephole and spied Lisa on the other side, practically bouncing up and down like she had to pee really bad.

"What are you doing here?" Sally asked when she opened the door.

Lisa just stood there for a moment, staring at Sally, a goofy grin on her face.

Sally frowned at her friend.

"What?" she asked impatiently.

Lisa squealed and then rushed into Sally's arms.

"Ohmygod, ohmygod, ohmyGOD!" Lisa screamed. "I can't believe it!"

Sally had no idea what was going on. Disentangling herself from Lisa, she asked exactly what it was that Lisa couldn't believe.

Lisa rushed into Sally's apartment.

"Hello?" Lisa began. "That *you're* Jillian Ashley!"

Sally's mouth dropped open.

Oh, shit!

In all the weirdness of the past twenty-four hours she had completely overlooked the fact that Lisa would see Amy's interview. But of course Lisa would see it. Lisa stayed hip to everything lesbian in the world. She had even found out somehow that Revlon's *If I Want To* matte lipstick was *the* shade for lesbians this season and so now always wore it. She was even wearing it now.

And if Lisa saw the interview…

It also meant that all of Sally's other queer female friends had seen it.

Shit!

She thought of her phone. It was still in the bedroom. Rushing past Lisa, she went into the still-darkened room, picked it up and turned it on.

Shit!

She had never seen so many notifications on her phone. In. Her. Life!

Missed calls, voicemails, text messages, emails, Facebook, Twitter, Instagram…it seemed like every gay woman Sally knew, even marginally, had tried to reach her today! She was going to *kill* Max for getting her mixed up in all this!

Thinking of whom, there was also a Venmo notification that said it was from him. She tapped it.

Max Tremont just paid you $500!

Holy shit!

That was her car payment *and* her normal electric bill taken care of this month! Or, put another way, more money for shoe shopping.

Okay, she decided, Max could live.

She turned to head back to the living room and gasped. Lisa was standing right next to her.

"Jesus, you scared me!" she hissed, smacking Lisa's arm.

"Why did you never tell me?" Lisa asked, still smiling like an idiot and looking at Sally with the same look people have when they spot their favorite movie star walking down the street.

Sally knew she needed to set the record straight but just as she was about to open her mouth to do so, she realized what a mistake that would be. Lisa was perhaps the most indiscreet person Sally knew. In fact, as much as Sally loved Lisa to bits, she also knew that telling her best friend any sensitive information was the same as taking out an ad on TV during the Super Bowl. If Sally now told Lisa the truth about what she and Max were doing, it would spread through the Lesbianverse like a dry-brush fire and not only would Max's writing career be finished but lesbians here in Carlsbad might actually throw rotten fruit at Sally whenever she went outside.

She needed to keep the truth from Lisa.

"Um…because you have a big mouth and would have told everyone," she stated, walking past her and back into the living room.

"But I'm your best friend!" Lisa whined.

"My best friend who has a big mouth and would have told everyone," Sally reiterated.

"So all those times we were reading Jillian Ashley books together…"

Fuck!

Sally thought quickly.

"I was just pretending because obviously I had read them already because obviously I wrote them. Have you eaten?" she asked, wanting to change the topic. "Because I'm starving and was about to order something."

"Ooh, let me do it for you!" Lisa exclaimed. "What kind of best friend to Jillian Ashley would I be if I didn't buy her dinner?"

Sally sighed and plopped down on the sofa. Lena finally made an appearance from wherever she had been hiding in apparent effort to determine what all the fuss was about. Evidently, the cat deemed the ruckus not worthy of her time because after glaring at the two women, she went back from whence she came.

Sally allowed Lisa to buy Jillian Ashley a pizza and while they waited for it to be delivered had to explain to her friend when it was she decided to start writing lesfic, where she got her ideas from and how it feels having so many fans. It was basically Amy's interview all over again, but Lisa was acting as if countless lesbians hadn't already heard these answers now; that Sally was giving her an exclusive peek into the mind of the great lesfic author.

"How did you come up with Jillian Ashley as a pen name, though?" Lisa eventually asked.

That one threw Sally and she felt a momentary panic. She couldn't use Max's story of how he came up with the name, her own mother being named Leslie and her own sister being named Camille.

"I, uh, just randomly picked some names off a baby-naming website."

"Oh, I see!" Lisa said, still in awe, as if Sally had just imparted to her the answer to the Sphinx's riddle.

"So, have you made a lot of money off the books?" Lisa asked.

Five-hundred dollars.

"Um...I mean, yeah, sure," Sally said, thinking of the image of Max's sales charts from the other day.

"Are you going to, like, buy a Porsche or a beach house or something?"

"Jesus, Lisa! Next you'll be expecting me to purchase a private plane!"

"What else is there to do with money, Sally?"

"Oh, I don't know...Pay off the mortgage on this place. Invest it. Save for retirement." Assuming there would be more than five-hundred dollars coming, of course. And the only way to ensure that was to keep the ruse going.

Sighing, Sally sat back and wondered how many more of these ridiculous questions she was going to have to answer tonight.

***

Lisa finally left at around eight o'clock, and quite frankly, Sally couldn't have been happier to see her go. Lisa on her best behavior was a handful. Lisa after recently discovering that she was the best friend of *the* Jillian Ashley was insufferable.

The day-long nap she had taken to cure her migraine meant that Sally was now wide awake. She had no idea how she would eventually fall asleep later but she'd cross that bridge when she came to it. Right now, with Lisa gone and her hunger sated with pizza, Sally was finally ready to curl up on the couch and watch British potters throw pottery.

Naturally, her phone rang.

"Hello?" she answered with a bit more edge to her voice than normal.

"Hello? Is this Sally?" a woman's voice replied.

"Yes, it is. Who's this?"

"Hi! This is Ainsley Janowicz. Um…our mothers work together and your mother gave me your phone number because she thought we might like to meet up, maybe have a drink?"

Fuck!

"Oh, Ainsley!" Sally said, trying hard to not sound like the pretentiousness of the name was grating on her every nerve. "Yes, Mom mentioned it. So glad you called!" It was a lie but Sally figured why be a bitch?

A breathed sigh of relief came over the connection.

"Oh, thank goodness! I'm pretty crap at doing this, you know. I mean, it's not how I normally meet women."

Sally figured Ainsley normally met women at tea parties on Mount Olympus. Still, though, she had to admit that Ainsley had a pretty sexy voice.

"Anyway," the doctor continued, "look, I know that the last thing you probably want is a blind date but I have a feeling we have something in common."

Nope! I've never been to Mount Olympus and I have a normal name!

"Really?" Sally asked. "And what do we have in common?"

"We both have overbearing mothers who will absolutely not let us live a moment in peace unless we meet for one drink."

Sally laughed at that, which surprised her. She didn't think anyone who dwelled on Mount Olympus even had a sense of humor.

"So, what do you say we at least meet for that drink, do our daughterly duty and get our two Moms off our backs? No pressure for anything else."

Sally was smiling. She liked the way Doctor Ainsley thought. And even though she was certain having one drink with anyone named Ainsley would be as enjoyable as spending time with a chihuahua, at least Ainsley was acknowledging that this blind date was simply a chore to be got done with in order to shut their mothers up.

"I think that's a great idea," Sally told her, knowing that her voice telegraphed the smile still on her face.

"Fabulous! You're in Carlsbad, right?" Ainsley then chuckled. "Don't get weirded out. My mother, no doubt coached by *your* mother, told me all your vitals: let's see, you live in Carlsbad; you're a graphic designer; you're five-foot-ten and have green eyes."

Sally laughed.

"Did she include my social security number?"

"No," Ainsley replied, "but at the least the criminal background check was negative."

Sally laughed again, which alarmed her. She wasn't *supposed* to enjoy talking to someone named Ainsley.

"Anyway," Ainsley went on, "I live in San Diego but I know a great coastal bar about halfway between us, in Solana Beach. How about tomorrow night?"

"Oh, tomorrow is no good," Sally said. "I hate to sound like an old lady but I have a super important meeting early on Friday morning with a client and I really want to make sure I get to bed early tomorrow night. I know that also sounds like the lamest excuse ever but I swear it's true."

Ainsley laughed.

"Fear not, I believe you and can relate. I always make a point to get to bed early the night before I have to do a procedure. How about Saturday afternoon, then?"

The woman really did have an amazing voice, Sally considered again. She told Ainsley that Saturday would be perfect. Ainsley told her the name of the bar and they agreed on a time.

When the call ended, Sally looked at the device and shrugged.

One drink.

Chapter 11

Nope! Way too much!

Amy shimmied out of the dress she had just put on in her bedroom. It was one of her favorites, a flirty blue number with a flared hem. It fit her perfectly, showed off her legs and with the right bra it even flattered her bustline. But it was too much…too fancy. It was perfect for a proper date out to dinner or dancing but she was meeting Jillian at La Vida Mocha, a laid-back and chill coffeeshop. Also…was this a date?

Amy seemed to think so. There was no doubting the chemistry her and Jillian practically oozed the other day during the podcast, and there was no doubting the flirting she and Jillian had engaged in either. In fact, many of the people who had commented on the interview even made mention of it. And even though Amy had made the invitation to coffee sound like it was merely a way of thanking Jillian for appearing on her show, she was certain that Jillian had cottoned on to the fact that that was just pretense.

Okay, so…a real date. This meant she must make an effort appearance-wise while also keeping her outfit laid-back and chill, La Vida Mocha style.

In another twenty minutes Amy was almost ready to go, dressed in black skinny jeans that were fashionably ripped at the knees and a simple lilac tee. She accessorized with a few bangles on her right arm and a colorful beaded necklace she had bought during a trip to Spain a few years ago.

Deciding on her footwear, however, required additional consideration. She wanted to go with a nice pair of high heels, wanting to add a classy and sexy finishing touch to the outfit but, again, she worried it would be too much. The operative words were *laid-back and casual.* So, after further debate, she went with one of her favorite pairs of lace ballet flats. She examined the final result in the full-length mirror in her bedroom.

Ready! Shit, and running late!

Grabbing her Michael Kors tote purse from where she had left it on her make-up table, Amy checked that it contained her car keys, tossed her phone inside as well as the lipstick she was wearing in case she needed to touch it up and fifteen seconds later she was out the door.

The traffic gods were kind to her and she made it to La Vida Mocha at ten minutes to four o'clock, which was perfect. It meant she had plenty of time to find a table for her and Jillian, hopefully one near the window so they could people-watch. Amy loved people-watching and she hoped Jillian did too. Pulling into the parking lot behind the coffeeshop, she wondered if any of the cars already parked belonged to Jillian. The Jeep she knew was Vanessa's and that Volkswagen she knew belonged to Chloë. What kind of car did Jillian drive? There was a Mercedes convertible, black and sleek, parked near a lamppost, that Amy could imagine a bestselling author tooling around town in. But it seemed too flash for Jillian. And she was positive the red Camaro must belong to some guy trying compensate for certain shortcomings.

Parking her own car, Amy shook her head, chiding herself. She knew next to nothing about Jillian. For all she knew, Jillian liked flashy cars and maybe even muscle cars. She reminded herself that she needed to not be starstruck on this date, that she needed to take the time to get to know Jillian and find out things about her—like what kind of car she drives.

Stepping into La Vida Mocha a few moments later, Amy stopped and did a quick scan of the customers already inside. Thanks to the lessening of Covid restrictions in California due to the rise of vaccinations and other measures, places like La Vida Mocha were starting to see the kind of patronage they had in the Before Times. This evening, La Vida Mocha was busy and there was a pleasant hubbub of conversation inside providing an accompaniment to the down-tempo electronic music Vanessa always enjoyed playing over the sound system. Amy quickly determined that Jillian's wasn't among the faces already here and she also quickly determined that there were only two tables currently unoccupied, including one by the window!

She hurried over to it in order to claim it.

Yay! Choice seat!

But after a minute, she bit her bottom lip, feeling self-conscious. Her usual routine when coming into La Vida Mocha was to head to the counter and immediately order her favorite drink, the one Vanessa named after her, the Amy's Jet Fuel, and then find a seat. Of course, her usual routine also involved coming into La Vida Mocha *alone*. The only exceptions were when she was with Rachel but on those occasions, they typically got their coffee to go. Amy had never met a date here and she quite frankly didn't know what to do. She didn't like occupying a seat in the coffeeshop without actually having any coffee in front of her to drink. She suddenly felt certain that perhaps Vanessa was glaring at her from behind the counter, wondering why Amy's ass was taking up valuable seating real estate when Amy hadn't bothered to buy anything yet. She also suddenly felt certain that other customers were whispering about her; things like, "Look at that freak sitting there without any coffee!" or "What does she think this is, a bus stop?"

Should she order a drink for herself? But what happens when Jillian arrives in—Amy checked her watch—four minutes? She didn't want Jillian feeling like she had to buy her own coffee; after all, Amy had invited her! Amy wanted to be the one who treated. But getting up from the table to go get Jillian's coffee right after Jillian arrived seemed awkward in Amy's mind; so did standing in line with Jillian and then ordering only one coffee.

Argh! Stop it!

Amy knew she was letting her anxiety about being on a date get the best of her. She also knew that she'd be feeling this anxiety no matter the woman she was meeting for the date, but the fact that she was meeting Jillian Ashley was making the anxiety that much worse.

"Hey, Amy!"

Amy looked up to see Chloë, the coffeeshop's manager standing next to her table. She was wearing a cute polka dot face mask and the dots were the same color as her pixie-cut platinum blonde hair.

"Hey, Chloë!" Amy said, at first relieved to be distracted from her thoughts. She liked Chloë a lot. In fact, she was hoping that Chloë and her girlfriend would one day be guests on her podcast because their relationship—which not only involved an age gap but also a first-time lesbian—would be perfect for her series of episodes on real-life lesfic tropes.

But then, Amy's mind couldn't help but wonder if Vanessa had instructed Chloë to come ask Amy why she was sitting here without any coffee.

"Um…I hope you don't mind," Amy began, "but I haven't ordered anything yet because I'm waiting for someone."

Chloë waved it off.

"Dude, you're fine," she said, making Amy feel a lot better. "By the way, I always tell Vanessa that we should put a sign on this table which says 'Reserved for Amy' because you, like, always sit here!"

Amy laughed. In her nervousness, she hadn't realized that this was, in fact, the table she usually snagged when she came to La Vida Mocha.

"Oh my god, that would be so awesome!" she said to Chloë. "It would make me feel like a celebrity! Oh, Vanessa told me you guys are opening another shop!"

Chloë beamed.

"We are! In fact, I'm going to be part-owner of it."

"No way! Congratulations!"

Amy stood up to hug her friend, genuinely happy for her.

They remained standing for a few minutes, chatting, Chloë telling Amy about the new coffeeshop, which was not going to be in Carlsbad but in Encinitas. Eventually, though, Chloë had to go tend to something behind the counter and Amy sat back down.

Checking her smartwatch, her heart plummeted.

During her pleasant chat with Chloë, Amy had lost sense of the passage of time and she now discovered that it was five minutes past four o'clock! And Jillian wasn't here yet!

Fuck!

She told herself to calm down. Her date was late, no big deal. Happens all the time. Right now, she reasoned, there were countless women around the world whose dates were late. It didn't mean anything and it certainly didn't mean that she had been stood up.

Her phone! Her phone was still in her bag and maybe she had missed a notification!

Rescuing the device from the depths of the purse, Amy's face fell when the phone's screen merely showed her the time, nothing else. Still not a big deal, she reassured herself, wishing that such thoughts could magically calm her nerves. But with each passing second, she grew more fearful, certain that she'd been stood up. Worse still, she had told Chloë that she was waiting for someone, which meant that Chloë could be, right this very second, stealing glances over at her, feeling sorry for her for being stood up!

But wait…Amy hadn't told Chloë that she was meeting a *date* here, just *someone*. She also hadn't told Chloë what time she was supposed to be meeting this person.

Amy rolled her eyes.

Of course Chloë would know she was waiting for a date! It was Friday evening. And of course Chloë would think she had been stood up! People don't say, "Hey, let's meet up at 4:07!" or "Great! See you there at 4:12!" Any idiot would know that Amy's date was supposed to show up at the top of the hour and not…Amy checked her watch again…

Fuck! 4:09!

She sighed.

So, now, she was the freak sitting in a coffeeshop without any coffee *and* no date! Fabulous!

Podcast idea: Lesbian dating protocols. How late is too late?

Oh well. She started consoling herself with the fact that she had at least gotten to interview Jillian on her podcast, which was something of a major coup in the lesfic world. And just because Jillian hadn't showed up for their date, that wasn't something to hold against her. Jillian was literally one of the top three lesfic authors *in the world*, even after only four books so far! Perfectly understandable, then, why she would find it a less than stimulating use of her time to meet a local blogger/podcaster for coffee on a primo date night.

Just then, though, the bell over the door to La Vida Mocha tinkled as the door was opened and a woman rushed in.

Amy gasped.

Jillian.

And suddenly, Amy felt a lot of the blood in her body flowing south and settling between her legs.

Jillian on video was gorgeous.

Jillian in real life was *spectacularly* gorgeous.

The first thing Amy noticed was how tall she was! Like, model tall. With legs that seemed interminable, making Amy subconsciously lick her lips. Her lean figure was dressed remarkably like her own: skinny jeans and a tee, though Jillian's tee was tan and sleeveless, showing off toned arms that weren't *too* toned.

Amy had to swallow when Jillian finally located her and those green eyes locked with hers.

"I am *soooooo* sorry!" Jillian said when she reached the table. Amy stood and was delighted beyond description when Jillian embraced her. Being several inches shorter than Jillian, Amy found her face nestled against where Jillian's long neck met her shoulders and Amy surreptitiously inhaled Jillian's fragrances of cherry blossoms, citrus and, most enigmatic of all, patchouli.

"Don't worry about it," Amy said with her best smile when they separated.

I'd have waited until midnight for you.

"I promise I am not usually late," Jillian insisted. "Well, I used to be but my friend Max got me out of the habit. Anyway, today I just got…careless with the time!" Her face lost some color and she hurriedly added, "Not that I didn't think meeting you was anything to care about! I totally cared, I promise! In fact, caring is what made me late! Please don't think I'm a geek but I just couldn't figure out what to wear!"

"Oh my god, me too!" Amy told her. "Like, a dress seemed too dressy…"

"Right! And even high heels seemed like too much."

Amy beamed. It made her feel a thousand percent better knowing that Jillian had gone through the same mental gymnastics trying to come up with an outfit for their date. It also helped that she seemed just as nervous about this date as Amy was. And Jillian's rambling was adorable!

And good lord! The thought of Jillian in high heels! The woman would be about seven feet tall! And now even more blood was flowing south at that image!

Only a few minutes into their date and Amy was already wet.

"Well, you look great," Amy said.

"You too. I think we both pulled off just the right amount of stylish-but-casual."

"Shall we get some coffee?" Amy asked.

"Oh, thank god, yes! I could use some. But let me treat you! I feel so horrible that I was this late."

But Amy shook her head.

"Nope," she replied. "I invited you and so it's on me." After a half-second's consideration, she decided to be bold and loop her arm around Jillian's, the contact sending a little electric thrill down her spine and straight to her clit. Not only that, but the contact felt...*perfect*. It felt like she had found a missing piece of herself.

She took a deep breath.

Too early. Too early. Too early!

Amy led her date to the ordering counter.

It was the new(ish) La Vida Mocha girl, Amber, who took their order. When Jillian asked for a white chocolate mocha, Amy decided to copy her, remembering reading somewhere that a surefire way to signal attraction to somebody was to subtly mimic their moves. While they waited, Jillian surveyed the surroundings.

"This is a cool spot," she eventually declared. "I knew this place was here but I've never come inside. I'm more of a Starbucks girl."

Amy crossed her arms and gave Jillian a faux stern expression.

"Okay, I am going to try my hardest *not* to hold that against you, but just so you know, it will be very difficult."

Jillian laughed.

"Oh, I know! I'm a slave to the chain places and I need to break free. Do you realize that my idea of going out for Mexican is a visit to Taco Bell?"

Amy couldn't help the look of surprise which came over her face. Taco Bell? Starbucks? Carlsbad wasn't a backwater town in the hills of Arkansas where options were limited. This was Southern California! There were all sorts of wonderful independent and local dining and caffeine-dispensing options everywhere!

"I see I have a lot of work to do with you," she said, arching an eyebrow.

"Is that right?" Jillian asked. "And how do you propose to start?"

Amy was certain the timbre of Jillian's voice had an undertone of flirtation and she bit her bottom lip, gratified when she noticed Jillian's eyes zero in on her mouth.

Unfortunately, it was at that moment when Amber, completely oblivious to the sexual tension which Amy would have thought was obvious to even a blind person, butted in.

"Here are your drinks, ladies," Amber said, placing the two coffees on the pick-up counter, her brown eyes crinkling with the smile that was hidden by her face mask.

Gee, thanks, Amber!

Back at their table, Amy said, "So, Jillian, tell me about yourself; I mean stuff we didn't go over during our interview the other day."

"Well," Jillian began, after a sip of her coffee, "I suppose the most earth-shattering thing I can tell you right now is that my name is Sally, not Jillian."

Amy smiled.

"Oh my god, that is such a cool name! It's, like, classic."

Amy regarded her companion anew, getting used to viewing her as a Sally, not a Jillian. She determined that the name suited her, even more so than Jillian did.

"Bet you can't guess who I'm named after," Sally prompted. "And, no, it's not a family member."

Amy considered the question.

"Sally Ride?" she ventured, naming America's first woman in space.

"Nope."

Oh god…what is the name of that old actress my mother likes…?

"Sally Field?" she asked when it suddenly came to her.

"Nope."

Amy twisted her features into an expression of being stumped.

"Oh gosh. Are there any other famous Sallys?"

Her date feigned surprise.

"I'm sure there are but you're forgetting the one mega-famous Sally!" she said.

Amy laughed.

"Who?"

"Charlie Brown's sister!"

"Oh my god, I totally forgot about her! That's hilarious!"

"I hope you made note of it," Sally said, "I will be quizzing you later."

Amy felt her pulse quicken.

"And if I fail the quiz?"

"You'll have to take the make-up exam, won't you?" Sally told her.

"I see. Well, I'm sure I don't want to do that."

Sally quirked an eyebrow and sucked her bottom lip between her teeth.

"Don't be so sure of that," she said.

Amy felt another delicious chill tickle her spine and which made all her nerve endings feel alive. She brought her coffee cup up to her mouth for a sip, more as an attempt to cover the blush she felt creeping up her neck to her cheeks than because she wanted a drink.

"So, how did you come up with Jillian Ashley as a pen name?" she asked.

A change came over Sally's features then, which Amy had trouble interpreting.

"Do you mind if we not talk about Jillian Ashley and writing and the books and all that?" Sally inquired. "I'd rather our time together be about getting to know one another instead." And then she gave Amy a smile that actually made Amy cross her legs under the table.

"I love that idea," she replied. What she didn't add was that she was currently rethinking her no-sex-on-a-first-date policy. It was a hard and fast rule for her. There were exceptions, of course—Amy had had her share of hook-ups and one-night-stands. But for proper first dates, the kind that were meant to be the start of a relationship, Amy made sure things never progressed to the bedroom.

Now, however, she was wondering if Sally also had a no-sex-on-a-first-date rule, and what she would need to do to get Sally to break it.

Chapter 12

Max was going to kill her.

And Sally had known that Max was going to kill her about fifteen seconds after she walked into this coffeeshop and saw Amy. In that instant, when her eyes had landed on Amy IRL, two things had happened...

The first was that Sally's heart had thumped hard enough that she felt a rush of warm blood course through her limbs.

The second was that her first thought was, *I finally found Her.*

Sally had been hoping to feel what she was feeling now on her date with Amy seemingly her entire adult life. She'd had plenty of girlfriends, of course; a couple of them had even been serious enough to make her wonder if marriage was in the cards. In the end, though, those relationships had fizzled out for one reason or another and when Sally was between girlfriends and thus had time to consider things, she had come to realize that those relationships had fizzled simply because there wasn't anything magical about them.

Because Sally really did believe there *was* a soulmate out there for her. The *one* woman who would make her feel the way Hollywood wanted people to believe they should feel in all those silly rom-coms and period romance dramas. This was a thought she had always kept to herself, though, knowing how pie-in-the-sky it all sounded.

But now she was sitting across from Amy in this cool coffeeshop she'd never been to before and everything about their date was firing on all cylinders.

It wasn't just that Amy was pretty, with chocolate-brown eyes which matched her chocolate-brown hair, lithe figure with small breasts and the most adorable dimples when she smiled. It was something else. Something between them which, like air, was invisible and also like air could only be felt when it was moving. And this *something* was moving, Sally determined. It was a current flowing between the two of them and it was something Sally had been waiting for all her life.

And Amy was proving to be a very impressive person. Sally almost wished her mother could be sitting here with them and learning that Amy was far more than just a blogger. So far, because

Sally had asked Amy to tell her about herself, Sally had discovered all of the important work Amy was doing for a women's rights organization based here in Carlsbad. The woman truly was in the trenches, helping others and fighting the good fight, trying on a daily basis to improve the lot of women in this region of California and undo a lot of the misogynistic poison of the Trump years. And Sally couldn't get enough of it. The stories Amy told, running the gamut from frustratingly sad to laugh out loud funny, put Amy's passion for her work on full display.

It was, quite frankly, sexy as hell.

"I'm having a really good time!" Amy said, with a smile, bringing those dimples to life, after relating to Sally the details of her upcoming meeting with a county supervisor about a women's rights bill.

"I am too!" Sally replied. "And I usually *hate* first dates."

"Same here. It always feels like—"

"An audition?" Sally offered.

"Exactly!" Amy enthused.

"I totally know what you're talking about! And then you're always wondering—"

"If the person you're with is truly being themselves?" Amy suggested.

Sally nodded.

"Exactly what I was going to say!"

They sat there staring at each other for a few silent moments that were not at all awkward.

"Get a load of us…" Sally started.

"…finishing each other's sentences." Amy concluded.

Sally's nipples hardened.

Eventually, she held up her coffee cup.

"Empty," she said. "Are you hungry? How about we finish each other's sentences over some food?"

"Love it!" Amy said. "Italian? I know a great place within walking distance."

"Please let it be Cicciotti's! I love that place!"

Amy leaned forward, holding Sally's eyes with her own.

"What a coincidence," she purred and even though Sally would have thought it impossible, her nipples got even harder.

***

Ten minutes later, they were at Cicciotti's, seated at one of the trattoria's sidewalk tables. The weather, as usual, was gorgeous; the daylight a lovely blue-orange as the sun began heading towards the horizon. There was an enormous tree just outside the establishment and the chorus of birds provided a pleasant accompaniment to the rustic Italian music playing softly on the trattoria's sound system.

Their waitress had just left them, having taken their order, promising to return soon with the bottle of pinot noir they had requested to enjoy with their meal.

Upon the waitress leaving, Amy had asked Sally what she did for a living, considering that they had spent all their time at La Vida Mocha discussing Amy's profession.

"Oh god, now I'm self-conscious!" Sally said.

"Why self-conscious?" Amy inquired, laughing.

Sally rolled her eyes.

"Because compared to what you do, my job is so unimportant!"

Amy laughed even more.

"Don't say that! I'm sure it's very important."

Sighing, because she knew she couldn't avoid this topic of conversation, Sally set about telling Amy about her job as a graphic designer, a job she really did love but which hardly had the world-changing potential of what Amy did. Still though, she explained how growing up she had been fascinated by things like signs and logos and how certain designs—even though they were incredibly simple—were so iconic and ubiquitous that even taken out of context, they were instantly recognizable.

"Take the Nike swoosh, for example," she said. "You don't have to see it on a pair of sneakers to know, instantly, that that symbol means Nike, right? And I love that! That symbol just looks like a fancy check mark—a child could have drawn it—but even so, when you see that simple swoosh, even if it's drawn on a napkin, you instantly know it's Nike."

"I totally get what you're saying," Amy said. "Like Milton Glaser's *I Love New York* logo. It's such a simple design and yet every time I see that, I picture everything awesome about New York City."

Sally blinked.

She knows who Milton Glaser is?

In the world of graphic design, Milton Glaser was God; yet very few people outside the industry knew his name, even though practically *everybody* around the world knew the *I Love New York* logo with that big red heart standing in for the word *love*.

Sally couldn't believe it but her center was getting slick. She was actually getting turned on because this gorgeous woman she was with knew the name of a renowned graphic designer and one of Sally's heroes.

Oh, Jesus…

The wine arrived then, which Sally knew wouldn't help. Wine, particularly good wine, always heightened her arousal.

Max is going to kill me.

"Anyway," Amy went on, after they had clinked glasses, "I think your job is super important."

Sally scoffed.

"Says the woman who literally improves other women's lives."

Amy waved that off, but Sally noticed Amy had blushed deeply.

"Fine, I help others, but so do you," she said. "People take comfort in familiarity. Things like the Nike swoosh and the *I Love New York* logo and even the golden arches, can make people feel safe in a world that is always changing. One day, you may also end up designing an image that is known worldwide and will give people comfort because of its familiarity."

Sally's heart was thudding.

"After dinner, let's go the beach," she said.

Amy arched an eyebrow and Sally knew, just knew, that Amy was reading her mind.

"Any particular reason why?"

Sally gave a little nod.

"Because I want our first kiss to be on the beach."

***

Dinner ended up being fabulous with great food and lots of instances of Sally and Amy finishing each other's sentences—a fact Sally appreciated more than the great food. She really had never felt this in tune with another woman; it was like her and Amy were vibing on the same frequency.

Luckily, Sally had had some fabulous girlfriends before—the major exception being Brooke, who had cheated on her—but all of those previous relationships had been lacking an undefinable thing which had contributed to those relationships eventually fizzling out and ending.

Had she found that undefinable thing now?

Was it synchronicity?

She had to remind herself that this was just date number one. Date number two could be a disaster. Date number ten could reveal that Amy was a psychopath.

That is, if Sally ever got to date number two with Amy, let alone date number ten.

That thought was preying on her mind now as her and Amy walked along Carlsbad Boulevard following their dinner, heading towards the entrance to the beach. Sunset was fast approaching and the sky was filled with small fluffy clouds that were tinted pink and lavender. Sally was genuinely worried that the decision she had made almost instantly when she had walked into that coffeeshop and laid eyes on Amy was going to cost her dearly. But she also knew the decision was the only right one.

Maybe I should just do it now…

But her thoughts were interrupted when Amy suddenly said, "I have to admit that I like first dates more when I know I can expect a kiss later."

Sally laughed, blushing.

"I hope I didn't ruin the surprise," she said, pushing aside her recent thoughts as she remembered her bold declaration back at the trattoria.

"Ruin? I thought it was hot."

Sally stopped just short of the pedestrian ramp which led from Carlsbad Boulevard down to the beach. Amy halted also and turned to face her.

"Hot, huh?" Sally said.

"Mm-hmm," Amy replied. She glanced over her shoulder. "But we're not technically on the beach yet, are we?"

"Nope."

After walking down the sloping footpath and just before stepping onto the sand of the beach, both women removed their shoes. As usual for a Friday evening at sunset, the section of the beach near the northern terminus of the seawall was crowded with people waiting to watch the sun disappear. This was the part of the beach near the restaurants and the hotels and timeshares. Sally noticed, though, that towards the south, close to the lagoon, the beach was less populated and so she started in that direction, Amy right beside her.

The two women walked in silence, close together. As their feet shifted in the sand, they would bump gently against one another and with each touch, Sally's excitement kept rising. Eventually, they reached a point near one of the empty lifeguard towers that was remarkably devoid of people. Not that they were completely alone, per se, just that other beachgoers were far enough away that Sally felt like her and Amy were in their own little haven.

Then, everything happened so fast.

No sooner had Sally stopped than Amy was right in front of her, pressing her body against hers as she wrapped her arms around Sally's neck. With a groan of lust, Sally abandoned her original of plan of saying what she wanted to say, cupped the back of Amy's head and brought their lips together for a hungry kiss that immediately made her curl her toes into the sand.

There was nothing tentative about this kiss, the way most first kisses are. Amy's soft lips moved against Sally's with an intensity that liquified Sally's center and when their tongues began playing together, Sally swore she was *thisclose* to coming as her clit pulsed in time with her escalated heartbeat.

But this was wrong.

She could kiss Amy like this for hours, she knew. She could kiss Amy like this from today's sunset until tomorrow's sunrise, but it was wrong.

She forced herself away from Amy.

"Wait!" she suddenly blurted out. Already she missed feeling Amy's lips against hers.

Amy was looking at her with a confused expression.

"Babe, what? If you're worried that you're moving too fast, don't be. I want this too."

Sally loved that Amy was already calling her *babe*.

"No, it's not that. I...I need to tell you something before we...Well, before anything else happens."

"Do you already have a girlfriend?" Amy practically screeched, stepping away from Sally.

"No! I swear, I don't. And before you ask, I don't have a wife either."

Amy knitted her brows.

"Are you straight?" she asked in a whisper.

Sally rolled her eyes.

"Of course not."

"Then what is it?"

Sally swallowed. This was going to be hard to get out but she knew she needed to do it and do it now before things with Amy went any further. This first date was fast heading toward the bedroom and Sally could *not* let that happen without first telling Amy the truth. In fact, she shouldn't have even started kissing Amy until she had come clean.

Of course, she understood the potential implications. There was a very good chance that in the next few moments she would see Amy walking out of her life forever. That scared Sally to no end. Sure, this was just their first date—ergo, they hardly had a long history; but Sally wanted to keep seeing Amy. Their connection was just...it was what people write about. In screenplays, in novels, in poems. And she knew Amy was feeling it too.

She felt a gentle touch on her arm. Amy had stepped forward again and was now within kissing distance once more.

"Hey," Amy said softly. "Whatever it is, just tell me. I'll understand."

You're speaking too soon.

"I'm not Jillian Ashley," Sally said.

She watched as Amy's featured morphed from one of gentle encouragement to utter confusion.

"What do you mean?"

Taking a deep breath, Sally ploughed on.

"I didn't write the Jillian Ashley books. My friend Max did; Jillian Ashley is *his* pen name. I just found out about it myself a week ago. Anyway, he asked me to impersonate Jillian for him because he knew Jillian needed to start doing some interviews before people started getting suspicious and so I said I would."

For twenty percent.

Sally decided to leave out that little tidbit.

She continued. She didn't want to give Amy a chance to interrupt. Not yet. And so she hurriedly told Amy how the interview was set up in Max's house, with Max feeding her the answers to Amy's questions as he sat off-screen.

"You have to believe me, Amy," she went on, "I figured I'd do the interview, one and done, that's it. But then…"

She sighed. How to explain this part?

"But then you asked me to join you for coffee. I should have said no, I know that, but I wanted to see you. I felt we had a connection that I've never felt with anyone ever before and I wanted to have a chance to see if it held up during an actual face-to-face meeting. And it did! I know you probably hate me now but I swear to god, Amy, I really do feel amazing just being with you. I see fireworks when we kiss and I want nothing more than to sit here on the beach holding you all night. Please believe me."

Sally stopped then to take another deep breath.

"I just wanted you to know that," she murmured.

There. It was done. Sally knew that compared to the courageous things countless other people have to do on a daily basis, this confession paled in comparison; yet to her, it felt like she had just done the most frightening thing she had ever done in her life.

And it was the right thing to do, even though she knew it might very well cost her.

Oh, and that Max was going to kill her.

Chapter 13

What the fuck just happened?
Amy was having a hard time wrapping her brain around this. Sally wasn't Jillian? The whole thing had been a lie?
Was this a joke?
But no matter how hard she scrutinized Sally's features now, Amy could detect no sign of mirth or humor. Sally was telling the truth. She wasn't Jillian. Even weirder than that: a *man* was Jillian!

She stepped away from Sally again, farther this time than when she had asked if Sally already had a girlfriend. Right now, she was compelled to give this…imposter the finger, tell her to fuck off and leave her standing here on the beach. But first, there were things to get off her chest.

"You came on my show!" she screamed, the volume of her voice somewhat tempered by the sound of the mighty Pacific's surf. "Do you have any idea how important that show is to me?"

Sally mutely nodded.

"Fuck, Sally!" Amy threw her hands up in the air and started pacing in the sand. Eventually, she stopped and stared at this woman who less than five minutes ago she had been kissing and had wanted to take home to fuck her brains out.

I still do.

She shook her head. She needed her brain to do the thinking now, not her vagina.

"Why?" she demanded. "Why did you do this?"

"I told you!" Sally said. "It was just going to be this one interview! Maybe a few others just to get people off Max's back and show them that, yes, Jillian Ashley really exists."

That made sense. Amy knew from various sources—Twitter, Facebook, comments made by readers of her blog and listeners of her podcast—that Jillian Ashley's Salinger-like reclusiveness, once part of her appeal, was beginning to make people suspicious. The question that was out there was, "Why wouldn't Jillian show herself?"

The theories about that were far-ranging. Most believed Jillian wasn't the seemingly young, shapely woman seen from behind in her author photo but was instead far older and heavier. Others considered that maybe Jillian had been disfigured in a horrible accident. More than one person—unbelievably—had even speculated that all of the Jillian Ashley novels had in fact been written by an AI computer secretly developed by the government.

Amy's eyes went wide as she suddenly remembered someone starting a thread on Twitter, postulating that Jillian might in fact be a man. The original poster had been shot down rather quickly and brutally for even suggesting it. Some of the comments could have even been categorized as bullying. Jillian Ashley had legions of devout and fiercely protective fans.

Another thought came to her, this one so frightening that she knew her legs would no longer support her and she quickly sat down on the sand before she fell down on the sand. She pulled her knees up against her chest and wrapped her arms around them. After a moment, when her nerves felt steady enough to allow her to speak, she looked over at Sally.

"Do you have any idea how many lesbians I just lied to?"

Lesbeing—the Podcast may not be on par with something like *This American Life* but it also wasn't small potatoes anymore. Twenty-five episodes in and she was already over ten-thousand subscribers and the interview with Jillian Ashley had increased the rate of new listeners signing up almost exponentially. She expected to break the fifteen-thousand mark by the end of next week. And her subscribers weren't just SoCal women—not anymore. Amy's podcast had listeners in Japan, Russia, Australia, and other countries, even Liechtenstein! Amy had had to Google that one. And now she was faced with telling all of them—even what had to be the only lesbian in Liechtenstein—that her exclusive Jillian Ashley interview had been a farce.

"Oh god," she groaned, resting her head on her knees and shutting her eyes.

Eventually—minutes later?—a voice said, "You don't have to tell anyone."

Amy opened her eyes and saw that Sally was also sitting on the sand. Despite everything, Amy almost laughed when she noticed that Sally had chosen a spot presumably out of her striking range, about fifteen feet away.

Little does she know how cat-like I can be.

"Who else knows about this?" she asked quietly.

"The whole story? Just me and Max."

Amy thought about that.

Three people.

Not telling anyone was plausible. If the true story was limited to three people—one of whom, this Max character, had a serious vested interest in *not* letting the secret out—then why not? It wasn't in her nature to be so willing to participate in a deception but, really, what did it matter in this case? She had given the lesfic community what it wanted, a look at "Jillian Ashley." And from the reaction to her interview, the lesfic community was satisfied and happy. What harm would it do for her to keep the ruse going? No one need ever know.

Besides, the alternative was horrible. It meant the end of her podcasting career. It had started as a hobby but was now not only a passion of hers, but a *money-making* passion because of the advertising spots she was able to sell on the show's website, not to mention the bits of *Lesbeing* merchandise she occasionally sold through the show's online store.

"Wait a minute," she said. "What did you mean just now when you said 'the whole story?'"

Sally sighed.

"My best friend Lisa watched our interview and now she thinks I'm Jillian Ashley."

Amy blinked.

"You didn't correct her?"

Sally scoffed.

"You don't tell Lisa secrets," she said. "That's how they stop being secrets."

"I see."

Amy bit her bottom lip, thinking things over.

"You could have avoided this whole conversation we're having if you had just turned me down for coffee. Why didn't you?"

Sally's green eyes, which were catching the orange and purple rays from the setting sun, pierced Amy's.

"I'm sorry," she said. "I know I should have turned you down but it was impossible. I wanted to go on a date with you. I just felt like there was something between us that was more than physical attraction and I felt like it would be a decision I'd regret if I didn't at least meet you for one lousy cup of coffee."

Amy sighed. She knew what Sally was referring to, that "something" between them, something which was more than physical attraction—although, Sally was *hot*. But during the interview on Tuesday and then while they were talking afterwards, Amy had felt insanely connected to this woman sitting on the beach with her, connected enough to feel like she finally understood when other people would tell her "I just knew" when talking about meeting their special someones.

"The coffee at La Vida Mocha is not lousy," Amy said.

"You know what I mean," Sally replied.

"And why did you tell me now?" Amy pressed. "I don't mind admitting that things were going your way tonight. Right now, we could have been at my place with a lot less clothes on."

Amy was gratified to hear Sally gasp and then work her mouth, trying to form sentences.

"I told you," Sally was finally able to say, "precisely because I knew things were going my way tonight. Amy, when I arrived at that coffeeshop, I didn't know what would happen. I figured, if our date fell flat and there was no chemistry then, fine, we go our separate ways and I let you keep thinking that you met Jillian Ashley. But our date didn't fall flat."

No, it didn't.

"Amy, I know you probably think I'm some kind of deceitful witch but I'm really not. There was never any malicious intent in any of this. I pretended to be Jillian to help out a friend, that's all. What I didn't count on was meeting you. Even over a stupid webcam I felt connected with you and then when we met in person…I just suddenly wanted to spend every minute of the rest of tonight with you. And I swear I've never felt that before."

"Fuck!" Amy exclaimed. "Why are you making this so hard!"

She sprang to her feet and resumed pacing. Everything Sally had just said, Amy had felt too, especially that bit about wanting to spend every minute of the rest of tonight together. Of course, Amy had planned to spend those minutes exploring every inch of Sally's body with her tongue, lips, fingers and anything else she could use, even her toes if Sally was kinky like that. But Amy also knew that if she and Sally had simply gone back to her place and spent the rest of the night together watching bad TV shows before finally falling asleep in each other's arm, she would have considered the night magical.

"I should be hating you right now!" she exclaimed, stopping in front of Sally, who stood up.

"I get that," Sally said. "I, um, wouldn't blame you. I wish you wouldn't, of course but I knew that telling you this carried the risk of you never wanting to see me again."

Amy suddenly found herself needing to exercise so much self-control. Sally's lips were so close and the memory of how they felt against her own so recent.

"I should go," Sally stated. "For what it's worth, again, I'm sorry."

And then Sally picked up her shoes and was walking away, just as the sun dipped below the horizon.

"Wait!" Amy called out.

Sally stopped and turned.

Amy swallowed. She wasn't completely sure that what she was doing was the right thing but something was telling her it was.

She walked over to where Sally had stopped and stood in front of her.

"Thank you for telling me," she said, meeting Sally's eyes with her own.

"I knew I was going to tell you fifteen seconds after I walked into the coffeeshop,"

"Then why didn't you tell me fifteen seconds after you walked into the coffeeshop?"

Sally shrugged.

"What if I was the only one who felt the way I did? I was hedging my bets, I guess. I figured if you were lukewarm to me or if you spent our entire date checking out that hot brunette behind the counter—"

"Vanessa," Amy supplied. "But you would have to give me a pass on her. Everybody checks out Vanessa. I even know a married lesbian couple who have a No-Cheating-Except-With-Vanessa policy."

Sally laughed.

"I could totally understand that. Anyway, the point is, if I felt that you weren't feeling the same way I was, I'd let you walk away none the wiser."

"But you knew I felt the same way?"
Sally nodded.
"I did," she confirmed. "And so here we are."
"Is everything else you told me true?"
"About my boring life? Yep."
"Don't forget the part about being named after Charlie Brown's sister," Amy added.
"I have her tattooed on my ribcage."
Amy's breath caught. She wanted to see that tattoo.
Actually, I just want to see her ribcage.
She pushed that thought away. It was counterproductive now.
"Before I decide if I never want to see you again," Amy began, "start from beginning and tell me *everything*."

***

How long it took, Amy didn't know, nor did she care. They had sat back down in the sand, facing each other as it grew dark, until the beach was illuminated only by moonlight. It could have been an incredibly romantic setting and she supposed to anyone passing by, it looked that way.

Sally did what Amy had asked and told her *everything*. How Sally herself had only found out the truth about Jillian Ashley just last week. How Sally had been just as shocked by the revelation that her favorite lesfic author was really a man. How this guy, Max, had come to write the books in the first place and how he had offered Sally twenty percent of his royalties to pretend to be Jillian from time to time.

"Wow! Twenty percent?" Amy was impressed. She didn't know the particulars of how many Jillian Ashley books had been sold, either in Kindle format or in paperback, but she figured a twenty percent cut was nothing to sneeze at.

"Amy, I swear," Sally began, "going on a date with you had nothing to do with money!"

"I totally believe you," Amy assured Sally. And she did. From the story which Sally had related, this whole her-pretending-to-be-Jillian-Ashley escapade was nothing sinister, nor had it been embarked upon with any evil intent. "But I'm still having trouble wrapping my mind around the fact that Jillian Ashley is actually a man."

"Tell me about it!" Sally agreed. "When Max told me, I was fucking floored! And a little sad, also. Like I had lost something."

Amy nodded. She felt the exact same way! Since the release of *The Fordham Road Fling,* Jillian Ashley had been an important part of Amy's life because reading was an important part of Amy's life. The escape which books—particularly lesfic books—had provided her, especially during the hardest days of the pandemic lockdowns, were immeasurable. And Jillian Ashley books had been the most important of all the books Amy had read. She had already re-read *The Fordham Road Fling* seven times since it was first released. It was her favorite lesfic book of all time.

How was she supposed to feel about *Fordham Road* now? As well as the other three books in the *Gotham* series released so far?

She decided that could wait. Right now, she had to decide how to feel about this woman sitting in front of her on the dark beach.

Thinking of which...

"We should go," she said, standing up. "I know Carlsbad is pretty safe but it's probably smart if two women don't sit around on a dark and quickly emptying beach."

She reached her hand down to help Sally up and as soon Sally took it, Amy knew what would happen next because the contact sent a thrill through her body which started at her arm and ended at her heart.

The act of pulling Sally up caused Sally to end up directly in front of Amy, with only a sliver of space separating them. And Amy erased that sliver of space immediately, claiming Sally's lips once more in a deep kiss, not caring about anything else except this moment. Jillian Ashley may be a man but Sally Whatever-her-last-name-is was a woman and Amy wanted every bit of her, as evidenced by the fact that her panties were now soaked, her pussy seemingly incapable of *not* producing liquid and pushing it out.

Sally pulled her lips away too soon. Amy mewled in protest.

"Are you sure?" Sally purred, nuzzling Amy's neck which made Amy want to collapse back onto the sand with pleasure.

"Positive," Amy stated, entangling her fingers in Sally's black hair. "Follow me back to my place."

She felt her earlobe get captured between Sally's teeth and then Sally's tongue circling the diamond stud she was wearing.

"What if I can't wait that long?" Sally whispered after a good tug on the lobe with her teeth.

Amy's heart thudded and her desire kicked into overdrive.

"Then don't wait," she practically growled.

Suddenly, Sally turned her around, pressing against her back and wrapping her arms around her. Her heart pounding in anticipation, Amy surveyed the setting.

Now that the sun had gone down, marking the end of another gorgeous day in Carlsbad, the beach had emptied considerably, though a few diehard beachgoers remained, most of them sitting with friends on the sand here and there. Amy could spot two joggers running together, heading away from them in the direction of Oceanside whose pier she could just make out the lights of three miles distant. However, in the immediate vicinity of where she was standing with Sally, right next to lifeguard tower #34, there was no one.

A good thing to, because Amy felt Sally's left hand start to slide up under her shirt. Amy gasped as the hand came to rest on her abdomen. Her breathing became shallower.

"Is this okay?" Sally asked.

Amy nodded and the hand slid a little further up until it was now resting on her chest just below the underwires of her bra.

"Still okay?"

Amy nodded again but this time, to show just how okay she was with what was happening, she also reached behind, finding the back of Sally's left thigh and squeezed it. The groan Sally gave in response made Amy groan as well.

Thus encouraged, Sally's hand now came up to cover the right cup of Amy's padded bra just before her fingers stole inside it, found her nipple and began pinching it.

"Oh god, Sally…"

"It's like a fucking diamond," Sally murmured.

That was hardly an exaggeration, Amy considered. Both of her nipples were achingly hard.

While Sally pinched and kneaded the electrified nub, she was kissing along Amy's neck, stopping every now and then to rake her teeth against the flesh as if she was going to take a big bite and Amy actually wished Sally was a vampire. She wanted to feel her neck punctured by sharp fangs while her clit was throbbing as it was now, knowing she would explode in orgasm at the pain and then the warmth as her blood was sucked.

After another few moments, Sally's hand left Amy's breast and slid back down. Amy thought maybe they would leave now, walk back to La Vida Mocha's parking lot, where they had left their cars, and finally head back to her place.

But she was wrong.

Sally wasn't done with her yet.

Now Sally had hooked both of her thumbs into Amy's jeans, right at the front, and the thumbs were playfully rubbing her lower abdomen just above her panties.

"Totally okay," Amy whispered before Sally asked. It had been too long since another woman had touched her like this and her center was now nothing but liquid.

"Are you *sure* sure?" Sally nonetheless asked.

Whereas Amy could appreciate Sally's consideration, she needed Sally to forget the question of consent right now.

"Yes! Please!" she croaked.

Sally didn't waste any more time and started unfastening Amy's jeans.

"Oh my god!" Amy whispered, her clit pulsing nearly as strongly as her heart as the cool night air found its way into her pants and softly caressed her most sensitive region.

Fingers slid into the unfastened pants and then slid under her panties and then, right there on the beach, out in the open, Sally's fingers were on Amy's pussy.

"Oh fuck, you're so wet!" Sally exclaimed.

Amy couldn't speak, she could only whimper as Sally played with all that wetness, sending waves of pleasure shooting out of Amy's core. Sally's other arm wrapped itself around Amy's midsection, making Amy feel captured, a prisoner of this woman who was taking her on the beach like this. She couldn't help but cry out when a finger was curled inside her. There was still no one around them, not close enough to have noticed the sound, and so Amy allowed herself to be a little vocal. It was getting impossible not to, anyway, because Sally's hand was pressing and rocking firmly against her clit while that lone finger wiggled inside her.

"I'm so close!" Amy said. "Oh shit, I'm coming! I'm coming!"

And then, euphoria.

Shuddering in Sally's arms, she surrendered to the orgasm which hit her, biting her lips to keep from screaming out. Her pussy throbbed and convulsed against Sally's hand, her come leaking out, soaking not only her panties but her thighs as well because the panties could no longer contain it.

Amy felt Sally tighten her grip with that arm she had around her, imprisoning her even more solidly.

"I got you," Sally whispered in her ear.

Good thing, too, because Sally's embrace was all that was keeping Amy upright. Her knees were now jelly and threatening to buckle. Being fucked in public like this, on a moonlit beach was adding to the intensity of the orgasm, making the muscles in all of her limbs weak. Finally she had to release her lips and allow a mewling moan to escape; it couldn't be helped.

Fuck, that was fast!

When it was done, Sally withdrew her hand and even very politely refastened Amy's jeans. For her part, Amy couldn't move, not just yet. She was trembling and whimpering softly while Sally held her in her arms, kissing her neck softly, letting Amy enjoy the last remnants of all that pleasure.

Chapter 14

It was Sally's idea to call a Lyft.

After bringing Amy to an orgasm right there on the beach, Sally's own center was on fire. It needed to be touched and kissed and penetrated and she was so wet and so desperate for Amy to do all of those things that the thought of walking all the way back to La Vida Mocha and then following Amy back to her place…no, it couldn't happen. That was going to take too long!

When Amy's climax had finished having its way with her, Sally had asked where she lived.

"The Arbors," Amy had whispered. "Over by the Buena Vista Lagoon."

"That's too far," Sally had said, still nuzzling Amy's neck. "My place is closer, if you'd like?"

"I'd like. I'd really, really like."

And so Sally had called for the Lyft and while they waited in the beach's parking lot for the car to arrive, they had stood under a streetlamp kissing non-stop as if they were teenagers in high school making out under the bleachers.

During the ride to her condo, they hadn't spoken, just cuddled in the back seat of the Kia Sportage driven by five-star driver Tyrone.

"Oh my god, this is so cute!" Amy now exclaimed, stepping into Sally's home.

"Thanks!"

Sally, like anyone who unexpectedly brought someone over to their dwelling, did a quick survey of the living room, dining room and kitchen, determining that, thankfully, her place wasn't a mess. Okay, she had left her much-loved and much-worn Carlsbad High sweatshirt on the sofa after taking it off last night when she had started feeling too warm. And, okay, she had also left an empty wine glass on the coffee table last night as well, but on the whole she didn't believe Amy would think her a slovenly person. Well, as long as Amy also didn't care about the pair of high heels that should have been in the bedroom closet but were in fact over by the dining room table where Sally had kicked them off back on…

Christ! Wednesday?

"Drink?" Sally asked as a way of hopefully diverting Amy's attention from her pigsty of a home.

Amy turned to her and their eyes locked. She shook her head. "No. I definitely don't want a drink."

And just like that, their lips were together again.

This was moving far, far faster than she normally preferred, Sally knew. This was supposed to be a proper date, after all; prelude to a relationship. Rapidly escalating things to the point of sex was fine back when she was twenty-one, but she was twenty-eight and craving more substantial bonds with women now. Yet, what was happening between her and Amy not only couldn't be stopped, it also felt so right.

Besides, the throbbing between her legs was telling her that now was not the time to be thinking about anything other than this moment. And she knew Amy felt the same too. God, the woman had been *soaked* when Sally fingered her on the beach…

Reluctantly breaking the kiss, Sally took hold of Amy's hand and practically sprinted with her into the bedroom where they disturbed Lena, who had been napping on the bed. After sussing out the situation, namely that her human had another human with her who looked to be staying a while, she jumped off the bed to go do cat-like things elsewhere in the condo.

As if they were of one mind, both women pulled off their shirts as soon as they were in the bedroom and then were back in each other's arms, kissing hungrily, Sally feeling Amy's cute soft pink padded bra pressing against her chest and Amy's hands reaching down and cupping her ass.

A moment later, Amy pulled Sally over to the bed, made her lay on it face down and then lowered her body on top of hers. Sally groaned when Amy started kissing the back of her neck, her clit reacting to each touch of her lips with tiny pulses of pleasure.

"I'm going to take my time with you, Sally," Amy purred, her lips now ghosting Sally's ear.

Yes!

"Do you have to be anywhere tomorrow?" Amy asked, her voice still a purr.

"Just here with you," Sally responded. "Doing this."

"Excellent…because this is going to take all night."

Amy's kisses then started falling on Sally's shoulder blades, first the left side, then the right, Amy interspersing licks with the flat of her tongue in with the kisses, making Sally feel electrified.

Next, Amy licked along the straps of Sally's bra, occasionally letting her tongue slide under the strap, lifting it just a skosh and letting it snap back down.

"Oh fuck!" Sally moaned each time this happened, the sudden tingle of the mild sting that was caused making her grind her hips against the mattress.

"Ooh, there she is!" Sally heard Amy say. At first, Sally didn't know what she was referring to but when Amy's lips and tongue started lavishing attention on a certain spot on her ribcage, Sally knew Amy had spotted the tattoo of Charlie Brown's sister. Somehow, even though Sally was quite ticklish, Amy's mouth on her ribcage did not cause her to break out into fits of giggles; instead, it made Sally's pussy even wetter and she moaned as her swollen clit twitched in her panties.

Her bra was unhooked and Amy kissed that bit of flesh which the closure had covered.

Sally decided it was time to let Amy know the gentleness could stop.

"You can bite," she murmured.

"Ooh, can I?"

"Please. And mark me."

"Oh, fuck…"

Permission thus given, Sally was pleased Amy didn't screw around. The first bite, right on her shoulder blade, was hard, painful. It caused Sally to cry out with the kind of sound which simultaneously telegraphed how much it hurt and how much it was close to making her come. The flesh was held in Amy's teeth and pulled, Sally riding out the pain, her core responding, until finally Amy released the skin.

"Okay?" Amy asked.

Sally nodded and so Amy chose another spot and clamped her teeth on it and again Sally cried out, her pussy pumping out more arousal, this bite just as hard as the previous one, Amy's sharp little teeth relentlessly holding onto Sally's skin and now Sally's inner walls started fluttering.

"Again…" she mewled when Amy was done.

This time, the bite came right above the waist of her jeans, Sally's eyes squeezing shut not only because of delicious pain but because now her center was positively going crazy. Amy's mouth was inches away and her pussy knew it.

"Amy, fuck me, please!" Sally cried out.

The teeth let go, lingering remnants of the pain still tingling Sally's core. Amy got off her back and turned her over. When Sally tossed off her bra, Amy gasped.

"Oh my god, Sally…" she said, eyeing Sally's breasts. She brought her face down to Sally's chest and this time, Sally reveled in how gentle Amy was as she pulled one of her nipples into her mouth, circling it with her tongue, softly suckling it, moaning as she did so. First the left, then the right…each hard and pebbled nipple was lavished with sensual attention, the pleasure only heightened for Sally by the visual of seeing Amy's lips puckered around her now incredibly sensitive buds.

When she apparently had her fill of Sally's breasts, Amy set about removing Sally's skinny jeans, hurriedly pulling them along with Sally's panties over Sally's hips and then down her legs so that the jeans came off inside-out with the panties still stuck to them.

Completely nude now, Sally pulled her knees up, opened her legs and pierced Amy's eyes with her own, daring Amy to come get her. She could see that Amy was trembling with desire, her mouth slack-jawed, her eyes wide and full of lust.

"Where's your vibrator?" Amy asked and Sally gasped.

Toys already? Yum!

"Clothes off first," she ordered.

Amy quickly opened her front-clasp bra and Sally licked her lips upon seeing Amy's small but pert breasts with rosy nipples.

"They're tiny," Amy said somewhat apologetically.

"Baby, they're perfection," Sally replied.

Amy then made quick work of her jeans, also removing her own panties simultaneously and Sally's clit pulsed at seeing Amy's completely shaved mound, the swollen lips of her pussy glistening with arousal.

With her companion now nude, Sally used her eyes and a slight tilt of her head to indicate the nightstand on the right side of her bed. Her favorite vibrator was kept in there, handy, ready for use anytime she needed it. If things kept progressing nicely, later she'd introduce Amy to the other magical items she kept in a plastic storage container under her bed.

With the purple slimline vibrator in hand, Amy got back on the queen-sized bed, settling herself comfortably with her head between Sally's legs.

Sally felt Amy's breath on her sex, caressing her clit, flowing over her wet lips, creating a cooling sensation which made Sally arch her head back as she waited for the inevitable.

"Fuck, babe, you smell so good!"

"Taste me, baby…"

And so Amy did, the flat of her tongue going up one side of Sally's pussy, up to her mound where Amy then licked the length of Sally's strip of hair, and then back down the other side of the pussy. Then, Sally felt Amy's tongue penetrate her and Sally's hands immediately gripped the bedsheets tightly, her back arching. She felt her pussy flooding even more, felt the liquid leaking out around that tongue which was swirling inside her, Amy moaning in pleasure as she tasted and drank.

"Fuck, Amy, I'm close!" Sally warned.

She heard a familiar *click* and then *bzzzzzzzzzz*. Sally groaned in anticipation, waiting to feel the touch of the buzzing toy on her sex. But Amy didn't press the vibe against her electrified pussy. Instead, she slid it in between the cheeks of Sally's ass.

Oh fuck!

Amy had positioned it perfectly, securing it tightly between Sally's cheeks. The toy, buzzing on its highest setting, was sending vibrations through Sally's entire ass, vibrations that were also felt a short distance away in her pussy. Amy's mouth was now on her clit, pulling on it gently, swiping it with her tongue.

How did she know?

Sally always enjoyed a bit of anal play in her sex life. And though Amy hadn't penetrated her ass with the vibrator, by sliding it between her cheeks as she did it was as if Amy was silently telling Sally, *I already know what you like!*

Sally was completely delirious now. She arched her back again but this time pushed down harder on the mattress with her ass, pressing that vibrator against it even more, making her bottom a tingling, energized part of everything sensational happening between her legs. And it was exquisite.

"Oh *fuuuuck*! The exclamation was screamed. "Oh *FUUUUCK*!" Screamed even louder.

Amy's tongue worked faster on Sally's button until…

Sally exploded.

"FUCKING CHRIST!"

Bursts of light popped behind her eyelids as her pussy came undone, her walls squeezing, her juices streaming out, her entire sex throbbing and convulsing rapidly as this climax became her world. The vibrations radiating through her ass thanks to the toy were adding layer upon layer on the orgasm until a second one hit her moments later, just as forceful as the first.

"Fuuuuuuck!"

And then she couldn't speak, only cry out with animal-like sounds. Nor could she control her own body any longer. Her long-limbed five-ten form started spasming, her hips bucking until she actually turned herself over, burying her face in the mattress, screaming until another big wave of pleasure hit her and turned her over again.

She felt Amy lay on top of her trembling, twitching body, pinning her arms down with her hands above her head. Sally's legs were parted with Amy's thigh and suddenly Sally had a surface to grind her demanding pussy against while Amy held her captive and kissed her with lips still slick with her come.

And soon Sally was coming again.

Chapter 15

"Aaaaahhhh! Fuck!"

Amy pounded the mattress with her fists as her latest orgasm rocked her, Sally's vibrator still being pumped in and out of her swollen pussy by Sally as the woman bit Amy's left nipple hard, the pain only adding to the fireworks happening below her waist.

"Oh my fucking god!" Amy finally gasped out. "Oh fuck, baby!"

She heard the vibrator click off, felt her nipple released from Sally's teeth and then her and Sally were cuddling while Amy recovered from the paroxysms of pleasure which were starting to slowly subside, Sally stroking her hair as she came down from the high.

What time was it? She had no idea. But her and Sally had been at it for a while now. They were both sweaty, rapidly breathing women, each with several bite marks all over their bodies now because fortune had finally smiled on Amy and she had found a woman who also saw the erotic fun of a little sexy pain.

After a while, Sally rolled over onto her back, staring at the ceiling.

"Yep, Max is definitely going to kill me," she said, shaking her head.

Amy felt her professional instincts kicked in.

"You're not in any real danger from this guy, are you?" she asked.

Sally looked at her with raised eyebrows and started chuckling.

"From Max? God no! I trust him with my life! I mean, he puts on this gruff exterior but in reality he's a big softie. And he would never dream of hurting me."

"I'd like to meet him," Amy said after a moment. She couldn't help it. She realized now that she just *had* to meet the guy who wrote all those Jillian Ashley books.

Sally rolled onto her side again, facing Amy.

"Please don't be upset with him," she said. "If you knew him like I know him, you'd realize that he didn't write those books to hurt anybody. He wasn't trying to play a trick on gay women and bamboozle us. Like I told you earlier, it started off as a silly personal challenge he gave himself as a writer and then it turned out he was good at it and was making money from it."

"I get that," Amy replied. It was still a big letdown that Jillian Ashley wasn't female, though. Even if Sally had been the beard for a woman who looked more like Danny DeVito than like, well, Sally, Amy would have been more at peace with that discovery than this one.

"I suppose," Amy continued, thoughtfully, "that it doesn't really matter if a man writes lesfic?"

"Honestly?" Sally began. "I don't see why it should. Of course, I've had a little longer to live with the truth about Jillian than you have, and at first, I was upset. But after thinking about it for a few days…"

She sat up then and Amy's eyes immediately went to Sally's breasts. Larger than her own and teardrop-shaped, with nipples that were a soft, almost-not-there pink, Amy was mesmerized by them. She licked her lips but controlled herself from touching them.

Sally went on.

"After a few days, I began to think, what difference does it make? Max wrote four really terrific books about lesbians. The stories were interesting and they brought me happiness when I read them, especially during the quarantine period of the pandemic."

Amy nodded, also adjusting herself so she was sitting up next to Sally against the padded headboard. Sally had a point: the Jillian Ashley novels brought her happiness also—and countless others as well.

"And what's super cool," Sally continued, "is that Max treats women with respect in all his books. I mean, as a guy, he could have written a smutty porno book about lesbians but instead he created strong female characters that aren't just sexual objects."

"True." Amy remembered being really impressed after finishing her first Jillian Ashley novel. The characters had seemed three-dimensional, with the concerns and struggles of real women everywhere. She started thinking now that some lesfic authors (who she knew were actually female) did a much worse job portraying women in their books, making them seem like sex-crazed, money-hungry prowlers who let their clitorises do all the thinking for them.

"But those sex scenes Jillian—I mean, your friend—wrote…" Amy murmured.

Next to her, Sally nodded.

"I know."

"Chapter twenty-five."

"Chapter twenty-five," Sally agreed.

"Anyway," Amy began, "never meet your heroes." She slid herself back down so she was once more prone on the bed, Sally doing the same. They lay there, facing each other.

Sally asked her what she meant by that.

"Just something I read somewhere," Amy said with a rueful smile. "Basically, never meet your heroes because if you do, they'll inevitably disappoint you. I don't know who said it but it applies to our situation. I wanted to meet my hero Jillian Ashley and practically begged her to be on my podcast. If I had left well enough alone, I would still think she was that mysterious, dark-haired woman who is only seen from behind in her author's photo."

Sally bit her lip.

"But then we wouldn't be here together right now."

Amy considered that.

"True," she said with a smile, knowing that she wouldn't have traded tonight for anything in the world. "So maybe the expression ought to be: 'Never meet your heroes unless they're supermodels with green eyes and incredibly long fingers that really, really, *really*, can reach in deep.'"

Sally laughed but then bit her lip again.

"Are you…are you going to tell anyone the real story?" she asked. "I just need to know exactly how much trouble I'm in with Max."

"Fuck no!" Amy insisted. "First of all, I have an archnemesis named Rhonda and she'll use this to destroy me! Secondly, it turns out there's at least one lesbian in Liechtenstein and she subscribes to my podcast and I don't want to disappoint her. The poor woman has enough problems being the only lesbian in an entire country. Thirdly, what's the point?"

She went on, explaining to Sally that telling the world that Jillian Ashley was in fact…

"What's Max's last name?" she asked Sally.

"Tremont," Sally provided.

…Max Tremont would be doing a disservice to the lesfic community. Why ruin it for everybody? Right now, Jillian Ashley books were important to a lot of people, for a lot of different reasons.

"I don't want to be the one who takes that away," Amy concluded. She paused then. "What I'm more concerned about…"

"Yes?"

Amy swallowed and pierced Sally's eyes with her own.

"I guess what I'm more concerned about is if this is the biggest surprise you have for me. Like, do you swear everything else about you is true?"

Sally's eyes went wide and she nodded vigorously.

"Yes! Oh my god, yes!"

"Because what happened tonight," Amy said, feeling shy all of a sudden, "is unusual for me. I don't usually have sex on first dates."

"Neither do I," Sally assured her.

"This wasn't a one-night thing, was it?" Amy asked.

"Only if you tell me you voted for Trump."

Amy laughed.

"As if. In fact, I almost moved to Finland when he was elected."

"Finland?"

"Uh-huh. They always get voted 'Happiest Country in the World.' I figured how could I go wrong there?"

"Sensible thinking," Sally agreed. "But if you had moved to Finland, then I wouldn't have ever met you and then I wouldn't be able to do this…"

Amy gasped when, quick as a flash, Sally's hand was between her legs and two incredibly long fingers were sliding between her slick folds. Moaning, Amy rotated her hips slightly so she could open her legs, submitting to Sally, letting her know she could do what she wanted.

"Fuck Finland," she murmured, closing her eyes.

Chapter 16

Max was pinching the bridge of his nose, his eyes squeezed shut. He had actually been doing it for nearly five minutes after Sally had stopped speaking and she was beginning to worry that maybe he had suffered a stroke. But she waited patiently. It was the least she could do.

"I would have been better off telling the New York Times," he finally muttered.

Sally sighed.

"I'm sorry!" she repeated for what felt like the trillionth time.

They were at Max's house, sitting together on his massive couch. Sally had driven over there right after she and Amy had retrieved their cars from the parking lot behind La Vida Mocha.

The morning had been amazing.

Sally had actually been woken up by Amy eating her out! In fact, she remembered clearly that just before she became fully awake, her last dream had been wildly pornographic—obviously her subconscious's way of telling her that wildly pornographic things were being done to her in real life, and when she finally snapped out of her slumber, she had already been so close to coming that it had only taken a few more swipes of Amy's tongue before the orgasm hit her.

Once she'd recovered, she had reciprocated on Amy, deciding also to leave yet another bite mark on her inner thigh. Then they'd had sex in the shower. Sally then loaned Amy one of her dresses—a short one which on Sally was actually short but on Amy looked like a maxi dress—so she wouldn't have to wear the same clothes as the night before and then cooked a breakfast of scrambled eggs, toast and sausage patties.

Eventually, they had used a Lyft to drive them back to their cars and after making plans to go on another date tonight, separated for the day, Sally deciding to head straight to Max's.

"After I met her," she now said after that trillionth apology, "I knew I wanted to keep seeing her and I also knew I wouldn't want to keep up the lie."

Max threw up his hands.

"Well, I knew it had to end someday," he said, getting up from his couch and pacing. "It's my own fault, really. I've seen *The*

L Word. Two cute lesbians get together for coffee, next thing you know they have a joint bank account and nuclear launch codes are being shared."

"No, check it out..." Sally said, standing up and stopping her friend's pacing by placing her hands on his shoulders. "Babe, listen...Amy isn't going to tell anyone that you're the author of the Jillian Ashley books. She doesn't want to blow your cover. Besides, it would kind of fuck things up for her and her podcast. And you know I won't let your secret out."

Max gave her an incredulous look.

"You already *let* my secret out, you looney toon!"

"Okay, good point," Sally conceded. "But I won't tell anyone else, I promise!" She paused. "Anyway...there's one other thing. Amy would like to meet you."

"Meet me?"

Sally nodded.

"No! Nothing doing!" Max exclaimed, stepping away from Sally and resuming his pacing.

Sally's face fell.

"Why not?" she asked.

"Why not?" Max stopped pacing and glared at her. "Are you outta your mind? It's clearly an assassination attempt! On behalf of all lesbians worldwide your new sweetheart is going to plunge a dagger into my heart!"

Sally rolled her eyes.

"Jesus, Max! Can you stop being a paranoid New Yorker for five minutes? Amy is really sweet! You'll like her."

Max gave her a look which clearly indicated that he was not buying what Sally was selling but Sally was grateful that for the moment, he seemed willing to drop the subject.

"I am *soooooo* super sorry," she repeated for the trillionth-and-one time. "Do you hate me?"

She really was worried about this. She didn't want to lose Max from her world, not because Fate had briefly created a perfect storm in her life of being entrusted with a huge secret while simultaneously meeting a fabulous woman she definitely wanted to keep seeing.

Max huffed and looked at her sternly.

"Stop worrying about silly shit like that," he told her gruffly. "You're annoying but I could never hate you."

"Yay!" Sally skipped over to him, giving him a hug. Keeping him wrapped in her arms, she looked at him. They were the same height when Sally was wearing flats as she was now and so she was able to meet his eyes directly. She said, "Aren't you at least happy that I apparently have a girlfriend now?"

"Well, it *will* be nice for me to have someone else to share the burden of putting up with you."

"Oh, shut up! You love me."

"I kind of like you; that's as far as I'll go."

It was their usual banter and it made Sally feel relieved. Just as she released Max from her grasp, her phone chirped.

Looking forward to later! See you at 2!!

"Shit!" Sally exclaimed. Ainsley.

"What's wrong now?" Max asked.

Sally looked at her watch.

"Fuck, I have to leave. I have a blind date in less than ninety minutes!" She gathered up her purse.

"A blind date? With *another woman?* Jesus, Sal!"

"It's not like that," Sally insisted, heading towards the front door. "My Mom…"

"Oh."

Sally knew Max understood. He had listened to enough of her tales about her mother's matchmaking attempts.

"Just don't go telling *her* about Jillian Ashley also!" Max called out as Sally exited the house.

***

At five minutes to two o'clock, pleased that she was early, Sally approached the entrance to the bar Ainsley had chosen. It was a laid-back, chill-vibe kind of place, fronting the beach, with a mid-century tropical décor aesthetic.

She had considered canceling this silly fix-up thing. She hadn't even bothered changing her clothes after rushing home from Max's to prepare. All she had done was apply some makeup—some mascara and a little eyeshadow—made sure Lena had some food and then left, figuring that her current outfit of denim shorts, pink tank and flip-flops was suitable enough. After all, she had just had an amazing night with Amy and wanted to take the time to explore having a relationship with her. *That's* who she wanted to be with right now, not here in Solana Beach about to meet some snooty doctor from Mount Olympus named *Ainsley*.

Opening the door to the bar, Sally rolled her eyes again at how pretentious that name was. She didn't care if earlier today, Ainsley had saved some little kid's life by performing some kind of radical emergency surgery. Good on her. But there was no way Sally was going to enjoy spending more than five minutes with someone named—

"Sally?"

Sally turned at the sound of her name.

Holy Jesus!

Standing near the hostess's station was a stunning blonde with eyes the color of sapphire. She was dressed much like Sally was: shorts and a tank (a blue one which Sally couldn't help noticing really brought out her eyes). And she was tall! Because the woman was also wearing flip-flops, Sally could assess that she was the same height as herself, a refreshing change because Sally was used to being the tall one.

The woman stepped forward, pink lips upturned and parted in a devastating smile.

"Hi, I'm Ainsley!"

Sally swallowed.

They know how to build them on Mount Olympus!

She suddenly remembered her manners.

"Sally," she said. "Nice to meet you!"

Ainsley pointed behind her, over her shoulder.

"I've already found us a spot. Shall we?"

Certain she was smiling goofily, Sally nodded and followed Ainsley to a small table near the window offering a view of the beach.

"So, I don't know what you like to drink," Ainsley began, "but this place makes the best margaritas! And they have, like, every flavor imaginable."

"I love margaritas!" Sally told her.

Ainsley smiled.

"Meddling mothers and a love of margaritas. Two things we have in common."

Sally laughed.

"If only meddling mothers were as easy to make disappear as margaritas," she joked.

A male server with the kind of chiseled good looks Sally knew straight women typically lost their minds over, stopped at their table and took their drinks order: a raspberry margarita for Ainsley and a watermelon one for Sally. Giving both of them his best flirting smile, having no idea what a waste of energy that was, he promised to be back soon with their drinks.

Left alone again, Ainsley was about to say something when Sally noticed a peculiar look come over her features. Suddenly, Ainsley's hands flew to her face and she gasped, looking at Sally with wide eyes.

"Oh my God! I just realized who you are!" she exclaimed.

Sally blinked.

"Um...Dr. Lassiter's daughter?"

"Jillian Ashley!"

Now, Sally's eyes widened.

Oh fuck!

"Um..."

"I watched your interview on *Lesbeing* the other day!"

Shit! Shit! Shit!

Seriously? In the most populated state in the union, the lesbian universe was still *this* small?

She gulped. There was no way she could tell yet another person—in less than twenty-four hours!—the truth about Jillian Ashley. Amy might be cool about it now—and Sally was certain that the several orgasms she had given Amy had played something of role in that—but Ainsley might not be cool with it and might start blabbing the truth to anyone who would listen. And Sally wasn't about to arrange things so that she would end up giving Ainsley several orgasms as a way of buying *her* silence (though, quite frankly, the thought of doing so made Sally cross her legs under the table).

"Yep!" she said. "I'm Jillian Ashley!"

"Sally, I'm not kidding, you are my favorite author! When I heard that you were going to be on Amy's show, I got so excited."

Sally started panicking a bit. She didn't have Max feeding her lines this time which meant she was going to have to come up with how to pretend to be a famous writer all on her own.

"I'm...I'm so glad you enjoy my work," she said, feeling rather pleased. That sounded like something a famous writer would say.

"Like it? I love it! My god, you have no idea! Reading is my favorite way to unwind after a long day at the hospital. And your books are the best. I've read *The Fordham Road Fling* six times now."

"Oh my god, me too!" Sally enthused.

Shit!

"I mean," she started her backtracking, "I...um...I *re-read* it six times while I was...editing it?" She smiled. She was going to have to remember all this great stuff to tell Max later so he could know what a great job she did. He'd be so proud of her.

Ainsley nodded.

"It shows," she complimented. "Your books don't have a lot of the silly mistakes other books have."

The server with the chiseled face returned then with their drinks. Sally was glad for the interruption. Maybe now they'd stop talking about what a great writer she was.

But no such luck.

After clinking their glasses, Ainsley leaned forward and said, "So, my meddling mother didn't tell me I was going on a blind date with a famous writer."

"Oh! Well, um...that's because your meddling mother doesn't know I'm a famous writer and that's because *my* meddling mother doesn't know I'm a famous writer."

Inwardly, she groaned because she knew that she had just started them down a rabbit hole of conversation. She knew—just knew!—Ainsley would then ask why Sally's mother didn't know about her writing. And sure enough, Ainsley asked that very question. Sally then had to come up with some balderdash about how she wasn't sure how her very image-conscious mother would react to learning her daughter was writing lesbian fiction books.

When she was done, Sally was amazed at herself. She was actually getting quite good at making shit up on her own!

And the best part was that Ainsley bought it!

"I totally understand," Ainsley said. "But, really, by now, I would think that Dr. Lassiter would be so proud of what you've accomplished. Your books do really well, don't they?"

Sally nodded.

"Yep. Really well."

It was when Ainsley's leg inadvertently brushed against hers under the table and Sally realized how much it thrilled her that she realized she needed to change the topic.

"Listen, Ainsley, there's something I need to tell you."

"Go right ahead," Ainsley replied, and Sally was certain her voice had a touch of a lascivious purr to it.

"Turns out that Amy—the host of the podcast, you know—and I really hit it off and, well, we started dating."

"Oh!"

Ainsley's face registered her disappointment.

"I'm so sorry!" Sally added. "It literally just happened last night! Our first date, I mean..."

And first orgasms together.

Smiling—and she really did have a devastatingly beautiful smile, Sally considered—Ainsley said, "No worries. We did agree to just meet up in order to get our mothers off our backs."

"Yeah, but..." Sally hesitated but decided to plow ahead. "Trust me, when I saw you...I was like, wow!"

"Oh god, don't tell me that!" Ainsley said, pretending to cover her ears, laughing. "Because I was, like, wow, too!"

Sally blushed.

Ainsley leaned forward again.

"Actually, thank you for telling me. Especially since..."

Sally quirked an eyebrow.

"Especially since...?"

Ainsley bit her lip and smiled.

"Especially since I've been giving you *fuck me* signals since we sat down. You could have kept me in the dark about you and Amy and after we were done here, we could have ended up at my place sharing a lot more than margaritas."

Chapter 17

Back in Carlsbad, Amy was at her apartment sitting on the floor of her living room, laptop on her lap, working on notes for her next episode of *Lesbeing—the Podcast*. This next show was going to be a discussion about depictions of lesbians in period dramas with particular focus on why such films tend to always have tragic endings for the main characters. Amy loved period dramas. Amy especially loved period dramas with lesbians in them. But she was growing impatient with filmmakers for not ever providing happy endings. Wasn't the world shitty enough?

She had already lined up a pair of really cool guests for the episode. One was a film archivist at a LGBTQ museum in New York City; the other was an up-and-coming young gay actress who had recently starred in an indie period piece about two lesbians in the eighteenth-century whose story—surprise, surprise—ends tragically.

After returning home from Sally's, Amy had taken a nap. It had been a long night, after all. She had ended up sleeping well for a couple of hours but had woken up absolutely soaked between her legs, her clit throbbing thanks to the dreams about Sally she'd had. At the time, she was torn between taking care of that urge right then and there or waiting. Tonight, she had another date with Sally and wouldn't it be fun to let Sally release this climax for her?

But lying there in bed, she had also realized that she had a lot of work to do today: notes for the next podcast episode, responding to fans' emails and laundry. She knew herself well enough to know that being incredibly horny was always counterproductive and so, after edging herself for a few minutes to really get the engine going, a few swipes of her finger over her clit in her panties was all it took before she was gasping and moaning as a strong orgasm took possession of her core. If things ended up well for her tonight after her date, there would plenty more for Sally to unleash.

Now, she finished writing the notes for the next podcast episode and closed her laptop, standing to stretch her body. The late afternoon sunlight was lying in streaks across her living room floor, filtered through the blinds of the window. Noticing how orange the sunlight was, Amy looked at the clock on the wall next to her flat-screen TV. It showed just past five-thirty. Her date with Sally was at seven. Well, their reservations were at seven; Sally was going to pick her up at six-thirty. They were going to Vigilucci's, an upscale Italian seafood restaurant on Carlsbad Boulevard. If she hurried, she'd have just enough time to get ready.

Naturally, her phone rang. Instead of being annoyed, however, when Amy saw who it was, she muttered, "Finally!"

Really, what was the point of having a best friend if said best friend wasn't around to talk to *immediately* after Amy had slept with a new woman for the first time? But Rachel, a junior realtor at a local agency, had spent the whole day at an open house for one of her listings and thus couldn't take any time to hear about the sapphic exploits of her best friend.

"I know, I know..." Rachel said as soon as the call connected, "but at least I got three solid offers on the place."

"Congratulations!" Amy was happy for her friend, who was working hard trying to establish herself in the SoCal real estate market—an incredibly competitive challenge. "I'm putting you on speakerphone because I need to get ready for my date."

"So, there will be a second date, huh? Spill the beans about last night!"

Amy had to pause then, standing in the hall, halfway between the living room and her bedroom.

All day long, what with lurid recollections of what her and Sally had gotten up to last night, combined with all the work she had had to do, Amy hadn't actually spent any time considering what she would tell her best friend regarding what she now referred to as the Jillian Ashley Thing.

On the one hand, she trusted Rachel. Moreover, Rachel wasn't part of the lesfic community and thus wouldn't really care that Jillian Ashley was in fact a man. Rachel would probably spend all of ten seconds laughing about it and then change the topic.

On the other hand, the Jillian Ashley Thing was a really big secret and even though Amy trusted Rachel, Rachel would nonetheless be another possible vector for the truth to be leaked out, and Amy really did not want this truth to be leaked. The ramifications to her reputation as a podcaster and commentator on all things lesbian would be harsh, sure, but they could possibly be mitigated and perhaps over time would fade. She was more concerned about playing a role in the lesfic community losing the books of Jillian Ashley.

Since Tuesday night, when she released her interview with "Jillian," Amy had been shocked at the response. Every day since then, her email inbox, her Twitter account, her Facebook page and her website had been flooded with messages from readers from all over the world—even that one lesbian in Liechtenstein. Many of the messages had been standard *good job!* compliments on how well she conducted the interview.

But the majority of the messages had been from women who had very emotionally explained to Amy how meaningful it had been to actually *see and hear* their favorite writer talking about her books, books that meant so much to them!

Amy had no idea how this guy Max had done it, but he—a man!—had somehow created a body of lesfic works which were super important to so many gay women. She really needed to meet this guy!

Now, though, she decided to keep Rachel in the dark. Well, in the dark about the Jillian Ashley Thing; not in the dark about what happened last night.

"Oh my god!" Rachel exclaimed a few minutes later, while Amy started getting ready in her bedroom for Sally's arrival. "You *slut*! On the beach? But you *never* have sex on the first date! Even in a bedroom!"

"I know!" Amy agreed. "But, Rach, it was *bam!* I just *wanted* her!"

"And it sounds like she wanted you, too!"

"I knew that five minutes after she sat down at La Vida Mocha. Basically, our date was one long session of both of us *not* tearing each other's clothes off."

"And how was the sex when it moved to the bedroom—you know, not out in public on our town's beach?"

Amy laughed, choosing the dress she was going to wear tonight from her walk-in closet.

"Rach, it was amazing! Of course, I won't bore you with the details of girl-on-girl sex. I don't want to make you cringe."

Shoes…which shoes?

"Whatever!" Rachel said. "I'll have you know that I am already familiar with descriptions of girl-on-girl sex because I've been reading your girlfriend's book for the past couple of days."

Amy, who had been crouching in her closet in front of her shoe rack, trying to decide on which heels to select, stood up.

"You have?" she asked. "Which one?"

"The first one, *Something Road Fling*," Rachel answered. "It's really good! She's a great writer! I'm, like, all into the whole 'Will Marisol and Karen get together?' thing. They'd better; I have feelings invested now."

"Have you read chapter twenty-five yet?" Amy asked, stifling a laugh.

"No, I'm only, like, up to chapter seventeen. Why?"

"You'll see," Amy told her.

"Okay, intriguing…Anyway, yay! I'm so happy for you! The dry spell is over! Does she have a brother for me?"

"I'll ask tonight," Amy said, laughing.

Chapter 18

Sally made it back from Solana Beach with plenty of time to get ready for tonight's date with Amy. Walking into her condo, she had to admit that she had enjoyed meeting Ainsley. For someone from Mount Olympus, Ainsley had been really down-to-earth and approachable.

And sexy as hell!

Sally allowed herself that thought, which seemed a bit sacrilegious considering how much she enjoyed this nascent thing with Amy and was, in point of fact, about to get ready for her second date with Amy, because it was undeniably true. Ainsley was definitely sexy as hell.

Only twenty-four hours…

Sally stopped walking towards her bedroom, thinking about that.

Only twenty-four hours separated Amy and Ainsley. If she had accepted Ainsley's original suggestion of meeting for drinks Thursday night—one night before her first date with Amy—who would she be getting ready to go on a date with tonight? Ainsley or Amy? Would she have sat in La Vida Mocha on Friday evening with Amy out of politeness, preparing to brush her off and make sure things didn't progress beyond a friendly cup of coffee?

Only twenty-four hours…

The realization sent a shudder down her spine now, especially as it proved, yet again, that the Universe worked in strange and mysterious ways.

No sooner had she stepped into her bedroom than her phone rang. Her mother.

"You're a *writer?*" was Leslie's greeting.

Fuck my life!

Word travels fast on the Meddling Mothers Hotline and Sally hated it.

"Um…" she began.

"Why have you never told me this?" Leslie screeched.

"Um…"

"My daughter has written four books—four!—and her mother is the last to know!"

And starring in the role of the Martyr…Dr. Leslie Lassiter.

Sally realized she could never tell her mother the truth. If telling Lisa the truth about Jillian Ashley would be like taking out an ad on Super Bowl Sunday, telling her Mom would be like somehow landing on the Moon and spray-painting "Max Tremont is Jillian Ashley" on the surface in letters large enough to be seen from Earth. Especially since her mother wasn't particularly fond of Max. Leslie never understood why a man Max's age (which was more or less her age) was such close friends with someone as young as her daughter and so always distrusted his motives, which always made Sally upset. In fact, the absolute only times Sally wished she was straight was when she would think of how fabulous it would be to marry Max and *really* piss her mother off.

"Well?" Leslie demanded.

Sally sighed.

"Mom, I never told you because…well, because I didn't think you'd like the books," she answered. "They're lesbian romances."

"I have nothing against lesbians!"

"Mom, obviously I know that! But—"

"Anyway," Leslie interrupted, "I downloaded the first book."

Sally almost dropped the phone.

The Jillian Ashley books weren't just pages and pages of sex, held together by the flimsiest of plots, like most of the erotica lesfic out there; but the sex scenes were…explicit. Sally's best friend, Lisa, even described them once as "pussy-clenching." The thought that her mother was going to read them—especially Chapter 25 in *Fordham Road!*—and think that she wrote them…

Seriously! Fuck my life!

"Mom…I really don't think—"

"And why did you pick a name like Jillian Ashley? How did you come up with that?"

"Baby name website," she said, using the same story she had told Lisa. "Anyway, Mom, I'll gladly explain all this to you some other time, but right now I need to get ready for a date! I'll call you in a few days."

Or maybe when your old and senile.

Leslie was reluctant to end the conversation but finally acquiesced and when Sally was finally able to tap the red button on her phone's screen, she let out a groan.

Seriously! Fuck my life!

***

"I suppose the *dream* dream is to open my own studio," Sally told Amy. They were at the restaurant, awaiting the arrival of their entrees, each woman enjoying a glass of the Riesling Sally had ordered a bottle of.

Sally was amazed at how good Amy looked. Her date was wearing an adorable off-shoulder floral print swing dress showing off her tanned legs, and cute high-heeled sandals. Sally had a shoe fetish—both as a shopper and as a lesbian. As a shopper, shoes were her drug of choice and she currently had over eighty pairs, lovingly displayed in an outrageously expensive shoe rack she'd had custom-built in the walk-in closet of her bedroom. As a lesbian, well…sexy shoes on sexy women turned her on immensely. On any given day, if she was out and about, Sally was often driven to distraction by seeing an attractive woman with cute footwear. It didn't even have to be high heels. Just the other day, Sally had found herself breathing a little more rapidly when she was in the grocery store, standing in line behind a yummy blonde in denim shorts who was wearing a pair of black ankle-strap ballet flats.

"But I'd want my studio to be more of a boutique operation, you know?" Sally continued, answering Amy's five-year-plan question. "I'd want our focus to be on doing smaller projects for a lot of smaller companies, with one, maybe two big national accounts to help keep the lights on."

"Sounds awesome," Amy said. "I like that you're not all about 'bigger is better.' It tells me that your craft is more important than your bottom line."

Sally licked her lips. She really liked that Amy got her.

"What about you? she asked.

"Well," Amy began, "I'd like to see my *Lesbeing* endeavors really take off, you know? But I promise I have altruistic reasons!"

Sally laughed. Amy was so fucking cute when she was excited about something she was talking about.

Amy explained that already, *Lesbeing*—both the blog and the podcast—was earning her money through advertising that she sold and various merchandise available on the show's website. But if she was able to increase that monetization, she wanted to use that income to help start a non-profit organization to provide support and counseling for at-risk LGBTQ youth in this part of California.

"I can't believe how hot you are," Sally couldn't help exclaiming.

Amy blushed a deep crimson.

"What? Why?"

Sally bit her lip, pleased that Amy watched it closely.

"Selflessness is sexy," she told Amy, practically purring.

Amy quirked an eyebrow.

"Well, in that case...I also regularly donate my blood plasma."

"Stop it or I'll start giving the other diners a show," Sally joked.

Their entrees arrived a moment later: *cioppino* for Sally and *grigliata di pesce* for Amy. Under the table, their legs were pressed together. At first, it had been an accidental touch caused by Sally shifting in her seat. But when the contact had occurred, Sally didn't break it and neither did Amy. Feeling the smooth and hairless skin of Amy's leg against hers had been keeping her pulse slightly elevated, and though initially Sally had been able to detect a temperature difference between their skin surfaces, with Amy's leg being a skosh warmer, that difference had since been equalized, with Sally taking on some of Amy's warmth and Amy taking on some of Sally's coolness until it was as if the connection between them made them one person.

Deciding to have a little fun, Sally ran her calf up Amy's lower leg, eliciting a gasp from her date just as Amy was about to take a bite of crab cake. The look Amy gave her—a mixture of *fuck me now* and *fuck me NOW!*—made Sally's clit twitch.

"Um...so..." Amy began, her face beginning to flush, "be honest with me...how likely is it that I can meet your friend?"

Sally knew she was talking about Max and wanting to give Amy a good answer, she considered it for a few moments while chewing on a bite of calamari.

"I already mentioned it to him," she said. "But I know him. He's going to want to know *why* you want to meet him."

"Fair enough," Amy said, nodding. "It's nothing sinister, though. I may not yet be one-hundred percent over the fact that my favorite lesfic author is a man but I'm over it enough to still want to meet my favorite lesfic author. Does that make sense?"

"Totally."

"I mean, it really is amazing what he managed to do," Amy went on, thoughtfully. "He's a guy who wrote books about lesbians that are better than some books written by actual lesbians. How the hell did he do that?"

"Beats me," Sally confessed. In the days since Max dropped that bomb on her, she had been wondering the same thing.

"Is he gay?" Amy asked. "Because for some reason that makes sense to me."

Sally laughed.

"Totally not gay," she assured Amy. In fact, she made a mental note to ask him about Tiffany. He had promised to call her and although Sally didn't expect that to lead to anything long-term, she still wanted Max to be out there dating.

Amy stared at her.

"Wait…you two never…?"

Sally blinked.

"Oh god no! No! I've known I was gay since junior high and never tried to prove otherwise!"

Amy giggled.

"God, that would be quite the story, wouldn't it?" she asked. "If I was currently fucking the woman who used to fuck the guy who is my favorite lesbian writer?"

Laughing, Sally said, "That would be the best podcast episode *ever!*" She took another sip of wine. "Oh, by the way…my mom now thinks I'm Jillian Ashley."

Amy's eyes became as wide as humanly possible and her mouth dropped open.

"No way! How?"

Sally fudged a little on the details. She wasn't about to tell Amy that earlier today she had been on a blind date with a hot doctor with a professional connection to her mother. Instead, she told Amy that she had run into a gay friend of her mother's who had seen Amy's podcast.

"And you didn't set her straight?" Amy asked.

"Too risky," Sally said. "I really don't want to blow Max's cover. I mean, I don't know how you feel about that but—"

"I think you did the right thing!" Amy interrupted.

Sally reached for Amy's hand.

"Are you sure?" she asked. Even though they had talked about keeping Max's secret during their first night together, Sally wasn't sure Amy understood how far this had spread and so she now told Amy about how, the day after the podcast interview, her social media accounts had been lit up, meaning *all* of her friends now believed she was Jillian Ashley.

"And if my mother thinks I'm Jillian Ashley," she went on, "then my entire family now thinks I'm Jillian Ashley."

Amy was nodding.

"I get that," she told Sally. "Basically, the whole world believes you wrote those books. But, baby, of course that was going to happen after you came on my show."

"Right, but…I feel like I'm now somehow roping you into this…deception."

"But the only reason you feel that way is because we're dating," Amy replied. "This whole thing with all of your friends and your mother knowing would have still happened after the show was uploaded even if we never saw each other again. The only difference is, I know the truth. And the only reason I know the truth is because you were honest enough to tell me."

"Because I wanted to keep seeing you," Sally said.

"And that is amazing!" Amy said, beaming a huge smile. "Because I wanted to keep seeing you as soon as you sat down in the coffeeshop."

Once again, Sally started moving her leg against Amy's. Amy's eyes grew stormy with lust.

"That's causing a reaction," Amy whispered.

Sally could believe it. She was experiencing her own reaction.

"Is that right?" she asked.

"Very much so," Amy confirmed.

"Let's finish eating.

***

"Leave the shoes on," Sally instructed.

They were at her condo again because, again, it was closer and after their dinner at Vigilucci's, it was all they could do to keep from *not* having sex in Sally's BMW as soon as the restaurant's valet returned it.

Her heart thudding, Sally watched Amy slide her panties over her hips and then let them fall to her ankles. She then expertly stepped out of them and suddenly Sally's breath was ragged as right before her was a gorgeous naked woman wearing only the cutest high heels.

Sally was sitting on the edge of her sofa in the living room. Her own dress was off, leaving her only wearing the purple lingerie she had chosen for tonight: a sheer-cup bra with lace straps and matching sheer panties. As Amy had undressed—slowly, provocatively—Sally had run her middle finger over her clit through the fabric of her panties, sending swoon-inducing tingles throughout her core. She had been wet throughout dinner but now she was flooded and she knew Amy could see the nice large damp spot on her underwear.

"I love how I can see your pussy through your panties," Amy whispered.

Sally groaned.

"Put your right foot on the coffee table," she said.

A high-heeled foot with perfectly pedicured toenails painted black clicked down atop the Scandinavian-designed coffee table and now, with Amy's foot lifted like that, her dripping pussy was on full display for Sally.

"Oh my god, baby!" Sally slid off the sofa, onto her knees before her guest, her face level with Amy's abdomen. The musk from Amy's arousal wafted up into her nostrils, making her groan and salivate. But Sally wasn't in a rush. She sat down on the floor, her legs tucked beneath her and kissed each of the toes of Amy's right foot, running her tongue along each lacquered nail, gratified to hear Amy whimper a bit at this attention.

Sally then slid her tongue up the top of Amy's foot and played it along the edge of the strap of Amy's shoe. Meanwhile, her hand traveled up Amy's leg, stopping at her thigh.

"Sally…" Amy moaned and Sally spared a look up at her date, seeing that Amy had her head thrown back, her mouth open and her eyes shut, huffs of excited breath escaping from between her lips.

Sally then looked back at Amy's pussy. The woman's clit was engorged—a pink and swollen button that made Sally lick her lips. And she nearly lost her mind when she saw a thin line of Amy's essence stretch down from her sexy folds, a glistening drop at the end of it, dangling from the lips, swaying a bit because of Amy's trembling.

With a moan of her own, Sally flicked out her tongue to catch that drop, savoring the flavor of it. She then quickly inserted two fingers inside the wetness.

"Oh fuck yes!" Amy squeaked.

Sally went back to lavishing kisses and licks on Amy's foot while fucking her slightly curled fingers slowly in and out of her girlfriend's soaked pussy, Amy's hips rocking in time with her thrusts. Gravity brought more Amy's arousal dripping out and Sally could feel the warm liquid roll down her fingers onto the rest of her hand. Looking up again, Sally saw Amy squeezing her tiny breasts with both hands, pinching her own nipples.

"Oh, fuck!" Amy exclaimed a minute or two later. "Sally! Oh, fuuuuuck! I'm coming!"

Sure enough, Sally felt her fingers clenched tightly by those soft inner walls when the orgasm first struck and Amy's pussy spasmed, just a moment before they were then kneaded rhythmically as the convulsions started, with Amy screaming lustily at this point, her come squirting out now. What didn't fall on Sally's wrist, fell on the shag area rug in shining droplets. Sally got back up onto her knees and snaked her free arm around Amy's waist to help support her while the climax tore through her. Amy grasped Sally's head and held it close to her trembling body and Sally peppered Amy's abdomen with light kisses and tiny nibbles.

Suddenly, Sally could sense Amy quickly losing her strength to remain standing and before she collapsed, began guiding her gently to the floor, laying her down on top of the area rug. Expertly, Sally kept her fingers buried inside Amy's center as she executed this maneuver and when they were both down on the floor, with Sally lying atop her, she began once more slowly fucking her fingers in and out.

Amy looked at Sally, her eyes smoky with lust.

"Make me come again!" she demanded.

Sally quirked an eyebrow.

"Only if you ask nicely," she responded, swiping Amy's clit once with her thumb which caused Amy to shudder and moan.

"Please!" Amy exclaimed.

Sally put a pout on her face.

"You can ask more nicely than that, can't you?" This time, her swipe of Amy's clit was feather-light but Sally was pleased that it still jolted Amy strongly.

"Oh, fuck!" Amy whispered. "Please, *please* make me come again!"

Sally shook her head.

"'Please' who?" she asked and then pressed her thumb against Amy's clit, holding it there.

She then had to wait a few moments because this act rendered Amy incapable of speech. Amy's head was now arched back, her mouth open wide as she half moaned/half whimpered.

"Please who?" Sally prodded again.

"Sally! Please, Sally!"

"Put it together properly," Sally instructed.

"Ohmyfuck! Please, Sally, please make me come again!"

Sally's panties were now overwhelmed, her arousal seeping past the fabric, coating her thighs, her pussy clenching at Amy's compliance. Smiling Sally, brought her lips down to give Amy a kiss.

"So much better," she purred after the kiss broke. She then gave Amy what she wanted and it wasn't long before the walls of Sally's condo were once more ringing with screams of delight.

Chapter 19

The next morning, Sally made them breakfast again. While Amy was sitting at the small table in the kitchen's breakfast nook and Sally was busy plating the food—this time, omelets and diced fruit—Amy's phone pinged. From the sound, she knew it was a notification of a new comment posted on her website. More than once over the past few days, she had considered turning off the notifications entirely because ever since the Jillian Ashley interview, her phone had been blowing up with them! As it was, she now found herself silencing her phone more during any given day just to avoid hearing that chime over and over again.

Opening the message, she started reading it as she took a sip of coffee.

Dear Amy,
My name is Gail and I just wanted to write to tell you how important it was for me to watch your interview of Jillian Ashley! Finally, I got to see and hear her! What a treat! It was particularly special for me because her books helped me through some difficult times recently, like when my girlfriend broke up with me and when I was unable to go visit my elderly parents for over a year because of the pandemic. I'm immunocompromised and so until all of this Covid stuff is done, I really have to be extra careful and stay inside! Jillian's books have been one of my main sources of escape from what has been a pretty dreary existence. Finally getting to see her was like finally meeting up again with an old friend!

"Babe, look at this," Amy said, just as Sally brought their plates to the table. Sally took the phone from her and read what was on the screen.

"Oh my God!" she said when she was done, handing the device back. "Wow!"

"I get messages like that all the time now." Amy said, putting the phone face down on the table. "This looks amazing, by the way!"

"Thank you," Sally said, sitting down. "I can eat breakfast three meals a day. I love it but I would need to be sure not to have blueberry muffins with it. Those are my weakness."

"Ah, so I can bribe you to do anything I want if I make you blueberry muffins?"

Sally looked at her.

"You can bribe me to do anything you want just by being topless," she said.

Amy laughed.

"Secondly," Sally went on, "if you actually *made* me blueberry muffins, I would think you're a goddess."

Amy resolved to buy the ingredients for muffins later that day.

They ate in silence for a bit. When it came to eggs, anyway, Sally was a really good cook. Cooking was something which Amy enjoyed immensely, though oftentimes her workaholic nature and the demands of her job, the blog and podcast meant that she frequently ordered take-out rather than cooked something. Nonetheless, she couldn't help her mind creating images now of her and Sally in her kitchen, working together to make a meal—perhaps something Italian, which was Amy's favorite. Imagining that felt good. In fact, perhaps it felt a little *too* good. She shook her head slightly to dispel the picture. This was only their second morning together…

Don't start thinking too far ahead, Aims!

No sooner had that though flitted through her mind when Sally's phone, which was lying on the table next to Amy's, chirped. Amy watched as Sally's eyebrows shot up after reading whatever the notification was.

"Everything okay?" she asked.

"Um…yeah," Sally replied. "It's a text from Max." She looked over at Amy. "He's agreed to meet you."

"Oh my god! No fucking way!"

"Way."

"When?" Amy's heart was thudding, which was really, really weird. The only time she'd been this excited at meeting a man was a few years ago when she had been invited to a meet-and-greet with Elton John who had been in San Diego performing at a benefit for abused women, a benefit Amy had played a role in organizing.

Sally looked at the message on her phone again.

"He says if we want to come over today, that's fine."

"OMG!" Amy forgot about her breakfast. The omelet was delicious but food was the last thing on her mind now. "I need to get home and change!"

Sally chuckled.

"You look fine!"

Amy knew she probably seemed silly. This time, she had thought ahead and brought a change of clothes with her on her date with Sally, just in case things ended up back here instead of her own apartment, the items fitting easily in her large Kate Spade tote. But faded denim shorts and a camouflage tank top were *not* what she wanted to be wearing when she met Jillian Ashley. Well, Max Tremont, who *was* Jillian Ashley.

"Please, please, please come with me to my place so I can change!" she pleaded.

Sally was laughing.

"Anything for a woman who hinted that she might bake me blueberry muffins one day."

***

"Holy shit! Is that you and Elton John?"

Amy poked her head out of her bedroom, where she was deciding what to change into and saw Sally in the living room holding a framed photo.

"Yeah, it is. I'll tell you all about that later. Come help me pick something!"

Amy went back to work, standing in her closet, trying to make a decision.

Dress? Or skirt? Leggings, maybe? Or skinny jeans?

Sally joined her in the closet.

"You know, you really don't have to stress about this," she told Amy, wrapping her arms around her from behind. "Max is just…Max."

"No, I want to look good," Amy said, leaning back into Sally, loving how it felt. A thought suddenly occurred to her and she quickly turned around to face her companion. "I just realized you're in my bedroom!"

Sally smirked.

"I am. And your place is super cute, by the way! I like your furniture."

"Thanks," Amy said. "But now I'm torn between getting ready to meet your friend and just having sex with you."

Sally pretended to think.

"Hmm. Sex first and then Max?"

Tempting, Amy realized.

"But what if Max changes his mind?" she asked. "No…sex later." She turned back around to once again survey her hanging clothes.

"But Amy…" Sally whined.

Amy giggled. Turning back around, she said, "You're a tall and demanding thing, aren't you?"

"Guilty."

A delicious idea started forming in Amy's mind. She reached up and cupped Sally's chin.

"How long do we have until we meet him?" she asked.

"He just said to come by whenever."

Amy bit her bottom lip.

"Get on my bed. Your pants and underwear off. Wait for me until I choose my outfit."

"Ooh!"

"But one more thing," Amy said, stopping Sally from leaving the closet. "Edge yourself while you're waiting. Go."

***

"Fuck, I am still *soaked!*" Sally exclaimed, driving her BMW into Oceanside about forty minutes later, wiggling in her seat.

In the passenger seat, Amy bit her lip remembering…

After choosing what to wear (dark skinny jeans and a black, grey and white long-sleeved top, with sophisticated heels completing the ensemble) Amy had found a pants-less Sally lying on her bed. Sally's eyes had been closed, her mouth ajar, her breathing shallow and rapid. The fingers of her right hand had been lightly playing along the edges of her pussy, on full view because her legs had been opened wide, and even from the closet, Amy could tell how wet Sally was.

Amy had tossed her selected garments onto the chair she used at her make-up table and got in the bed with Sally.

"Keep doing what you're doing," Amy had instructed. "But don't you dare touch your clit."

Once Sally had nodded her compliance, Amy had shucked off her shorts and panties and then straddled Sally, very carefully positioning her pussy over Sally's head. Looking down between her legs, Amy had seen Sally's eyes open wide, taking in the sight of Amy's sex hovering above her face.

"Keep edging," Amy had said. "No clit, understand?"

"Understood," Sally had murmured, her eyes not moving from Amy pussy.

And then Amy had gently lowered her pussy down until Sally could reach it and Amy then submitted herself for a good fifteen minutes or so to Sally's expert mouth and tongue, orgasming twice on her lover's face. Afterwards, she had lifted herself off and stood beside the bed, looking down at Sally, the entire lower half of her face glossed with Amy's arousal. Sally had still been edging herself and her pussy had been so obviously turned-on by that point that it had created a wet spot on Amy's sheets. Amy had then put her face between Sally's legs, latched onto her clit with her lips and made her girlfriend come undone in just a few seconds.

Now, as Sally turned her car onto a residential street in Oceanside, Amy considered how lucky she was. After only two incredible nights of sex together so far, she was learning that her and Sally enjoyed the same sexual predilections: teasing mixed with a bit of bossiness. She didn't know about Sally, but Amy wasn't interested in a full-bore domme/submissive lifestyle. Nonetheless, it did turn her on so much when she got to be a little demanding in the bedroom.

"Okay, we're here," Sally announced, yanking Amy out of her reverie. Instantly, Amy's mind shifted gear from lurid sexual thoughts to realizing that she was moments away from meeting her favorite lesfic author.

Sally had pulled into the driveway of a really nice-looking house on a quiet, tree-lined street close to the beach. The house was very mid-century modern and seemed to be built almost entirely of windows.

"Anything I should know?" Amy asked Sally.

"Yes, come to think of it," Sally said, turning to her. "Max 101: say nothing but good things about the New York Yankees; say nothing but bad things about the Boston Red Sox."

Amy laughed.

"Oh my god, if men are so easy to manipulate, why do straight women complain about them so much?"

***

"Hi! You must be Amy! Max Tremont."

The man who opened the door was one of those older guys who hadn't let himself go. He was still trim and fit, dressed stylishly in black jeans and a tight-fitting charcoal grey t-shirt which complemented the silver streaks in his black hair.

"Nice to meet you," Amy said, feeling stupid at how nervous she sounded.

"Come on in," Max invited, stepping aside to let her and Sally enter.

"Your house is fantastic!" Amy said. Even though she hadn't seen much of it yet, what she was seeing now showed that Max had good taste in both furnishings and décor. "I love your style!"

"Thank you," Max said, guiding them towards a large room with a sunken floor. "I suspect in a previous life I was an interior decorator. Whether I was a *gay* interior decorator, I do not remember nor do I care. I just hope I was happy."

Amy laughed. This guy was super charming but not in a trying-to-get-in-her-pants kind of way, like a lot of "charming" guys she encountered.

He offered his guests drinks. From the well-stocked bar Amy saw at the far side of the room, she knew she could probably ask for just about anything, so she told Max to surprise her.

"Hmm…" Max said, sizing her up. "Okay, I've got just the thing." He turned to Sally. "Your usual?" he asked, and Amy felt a bit jealous that Sally and Max were so close that Sally had a *usual* at his house. As silly as it was, Amy now wanted a *usual* here at Max's.

"Yes, please," Sally responded.

"Wait, what's your usual?" Amy asked, but Max *tsked* her.

"No, no, no, young lady," he chided. "I don't want you changing your mind. You asked to be surprised and you shall be surprised." And off he went to the bar.

"Oh my god, he's *awesome!*" Amy whispered to Sally when they were alone.

Sally laughed.

"Told you!" she whispered back. "Well…he is awesome, yes; but he's also a wise-ass New Yorker who can make you crazy with just how much of a wise-ass he is."

"I don't care! I love him!"

"Were you worried you'd hate him? Here, let's sit down." And Sally led them to an incredibly large leather sofa which Amy figured cost as much as three months of her rent.

"I don't know," Amy confessed once they had sat down. "I mean, I'm still in shock that Jillian Ashley is a man but I wasn't sure if that shock would become resentment once I actually met the man, you know? But it hasn't. Which is good. Now I'm just happy to be meeting the person who wrote all those great books."

A few minutes later, Max returned with their drinks. Sally's was in a standard cocktail glass.

"A cherry Manhattan," Sally told her after Max handed her the drink.

Amy's cocktail was in a margarita glass, though clearly it wasn't a margarita. It was white, somewhat creamy and had a sugared rim. Eagerly, Amy brought it to her lips and took a sip. Her eyes rolled back in her head.

"Oh my fucking *god!*" she exclaimed. "This is *soooooo* good!" She took another sip and then turned to Sally. "Sweetie, taste this!"

"Holy fuck!" Sally gasped, staring up at Max. "Babe, what is that?"

Amy clocked Sally calling Max "babe." Again, she felt a pang of jealousy but not because she suddenly suspected Sally and Max were lovers. If the past two nights had shown Amy anything, it was that Sally is as lesbian as they come. No, again, as silly as it was, Amy wanted to be close enough friends with Max to call him a pet name.

This is ridiculous!

"So, Amy..." Max began, taking a seat in an easy chair which looked like it could belong on a spaceship. "Let's address the elephant in the room. I hope you're not pissed at Sally for the role she played in my little deception on your podcast. It was my idea and my idea alone."

Amy smiled, impressed. It was big of him to be sure to let her know it had all been his idea.

"I just hope you're not pissed at Sally for telling me almost right away," Amy returned.

"I am," Max said. "In fact, I poisoned her drink."

And Amy burst out laughing when Sally started to choke after having just taken a sip.

"Anyway," Max continued. "I hope you understand my motivations. I'm proud of the Jillian Ashley books, I am; but let's face it—a straight *man* putting his name on a lesfic book? What do you think would have happened?"

That was too easy. Amy knew that if Max had published the first book, *The Fordham Fling*, using his own name and bio...the lesbians would have closed ranks and made sure he never tried to do something that stupid again.

"Exactly," Max said, even though Amy had not spoken a word in response to his question. Her answer must have been written on her face. "The problem was, after all this time, Jillian needed to be seen, and that's where Sally came in. But it was all my idea, not hers. The only thing I didn't factor into my calculations was you being so beautiful and this one..." he tilted his head towards Sally "...going nuts for you."

Again, Amy burst out laughing when, once more, Sally started choking.

Chapter 20

Sally was breathing easier. Things were going well.

Even though she hadn't admitted it to Amy, she had been incredibly nervous about her meeting Max, afraid that Amy would just go off on him for dashing her expectations of who Jillian Ashley really was and for his role in putting Sally on camera for the podcast interview. It would have been Amy's prerogative, Sally supposed, considering…but Sally didn't want to ambush Max with an angry lesbian. Thus, ever since arriving at his house nearly twenty minutes ago now, Sally had been on tenterhooks, wondering if at any moment Amy would venomously start chastising Max for daring to infiltrate the sacred world of lesfic with his testosterone and testicles and then blaming him for everything from global warming to John F. Kennedy's assassination.

Instead, Amy was obviously having a blast here at Max's house and it was clear Max had charmed the pants off of her. In fact, if Sally hadn't known just how gay Amy was, she would swear that there was a chance Amy would opt to spend the night here with their host. And not in the spare bedroom either.

Currently, Amy was laughing at yet another funny story Max was telling about his childhood in the Bronx. It made Sally extremely happy to see the interaction between the two of them. Max was just as important to Sally's life as Lisa was: an indispensable friend she couldn't imagine being without. And Amy…

Well, it was still *waaaaaaay* too early to consider anything about Amy! she reminded herself. Sally didn't want to let her mind wander down that rabbit hole. She'd made that mistake before! Finding herself deeply smitten early on with a fabulous and sexy woman only to find out later that either A: said woman was not really so fabulous (although she *was* still sexy), or B: said woman was not even close to being as deeply smitten yet, which inevitably creates all sorts of awkwardness in a relationship.

All Sally would commit to now was that it was wonderful to see that Amy got along with one of her best friends.

"So, guess what?" Sally interjected when there was a lull in the conversation between Amy and Max. "My Mom now thinks I'm a bestselling writer of lesbian romances."

Max laughed.

"The great Dr. Lassiter got wind of it?" he asked. "How did you explain that?" He looked at Amy. "Her mother hates me, by the way."

Amy turned to Sally, an expression of surprise on her face. "She does?"

"She doesn't *hate* you," Sally insisted. "She just doesn't understand our friendship. If you really want to know the truth, I think she has a crush on you and is annoyed that you've never asked her out."

That made Max laugh even harder.

"I would marry your mother just for the sake of becoming your stepfather and then having the power to ground you whenever I wanted."

"Oh my god, shut up!" Sally retorted, laughing. "Anyway, have you gotten more requests for interviews?"

"Are you kidding?" Max asked, getting up to make Amy another one of those amazing white cocktails. Amy snuggled back against Sally on the sofa while she waited. "The floodgates have opened, my dear!" From behind his bar, while he concocted Amy's drink, he explained that thanks to Sally being on *Lesbeing—the Podcast*, every lesbian with a webcam and just a handful of Twitter followers had been emailing "Jillian," asking for the privilege of her presence on their podcasts, panel discussions, you name it.

"You, young lady," he said to Sally, reapproaching with Amy's drink, Amy eagerly reaching out for it and taking it from him, "are in high demand. Well, *I'm* in high demand but your face and that wonderfully awkward-somewhat-geeky manner you have is also in high demand."

Still snuggled against her, Amy giggled after taking a long sip from her drink.

"Awkward-somewhat-geeky!" she exclaimed with another giggle. "That's totally you!"

Sally was certain Amy was getting drunk. Over Amy's head, she mouthed *No more drinks for her!* to Max. He acknowledged with a bemused expression and a slight nod.

"Anyway," Max went on, taking his seat in his Saarinen-designed easy chair that Sally knew he was so fond of, crossing one leg over the other, "I'll be sure to turn them all down when I get around to it."

"Wait! No!" This came from Amy, who sat up now. "You can't."

Max cocked an eyebrow.

"And why not?"

Sally was wondering the same thing, surprised at Amy's comment. Even though Amy had agreed to keep the truth about Jillian Ashley's real identity under wraps, Sally figured that was as far as Amy was willing to go to perpetuate the deception.

Amy turned to face Sally.

"I'm not saying you have to keep this up forever and ever, but you do need to keep it up for a little while at least. It meant so much to a lot of women seeing you on my podcast—actually *seeing* you!"

Amy then turned back to Max.

"Max, I don't think you fully understand what you've done."

"Meaning?" he prodded.

"Meaning that for you, the Jillian Ashley books are simply a way to express your creativity and earn some money doing it. Which is fine. But do you ever spend any time online in lesfic chat groups on Facebook or on Goodreads?"

Max shrugged.

"Here and there," he said. "Now and again."

Suddenly, Sally knew where Amy was going with this because *she* spent time on lesfic chat groups on Facebook, Goodreads and other sites—a lot more than here and there or now and again. She thought back to that email message Amy had shown her earlier this morning.

She sat forward now, taking Amy's hand, conveying to her that she was united with her on this.

"I don't know how you did it," Amy went on, "but you've created a series of lesfic books which have become super important to the community. I know because they're super important to *me!* But forget about me. Since Tuesday, when we did the interview, I have been getting bombarded with messages from women who are so happy because they felt like they had finally gotten to meet Jillian! Like they had finally gotten to meet an old friend! You can't just put Jillian back into hiding now!"

Max sighed.

"Look ladies," he began, "it makes no difference to me, okay? But I suppose it's up to her." And he pointed at Sally.

Sally was now the center of attention in the room, with both Amy and Max looking at her. It made her natural shyness kick in and she suddenly felt like she did back in her schooldays whenever she had to stand in front of the class to deliver an oral book report.

"You're so fucking cute when you blush," Amy said, with her thousand-watt smile. A simple statement but it went a long towards helping Sally's nerves dissipate.

"I already agreed I'd help you by pretending to be Jillian for a while," she told Max. "Besides…since everybody in my life already thinks I'm her, it will be good practice."

Chapter 21

Amy put her desk phone down and looked at the masked woman sitting in her guest chair.

"He can take the case," she told her client, Patricia, her voice slightly muffled by her own mask. Even though the organization she worked for had re-opened their office in Carlsbad a couple of months ago, following over a year of having their employees work from home, and even though all of the staff, including Amy, was fully vaccinated by now, everyone who entered the building was still required to wear masks.

"And don't let the fact that he's a man fool you," Amy said with a chuckle. "Trust me, he's one of the good guys."

Amy had just fixed Patricia up with a lawyer who agreed to take her case pro-bono. Patricia, who worked for an office supply company, had been passed over for promotion several times by her boss, each time in favor of a less-qualified man. She had finally had enough and wanted to sue but couldn't even dream of affording a lawyer on her salary, especially with three children to support.

Amy printed information about the lawyer and gave it to her client, promising to stay in touch and be available for her if needed. In truth, Amy wanted to keep abreast of this case. She had seen far too many of them during her career so far. What she couldn't understand was why such things were still happening. How was it possible that there are men out there—in charge of companies, no less—who still had such *Mad Men*-era concepts of gender roles?

After seeing Patricia out, Amy returned to her office, sat down and sighed. It was Wednesday afternoon and she was ready for the day to be over. She loved her job but on certain days, like this one, it really hit her what a Sisyphean task it is trying to make the world a better place for women. Patricia had only been the last of several appointments she'd had today with all sorts of women who needed her organization's help.

"Knock-knock."

Amy was snapped from her reverie by her boss, Makeda, standing just outside her open office door.

"Hey!" Amy said. "Come in."

Makeda did so, taking a seat in front of Amy's desk.

Makeda was the director of the North County Women's Rights Group, a middle-aged African-American woman with a slight southern accent left over from her childhood in Louisiana.

"Guess what?" Makeda asked.

"Um...we're all living in the Matrix?"

Makeda laughed.

"No. You're running point on the Edelmann meeting."

Amy was shocked and she knew her face showed it.

The "Edelmann meeting" referred to the meeting which Makeda and Amy had secured with Christine Edelmann, one of San Diego County's supervisors. The topic of discussion was about advancing debate on adding an amendment to the county's constitution guaranteeing equal rights for women.

"Wow! Thank you!" Amy really was appreciative of what a huge gesture of faith and trust this meant Makeda was showing.

"You earned it," Makeda told her. "I'll be there too, of course, but I think you'll do a great job of presenting our case and getting Edelmann on board to work with us on this. And if we can get her on board..."

Amy nodded, not needing Makeda to finish that statement. Supervisor Edelmann had influence, to put it mildly—and if she really *did* decide to run for mayor of San Diego like the rumors were suggesting...

"I'll admit that I'm being strategic, as well, with giving you this assignment," Makeda went on. "I think your youth will be our ace in the hole. Too many politicians think that equal rights amendments are something only women who were around during the seventies care about but we need to start showing them that young women like you are just as passionate about it."

"Definitely," Amy agreed, feeling incredibly excited about this. In fact, this conversation was giving her an idea for a podcast episode—one that would somehow tie the struggle for LGBTQ rights with women's rights in general. As soon as she got home, she resolved to start doing some research and making some notes for it.

"I'll start preparing for the meeting right away," she told Makeda. She reminded herself of today's date, realizing she'd have less than a week to put together a kick-ass presentation for Supervisor Edelmann.

"You do that," Makeda said, rising and heading for the door. But at the door she stopped. "And once we're done with that meeting, you're going on vacation."

Amy blinked.

"Wait. What?"

Makeda gave her a bemused look.

"You heard me," she said. "I took a look and you have too much time saved up. Which reminds me…What have you been saving it for? A special trip?"

"No," Amy replied. Her and Rachel *had* wanted to take a trip to Italy together in 2020 but of course that plan got shot down by a microscopic virus and so she had ended up only taking a few days off here and there last year, staying local each time. Italy still wasn't an option because of Europe's problems with the vaccination rollout, she considered. But, if she was going to be forced to take a vacation, perhaps she could find somewhere domestic to go. San Francisco came to mind immediately. It was one of her favorite cities and she supposed she could tear herself away from work enough to enjoy visiting the wonderful museums and parks there; hanging out at the wharf and, of course, eating some spectacular seafood.

It might be fun to take that trip with Sally.

She tried to shake that thought out of her head immediately. Sally? Really? Today was Wednesday, which meant their first date was five days ago. You don't plan on taking a trip with somebody you first started seeing five days ago.

But why had she (briefly) thought about it?

And why was her mind still trying to get her to *keep* thinking about it?

***

"*Jesus God!*"

Amy screamed as the orgasm exploded through her pelvis, her pussy squeezing those wonderfully long fingers of Sally's. She then couldn't scream anymore because Sally's lips suddenly covered hers for a deep and hungry kiss and so all of the other sounds she was now making went directly into Sally's mouth.

When the orgasm subsided, Sally left Amy's lips to kiss her way down her neck and then to her chest. Nipples that were already practically marble became even harder when Sally began sucking on them one by one, raking her teeth against them occasionally as she did so, eliciting yearning groans from Amy.

The three fingers that were still inside her began gently moving again, in and out, in and out; curling and straightening, curling and straightening…

Amy felt her come leaking out, running down and coating her rear opening. She tried to telepathically tell Sally it would be perfectly okay if one of her come-slicked fingers found its way in there. She'd enjoy it. She'd come that much harder. But she didn't dare voice that request yet. She first needed to suss out if Sally was into that. It wasn't every woman's cup of tea, after all.

"Oh my god, baby!" she grunted as her next climax was expertly brought closer and closer to the surface. Now Sally started pumping her fingers in and out with more vigor, Amy matching her rhythm with her thrusting hips until…

"Fucking god!!" she half screamed/half gasped, psychedelic colors popping behind her eyelids as her entire universe condensed down to the explosions of pleasure happening in her core.

When it was over, Sally withdrew her fingers slowly and then lay down next to the still quivering Amy who felt she needed a few moments before she could move again. When she was finally able to, she rolled onto her side to face Sally and cuddle with her, Sally wrapping those long legs of hers around Amy's lower half.

They were at Amy's tonight; Sally having come over after work. They had meant to order in dinner when Sally arrived but almost as soon as Amy had let her in, they were all over each other and then it was very *Who needs food?* as the foreplay started in the living room and the actual fucking started in the bedroom.

But now, at almost six o'clock, Amy's stomach let out a low growl, causing both women to giggle.

"What do you want to order?" Sally asked.

"No, let me cook us something," Amy insisted, reluctantly making her way off the bed.

"As long as I can help," Sally replied, also standing up. Amy tossed Sally her shirt which had been hurriedly taken off earlier and tossed to the floor. For herself, she pulled out a comfy pj set from her dresser and doing so prompted a question to come to her mind.

"Are you staying?" she asked Sally.

"It's your apartment; you tell me," Sally answered with a smirk.

"You're staying," Amy declared.

Sally approached and wrapped her arms around the still nude Amy.

"Ooh, bossy!"

Amy smiled.

"And horny. But hungry. Go change into your pjs so I don't feel underdressed."

A few minutes later, the two pj-clad women were in Amy's kitchen. Breakfast for dinner sounded good to both of them and while Amy made omelets with diced green peppers, Sally took care of making bacon. While they cooked, Amy told Sally about Makeda's decision to make her the point person for the meeting with County Supervisor Edelmann.

"Babe, that's huge!" Sally said. "Congrats!"

"Thank you. I'm going to have to work really super-*duper* hard to get our presentation ready in time."

"When is the meeting?"

"Tuesday."

"Fuck!" Sally exclaimed, taking her eyes off the sizzling bacon still in the pan. "That's, like, soon!"

"I know," Amy replied, nodding. In truth, ever since her discussion with Makeda, she had hardly stopped thinking about the presentation and all the work she still needed to do to complete it and make it as kick-ass as possible. She not only wanted to prove to Makeda that Makeda's trust in her was well-placed, but she also really, really wanted to get this amendment added to the county constitution. Okay, it wasn't like amending the sacred U.S constitution but it would be a triumph nonetheless and would also be a warning shot across the bows of other municipalities across the nation that women were not going to sit idle while basic guarantees of equal rights were still missing from the charter documents of states, counties, cities and towns all over America.

"I know for sure I'm going to end up working on it after hours the next couple of days," she went on. The omelets were ready and so she started plating them.

"For sure," Sally said. "I should probably make sure to leave you in peace until you get it done."

Fuck!

Keeping her eyes focused on plating the omelets, Amy pursed her lips. That hadn't been what she meant when she mentioned to Sally how much effort and time the presentation would take. On the other hand, it *would* be better not to have any distractions around.

"Um…yeah, I guess so," she told Sally. She hoped her voice wasn't telegraphing her disappointment at the possibility of not seeing Sally the rest of the week.

Jesus, get a grip! It's only a few days!

"I often have to bring work home when we're doing a big job for a huge client, so I know what it's like," Sally said. "Do you think you'll have any time this coming weekend to hang out, even if it's just for a little while?"

Amy told herself to look on the bright side. At least the woman she was seeing was understanding about professional obligations and not getting bent out of shape because Amy wouldn't be able to pay much attention to her. It was actually really, really sweet of Sally to suggest giving her some space.

"Of course," Amy answered, giving Sally a full smile.

By the weekend, I'm going to want to eat you alive!

Chapter 22

Two days later, Sally logged into Facebook on her phone for the first time in over a week. The day after the interview on Amy's podcast, Sally had turned off notifications from all of her social media apps because there were just too many of them. Now, looking at her Facebook account, she sighed.

There were over 500 notifications and by quickly skimming through them she could tell they were all about her circle of followers discovering that she was Jillian Ashley. What's more, word was getting out beyond her normal Facebook bunch. Many of the notifications showed that she had been tagged in posts made by her Facebook friends to other people, identifying her as the extremely popular lesfic author. This in turn had led to countless friend requests as well as her Facebook inbox being jammed with direct messages from people she didn't know.

Of all the notifications, she noticed three that were important to her: pictures of her six-year-old niece, Jodi, that had been shared by Sally's sister, Camille.

Twitter and Instagram were the same: both accounts, which she had assiduously avoided over the past ten days, were overloaded with notifications and the discovery that she had gained *thousands* of new followers.

She closed the apps and set the phone down on her desk at BRX Graphic Design. A few weeks ago, the company had initiated a return-to-office scheme which was a hybrid model of working in the office one week and working from home the next week. Just until the pandemic was well and truly done. This was one of the work-from-office weeks.

Arrayed on her desktop were a collection of concept images her team had put together for one of their clients, a boutique music label which produced vinyl record albums. The client needed artwork for a new limited-edition series of LPs they were getting ready to release and Sally knew none of the concepts she was looking at would make the cut. Jamal's concept was the most promising and so Sally spent some time making notes on his print and drawing some quick sketches which would demonstrate to the team how to take Jamal's idea and enhance it until it became something more likely to match the client's brief.

Done with that, she got up for some more coffee. In the breakroom, she had just popped her K-cup into the Keurig and hit *Start* when the new intern, Clara, came in. Clara had just joined the team on Wednesday and was still learning the ropes. Sally, as manager of the team and remembering her days as an intern had taken on the role of Clara's mentor, making sure the super young college student wasn't overwhelmed while still having interesting things to do each day.

"Hey, Clara, what's up?" Sally greeted her.

Above the Spongebob Squarepants face mask Clara had on, her eyes were wide as she looked at Sally. She seemed too scared to approach her boss.

Sally frowned. Clara was very cute and Sally hoped none of the guys in the building had been behaving inappropriately towards her.

"Um...is everything okay?"

Clara nodded.

"Yeah, everything's fine. I just wanted to say that I'm a big fan of yours!"

Sally blinked. Sure, during her time at BRX she had worked on a few high-profile ad campaigns for some pretty big clients, and it still thrilled her each time she saw one of her designs out in the wild, but she had hardly made a name for herself. Then again, the world of graphic design *was* kind of niche. Maybe Clara had done some research before applying for one of the coveted internship slots here at BRX and had actually seen some of Sally's work.

She smiled behind her mask.

"Thank you! That's sweet!"

"I have read all your books!" Clara gushed.

Books?

It took a moment, but then...

Oh, good lord! Seriously?

"When I started here on Wednesday," Clara went on, "I was, like, 'Wait, I know her from somewhere!' and then I was, like, 'She's Jillian Ashley!'"

Behind her mask, Sally's lips were tightly pressed together.

Of course we'd get an intern who's a lesbian and of course she saw my interview.

Sally had learned that a woman didn't even need to be a subscriber to Amy's podcast to have seen the interview. It was now just *out there*...out in the ether of the internet, completely unattached to Amy's website, an unstoppable force that was reaching audiences far and wide, all because Amy had scored a rare in-person interview with Jillian Ashley.

Well, with Sally *pretending* to be Jillian Ashley.

"Thanks," Sally managed to say. "I'm glad you like my books."

"Like them? I *love* them! You and Suzanne Collins are my favorite writers."

Sally chuckled. Max should get a kick out of learning that for at least one person, his books are right up there with *The Hunger Games*.

"I know it's probably completely unprofessional," Clara continued, "but would you...?" And she held out a book and a Sharpie.

It was the paperback version of *The Fordham Road Fling*. Sally had a copy of it herself, buying it after first reading the novel on her Kindle. Sally had never so much as opened the book. When it arrived from Amazon, she had wanted to keep it pristine, untouched, in mint condition. Each re-reading of *Fordham Road* that she had done—and so far, she was up to six times doing that—had been done using her Oasis.

"Sure, no problem," Sally muttered, taking the book and Sharpie from Clara.

Wait. How did writers do this? Did they autograph the cover or one of the pages inside? She hurriedly tried to remember a movie or a TV show or something showing a writer autographing a book and for some reason a scene from some movie starring John Cusack popped into her head. She remembered that he opened the books fans gave him to sign. So she did that. The first page displayed the title and "by Jillian Ashley" and so that seemed as good a place as any.

Crap!

Don't authors usually write something other than their names? Like, a personal message? Something witty?

Sally's mouth went dry. She didn't know anything witty to write! And she'd only known Clara all of two days! That certainly wasn't long enough to jot down something personal.

Suddenly, it came to her and she wrote *To Clara, a future star in the world of graphic arts!*

Not witty, perhaps, but certainly personal and encouraging!

Then another problem presented itself. Looking up at Clara, she asked, "Do you want me to sign it with my real name or as Jillian Ashley?"

"As Jillian, please!" Clara said. "No! Wait! Can you sign it as Jillian and then put your real name in parentheses underneath it? That would be so cool!"

"Sure," Sally answered and then was faced with yet another problem; one she never thought she'd ever have in her entire life, even if she lived to be one-hundred: On the fly, and with someone watching her, she had to come up with a convincing signature using a different name. Somehow, she managed to scrawl a glyph-like signature that looked like it had a J, what might be two Ls and the first three letters of the name Ashley, but only if you squinted just right. In truth, it was illegible, but then again, isn't that what most signatures are?

"There you are," Sally said, handing the book back to Clara, who read the inscription and then clutched the book to her chest.

"Thank you so much! You're the best! God, I can't believe I got to meet you! And now I get to work with you too!"

"Well…um…just keep reading!" Sally said because it sounded like an authorly thing to say.

Fortunately, Clara left her alone then and Sally took a big slug of her freshly-brewed coffee, figuring that was probably the weirdest thing that would happen to her today.

***

She was wrong.

No sooner had she reached home after work when her mother called.

"Hey, Mom," she answered, toeing off her shoes by the front door. Lena sat up on the couch, a disapproving look on her face, as if the cat had been thinking that today was the day the human would finally not come back, leaving the entire condo for herself.

"I can't read any more of your book," Leslie stated. "I just got to the first sex part and, uh-uh, I just can't."

Sally groaned inwardly, blushing hotly. With her free hand, she pinched the bridge of her nose.

Fuck!

Jillian Ashley sex scenes were legendary. Sure, people loved the books because of the strong plots and well-developed characters, but what they talked about—on Twitter, Facebook, podcasts…basically anywhere lesbians gathered—were the sex scenes.

Having read *The Fordham Road Fling* so many times, Sally knew—by heart—the first sex scene in that book. And how graphic it was. Especially the bit about the finger vibe.

And now her mother thought she had written it.

What did I do to deserve this?

Sally sighed.

"Yeah, Mom, it's probably best if you stop reading," she said.

"Are all the books like that?" Leslie asked. "Did you have to be so…*detailed*?"

"Mom, the books aren't just about sex! Did you not pay attention to how Jilli—I mean, *I*—did a great job introducing the characters and setting up the story and all that?"

"I will hand it to you," Leslie said, as if reluctantly conceding a point, "that, yes, the writing is excellent and you did get me interested in the story, but once I got to this sex scene…I guess I'm just not used to that in the books I normally read."

"Yeah, well, the women who read lesbian romances tend to like graphic sex scenes, Mom. If I stopped writing them, I may have to leave the country. Although, I don't know where I'd go because I have fans all over the world."

"Really?" Leslie asked, obviously not believing her daughter.

Sally rolled her eyes. Of course her snobbish surgeon mother would have trouble believing that books like *The Fordham Road Fling* would be popular the world over because her snobbish surgeon mother only read books shortlisted for the Pulitzer Prize.

So, taking a seat next to Lena on the sofa (the cat, by the way, still looking like she still hadn't forgiven the human for coming home), Sally put her feet up on the coffee table.

"Yes, Mom, really," Sally said, letting a little exasperation creep into her voice. "Lesbian romance is a thriving genre of fiction because it gives women like me a chance to read books that feature characters we can relate to and so, yes, the Jillian Ashley books are read all over the planet."

"Well, fine," her mother began, "but what am I supposed to do about reading the rest of your book?"

"Just skip the sex scenes, Mom," Sally said with a sigh. "That means skipping chapters seven, ten, eleven, seventeen, twenty-one, twenty-five, thirty-two, thirty-nine and forty-three."

She suddenly sat upright.

God, should she be worried that she could rattle off the sex chapters in a single book without stopping for breath? That didn't seem…healthy.

"Whatever you do, don't read chapter twenty-five," she added sternly. "Like, seriously, Mom…When you get to chapter twenty-five, *skip it.*"

"Why did you bother writing it, then?" Leslie asked.

Putting aside the fact that I actually didn't write it…

"Because lesbians like things like chapter twenty-five, Mom!"

You have no idea *how much lesbians like things like chapter twenty-five!*

"Well, I suppose they are your audience…"

Eventually, Sally managed to steer the conversation away from "her" books and onto other topics, including Camille and her family. Finally, Sally was able to get her mother off the phone and then she sat there, trying to figure out what to do with the rest of her night.

Lisa had a date and even Max was "indisposed"—his term, which Sally took to mean having a date of his own.

What Sally really wanted to do was Amy. That is, what she really wanted to do was hang out with Amy, although, truth be told, she also wanted to *do* Amy. The problem was, Amy was also indisposed tonight. Apparently, she had underestimated the amount of effort it was going to take to craft that presentation for…who was it again? A councilwoman or something? Sally couldn't remember. Anyway, to craft that super important presentation about the equal rights amendment. Earlier, Amy had texted Sally, telling her that her boss was coming over this evening to help and that it was unlikely she'd be able to go on a date tonight or do anything else fun.

Sally, though disappointed, understood. What Amy was striving for was important and if she could support her by simply staying out of the way, then that is what she would do.

So, her Friday night was going to be one of her typical home alone Friday nights.

After taking a shower and changing into pink pj shorts and a tank, she heated up some leftovers for dinner and put on her new favorite show on Netflix: *Kim's Convenience*. It didn't have any lesbians in it but it was hilarious. She binged two seasons worth of it, having some chocolate chip ice cream with caramel sauce dribbled on top of it halfway through season three.

Having had enough TV, she told Alexa to play her favorite reading playlist, picked up her Kindle and continued reading a fun f/f sci-fi adventure one of her Twitter friends had recommended. She wondered if Max would consider having Jillian write a sci-fi lesbian romance. She'd have to mention it to him.

Finally, she started yawning. The clock told her it was just past eleven and since she had no real reason to stay up super late, decided to head to bed. Tomorrow morning she'd get up early, go for a run and maybe have coffee down at the beach.

Then her phone pinged.

Amy!

You still up?

Sally eagerly texted back.

I am!

Thank god! was Amy's reply.

LOL! Why?

Amy's answer came quickly…

I need RELEASE!

Chapter 23

Amy couldn't sit still.

Sally was on her way and the anticipation of her arrival was making Amy's body practically buzz with excitement because she *needed* Sally!

The past two days had been hell. But a good hell, she supposed, because though it had been hard work, the cause was important. Yesterday and today, both at the office and at home, Amy had been busting her ass getting ready for her and Makeda's meeting on Tuesday with Supervisor Edelmann. They weren't going to be able to just walk into her office and say, "Make it happen!" Amy knew that most politicians today think the ERA is a relic from the past and a waste of time. They argue that much of what the ERA proposes is already guaranteed by the 14th Amendment of the US constitution, which grants equal protection of the laws to everyone. What's more, there are already numerous protections against discrimination for women, such as Title IX, for example, and statutory protections against pay discrimination and gender-based violence. The problem, however, is that there are still too many conservative-minded politicians and jurists—with *real power*—who actively work at undermining those protections. Therefore, until the ERA is officially ratified and thus made federal law, women's rights were technically still at risk.

In the meantime, until the ERA is ratified at the federal level, a movement has been occurring throughout the country to at least get counties, cities and other such entities to add equal rights amendments to *their* constitutions and charters in the hope that getting enough of these smaller pieces of America to officially declare that women have the same rights and protections as men—*by law*—the federal government will finally take action and make the Equal Rights Amendment part of the U.S. constitution.

The trick would be convincing Supervisor Edelmann to help push this cause forward at the county level. Amy and Makeda knew they had a potential champion in Christine Edelmann because of on-the-record comments she had made in the past supporting not only the federal ERA but also an ERA for San Diego County.

Yesterday and today, Amy had worked long hours, both at the office and at home. This evening, Makeda had come over to help with some of the research to include in their presentation on Tuesday and to offer insight into and critique of Amy's work so far. The session had been a success, in Amy's opinion, and she felt like she was finally taming this beast of a project.

She still wasn't done, though. She would need to continue working through the weekend, which she was more than willing to do. But for tonight…she needed to be fucked. Getting herself off wasn't going to cut it; not this time.

Her doorbell rang and she practically sprinted to open it. When she did, she pulled Sally inside and started kissing her straight away. She didn't care if it was rude and by Sally's reaction, neither did Sally. They hadn't seen each other since Thursday morning, when Sally had left Amy's apartment to go to work and though Amy had been super busy since then, she had missed Sally. Having sex with her was like taking a drug.

"Hi," Amy said when their lips separated briefly for air.

"Hi," Sally returned, and then that was it for talking. Never breaking their lip lock, Amy expertly—and walking backwards—guided them both to her bedroom and once inside, the two women began undressing themselves until, nude, they fell on the bed, Amy pulling Sally on top of her.

"Babe, I need hard and rough," Amy growled and then groaned when Sally gave her an absolutely predatory look with those emerald-green eyes.

"Where do you keep them?" Sally asked and Amy knew exactly what she meant.

"Container just inside the closet," she answered.

Sally scampered off the bed and Amy watched her locate her toybox—a large plastic storage bin. She saw Sally pull the lid off, survey the contents and then turn to look at her again and Amy almost came right then at the pure depravity in those eyes. Her already rapidly beating heart started beating faster in anticipation.

The harness was pulled out and pulled on—exactly what Amy was hoping for. The pink dildo, the one with the large and bulbous head was attached to it.

That will do nicely!

But when Sally walked back, she had something else in her hand and she held it up for Amy to see and Amy, as turned on and horny as she was, felt dizzy with expectation.

Oh, my god, yes!

"What a coincidence," Sally purred. "I have the exact same one."

The lube was in her nightstand drawer and Amy hurriedly took it out.

"I'll take that," Sally instructed, holding out her hand and then taking it from Amy.

"How do you want me?" Amy squeaked.

"No, no…" Sally said, shaking her head. "How do *you* want it?"

That required no thought. Amy got on all fours, raising her ass high, presenting herself, all of herself, to her lover.

She felt the mattress shift as Sally got back on the bed and then…

"Oh, fuuuuuck, yes!" Amy called out as she felt Sally push the dildo into her, that bulbous head stretching her as it penetrated deeper and deeper. And then Sally was fucking her, the thrusts long and deep, Amy's core lubricating the passage for the dildo, so much so that each time Sally pulled back, Amy felt her upper thighs sprayed with arousal.

But this was just the teaser, Amy knew, because after no more than a couple of minutes of Sally pounding her and just before Amy felt herself nearing that point of no return, Sally slowed and stopped.

"Yes?" Sally asked.

"Yes! Fuck, yes!" Amy exclaimed.

She felt the viscous wetness of the lube fall on her rear opening and then…

"Oh, *fuuuuuck, yes!*" Amy called out again, this time as the aluminum butt plug, the one with the heart shaped gem in the base was slowly slid in.

"So pretty…" Sally murmured when it was securely inside.

Now, double-penetrated, Amy was fucked again with the dildo, the pleasing weight of the metal plug adding another dimension to the pleasures shooting throughout her entire lower half. Her hair was grabbed, used by Sally for extra leverage to drive the pink toy in as far as it could go, Amy grunting or crying out ecstatically with each thrust, calling Sally's name this time, God's name that time, ordering Sally not to stop, telling her to go faster.

Finally, she came undone.

"Fuuuuuuuuuuuuuuuuuck!" she screamed. "Fuuuuuck! I'm coming!"

It was an explosion between her legs.

Her pussy was the purest form of pleasure imaginable as it spasmed and clutched at the invader inside it at the same time her ass was clenching around that plug. Her orgasm kept her screaming, louder than she normally did, both of her openings radiating rapture, her pussy squirting as Sally kept fucking her throughout it.

"There's another one in there, baby, let it out!" Sally ordered.

And sure enough, the second orgasm hit her then. Her screams reached new decibel levels and she would swear that everything below her waist was liquid.

Sally yanked her hair a bit harder.

"Rub your clit!" she commanded. "There's another one in there! Give it to me!"

Her clit was a swollen, electrified button, almost too sensitive to touch by now but as soon as Amy's finger pressed hard against it she grunted as the next orgasm burst free and as its waves roiled through her she collapsed on the bed, Sally adroitly falling with her, now lying right on top of her, that pink dildo buried completely in her pussy, the plug still in her ass, a satisfying feeling of fullness adding to the explosions of her climax.

Amy, trembling, screamed into her pillow, never wanting this night to end.

***

Amy licked her lips, Sally's come all over them, and swallowed.

Sally tasted so damn good. And, heavens, when the woman came, the floodgates opened, giving Amy all she could care to coat her tongue with.

Coming up from between Sally's long legs, Amy snuggled against her, holding Sally as she rode out this latest orgasm Amy had given her.

Were they finally done? Amy had no idea. She had thought they might be done a while ago but then more of her toys were brought out and things picked right back up again.

"Jesus, baby..." Sally muttered.

Amy responded by nuzzling her neck.

"Did you get the release you needed?" Sally asked.

"And then some," Amy purred.

Christ, and then some!

Their sex had been exactly what she had wanted when she had sent that text to Sally just after Makeda left. It had been hard and rough with fast orgasms that had shaken her bones. She had been demanding, so demanding. But so had Sally. And through it all, hair had been pulled, asses spanked and new bite marks made all over their bodies. Amy felt like a new woman now after all the pressure of the past two days.

"I still have to work during the weekend, though," Amy told Sally now. "Much of it anyway."

"That's cool," Sally replied. "I have a bunch of errands I need to run anyway and then maybe I'll hang out with my best friend a bit."

"Is she pretty?" Amy asked, suddenly feeling a little jealous.

"Lisa? She's gorgeous."

"Ugh! You're supposed to tell me she looks like a troll!"

"Oh, right, sorry. Yeah, Lisa is practically Shrek's twin."

"Shrek's an ogre but I'll accept your answer." Amy rose up on her elbow just enough to be able to kiss Sally.

"Lisa is harmless," Sally reassured her. "If something was going to happen between us, it would have happened a long time ago. Besides, I bet you have a cute friend or two."

"Okay, okay, I'll stop being jealous. But I'd like to see you later today."

"How about a dinner date?" Sally suggested. "Roosevelt Pizza?"

Amy liked that idea and agreed immediately.

The sheets and blanket were pulled up over them by Sally and then the two women snuggled together and Amy felt sleep finally begin to overtake her.

Being here like this with Sally felt so familiar already, which was mildly alarming. Sure, they had just had sex and it was really late—it was only natural that Sally stay the night. But the thing was, Amy was realizing with the last bit of brainpower she had left before

losing consciousness, that she felt Sally *belonged* with her in bed—
any bed—falling asleep alongside her.

Chapter 24

When Sally awoke the next morning, the bed was empty beside her. A diffused sunlight was making its way into the room but Sally could tell by the light that it was still early. The digital clock on the nightstand confirmed it, telling her it was only 6:38 a.m.

What time had they finally gone to sleep last night, she wondered? Or rather—technically—this morning? Definitely after two o'clock. No matter. She felt rested enough now, though she suspected she'd want a nap later on.

Getting out of bed, she took her small travel toiletries bag out of her tote purse, freshened up in the bathroom and put on the clean underwear, black leggings and white tee which she also took out of her bag. Then she went to find Amy.

"Hey, good morning," she said, discovering Amy in the living room of the apartment, sitting on the floor, tapping away on her laptop which was on the coffee table.

"Good morning!" Amy said, not sparing Sally a look. "I didn't wake you, did I?"

"No. How long have you been up?" Sally sat on the couch behind Amy, her legs on either side of the woman on the floor. She leaned forward and draped her arms over Amy's shoulders, resting her cheek against Amy's head.

"About an hour," Amy replied.

Sally blinked.

"Jesus! Babe, that means you hardly got any sleep!"

"I slept fine, I swear. I just knew I wanted to get back to work on this presentation."

Sally frowned. Almost right from the start of their first date last week, Sally had sensed that Amy was a driven person, but did she ever just relax? Fine, the presentation was important…Sally got that; but would it all go down the toilet if Amy had stayed in bed a couple of more hours and gotten some more rest?

She mentally shrugged.

Let Amy do Amy.

"Well, I don't want to disrupt you," Sally told her. Actually, she *did* want to disrupt her. Amy looked incredibly cute wearing an oversized pink satin button-up pajama top and what looked like nothing but panties underneath because her lean legs were bare all the way up to her hips. And she had the most adorable pair of pink fuzzy socks on her feet. "How about I make you some coffee and then I'll head out?"

That finally made Amy look away from her laptop's screen.

"Oh my god, would you do me the super biggest favor on the planet?" she asked.

Sally laughed.

"Name it."

"Run to La Vida Mocha for me and get me an Amy's Jet Fuel? Pleasepleaseplease?"

"That's a thing?"

Seriously? The woman has a coffee drink named after her?

"Trust me, it is. And get yourself whatever you want. You can take money from my purse."

Laughing, Sally said, "Don't worry about it, I'll get it. But let me know when you have a million bucks in your purse; *then* I'll take some money from it."

"You're the best," Amy said, returning her focus back to her work.

Amy's place was literally a three-minute drive to La Vida Mocha. If Sally had realized that, she would have walked it. That super-gorgeous barista, Vanessa, was behind the counter when Sally arrived and it didn't escape her notice that even though she had been a loyal Starbucks customer for years now, she couldn't name a single barista who worked there. Yet she knew Vanessa's name after only one coffee date in this place.

Scanning the chalkboard menu mounted on the wall above the coffee machines as she approached the counter, Sally didn't see what she was looking for and so it was with some trepidation that she said to Vanessa, "Um…this might sound crazy but I need an 'Amy's Jet Fuel?'"

Thankfully, Vanessa was anything but flummoxed at the request.

"Oh, is this for Amy?" she asked, already punching the order into the ordering thingamajig. "How's she doing? She must be busy if she didn't come herself."

"You know her well," Sally replied, adding that she had left Amy tapping away on her laptop.

"Well, I rarely see her *without* her laptop," Vanessa replied. "And can I get anything for—"

Suddenly, Vanessa's eyes went wide above the Darth Vader face mask she was wearing.

"Hey, wait a minute," she began before blushing and giggling. "You're Jillian Ashley! Even with the mask I recognize you from Amy's show!"

By now, Sally had resigned herself to the fact that apparently, every woman she was going to encounter from now on was A: a lesbian and B: a huge fan of Jillian Ashley books; huge enough to have watched the ultra-exclusive interview with Amy Broadnax.

Nodding, she said, "Yep! That's me!"

"Your books are amazing!" Vanessa gushed. "And you're so young! I mean this as a compliment but you write like someone much older."

Like, someone who's, say, fifty-one? Oh, and a man?

"Thanks," Sally said. "That means a lot. I try to make sure the reader focuses more on the story and not on how my youth may affect the tone of the narrative."

Holy shit!

Sally gave herself a mental pat on the back. She was getting really good at this bullshitting about being a famous author thing.

She then made an excuse about needing to get back to Amy quickly, even though she was willing to bet money that Amy wasn't even aware she had gone, and gave Vanessa her coffee order. When she opened her purse to pull out her wallet, Vanessa waved her off.

"On the house, please," Vanessa told her.

"No!" Sally exclaimed.

She was perfectly fine pretending to be Jillian Ashley to the occasional woman here and there who recognized her. And she was perfectly fine with autographing a fawning intern's book or coming up with nonsense about "the tone of the narrative," but she was *not* going to start accepting freebies using Jillian's name!

"I insist, really," Vanessa said…insistently.

Sally thought fast. She knew she was at risk of offending Vanessa and she didn't want that.

"It's so super sweet," she said. "But I have this hard and fast rule that I won't trade on my celebrity." Another idea came to her and she quickly pulled out a twenty. "Look, you agree to take this money and I'll even autograph it for you!"

Vanessa laughed but before she could again insist that the coffees were on the house, Sally grabbed a pen from the collection in the holder on the counter and which were provided for customers to sign their credit card receipts and started scribbling on the bill.

"To Vanessa," Sally recited as she wrote, "the most gorgeous barista in Carlsbad! Love, Jillian Ashley!"

The signature was still *blech* but as it was only the second time she ever wrote it, Sally cut herself some slack.

And Vanessa certainly didn't seem to mind. Picking up the twenty-dollar bill, she stared at the inscription, her eyes telegraphing her pleasure.

"FYI," Vanessa said, "a jealous little woman with auburn hair may show up at your house wanting to pick a fight one day. That will be my fiancée, Megan. Ignore her."

"No problem," Sally said with a laugh.

Vanessa carefully folded the autographed bill and put it in one of the pockets of her skinny jeans.

"Thanks for the autograph," she said. "You made my day. I'll get your change."

Sally wanted to scream.

She knew Vanessa was going to keep that twenty-dollar bill as a prized possession. Which meant that—as odd as it was—even though Sally was now twenty dollars poorer, she still hadn't *technically* paid for the coffee as the money hadn't gone into the register. That didn't bother her so much; she was still out twenty bucks and thus could go to sleep tonight feeling like she hadn't traded on her fake fame as a top lesfic author.

But…if she allowed Vanessa to give her the change, Vanessa would be out even more money.

"A tip!" she said. "Please, keep the change!"

It was too early in the morning for all these mental gymnastics.

Vanessa frowned.

"Are you sure? That's a big tip…"

"Totally sure!" Sally said. "I'm a big tipper! You know, all those…"

Fuck! What were they called again? Revenues…proceeds…?

"Royalties!" she blurted out, suddenly remembering the word. She really needed her coffee. "Yep. Just such a big tipper because of that."

"Okay, then...well, thanks again," Vanessa said. "You really are as nice as you seemed on the podcast."

"Thank you! By the way, what's an Amy's Jet Fuel?"

Vanessa said, "Do you know what a dead eye is?"

A non-functioning eye?

"Nope."

"A dead eye is a cup of coffee with three shots of espresso," Vanessa explained. "An Amy's Jet Fuel is a cup of coffee with four shots of espresso."

***

"I am *soooooo* glad you like pizza!" Amy exclaimed that night at Roosevelt Pizzeria. "When I first saw you walk into La Vida Mocha on our first date I was worried you were one of those women who only ate, like, kale sandwiches or something like that.'

Sally laughed.

"Is that the impression I make?" she asked.

"It's just that you're so tall," Amy answered. "You have this, like, model thing going on and so I imagined you not even knowing what a pizza is."

"I will have you know that I am actually something of a pizza snob, thanks to Max. He knows all the best places to go in SoCal and this is one of them."

Sally had had a fairly low-key day after leaving Amy's early this morning, Amy still sitting on the floor of the living room, tapping away at her laptop, her coffee with *four shots* of espresso—enough to reawaken an extinct dinosaur—within reach. She had gone home, showered and then made lunch plans with Lisa. During lunch, she had indulged Lisa's fangirling for a little while, just to let Lisa get it out of her system, before finally managing to steer her best friend away from all things Jillian Ashley and onto Lisa's favorite topic: Lisa. Then she had returned home and taken a nap—something she figured Amy would never be able to do after drinking all that espresso—woke up at around three o'clock and then just chillaxed at home, watching movies until Amy showed up for their date.

When Amy had arrived, Sally had then had cause to re-evaluate her negative assessment of the sanity of a person who ingests four shots of espresso because as soon as Amy flitted into the condo, she had taken Sally's hand and wordlessly led her to the bedroom. Once there, Amy pushed Sally onto the bed, hiked up Sally's dress, pulled aside the crotch of Sally's panties and then proceeded to eat her out to a gushing orgasm.

"Caffeine makes me so fucking horny!" Amy had then said afterwards, slipping off her own panties and coming up to straddle Sally's face. Sally then made sure Amy's caffeine-induced horniness was taken care of.

Naturally, Sally had suggested they order their dinner for delivery but Amy had smiled and said, "No, I want to go out. But while we're out, you can think about what else you'd like to do to me later."

And Sally *had* often thought about what else she'd like to do, which, combined with the lingering effects of her recent climax, made Sally's pussy a veritable faucet.

"So," Sally now said, wanting to get her mind off sex because, really, her clit's pulsing was becoming distracting, "did you get a lot done today?"

"I did," Amy said, nodding. "So much done. I worked on the presentation until about one o'clock, I guess, and then I switched gears and did some prep work for the next podcast episode, which I'm super stoked about."

"Good for you," Sally said. Silently, however, she was thinking that what Amy had just described hardly sounded like a day off. "So, after this big presentation on Tuesday, what's next?"

Amy pouted, which Sally found both odd and cute.

"I'm being forced to take a vacation," Amy said.

Sally laughed.

"Forced? You poor thing!"

"I know, I know…" Amy began in a conciliatory tone, "First World problem." She bit into one of the complimentary breadsticks the restaurant provided each table. "I just have a lot to do and so I don't really feel like switching off right now. But my boss is basically holding a gun to my head, so…"

"How long a vacation?"

"At least a week," Amy said, still pouting.

Sally laughed again.

"Oh my god, you are hopeless!" she said. "Babe, a week off will do you good. I mean, I know I've only known you for, like, five minutes, but I can already tell that you work too hard."

"I know…"

"So, what are you going to do on your vacation?"

Amy shrugged.

"I was thinking of taking a trip to San Francisco. I love it there and since I can't do any of the European traveling I had wanted to do, it's the next best thing. Have you ever been?"

"Oh my god, the clam chowder at Scoma's?" Sally enthused. "I love it! My grandparents live in San Francisco and so I've been up there lots."

Their server arrived with their pizza and throughout dinner, the two women talked San Francisco: favorite restaurants, favorite things to do, various misadventures on the BART or Muni. Amy told Sally about her plans to visit her favorite art museums and also to just wander around the city, taking photos with her SLR camera.

"SLR? That's, like, one of those cameras that doesn't have cellphone attached to it, right?" Sally asked.

Amy laughed.

"Precisely," she said. "Photography is a hobby of mine."

"When are you going to leave?" Sally asked.

"I don't know. Maybe next weekend. My boss says she won't let me back in the office building if I put it off too long."

"Well, I can't wait to see all your pictures when you get back."

Sally really was happy Amy was taking some time off. Well, she was happy that Amy was being *forced* to take some time off. The woman was a workaholic. Nonetheless, Sally was also realizing that she was disappointed that she wouldn't be able to see Amy while she was up north. This new relationship of theirs was fun and exciting. And *hot*. Okay, it had only been a week and Sally knew she needed to keep that in mind because virtually all new relationships started off fun, exciting and hot. The trick was keeping it that way when one week eventually morphed into three and three weeks eventually morphed into two months and two months eventually became six.

So, she knew she had to temper her expectations.

But, Sally also knew that her and Amy just *clicked*. Like, incredibly well. Sally could remember in 8K-level clarity that exact moment she had first locked eyes with Amy over the internet just before the podcast interview started. And it wasn't just that Amy was beautiful—Sally literally locked eyes with scores of beautiful women on a daily basis…That first moment she had locked eyes with Amy had been as if Sally had suddenly seen her future and in the time since then, Sally had sensed that feeling growing stronger and stronger.

Admittedly, Amy's need to always be doing something was a little alarming but Sally was thinking that maybe she had simply come into Amy's life at one of those crazy-hectic times everybody goes through occasionally. Maybe, once Tuesday's meeting had passed and Amy had her week in Frisco, Sally would discover that her new girlfriend was actually not as tightly wound as she could seem to be.

Chapter 25

On Tuesday afternoon, Amy was elated.

No, scratch that.

She was *fucking* elated!

Her and Makeda were driving back to Carlsbad from San Diego in Makeda's Cadillac after meeting with Supervisor Edelmann and they had knocked it out of the park! The discussion with Edelmann had been a meeting of like minds and all the work Amy had done to prepare for it paid off. Edelmann had determined to be the champion for amending the San Diego County constitution to include equal rights for women, telling Amy and Makeda that if she could count on their organization to help with the lobbying, she was certain she could get enough support to make it happen.

But Amy and Makeda wanted to do even more and as soon as they had started the drive back north, had begun strategizing on how to engineer a grassroots campaign that would harness the power of women in San Diego County as a voting bloc and really draw attention to this effort.

"But first, you're going on vacation," Makeda reminded her as they approached the exits for Del Mar.

Amy rolled her eyes but didn't argue, knowing *that* battle was lost.

"I know," she said.

"It will give the rest of us a chance to prove to you that we can survive without you for a little while," Makeda joked. "Next week I don't want to see you. Will it be a staycation or are you going somewhere?"

"San Francisco," Amy answered, reminding herself that she still needed to book the trip. Because she hated long drives, she wanted to fly, so there were airline tickets to purchase, along with finding and booking a hotel. Whenever she traveled to Frisco, she always preferred staying right in the downtown area so she could be near everything. Doing so also relieved her of the hassle of renting a car because she could either walk, Lyft or BART anywhere she needed to go.

In any case, she needed to get all those travel arrangements taken care of and so she resolved that tonight she'd spend time on her Travelocity account.

Well, she'd do that *after* she spent time *on* Sally.

Amy didn't know what it was—perhaps it was the relief that the meeting with Edelmann was finally over; perhaps it was the feeling of success that came with a job well done; perhaps it was the still lingering effects of her morning Jet Fuel—but ever since the meeting ended, Amy had been very much aware of being incredibly horny.

***

After Makeda drove them back to the office, the two women said their goodbyes, with Makeda congratulating Amy again on a job well done. Before she got in her car, Amy sent a text to Sally and discovered that Sally had just gotten home from work and so Amy drove straight to the condo.

"Hi," Amy purred after Sally let her in and they had shared a deep kiss with probing tongues.

"Hi," Sally said, catching her breath. "There's *soooooo* much I want to do to you right now but first tell me how the meeting went; I've been dying to know all day."

Amy's clit was still pulsing from the intensity of their kiss hello and so she said, "Cliff's Notes version: it went awesome and we got Edelmann's full support."

"Yay! Babe, that's amazing!"

"I'll give you the full story after you do all those things you want to do to me," Amy then said. "Please!"

Sally pulled Amy into another kiss, pressing Amy against the entryway wall.

"Thank god you said that," Sally eventually said. "You look so fucking hot in that suit."

Amy smiled. She was wearing one of her favorite professional outfits: a dark-blue skirt-suit set with a fitted jacket. She also had on black pantyhose and her Amy-means-business high heels—black pumps with a metallic stiletto heel. It was the outfit she always chose when she wanted to feel like Darth Vader's lawyer.

Taking Amy's hand, Sally quickly led her into the bedroom and Amy stood still while Sally first removed Amy's suit jacket, nibbling on her neck as she did so, and then began unbuttoning the white blouse underneath it. She started trembling when Sally bit her left nipple through the fabric of her white bralette. Sally then pulled the left strap of the garment off Amy's shoulder and exposed the breast, bringing her lips onto the stone-like nipple and bringing a moan from Amy's lips.

Her mouth was then claimed in another kiss but this time, Amy felt Sally's hand sneak up under pencil skirt and in a less than a moment that hand was rubbing Amy's center through the fabric of her pantyhose and panties and all Amy could do was mewl into Sally's mouth as her pussy reacted, her inner walls clenching, her clit swelling and throbbing.

Finally, Sally guided Amy down onto the bed. Amy was in an odd state of undress: her jacket and shirt were off but her bralette was only halfway off and her skirt and everything underneath it was still on. Nonetheless, once Amy was down on the bed, Sally quickly brought her head down between Amy's legs, pushing up the hem of her skirt and gently kissing Amy's stockings-clad thighs. Amy pulled up the skirt even further so she could spread her legs more.

After a moment, Sally looked up with a wicked smile and said, "I owe you ten dollars."

In her hyper-aroused state, Amy was confused. She had no idea what Sally was talking about.

"Wh-What?" she stammered. "Why?"

And then Sally provided the answer.

Amy felt Sally's fingers dig into the fabric of the pantyhose and then with a loud *rrrrripppp!* the crotch of the hose was torn open.

"Oh my fuck!" Amy gasped, her arousal kicking up several *big* notches. That sound of the fabric tearing, the violence of it, the sheer animalistic nature of it, her pantyhose destroyed by a woman who wanted to get to her pussy that much quicker—all of that brought her to the brink of coming undone and her hips twitched reflexively as her center—her entire center—spasmed with pleasure that took her right to the edge and Amy had to clutch the bedsheets because she felt as if she was about to rocket upwards.

Her panties were aggressively pulled aside and just like that, Sally's mouth was on her pussy. It started with Sally's tongue pushing inside her and then swirling around, catching all of the warm liquid Amy knew her pussy was flooded with and then the tongue was removed and the flat of it slid upwards until it settled on her clit, licking it over and over again.

"Oh my fuck!" Amy repeated, louder this time. She knew she wasn't going to last long.

Fingers slid inside her, a jolt of pleasure shot up her spine. Her clit was encircled by Sally's lips now and sucked once…twice…

"I'm coming!" Amy screamed out, her hips bucking, her back arching, her pussy contracting around those fingers as the almost unbearably delightful waves of the climax tore through her.

"Sallyohmyfuuuuuuuuuck!"

Her scream was now a keening wail.

Releasing her clit but keeping her fingers inside her spasming core, Sally came up from between Amy's legs to lay on top of her. As her body kept quaking, Amy grabbed the sides of Sally's head and brought Sally's face down for a hungry and possessive kiss. She smelled and tasted herself on Sally's lips and she craved it, breathing it in, licking it off with her quickly swiping tongue.

But Sally ruthlessly broke the kiss and before Amy knew it, she was turned over on the bed, Sally's fingers were re-inserted and then Sally was biting her ass through the fabric of the pantyhose, the flesh of Amy's ass separated from Sally's sharp teeth only by that oh-so-thin layer of nylon because of the fact that she had chosen to wear a thong today.

While she bit, Sally fucked Amy with those long fingers, pumping them in and out while her mouth administered the bites all over Amy's ass, both cheeks getting equal attention.

Amy grunted in both pleasure and pain and screamed directly into the mattress when she came again, feeling her come squirt out, feeling her pussy clutch at those fingers. She continued screaming until she had to come up for air, dizzy both with the pleasure consuming her and from having almost suffocated herself.

There was another loud *rrrrripppp!* Sally had torn the pantyhose away even more and Amy felt her bite-ridden ass exposed properly now. The third orgasm hit her right when Sally pulled her soaked fingers out and then used them to rub her engorged clit right at the same moment those wonderfully sharp teeth clamped down again on her ass.

Amy felt her body convulsing like something from a scene in a movie about a woman possessed by evil spirits. This third climax had total control of her from within and when it finally subsided, all she could do was lay there with her eyes closed, panting, feeling spent, unable to move, her pantyhose in shreds. Occasionally she would twitch as a few latent pulses of pleasure would sneakily hit her just when she thought it was over.

***

Eventually, all of her clothes had been removed; Sally's too.
Eventually, toys had been brought out.
Eventually, Amy had her way with Sally; Sally had her way with Amy again; Amy had her way with Sally again…et cetera, et cetera.
And eventually, they had to stop for food.
Going out was not an option—neither of them wanted to get dressed. Nor was cooking an option—by the time they'd finished with each other, both women were too drained to put in that kind of effort on anything.
When the Chinese food arrived, no sooner had they sat down at Sally's dining table, both wearing bathrobes, than Amy suddenly said, "Come to San Francisco with me."
She knew it was a risky thing to say, but she also knew it was what she wanted. She may not know where Sally and her were headed; she may not know if Sally and her would even be speaking to each other in six months but what she did know was that her and Sally were on a fantastic ride right now and Amy did not want the momentum of it to stop because she disappeared for a week to San Francisco.
And she was perfectly prepared for Sally to say no; for Sally to say it was too soon for such an idea. If that happened, Amy would be disappointed, yes, but it would hardly be a life-ending event; she would just do whatever it takes to ensure that the momentum was regained once she returned.
But Sally gave her an encouraging sign when her face lit up with a full-blown smile.
"Really?" Sally asked. "A trip together?"
Amy licked her lips.
"I know…it's kind of crazy," she began, "but I swear I'm not trying to move things along too fast."

"I believe you," Sally stated.

"It's just…I'm being forced to take this vacation, you know that, and I suppose I could just stay here in Carlsbad but I'm kind of sick of Carlsbad because of the pandemic. I really want to go to Europe but obviously that can't happen."

Sally gave a groan.

"I know what you mean," she said. "I wanted to go to Amsterdam this year."

"Oh my god, I would *looooove* to go to Amsterdam!" Amy said "Definitely on my bucket list. Anyway, it's just that I've been having a lot of fun with you the past almost two weeks and I'm thinking why can't we continue having fun up in Frisco? But I swear…like I said, I'm so not trying to move things along too fast! I just think it would be a lot of fun and it would also be a great way for us to continue getting to know each other."

And to keep fucking our brains out…

Amy wasn't sure she wanted to use that as a selling point for her suggestion that both of them go to San Francisco, but it was true nonetheless. The thought of going a week without this amazing sex she had with Sally…nope, not worth thinking about.

Chapter 26

Amy had a point, Sally was thinking. Taking a trip together *would* be a great way to continue getting to know one another.

But, goddamn…

A trip together? Already?

They haven't even been dating for two weeks yet!

But why should that matter, she wondered? A trip to San Francisco wasn't like buying a house together. Amy wasn't proposing marriage or suggesting names for their future children. No one was calling U-Haul.

Sally recalled how she felt when Amy first told her about being forced to take a vacation and that she was planning on going to Frisco. She'd been a little disappointed. Disappointed that suddenly, they would have to press *Pause* on this fledgling relationship of theirs while Amy was nearly five-hundred miles away.

Of course, she'd have gotten over it, Sally realized. That week or so while Amy was gone would have passed and most likely they would have picked up right where they left off when Amy returned. But now she had the opportunity to ignore the *Pause* button altogether.

Besides, she was tired of being Sensible Sally. She really liked Amy and the idea of getting out of Carlsbad with her was exciting. Oh, and going to San Francisco had the added benefit of her not missing out on their incredible sex life! Sex with Amy, Sally had thought more than once, was like a drug and she was a full-blown addict by now.

"Let's do it," she stated and was instantly rewarded with that gorgeous smile of Amy's.

"Really?"

"Really!"

"Yay!" Amy clapped her hands and then leaned across the table to give Sally a quick kiss. "So, I know it's short notice and all…will you be able to get the time off?"

With a dismissive wave of her hand, Sally indicated that that was a non-problem. She told Amy that she had plenty of vacation time available and that as it turns out, this was the perfect time to use some of it because her team's projects were not only running smoothly but she had trusted lieutenants she could delegate responsibilities to in her absence.

"Oh my god, we have *soooooo* much planning to do!" Amy enthused and Sally had to laugh because Amy's enthusiasm was infectious and also because Sally could just tell that Amy loved anything that would get her in front of her laptop doing something.

"It's kind of like online shopping, when you think about it," Sally suggested. "Finding the best airline to use; finding the best hotel with all the right amenities…"

"Totally!"

After they had finished eating, they got to work.

They decided on a Saturday-to-Saturday trip, catching a flight out of San Diego this coming weekend. That portion of the planning was a piece of cake. They were able to easily secure two roundtrip tickets on a major carrier and the best part was, because the airlines were still reeling from the pandemic's effect on travel, Sally and Amy were able to buy first-class seats both ways for reasonable prices.

The matter of where they would stay was a little more complicated. Amy told Sally about her preference of staying right in the downtown area, which Sally was completely on board with. What was the point of traveling to such a magnificent city if they were going to stay anywhere but *in* the magnificent city? The problem was, there were so many hotels to choose from. However, after talking about it and each woman coming up with a list of must-have amenities (wi-fi for Amy; a balcony for Sally), and determining their budget—which was pretty high considering they were two single women with well-paying jobs and absolutely zero financial dependents (Lena hardly counted)—they agreed on an upscale Hyatt hotel in the Embarcadero district. Not only did it have wi-fi but they splurged on a suite which faced the water and had a balcony. Sally was already imagining spending lovely evenings on it, in a bathrobe, sipping wine and looking out over the harbor.

With their flight and hotel arrangements squared away, Sally was certain their planning was done. Besides, it was almost ten o'clock and the only screen Sally wanted to continue looking at was the one on her Kindle while she read herself to sleep. But Amy insisted on staying up a little longer, wanting to find out what current exhibitions the art museums were showing and also wanting to make reservations for them at some of Frisco's nicest restaurants. She even talked about planning some boating excursions for them.

"All of that *tonight*?" Sally had asked, surprised, getting to her feet to head to the bedroom, her own laptop already closed. "It's practically ten o'clock!"

"It won't take long," Amy promised, not looking up from her laptop's screen.

Sally crossed her arms and looked down at Amy who was sitting on the floor in front of her laptop which was resting on Sally's coffee table. She suddenly flashbacked to the other day, when she had left Amy's apartment with Amy sitting on *her* floor, her laptop on *her* coffee table and that high-octane, ought-to-be-illegal-in-all-fifty-states Amy's Jet Fuel drink beside her.

"Babe!" Sally said sternly.

Amy looked up at her.

Sally decided to soften her approach.

"Babe," she said less sternly, "you can either do that or we can both drift off to sleep together after having made each other come. Choose now."

Amy's mouth dropped open but Sally was gratified to see lust cloud those chocolate-brown eyes of hers.

Sally smiled.

"Now, close your laptop," she ordered.

Amy did.

"Stand up."

Amy stood.

"Let's go to bed," Sally said, holding out her hand for Amy to take.

Chapter 27

The next evening, the doorbell at Amy's apartment rang and Amy got up from her sofa to let Rachel in. Sally had decided to work a little later this evening due to her suddenly deciding to take a vacation and she told Amy she wanted to be sure things were in order before they left for San Francisco; also, Sally had dinner plans with her mother later, so it was doubtful Amy was going to get to see her tonight anyway. Thus, Amy had invited Rachel over to cook Thai food together and watch TV.

"Okay, my mind is officially blown!" Rachel said as she walked into Amy's place carrying some groceries.

Amy giggled.

"Blown about what?" she asked, following her best friend into the kitchen.

After settling the grocery bags on the counter near the stove, Rachel looked at her.

"That book by your new main squeeze! Holy fuck! Chapter twenty-five was…holy fuck!"

"I told you!"

"I wish I was a lesbian!" Rachel exclaimed.

Amy laughed.

"No, I'm serious!" Rachel continued. "I just can't believe what I read! That chapter has changed my life about what sex could actually be like! Actually, the whole book has done that, but especially that chapter. You don't understand, sweetie. Sex with men is *never* like that!"

Amy pulled out her wok and two cutting boards.

"Yeah, well, you need to understand that there are plenty of women out there who are lousy in bed also," she told Rachel. And Amy had had her fair share of them. Gwen, for one. Amy was a big believer in *to each her own*, but a lesbian who didn't like going down on women? Seriously?

Rachel placed the prawns she had brought over on one of the cutting boards and started slicing them in half while Amy began chopping the onion and red chilis on the other.

"But how is it with Sally?" Rachel asked. "She's not lousy, is she? I mean, she can't possibly be! She wrote that book! She wrote chapter twenty-five, which, by the way, is now my favorite chapter in any book written by any author, male or female, straight or lesbian."

Amy laughed and told Rachel—without providing too many details—that Sally was beyond fabulous in bed and that their sex life was phenomenal.

"In fact, I invited her to San Francisco with me," she added.

Having finished with the prawns, Rachel had just started preparing the stir-fry sauce by mixing oyster and soy sauces with some sugar. Briefly looking up from her stirring duties, she asked, "Really?"

But Amy could read the subtext of that one word question.

"I know, I know; it seems super-fast but…"

"What?"

Amy started heating up some oil in the wok.

"Okay," she began, "so I'll admit that part of the reason I invited her is because our sex is amazing. I did *not* want to go a whole week without it."

"See?" Rachel interjected. "That's what I'm talking about! I have *never* had a guy so good in bed that I couldn't imagine going a week without his services! Anyway, continue…"

"So, yeah, sex played a big role in the invitation," Amy went on, "but…I don't know…I have a really good feeling about this one, Rach."

"Already?"

Amy nodded.

"Already. And you know me…I *never* say that! It usually takes me longer but…" A small smile formed on her face as she started measuring out rice. "…Sally is amazing. She gets me. I get her. I just didn't want to be up in San Francisco without her."

"Well, I'm just surprised you allowed yourself time away from everything you're always working on to actually have a girlfriend."

Amy wanted to reply back with something sarcastic, but found she couldn't. Rachel was speaking the truth, after all. Amy knew she worked too much. If it wasn't something for the Women's Resource Center it was something for her blog or her podcast—which reminded her, she needed to sort out all the research for her next episode of *Lesbeing—the Podcast*, the episode about lesbian period dramas, before she left for Frisco and—

She shook her head. She was doing it again. Instead of being here in the moment with her best friend and having fun cooking, she was thinking about work she needed to do. What's more, she was certain that Sally was beginning to notice just how much of a workaholic she was. Last night, Sally had had to lure her away from her laptop with sex—and that had turned into another amazing time in the bedroom. Still, though, Sally hadn't exactly complained or anything, Amy considered…

Perhaps Sally didn't think it was such a big deal. After all, Sally was a professional who also took her job seriously and worked hard.

Anyway, Amy put all of that out of her mind. Her best friend was here in her home and they were cooking together; *this* was what she needed to focus on.

***

"Have you started packing yet?" Amy asked Sally later that night over the phone.

Sally scoffed.

"Hello? It's Wednesday, we're leaving on Saturday and I'm a woman! That means I actually built a time machine today and zapped myself back to three days ago and started packing then!"

Amy laughed.

It was almost nine o'clock and she was in her bedroom, her suitcase open on her bed, several outfits on the mattress next to it.

"In fact," Sally went on, "I'm packing now."

"No way, me too!" Amy replied.

"Are you bringing any bathing suits?"

"I checked," Amy began, "the hotel's pool *is* open and so I figured I'd bring at least one. It might be fun to just chill poolside one day."

"*Please* bring those stilettos you were wearing yesterday!" Sally said.

"Liked those, did you?" Amy asked, tossing a collection of bras she had just removed from her bra drawer onto the bed. "I think I'll also bring some pantyhose I don't care about just so you can go savage on me again."

"Liked that, did you?" Sally replied.

"Fuck, that was hot," Amy breathed, her clit pulsing at the memory.

"Actually, since we're kinda-sorta on this topic," Sally began, "what about toys?"

"Wait, hold on a sec…"

Amy opened her phone's camera and snapped a pic of her open toybox, also on the bed, and sent it to Sally. A moment later she heard Sally laughing.

"I just haven't decided which ones to pack yet," Amy said.

"First World problem," Sally chuckled. "As long as one of us remembers a harness."

"God, yes! Of course, the great thing about a place like San Francisco is if we forget to pack anything…"

"…they'll be a place there that sells it," Sally finished for her.

"Okay, we have to change the topic," Amy said, "I'm getting excited and I'm *soooooo* not dressed for it!"

Sally laughed.

"Why? What are you wearing?"

"Just pj shorts and a tank, but no underwear. I'll be a dripping mess pretty soon."

"Exactly how I like you."

Amy groaned.

"Then maybe you should come over and make sure I'm exactly how you like me."

"No, no, no…" Sally said. "We agreed."

Amy sighed. They *had* agreed.

Much earlier, when the two of them had discussed their plans for the day and Sally had mentioned not only working late but also the dinner date with her mother, the question had come up about whether they'd get to see each other at all today. That naturally led to the discovery that ever since they had started dating nearly two weeks ago, they'd spent every night together but one.

What amazed Amy was, she hadn't realized that was the case! Normally, a new woman suddenly guest-starring in her life was something she had to adjust to. Even those women with whom she didn't start off spending practically *every* night with, like she had done with Sally so far, required Amy to recalibrate herself to a degree—especially mentally—in order to accommodate this new person occupying her time and personal space.

But with Sally, there had been no feeling that recalibration was needed. Sally had just *fit in* so seamlessly. A thrilling and somewhat scary prospect.

Podcast idea: Something about lesbians compared to other women when it comes to time spent with a new lover in the early days of a relationship.

And she could write an accompanying blog article to go with it! It was still a very nebulous idea but Amy resolved to firm it up more later after she finished what she was doing.

In any case, her and Sally had agreed that tonight they'd spend apart, if only as a token gesture to avoid becoming a lesbian cliché. Besides, they were about to spend a week together in a hotel room in San Francisco—one night apart wouldn't kill them.

But Amy knew it was too late to turn her libido off now. Even that brief discussion about what toys to bring on their trip was enough to ensure her center would remain aroused for quite some time—she just had that kind of sex drive. Nor did it help that because of this arousal she was suddenly hyper-aware of the way the fabric of her shorts would softly brush or swish against the folds between her legs as she moved about the room to continue packing.

Yep, she was going to be a dripping mess, *real* soon.

Chapter 28

On Saturday morning, Sally had a wickedly delicious idea.

It came to her as she stepped out of the shower at her condo and saw a topless Amy brushing her teeth at the sink. Just as Amy finished, Sally dropped her towel and pressed herself against Amy's back, loving how Amy groaned when Sally's hard nipples made contact with her skin.

"God, I was hoping you were going to wake up horny," Amy whispered, tilting her head back, exposing more of her neck to Sally's lips. "We have time…"

"I know," Sally said. Amy, she was discovering, was a consummate planner and when it came to determining when they should wake up today to get to the airport all the way in San Diego, Sally had let Amy do all that calculating, knowing that if she herself did it, they'd be lucky to make it in time to catch the flight.

"Tell me the truth," Sally said, after raking her teeth along Amy's neck, eliciting a purr from the other woman. "You factored in morning sex when you determined what time we should get up today, didn't you?"

"Only two weeks in and you know me so well," Amy murmured. "We have approximately forty-five minutes of Whatever Time."

"Come on," Sally said, leading Amy back to the bedroom.

"Yay!"

Sally laid Amy on the bed and topped her, looking down into her chocolate-brown eyes.

"Not so fast," she said. "Let's play a game."

Biting her lip, Amy smiled up at Sally.

"What kind of game?"

Sally sucked a hard nipple into her mouth and when she released it, said, "Let's bring each other to the brink. *Only* to the brink. No coming until we get to the hotel."

Amy sucked in a breath.

"Fuck, yes!" she uttered. "I love a good tease!"

"It means being sopping, liquid messes all morning," Sally warned after nibbling on Amy's second nipple.

"But it also means a holy-fuck-I'm-gonna-pass-out orgasm later," Amy whispered.

"Exactly!" Sally stared down into Amy's eyes again. "Shall we…?"

And with that, Amy's pj shorts were yanked off. In a mere moment, the two women quickly repositioned themselves into a sixty-nine, with Sally on top. Sally lustily uttered an "Oh fuck!" when Amy's scent filled her nostrils and she saw how wet Amy's pussy already was. A crystal clear droplet of arousal was slowly dribbling out and Sally quickly darted out her tongue to catch it to let it sit on her tongue. Meanwhile, she felt her clit pulled on by Amy's lips and her own pussy contract in response.

Groaning, she pushed her tongue through her girlfriend's folds and into the warmth beyond, hearing Amy's whimpers of pleasure as her tongue swirled, Sally coating it with as much of Amy's essence as possible and then swallowing, wanting those juices inside her.

Who needs coffee?

She felt Amy's fingers dig into the flesh of her ass and spread the cheeks wider. This opened her pussy more and Sally could feel her arousal stream out, Amy's tongue lapping it up. Sally brought her own tongue to Amy's clit and started slowly circling the bud.

"Oh my fuck!" Amy cried out. "Careful!"

But Sally didn't want to relinquish the clit. She slowed her circling, yes; she lightened her tongue's touch, yes; but the feel of the swollen button in her mouth was too good to give up just now.

Fingers entered her and Sally's eyes rolled back in her head. Amy's clit was relinquished just then because Sally had to take her mouth away and moan loudly.

"Babe! I'm close!" she warned and felt Amy still the fingers inside her but not remove them. Sally had to squeeze her eyes shut and concentrate to walk her pussy back from bursting in a climax.

Two can play at that game!

She slid her middle finger into Amy first and then her ring finger. Instantly, Amy's inner walls grabbed them while simultaneously her own clit was once more captured by Amy's lips.

After making sure her fingers were good and coated, Sally slid them out and immediately put them in her mouth, tasting the liquid pleasure from deeper in Amy's pussy.

"Oh shit! Careful!" she called out when the sensations from this tasting, combined with what Amy was doing to her clit once more brought her to the brink.

In lust-filled hunger she brought her mouth back to Amy's pussy, the flat of her tongue swiping across the entirety of it, starting at her clit and then over the shiny wet lips and then down to the leaking opening. And now it was Amy warning her; pleading, really, for Sally to stop or she'd come.

It continued like this for a good twenty minutes until finally, Sally had to call it quits. It had gotten to the point where if Amy so much as breathed on her clit, she'd explode.

"Oh, thank god!" Amy exclaimed when Sally rolled off her, Sally trying not to put any pressure on her clit with her legs or else there would be no stopping the dam from bursting. "I don't know how much more I could have taken," Amy added.

Sally laughed.

"Fun game, then?"

"Very fun!" Amy said after a couple of deep breaths. "God, why can't we just teleport to San Francisco?" she added with a whine.

Sally understood. Amy had expertly turned her pussy into a tingling, vibing, dripping living entity that *needed* to come! But that was the fun part, wasn't it?

As she lay on the bed, next to Amy, both of them recovering, both of them trying to regain control enough to be able to function and get to the airport, Sally smiled to herself.

It was going to be a fun trip!

***

"Wait, you're bringing your laptop?" Sally asked.

When Amy had arrived last night to spend the night, toting her luggage for the trip, Sally hadn't noticed that one of the bags Amy had been carrying was her nice, leather laptop bag. Now, as they were preparing to leave the condo because their Lyft was due to arrive in six minutes, Sally *did* notice it.

"Yeah," Amy said, following Sally's gaze to where the laptop bag was resting near the front door. "Well, I mean…"

"You're not actually going to do any work, are you?" Sally challenged her.

"No!" Amy returned. "But, I mean, we're going to have downtime, right? We're not *always* going to be out doing stuff, right? I figure that when we're not really doing anything in particular, I can maybe just take some notes for my *Lesbeing* stuff."

Sally considered that. It made sense. They *would* have downtime—they were going to be there for a week, after all. And Sally was even hoping to use some of that downtime to catch up on her reading. But bringing a Kindle loaded with books and bringing a laptop seemed like two different things.

"I suppose..." she agreed, somewhat reluctantly.

"Also," Amy added hurriedly, "I figure we can hook the laptop up to the TV in the room and use it to stream stuff to watch."

That also made sense. Hotel TV sucked. Having a way to stream Netflix or Prime would be awesome.

She smiled.

"Cool," she said. She knew she wasn't one-hundred percent convinced, but at least she was close. Just then her phone chirped. "Ooh, Lucinda is here! Let's go!"

Sally had to hand it to Amy: her planning had been spot-on so far. Their Lyft driver, Lucinda, dropped them off at San Diego International Airport two hours before their flight departed and even though there was a bit of wait to check their bags, their first-class tickets allowed them to use the much shorter security line and reach their gate with plenty of time to spare before boarding.

Finally sitting in the gate area, Sally leaned over to Amy and whispered, "My god, I am horny as fuck!"

Amy laughed.

"Preaching to the choir," she murmured, placing her hand on Sally's thigh.

Sally couldn't believe what was going on south of her waist. Despite all the non-erotic things that had happened since leaving her condo: the ride to the airport, the hassle of checking their luggage and getting through security...Sally's core was still just as lubricated as when she had rolled off Amy over an hour ago now, and her clit was still just as swollen and energized. She realized it was simply Amy's presence near her doing it. Every time Sally looked at her stunning girlfriend; every time she caught a whiff of Amy's perfume mixed with the body lotion she used; every time Amy took her hand or simply smiled at her, Sally's body reacted lasciviously.

She felt Amy use the tips of her fingers to stroke her thigh over the fabric of the leggings she was wearing. Sally snapped her head to look at Amy, who was pretending to be nonchalantly checking notifications on her phone. But the tiny wicked smile Amy was trying to hide gave her away.

"Are you doing that on purpose?" Sally asked.

"Hmm? I have no idea what you're talking about," Amy said, not looking away from her phone.

"Fine," Sally stated. She then rested her own hand on Amy's leggings-clad thigh and also played her fingers over the fabric, gratified to see Amy shut her eyes briefly and give a little gasp in response, which only made Sally's clit pulse harder.

Fuck, this is going to be a long flight!

Chapter 29

As soon as they entered their hotel suite, they were all over each other. Amy quickly determined which way the bedroom was and practically yanked Sally into it.

Normally, after a day of traveling, Amy would have wanted to first hop in the shower before having sex but this time she didn't care. Showering took time, time she didn't want to waste and considering how quickly Sally was trying to get her clothes off, Sally felt the same way.

Both women were naked in seemingly record time, their clothes left in a jumbled pile on the floor, and they clambered onto the bed.

"I want to be on top this time," Amy insisted.

"Anything you want," Sally panted, lying on her back while Amy positioned herself over her.

"Oh my fucking god!" Amy mewled when, in the sixty-nine position, Sally's nude pussy was right there in front of her face. It was the most beautiful thing in the world to her hyper-aroused mind: pink, dripping, the musky scent of its arousal—contained these last few hours during their journey, slamming into her nostrils, turning her on even more and making her own pussy contract and squeeze out more of her own juices.

She felt Sally grab her ass and bury her face into her center, lips and tongue working furiously and so Amy did the same. No fucking around this time. No warnings. No stopping.

Fuck the brink.

She latched onto Sally's clit with her lips, humming contentedly at the taste of it, and with a few flicks of her tongue over the swollen organ heard Sally give a high-pitched moan just as her pussy started convulsing and squirting out come against Amy's face.

A second later, Amy orgasmed hard also and she grunted with the release, her mouth still pressed against Sally's center, her hips twitching as she came. She pressed her pussy hard against the mouth giving her this pleasure, feeling her slick sex slide easily along Sally's features. She screamed against Sally's pussy as her core was rocked by the intensity of the climax—an intensity that had been built up hours ago in Sally's bedroom and was now finally being released.

But no matter how hard she was coming, still she licked her girlfriend's throbbing pussy, trying to catch and swallow as much of Sally's essence as her tongue could find.

They came together a second time quickly after the first and now Amy was seeing flashes of light behind her eyelids. She felt all that arousal which had been flooding her insides throughout the trip gush out while her entire core contracted with pure pleasure that forced her reluctantly to pull her face away from Sally's sex, lift her head and cry out with a guttural yell.

Still they weren't done. Fingers were inserted next. But Amy wasn't going to be satisfied with plain vanilla finger play this time. Delirious with the pleasure already coursing through her and the pleasure yet to be released, she indicated without words what she wanted Sally to do.

With her forefinger and middle finger stuck deep into Sally's liquid pussy, Amy curled her ring finger around, found Sally's rear opening, which was already lubricated with the woman's come and easily slid it inside.

"Ohhhhhhhh FUCK!" Sally screamed before mimicking the action on Amy and now, with both of them double-penetrated, they exploded in yet another shared orgasm and this one was making Amy's entire body quake as if she was shivering from being out in the cold. Again, she screamed against Sally's pussy as she sucked on her girlfriend's clit, Sally bucking slightly beneath her, held down and controlled only by Amy's weight.

"Holy fuck!" Amy eventually had to call out, her body lost in the throes of the climax.

When it finally released her, she went limp atop Sally, the side of her face resting lifelessly against Sally's convulsing, streaming core.

She was done. Sally was too. It was so fast and so primal but it was what they needed.

The fingers from all openings were removed and Amy somehow managed to find the strength to roll off Sally's slack, panting form.

Amy knew she had never experienced anything like that before. The intensity of the orgasms she had just been given had robbed other parts of her body of feeling. Her toes and fingers were numb. Her cheeks were tingling in the way a body part feels when it has lost its source of blood. Her legs and arms were all jelly.

Without speaking, Amy and Sally spent time recovering, both of them panting hard, both of them unable to move.

My god in heaven!

***

"We scored ourselves a nice room, by the way," Amy said after they both shared a shower and put on the hotel's oh-so-soft bathrobes.

They were in one of the hotel's luxury suites with a bedroom, living and dining areas and a private balcony facing the bay—all artfully decorated with mid-century modern furnishings. Amy didn't have a tape measure but she suspected the suite was as large as her apartment in Carlsbad.

It was now late afternoon and a wonderfully orange-tinged sunlight was streaming into the suite from the window.

"Yeah," Sally agreed. "I would say we shouldn't feel too cramped here. Although, if we really wanted to stress-test this relationship, we should've gotten one of the basic rooms."

Amy laughed.

"Whatever! You find me irresistible and living in a veritable shoebox of a hotel room wouldn't change that."

Sally smiled and put her arms around Amy's waist and gave her a quick kiss.

"I think you're right," Sally said.

"Anyway, what do you want to do now?" she asked Sally.

"Food!" Sally exclaimed.

"Oh, thank god! Me too! You taste good but you aren't very filling!"

"Hmm," Sally began, a mischievous gleam in her eyes, "strangely enough, you *are* filling; like a high-calorie meal."

Amy gasped and playfully swatted at Sally while laughing.

"You bitch! Take that back!"

The weather was pleasant but San Francisco was nonetheless living up to its reputation weather-wise and so Amy and Sally had to dress as if it was autumn even though by the time they would leave this city to return home, it would be May. Both women had on light coats. Sally was also wearing skinny jeans and a sweater; Amy had on a casual dress with tights and boots.

They found a hip seafood place on Embarcadero which Amy had discovered on Yelp during her pre-trip research. Once they had been shown to their table, Amy said, "I still can't believe you agreed to come with me on this trip."

Sally smiled.

"I'm serious," Amy went on. "I really am glad you're here with me."

If it was possible, Sally's smile got bigger.

"Babe, I'm glad I'm here with you too," she said, reaching across the table and taking her hand.

"So…I have a serious question," Amy began but was interrupted when their server arrived to take their drinks order.

"Call me crazy," Amy said to Sally, switching gears, "but I often like beer with my seafood."

"I'm game," Sally replied.

"We have a really large selection of beers," their server offered. "A lot of them are from local microbreweries."

"Perfect," Amy said, quickly scanning the list. "Ooh! I'll have that coffee IPA, please."

"Aaaand it doesn't surprise me that you'd order a beer with coffee in it," Sally snarked. "I'll have the same," Sally then told the server. When she left to get their drinks, Sally said, "I'm afraid I don't know much about beer. I usually stick with wine."

"Snob," Amy said jokingly.

"So, what was your serious question?" Sally asked.

"Oh! Right! Um…Do you think things are moving too fast between us? For the record, I totally don't! I mean, I know we've practically spent every night together since we met and I know that—Oh my god!—we're suddenly taking a vacation together! But, I don't know, I don't *feel* like things are moving way too fast. I feel like this is totally normal for us! Like, it's the pace we're meant to follow! And it's not like we've U-Hauled—which, by the way, if we do…your place! So much bigger! But I'm not suggesting we do that! I'm just saying…Anyway, forget that! I don't think we're moving too fast but I'm kind of worried that you might feel that way and if you do, tell me because I'd rather you be honest so we can make adjustments and whatnot."

Amy finally had to stop because somehow, she said all that in one breath and her lungs were starting to ache.

Meanwhile, Sally was laughing.

"Holy fuck, why do so many lesbians ramble?" Sally asked, staring at Amy with wide eyes.

"Do they?" Amy asked, interested, already wondering if this could be a blog post. Communication idiosyncrasies of gay women.

"Well, I don't know, actually," Sally said. "I probably just *think* so many lesbians ramble because I pretty much only hang out with lesbians. Anyway, you're now added to my collection of rambling lesbians."

Amy blushed.

"I know…I just had diarrhea of the mouth there."

"Well, before you have another bout of diarrhea, let me answer you," Sally said quickly.

Amy folded her hands on the tabletop and forced herself to stay quiet.

"No, I don't think we've been moving too fast," Sally said, smiling. "I like our pace."

"Really?"

"Really. Like you said, it feels like it's the pace we're meant to follow. At least I think that's what you said…You can talk really, really fast, did you know that? Anyway, before *I* become a rambling lesbian…No, I don't think we're moving too fast and so now we can both relax about that."

"Yay!" Amy replied, feeling relieved and feeling that, yes, she could now relax about it.

Chapter 30

The next morning, Sunday, something pulled Sally out of a deep sleep. It wasn't a noise or other disturbance which did it, and as she lay there in that fog-like, in-between state of being somewhat awake, somewhat asleep, she tried to puzzle out what it was. Finally, she determined that it was the absence of something. Or rather, someone.

Amy wasn't next to her.

Groggily, she opened her eyes and then had to wait until her brain recognized the unfamiliar surroundings.

San Francisco. I'm in a hotel suite in San Francisco.

That done, her eyes located the clock on the nightstand. It was only just past six a.m. She groaned, wondering why, when she was on vacation, she couldn't sleep in later than dawn.

Must be the new bed.

It always took her a while to adjust to a new bed. The first few mornings she awoke at Amy's had been super early also. Even those mornings she had had to go to work, she had woken up before her normal alarm.

She wanted to just snuggle her face back into the pillows but she knew the mystery of where Amy was would keep her awake and so she needed to solve that first and so, after wrapping herself in that amazing Hyatt bathrobe—And, seriously, did they *sell* these? Because she wanted one. She made a mental note to ask. —she padded out of the bedroom.

She found Amy in the dining area, sitting at the table, tapping away on her laptop.

Seriously?

"How long have you been up?" Sally asked, standing before the table with her arms crossed.

"I think since four-thirty-ish," Amy said. "I couldn't sleep anymore and so I figured I'd get some work done on my blog and answer some emails from fans."

Sally sighed. This woman really needed to learn to switch off.

On the one hand, Sally was annoyed. If she wanted to wake up to an empty bed only to find Amy working on something in another room, they could have stayed in Carlsbad. But part of what she had been looking forward to on this trip was waking up next to Amy, knowing that they both could just stay in bed all day if they wanted.

On the other hand, she reminded herself that her and Amy had had a fabulous time last night. After dinner, they had walked in the city, just talking and enjoying being in a new town. They had come across a local ice cream shop and gotten ice cream, despite the night being chilly. Eventually, they returned to the hotel, had amazing sex, and fell asleep.

The point was, Sally considered, Amy wasn't really doing anything wrong. So she had gotten up early and decided to be productive. Was that the worst thing she could have done? No. But Sally could think of one or two *better* things Amy could have done.

She approached Amy and started rubbing her shoulders, Amy groaning in appreciation.

"Babe, you need to relax," Sally said, gratified that Amy stopped typing and was now lolling her head back, eyes closed, apparently enjoying the ministrations of Sally's fingers.

"I know," Amy practically sighed.

"We're on vacation."

"I know. Oh, god, that feels good!"

Sally smiled to herself.

"The next time you can't sleep at four-thirty…" She started moving her hands lower, down Amy's chest and then underneath the cami top Amy was wearing. Amy gave a little gasp of anticipation. "…You can wake me up and maybe we can find other things for you to do," Sally continued. Both of her hands now covered Amy's small breasts. She gave them a gentle squeeze and then began softly pinching the two nipples.

"Okay," Amy squeaked.

"Good girl," Sally said and then kissed the top of Amy's head. "Now, come back to bed."

***

After getting out of bed—again—it was still early. Once they left their hotel to go to breakfast, they didn't end up returning until almost ten p.m. In between, they packed the day with a walk across the Golden Gate Bridge—taking selfies galore; a visit to the windmills in Golden Gate Park (more selfies); a visit to the de Young Museum (selfies in front of Picassos); two cable car rides (Sally almost dropped her phone taking selfies); an amazing crab lunch; cocktails at a cool bar near the vicinity of the Painted Ladies (and then selfies in front of the Painted Ladies) and a visit to Little Italy.

They had an incredible Italian feast for dinner and then went shopping on Market Street to walk it off before heading back to their hotel.

"Oh, my god, baby!" Sally groaned when they finally returned to their suite. After dropping her purse and her bags of shopping by the door, she trudged over to the sofa and plopped face-down on it.

"I am *soooooo* fucking exhausted!" Amy complained. She also dropped her belongings at the door, went to the sofa and made Sally scootch over to make room so she could lie down next to her.

"You'll forgive me if I don't make mad, passionate love to you tonight, won't you?" Sally murmured, her face half-buried in the sofa cushions.

"I *insist* you don't make mad, passionate love to me tonight," Amy replied. Nonetheless, she snuggled closer to Sally and Sally felt as if all was right with the world.

"I had a great day with you," Sally said, kissing the tip of Amy's nose.

"Me too. You're fun to explore with."

"I can't wait until the world opens up again," Sally replied. "Wouldn't it be fun to explore a city both of us have never been to?"

She wondered if she was being too presumptuous by stating that. It suggested a future—a future with Amy in a world in which they could move freely around. But Sally wanted to imagine that future and judging from Amy's megawatt smile, so did Amy.

"I would love that!" Amy said and then closed her eyes. "But after we get some sleep."

***

They decided to spend the early part of Monday in the Castro, San Francisco's gay mecca, to take pictures, enjoy thrift shopping and do a lot of people-watching, and also to visit the Rainbow Honor Walk.

"Ooh! Have you been there?" Amy asked after they had lunch at a place which made incredible Cuban sandwiches.

Sally looked at where Amy was pointing. It was a bookstore across the street and, judging by the rainbow-colored paint job on the exterior as well as the three huge rainbow flags flying over its doorway, a bookstore that was very proudly LGBTQ-centric.

Sally smiled. Despite doing virtually all of her reading on her Kindle, she still liked browsing bookshops and would often find a nice coffee table book or two to add to her collection.

The shop was large and well-lit and Sally loved that familiar and comforting smell of new books. The Kindle was an amazing device but it lacked that special something which can only be felt by holding a real book in her hands and lately she'd been thinking more and more that every now and then she ought to put her Kindle aside and read books with actual pages.

As her and Amy were silently browsing the titles on a table marked "Lesbian New Releases," a woman approached Amy.

"I like your bag," the woman said. She was in her thirties, dressed in jeans and a flannel shirt, with a paisley-patterned headscarf holding her brown hair away from her face. Sally's threat detector sensed no danger. She was certain this woman wasn't hitting on Amy but was genuinely complimenting her on the tote bag Amy had brought with her.

The bag was a large, pink canvas tote with the words *Lesbeing—the Podcast* printed on it, along with the show's logo. It was one of the items of merch from the podcast's online shop.

"I love that show," the woman said, pointing at the bag. Sally had to hold in her laughter as she watched Amy's eyes go wide over her face mask. The woman continued. "A lot of other lesbian podcasts just talk about fluffy stuff like sex scenes in books and movies, or who's hotter, Kate Winslet or Cate Blanchett, but *Lesbeing* talks about more cerebral topics pertaining to the lesbian experience. Like that episode where Amy compared lesbian representation in American government compared to other countries…"

Sally was beginning to wonder if Amy was going to survive this encounter. Standing next to her, Sally could almost feel Amy vibrating with excitement and she worried that Amy might literally explode.

"I take it you're a fan?" the woman prodded.

"It's *my* show!" Amy blurted out. "I'm Amy Broadnax!"

Now it was the woman's turn for a display of wide-eyed wonder.

"No way!" she exclaimed, laughing. "That's amazing!" She took a closer look at Amy. "Oh my goodness, I recognize you now! Well, I meant what I said…I'm a huge fan, really! I absolutely love your show."

"Thank you so much!"

Behind her mask, Sally was grinning ear to ear. This was so cool! And it made her feel super proud. She was rather enjoying being the girlfriend of a woman whose podcast talks about "cerebral topics pertaining to lesbianism." And who was incredibly cute to boot.

And then…

"I'm Pam, by the way," the woman said, offering her fist to bump. "This is my store."

"I love this place!" Amy enthused. "I always visit when I come to San Francisco."

"Thank you," Pam said. "Really, though…you're the best!"

"And this is my girlfriend, Sally," Amy said, turning and indicating Sally next to her.

Again, the fist was raised for a bump but before Sally had a chance to do so, Pam gasped and her hands flew to her face.

"Jillian!" she said.

Shit!

"I watched that interview three times!" Pam said. "Oh my goodness, you're actually in my store!"

Sally shrugged.

"Yep, I guess I am," she said. "So much for my mask keeping my identity a secret. Batman makes it look so easy."

"It's your black hair and green eyes," Pam said. "They give you away."

Great…

She looked at Amy, silently pleading with her eyes to help her, but Amy seemed too amused to want to do anything like that.

"Amy," Pam began, "you did such a great job with that interview! Your questions were…perfect."

"Thank you, that means a lot."

"Goodness, did you two start dating after that interview?"

"Yep," Amy answered.

"I could tell there was chemistry between you two! Everybody was commenting on it afterwards."

This was true. Once Sally's "secret identity" was revealed, her social media feeds had been full of remarks by people commenting on how obvious it was that her and Amy had the hots for each other during the interview.

If they only knew…

"Excuse me," another woman said, approaching the trio. "Did I hear you say you're Jillian Ashley?"

Sally nodded, glad that her face mask was hiding her clenched jaw. She really didn't feel like being Jillian today.

"Huh!" The woman uttered. "I'm actually not a big fan of your books."

Sally didn't know how to respond to that.

"No…Actually, I hate them. I stopped reading them after the second one."

Oh, good lord!

"No," the woman went on, "I'm more of a Kitty Karlyle fan myself."

It took all of Sally's self-control to not burst out in righteous indignation. Kitty Karlyle? This…person…preferred Kitty Karlyle to Jillian Ashley? It was like comparing the sonnets of Shakespeare to the instructions on a bottle of shampoo!

But Sally smiled and said, "Well, to each her own, right?"

"But my wife is a huge fan of yours!" the woman stated. "Too bad she's not here with me."

"Yeah, too bad," Sally murmured.

"Hey, can you do me a favor, though?" The woman held out the book in her hand. "Can you autograph this for her? She'll get a kick out of that."

The book was a collection of lesbian sex positions—exactly what someone who was a fan of Kitty Karlyle *would* buy. Taking the proffered pen, Sally didn't bother trying to come up with a cute message and simply scrawled Jillian's name inside the front cover before handing the book back.

The woman then turned to Amy.

"Can you autograph it too?" she asked, holding out the book. "I overheard…You're the one who runs that podcast, right? My wife listens to that too."

"What about you?" Amy inquired.

"Nah. No offense, but your show's too smart. I lose interest after five minutes."

After Amy had autographed the book and the woman went away to pay for it, Sally said, "Well! Her wife sounds like a perfectly delightful person!"

Chapter 31

The next night, Amy and Sally went on a romantic sunset wine-tasting cruise in San Francisco Bay on a catamaran which left from Fisherman's Wharf and sailed past Alcatraz and the Golden Gate Bridge. There were three other couples on board with them and they all got to sample some fabulous wines from the nearby wine-producing counties of California, like Napa.

At one point on the boat, while Sally was embracing her from behind as they stood at the port gunwales looking out over the water at the twinkling lights of San Francisco, Amy wondered if she could possibly feel happier. Perhaps it was the wine but Amy simply felt as if the woman who was now holding her was the woman who was *meant* to hold her and all those other women who had come before Sally had just been…what, exactly? Practice? That idea almost caused her to laugh out loud but she didn't want to ruin this moment. Her and Sally were both quiet, silently enjoying the view as the boat rocked beneath their feet; both of them obviously feeling that not only was there nothing to be said, but also that there didn't *need* to be anything said.

Not practice, exactly, Amy considered. More like…guides on her journey of discovery.

She'd been pretty lucky in the girlfriend department. Her exes had all been bright, beautiful women and each of them had added a measure of joy and excitement to Amy's life—no matter how temporarily each one remained. But though she'd been happy with most of these women, the relationships had always lacked something. The problem was, that *something* was always hard to identify. Now, however, on this boat, she felt she could identify it.

All of her exes had lacked Sallyness.

Again, she almost laughed, this time at her totally made up word, but it was true. Her exes had been lacking in Sallyness—at not being Sally. And Amy now knew that it had taken having all those exes for her to reach this point of discovery of what those women had been missing.

She felt Sally tighten her embrace ever so slightly around her as the boat rocked a smidge harder than normal after riding a swell.

"Mm," Amy purred, loving how being in Sally's arms was like being under the most fabulous comforter in bed.

"I got you," Sally said.

Amy's mind instantly went back to their first date, to just after Sally had made her come on the beach and her legs had been weak. Sally had tightened her embrace around her then too and said, "I got you."

The memory instantly made her center start becoming wet and her clit to swell. She would have given anything for Sally to be able to fuck her right here on the boat but it wasn't a huge boat and there were too many people on it. Oh well. They'd be back at the hotel soon enough.

***

They started making out in the elevator ride up to the eleventh floor. Fortunately, they had the car to themselves and even before the elevator doors had completely shut down in the lobby, Amy had Sally pressed against the wall of the lift and they were kissing each other with passion and lust and moans and roaming hands.

When the elevator reached eleven and the doors opened, they stumbled out, hardly breaking their lip lock as they did.

The first thing Amy noticed was how quiet it was on the floor. After being out in the noise of San Francisco, it was as quiet as an empty church up here on eleven. It was only just past ten o'clock but it was also a weeknight and so maybe that explained it. Whatever the reason, Amy decided she wanted to be naughty.

Still kissing Sally, she pushed her girlfriend backwards until Sally's ass bumped up against a console table the hotel had in the elevator bank (like most hotels do for no apparent reason). Amy quickly unfastened Sally's coat and got it off her in a flash, letting it fall off her shoulders and arms and onto the floor. This revealed Sally's tight-fitting crewneck pullover sweater, the bottom of which Amy started pulling up until Sally's bra was revealed, two very hard nipples looking as if they were going to poke right through the lace fabric of the cups. Amy hurriedly pulled aside one of those cups to free a nipple which was then sucked into her mouth and bitten gently.

"Mm..." Sally moaned softly, gripping Amy's head. "Oh my god..."

Amy sucked harder, interspersing more bites with soft swirls of her tongue around the hard bud.

"Amy..." Sally mewled.

Amy released the breast and looked up at Sally. She lifted Sally's denim maxi skirt until the fabric was bunched up at Sally's waist.

"Get on the table" Amy whispered, and without any objection, Sally hoisted herself up until she was sitting on the sturdy piece of furniture.

Kneeling before it, Amy spread Sally's legs apart and looked at the brown tights her girlfriend had worn to help ward off the San Francisco nighttime chill. Just beyond that fabric was the prize and Amy wanted to reach it. Quickly.

"We're even," Amy murmured and then *rrrrripppp!* She tore open the crotch of Sally's tights viciously, pulled aside Sally's nude panties that were already showing a damp spot and clamped her mouth on Sally's engorged clit.

"Oh shit!" Sally squawked, obviously trying to stay quiet. "Fuck, Amy, yes!"

That intoxicating tang of Sally's pussy tickled Amy's tongue as she slavishly bathed Sally's sex with it, right there in the elevator bank of the eleventh floor. Despite all the sexual sensations her body was flooded with, Amy still kept her ears attuned for danger: the *ding* announcing another elevator arriving on eleven, perhaps; or the sound of a room door opening and closing somewhere else on this level.

Up Amy's tongue went to circle her girlfriend's electrified clit. Down her tongue went to part the pink lips and lap up Sally's juices. Back up to the clit for a few determined swipes. Back down to the warm and wet opening to poke inside and explore.

When she went back up to the clit, Sally grunted and expelled a breath she had evidently been holding.

"Oh fuck, Amy! Don't stop! I'm gonna come!"

The words came out strangled, with effort, but Amy heard them clearly and then...

Sally gasped as her pussy came alive against Amy's mouth, throbbing, convulsing, pushing out that nectar Amy craved and which she now licked up and swallowed.

Just in time too.

They heard a door open and then quickly shut somewhere on the floor, the sounds practically echoing in the stillness, and then voices. A man and a woman.

Amy couldn't resist. She gave Sally's clit one last good suck, which made Sally's legs quiver, before quickly rising from her knees, handing Sally her coat as she did so. Sally hopped off the table and adjusted her clothes in double-fast time. As they started walking away from the elevator bank, the couple they heard turned the corner.

"Hello!" the male half said; his partner giving them a pleasant smile.

"Hi!" Amy and Sally both said cheerily and simultaneously as they walked past them, both of them holding in their laughter.

***

Ten minutes later, Amy's pussy was filled with the largest dildo she owned which was now attached to the harness Sally was wearing.

She was straddling Sally on the bed and her back was arched, her head upturned toward the ceiling, her mouth agape, her pussy clenching, her entire body an epicenter of pleasure. She was *stuffed*! The dildo was all the way in, her nether lips stretched snugly around its girth, its eight-inch length touching parts of her insides that were too often ignored.

She started rocking her hips, crying out unintelligible sounds as she did so, her clit rubbing against the base of the dildo, her pussy lubricating and shaping itself around the stiff yet pliant toy as she rode it.

She felt Sally's hands on her hips. She started rocking faster. She brought her hands up to her hair, entangling her fingers in her brown locks as she rode and rode. The sounds coming from her mouth got louder. She felt her clit pulse quicker. She felt her inner walls flutter faster.

She wanted to open her eyes and stare down at the nude perfection that was Sally but she couldn't. The pleasure rocketing through her made it impossible as she fucked herself atop Sally. It was a mix of pure sexual bliss combined perfectly with the gentle ache of being so fucking *stuffed*!

This was it!

An animal yell escaped her lips as she came, her hips now rocking insanely fast, as if they were out of her control. Her shouts increased in volume as the intensity of the orgasm increased. She felt how much come was leaking out of her, finding its way past the dildo her pussy lips were sealed against. She felt how much come was still inside her; how the dildo was practically sloshing around in it.

When she felt the second orgasm right on the heels of the first, she leaned forward, supporting herself on her arms and started lifting her hips and ass, pounding the dildo into herself ferociously, wanting to be *fucked* by it. Out she would make it slide only to force it back in by lowering her ass. She was in excellent physical condition but still her thighs burned with this workout because she wasn't being gentle and she wasn't moving slowly. The dildo was a piston, jamming in and out of her as if her pussy was part of an engine.

She came again. Hard. Blindingly hard.

"Oh my FUCKING GOD!" she screamed and then repeated it when she came yet again.

Somehow, she found Sally's lips, kissing her sloppily and hungrily while the latest orgasm sent shockwaves through her entire being.

In the throes of the ludicrous amount of pleasure, she miscalculated one of her upward thrusts and with a wet sucking sound the dildo popped out of her. But she didn't lament. Instead, she released Sally's lips and hurriedly slid up Sally's body until she was sitting on her face, her gushing pussy directly over Sally's mouth.

Sally grabbed onto Amy's ass cheeks and, squeezing them, started working her mouth on Amy's electrified center.

"Fuck yes!" Amy called out. Did this woman have more than one tongue? It felt like it was everywhere! Simultaneously poking inside her while also flicking her clit.

"Fuuuuuuck!" she shouted, feeling the liquid practically pouring out of her, Sally humming against her pussy as her tongue worked.

Amy stayed there, making sure Sally's face was slick with her arousal until she came yet again, screaming Sally's name, pounding on the headboard as her pussy spasmed and shot out those delicious, radiating waves of carnal joy.

Four times! Practically one after the other! Bang! Bang! Bang! BANG!

When it was over, she collapsed on the mattress, instantly folding herself into the fetal position as she trembled and quaked, knowing this wasn't going to end quickly, hoping it was going to last forever.

Chapter 32

The next morning, before sunrise, Sally breathed out a puff of air as her center finally stopped contracting, settling itself down after Amy had expertly licked her to orgasm. Clutching the sheets tightly, she whimpered as Amy took her time cleaning her up. Amy had told her how much she loved how wet she got during sex and how much she loved Sally's taste, and therefore after practically every climax that Amy gave her with her mouth, she would remain with her face between Sally's legs, continuing to taste and get her fill.

Eventually, Amy gave Sally's mound a kiss.

"That was a nice way to be woken up," Sally murmured when Amy laid down beside her once more.

"Glad you think so," Amy said, giving her a peck on the lips, Sally getting a brief taste of herself. "Now, I am going to go in the other room and do some work on my blog." Quick as a flash, she got up and out of the bed.

Sally blinked.

"Um…" Sally began, raising herself up on her elbow, not quite knowing what to say, watching as Amy started to put on shorts and a tee.

Amy looked over at her.

"I can't sleep anymore," she said, apologetically, and then she disappeared into the bathroom.

Sally checked the clock. It showed *4:49 a.m.* She fell back onto the mattress, sighing, staring up at the ceiling. From behind the closed bathroom door she heard Amy brushing her teeth.

She was upset. Was it really too much to expect that Amy stay in bed with her, especially after being brought to orgasm? And even though Sally had just come, she was all charged up now, ready for more; ergo, it would have been nice if instead of hurrying to get dressed, anxious to go into the other room and work on her *blog*, Amy had instead remained with Sally and let even more carnal things develop.

But no; rather than *that* happening, Amy had hopped up and skedaddled into the bathroom as if she couldn't wait to get the hell out of the bedroom.

Sally's mouth tightened.

It was as if the great orgasm Amy had just given her had been…

Obligatory.

Yes! That was it. It now had this obligatory feeling to it. Sally recalled their conversation from a couple of mornings ago—the morning Sally had woken up and found Amy working on her blog in the other room; the morning Sally told her that if Amy couldn't sleep at four-whatever in the morning that Amy could wake her up and they'd find other things to do.

So…did Amy eat her out just now only so that Sally wouldn't complain about her wanting to work on her blog?

Seriously?

The door to the bathroom opened and Amy came out, humming. Sally sat up against the headboard.

"Hey," she said, stopping Amy from heading out of the bedroom.

"Hey, what's up?"

"Tell me the truth. Did you *want* to go down on me just then?"

Amy's eyebrows raised.

"What are you talking about?" she asked.

Sally stared at her.

"I just want to know if when you woke up, unable to sleep anymore, if your first thought was, 'God, I want to go down on my sexy girlfriend' or was it, 'I really want to go work on my blog but I'd better go down on Sally first or else she'll come out there and complain'?"

Amy's jaw dropped open.

"Fuck, what do you want from me, Sally?" she exclaimed. "First you tell me that if I wake up super early there are certain better things I can do than just go work on something, but now you're telling me that you're not happy that I did one of those certain things!"

"So you *didn't* want to go down on me!"

"Fuck! I *always* want to go down on you, Sally! Was that my first thought as soon as I woke up? Fine, no, it wasn't. But who cares? I did it, didn't I?"

Sally felt like she'd been slapped.

"You *did* it?" she scoffed. "Way to make it sound like doing the laundry!"

"Aargh!" Amy stomped her foot in frustration. "That's not what I meant and you know it!"

Sally crossed her arms.

"Don't fucking touch me if it's going to be an obligation!" she said.

Amy's eyes flashed.

"Oh my god, are you serious? What is wrong with you?"

"Nothing is wrong with me except the fact that my girlfriend just went down on me only so I'd give her permission to go work on her blog!"

"Permission? I don't need permission from you to work on *anything!*"

"Fine, then go work on *anything*," Sally said, lying back down and turning on her side.

"Fine, I will."

"Fine."

"Fine."

"Close the door so I don't have to hear you typing while I go back to sleep."

"Fine."

"Fine."

Sally pulled the covers over her head just as she heard the bedroom door shut.

Put that in your fucking blog!

***

Despite being upset, Sally did manage to fall back asleep and when she woke again, the clock told her it was now past nine a.m.

Rubbing her eyes, she sat up and as soon as the fog of sleep and uneasy dreams cleared from her mind, was able to recall the argument with Amy.

With the benefit of time and more sleep, she felt calmer and even remorseful for her part in the disagreement. Things shouldn't have escalated to the point they had and with hindsight, she saw how she could have said certain things differently or in a manner that would have prevented the small-scale war.

But wasn't that often the way with arguments? The feelings and thoughts which start them are just spurted out and it's only until later when one can re-evaluate and say to themselves, "Oh, crap; I could have approached that better"?

Still though, Sally was also feeling that she'd had a right to tell Amy what was on her mind back then because she still wasn't happy with what had transpired earlier. It was just that now, Sally could come up with at least a dozen better ways to have done it.

Sighing, she got out of bed and though she wanted to immediately go find Amy, she determined that having a heart-to-heart chat with your girlfriend was best done without morning breath.

Expecting to find Amy typing away on her laptop in the living room of the suite, Sally instead discovered her curled up on the couch, fast asleep. Instantly, Sally felt her heart break. Okay, they had had an argument—and they were sure to have plenty more if they kept seeing each other—but she would *never* want Amy to feel that she couldn't share a bed with her! Or, even worse, to *not* want to share a bed with her!

Right then, she realized that there were far worse things than having a girlfriend who liked to blog at ungodly hours of the morning.

Sally lowered herself to the floor beside the couch, folding her legs under her, and gently stroked Amy's hair. At her touch, Amy stirred, opened her eyes slowly and smiled an adorable sleepy smile.

"Good morning," Sally whispered.
"Good morning," Amy replied and then yawned.
"Sorry to wake you."
"I'm glad you did," Amy said.
"And I'm sorry for everything else too."
"Me too, baby."

Amy scootched over to make room for Sally on the couch and Sally happily laid down next to her, tucking some stray locks of Amy's brown hair behind her ear.

"I shouldn't have attacked you like I did," Sally said, and then grinned impishly. "I promise I won't complain the next time you wake me up by going down on me."

Amy giggled. But then she sucked her lips between her teeth and shyly met Sally's eyes.

"I have a confession to make," she began. "I kind of did go down on you as a sort of insurance policy. I *wanted* to!" she hurriedly added. "And I totally loved it. But I was also thinking it would—"

"—get me off your back?" Sally finished for her.

"Yeah. Sorry."

"It's okay."

"It's just that I have trouble shutting my mind off sometimes."

"I've noticed," Sally said.

"And when that happens, I just can't stay in bed doing nothing."

Sally nodded. She could see Amy's point. It wasn't ideal, admittedly. Sally always was the type who enjoyed waking up next to girlfriends, feeling the weight of another body next to her on the mattress, feeling the heat radiating off them onto her…Even if the woman was zonked out cold and snoring like a chainsaw, oblivious to the world around her, it was still companionship.

But wasn't it still companionship if when she woke up, she found her girlfriend in another room, ready to say "good morning" to her and blow her a kiss? What's more, Sally didn't want Amy to feel constrained around her. Amy was bright, ambitious, creative and motivated, all of which Sally found super attractive. And, Amy had this really cool activist streak in her, which Sally found hot as fuck for some reason.

"It's all good," Sally said, running her thumb along Amy's bottom lip.

"But I totally see your point too," Amy said right away. "I'm, like, this weirdo girlfriend who hops out of bed at strange hours, like I can't stand being next to you anymore."

Sally laughed.

"So, that's not how I see it," she stated. "At least not anymore."

"Wait, you saw it that way?" Amy asked, panic in her eyes.

"Well, maybe not quite that way," Sally amended. "But I was kind of bothered by the fact that you can't seem to switch off sometimes, even while on vacation."

Amy nodded.

"I know," she said ruefully.

"But you know what? You're just being you and I could get used to it."

"Really?"

"Really."

"Because it's not like I *don't* want to stay in bed with you! It's just that you're sleeping and I'm wide awake and…" Amy sighed deeply. "There's just so much I want to *do!*"

"Is this one of things you'd like to do?" Sally asked, sliding her hand into Amy's shorts, over her shaved mound, until her fingers found those silky lips.

Amy gasped and her eyes rolled back in her head.

Sally bit her lip.

"Erotic dreams?" she asked when her fingers discovered just how incredibly wet Amy was.

Slack-jawed, Amy nodded and started rocking her pelvis against Sally's hand.

"I was horny when I came out here after eating you out—Oh, fuck!"

Sally had just slipped two fingers inside and now Amy's swollen clit was also being swiped gently with her thumb.

"Oh, fuck, Sally…"

Amy buried her face against Sally's chest, whimpering until the whimpers became rapid puffs of breath and the rapid puffs of breath became cute little mewling sounds which kept increasing in pitch until…

"I'm coming!" Amy told Sally's breasts.

And then Amy was shuddering next to her and Sally was feeling her fingers inundated with more arousal and squeezed by Amy's inner walls.

"Back to bed?" Sally whispered when Amy came down from the high.

"Yes, please."

Chapter 33

Saturday morning arrived and it was time to go back home.

"Ready, baby?" Amy asked, standing by the door to their suite with her luggage. "Lyft will be here in ten."

"I'm coming!" was Sally's reply, called out from the bedroom.

Amy smirked to herself.

"But I haven't even touched you!" she called back.

Sally emerged from the direction of the bedroom.

"Very funny," she said. "Anyway, that's everything."

"Yay! One last kiss before we depart our magnificent palace?"

"Most definitely."

Amy looped her arms around the taller Sally's neck and brought their lips together, tasting Sally's lip gloss as she slid her tongue into her girlfriend's mouth and the kiss deepened.

Breaking for air after a few moments, Amy turned to the room and said, "Bye, room! Thanks for everything!"

As the Lyft driver maneuvered through the city on the way to the airport, Amy watched the passing urban scenery, ruminating on things while Sally took a phone call from her mother.

They had survived their first trip together, which Amy took to be a good sign. And the trip had been fabulous! Amy was so relieved that in Sally, she had found a girlfriend who loved exploring and wandering around a city like San Francisco as much as she did. Every day they had been out, visiting, seeing and doing all manner of things in all parts of the city. Even Thursday, when it rained all day, they had bought umbrellas in the hotel's gift shop and spent the day visiting another art museum and then riding the BART to different parts of town to enjoy shopping or eating seafood or just walking in the rain.

And the sex…

In the back seat of the Honda Passport they were riding in, Amy had to cross her legs at the memory of all the sex they'd had. Their carnal fun had certainly been kicked up a notch during this trip. Eating Sally out in the elevator bank on the eleventh floor had been but one example of their daring public or quasi-public sexual exploits. Well past midnight one night, Sally had pulled a completely nude Amy out onto their suite's balcony and fucked her mercilessly with the strap-on, Amy covering her mouth with her hand so as not to scream out in ecstasy with each thrust. And on that rainy Thursday, because the city had been remarkably devoid of people who were out and about, they had ended up in Golden Gate Park fingering each other under an enormous tree.

The only black mark during their trip had been that slight blip of an argument on Wednesday morning. Amy had to admit to herself that it had not only scared her at the time but it was still scaring her now.

Annabeth.

Three years ago, Amy had been in a serious relationship with a woman from Oceanside named Annabeth. They had even lived together in Oceanside in a cute little apartment within walking distance of the pier. But then Annabeth had started getting annoyed with how much work Amy would bring home from the office and then when that was done, how much work Amy would put in writing her then nascent *Lesbeing* blog.

They started fighting a lot, with Annabeth accusing Amy of only being half-invested in their relationship; asking her why they had even bothered moving in together.

Naturally, Amy had defended herself. In those days, she had been relatively new at the North County Women's Rights Group and so had felt a need to work extra in order to prove herself. And her new blog was her way of decompressing.

Both of those explanations were true. But even back then, Amy had known that they were true…to a point. Yes, she had been new at her job but she hadn't been expected to work beyond office hours as much as she did. And, yes, the blog was a great decompression activity but spending more time with Annabeth doing almost anything else would have also been a great way to decompress too.

No, the real truth was, that Amy *liked* working as much as she did—it was almost like a drug for her—and in the end, her relationship with Annabeth had become a casualty of that.

Was history going to repeat itself with Sally, she wondered? Okay, Sally had ended up being cool about the whole getting-up-in-the-middle-of-the-night-to-work-on-the-blog thing. But Amy was worried. She was worried because over the past couple of days, as their vacation was getting closer and closer to ending, she had recognized the familiar stirrings in herself, the familiar *need* to get stuff done. She had even spent quite a bit of brainpower on considering what she was going to get working on as soon as Monday came around and she returned to the office.

Shit…

"Is everything okay?" Amy asked when she heard Sally tell her mother goodbye.

"Yeah, fine. She was just calling to invite me out to dinner tonight but I told her that we're flying back from San Francisco and that I most likely will just want to relax the rest of the day. Then I got an earful because I hadn't told her I was even going to San Francisco."

Amy was surprised.

"You didn't tell your mother?"

Sally rolled her eyes.

"Trust me, if I had, all she would have done was tell me which doctor friends of hers have lesbian daughters living in the Bay Area and how I should give one of them a call."

Amy smirked.

"Oh my goodness. Your mother and I definitely need to have a talk. Because you are *soooooo* taken!"

***

While waiting in the line to show their IDs and boarding passes to the TSA agent, Sally leaned over and whispered to Amy, "Oh, by the way, you had left your blue vibe on the nightstand back at the hotel and so I just popped it into my carry-on bag." And here, Sally patted the handle of the Coach roll-away suitcase by her side. "When we get home, remind me to give it back to you."

Amy swallowed, her mouth suddenly dry.

"Wait…what?" she asked.

Sally took a moment to look around to make sure no one else was listening and repeated what she had just told Amy.

Amy blinked.

"It's in *there?*" she asked, using her eyes to indicate the bag.

"Uh-huh."

"Next!" the TSA agent called out in a Southern drawl.

Sally stepped forward, presented her I'm-not-a-terrorist documents and was waved forward, Amy keeping her eyes on the Coach bag as Sally wheeled it towards the X-ray line.

"Next!" the same TSA agent repeated.

Still keeping her eyes on Sally's bag, Amy stepped forward and wordlessly handed over her driver's license.

"Ma'am?" the TSA agent prodded. When Amy didn't respond, he repeated the one word, more forcefully this time. "*Ma'am!*"

Amy looked at him.

"Ma'am, I need you to look at me, please, and lower your mask," Holding up Amy's license, the man compared the photo on it to Amy's actual face. He then instructed her to hold her phone face-down on the scanner so her boarding pass could be read and then waved her on.

Catching up to Sally on the X-ray line, she whispered, "Don't you remember what happened in *The L Word*?"

Above her face mask, Sally cocked an eyebrow in puzzlement.

"Um…the old *L Word* or the new *L Word*?" she asked.

"The old one."

"Okaaaay…can you be more specific?" Sally asked.

"Season two, episode ten," Amy stated.

"Wow, that *is* specific," Sally said. Together, they took a few steps forward as the line advanced. "Unfortunately, I'm apparently not as up on *L Word* lore as you are."

Amy sighed.

"Dana and Alice packed…" Amy looked around, but no one else on line was paying them the slightest attention "…sex toys in their carry-on luggage and then the TSA agent at the X-ray machine was all like, 'What the hell are these?' Remember? And then the TSA opened their bag and was displaying all their toys to everyone."

Sally scoffed.

"Sweetie, that was a TV show! Besides, I seem to remember that Dana and Alice had things in that bag which could actually be used to commandeer an airplane. Like, nipple clamps."

"How do you take over an airplane with nipple clamps?" Amy asked, certain that Sally wasn't taking this seriously.

"I don't know, Amy! How do you take over an airplane with a vibrator?"

"I don't know!" Amy whisper-hissed. "Maybe it could be used as a club. Anyway, in an X-ray machine it probably looks like a pipe bomb or something."

They moved forward a few more steps again.

"Babe," Sally began, "I hate to throw your genetic privilege in your face but we're two cute white girls from Carlsbad. The vibrator-slash-pipe bomb is in a Coach bag that cost more than some people's car payment and you're wearing Balenciaga jeans. The way our fucked-up country's system works, we could actually *have* a pipe bomb in the bag and the TSA would just wave us on through."

They had reached the checkpoint and had to remove their shoes and place those and their other items in those hideous gray plastic bins. Amy watched Sally lift her Coach bag onto the conveyor for the trip through the X-ray machine.

"I just don't want everyone in this airport knowing I happen to like vibrators with attached clit stimulators."

"So, we'll tell them it's mine," Sally whispered back. "Besides, *everybody* ought to know that women like vibes with clit stims. The world would be a better place."

First Sally went through the body scanner machine and then Amy followed. When it was determined she didn't have explosives hidden in her bra and had been cleared to proceed through, the Coach bag was already in the X-ray machine. Amy watched the face of the TSA agent on X-ray duty. It was a middle-aged woman with long blonde hair tied back in a ponytail and at first she seemed bored at what she was looking at on her screen. But then suddenly, her brows knitted and her eyes squinted as she peered more closely at the monitor. She pressed a button and the conveyor belt moved backward, then forward, then backward again. Just like in season two, episode ten! Finally, she glanced over at Amy.

Amy could think of nothing better to do than shrug and smile.

With an amused look on her face, the TSA agent pressed the button to start the conveyor moving forward again.

"I think I have the same one," she said, her eyes scanning the next object in the machine.

***

"That is so totally a podcast episode!" Amy said, slipping her ballet flats back on and gathering up the items she had sent through the X-ray machine. She and Sally started walking towards the gate. "Lesbian travel tips and what kind of toys are allowed in carry-on luggage. We already know—thanks to the *L Word*—that nipple clamps aren't allowed; but, like, how *big* a vibrator can you bring on board? What about one with a rechargeable battery? What about dildos or anal beads?"

Sally laughed.

"That is a really good idea, babe," she said.

"Thank you. Ooh! Do you think I can get a representative from the TSA to be a guest?"

"I don't see why not," Sally said after a moment. "I would think the TSA would welcome any chance they get to inform the public about their policies, especially in a gay-friendly forum."

"Totally doing it," Amy decided, feeling excited.

They were on the plane in forty minutes, comfortably ensconced in their first class seats, waiting for takeoff.

"Soooooo," Amy began after the flight attendant finished his safety demonstration. "What happens when we get home? Do you want to hang out later?"

"Well, the first thing I have to do," Sally answered, as the engines revved and the plane started backing away from the gate, "is go pick up Lena from Lisa's. After that, I'll just be relaxing. I love to travel but I hate the *traveling* part, you know? So, once I get home I usually just like to chill and veg out. Why don't you come over later and we'll order in and watch Netflix?"

"Love to! Provided you're not sick of me yet?"

Sally pulled her mask down just quick enough to blow her a kiss.

"Sick of you?" she asked. "If anything, I want more of you."

Amy gasped and felt her heart flutter. The truth was, she felt exactly the same way. Spending a week in San Francisco with Sally had done nothing to diminish her desire for wanting to *keep* spending time with Sally. It was really crazy. Even things with Annabeth hadn't started like this. In the beginning of that relationship, her and Annabeth would often go a few days without seeing each other or spending nights together. But with Sally…Amy was already at the point of feeling that there was no such thing as too much time together with her.

Chapter 34

Sally was reading on her Kindle, Amy sitting next to her typing on her laptop. She had no idea how long they'd been in the air but it felt like it could only have been about forty-five minutes or so, which meant there was still close to an hour before they landed in San Diego.

Despite trying to concentrate on her book, thoughts of this recent change in her life kept creeping in, making her smile slightly to herself.

She was on a plane after spending a week away with her girlfriend! And it had been so long since she'd felt this happy with another woman. Who was the last one, she wondered? Not just *girlfriend*, per se, but girlfriend she'd felt happy and content with. It had to have been Emily, she figured. That had been her last "serious" relationship, a little more than two years ago. Unfortunately, that feeling of happiness and contentment with Emily didn't last.

Sally could never understand exactly what went wrong with her and Emily. There wasn't that *one* thing which drove them apart like cheating or mistreatment of some form. It was just…one day they were happy and nuts for each other and then suddenly they weren't. It was as if both of them, simultaneously, had lost all motivation to keep their romance alive and fresh and exciting. Towards the end, she and Emily were both just going through the motions until finally, they tearfully said goodbye to one another.

Other girlfriends Sally had had since Emily had been fun, sure; delightful in their unique ways; but those relationships hadn't brought her that early-Emily-like happiness. Until now. With Amy.

Were her and Amy, though, doomed for the same ending Sally and Emily had suffered? Post-Emily, Sally had discovered that the problem with not having one definitive *thing* to point to as the cause of the end of a relationship is that at night, lying in bed along, wide awake, a woman's mind starts to wonder, "Was it my fault? Was it something about me?"

But Sally didn't feel that her Amy were going to end up like her and Emily. Don't ask her why. All she knew was that this felt different; it felt like what the movies and the lesfic books and even some TV shows wanted one to believe it should feel like when you finally discover your soulmate. With Emily, Sally had been happy and content. With Amy, Sally was happy, content and *whole*.

The plane suddenly rocked a bit, pulling Sally from her reverie.

Turbulence.

Sally went back to reading her book.

Then the plane rocked again. Harder.

A nervous energy now filled the first-class cabin. Other passengers were looking up from their books or tablet screens. Next to her, Amy stopped typing. The fasten-seat-belt indicator chimed and lit up. The first-class flight attendant, who had been about to deliver a drink to a passenger quickly turned around and went back to the galley.

For a few moments, nothing else happened. The aircraft resumed its smooth journey through the air. Sally shared a quick *no big deal* smile with Amy and went back to reading.

And then…

Wham!

It was as if the hand of a god had swatted the plane from above. With gut-lurching suddenness, the plane shuddered and then plummeted. Screams filled the cabin, mixing with the sounds of banging that seemed to be coming from the underbelly of the craft, while the whine of the engines kicked up many decibels, as if the engines were being pushed to their max.

Sally dropped her Kindle and gripped the armrests of her seat. She could feel her body actually trying to lift off the seat as the rapid descent continued, her seatbelt the only thing keeping her in place.

"Sally!" Amy called out, her voice strained, like a character in a horror movie upon seeing the featured monster.

It got worse.

Suddenly the plane banked sharply. The screams—Sally's included—rose in volume. The lights in the cabin went out. The overhead bins burst open and Sally felt something punch her in the head but with her eyes squeezed shut she had no idea what it was. A suitcase? A duffel bag?

"OhfuckOhfuckOhfuckOhfuckOhfuck!" she chanted, pausing only to scream again when the plane lurched violently again.

She knew this wasn't turbulence. Something was mechanically or structurally wrong with their aircraft!

Fuck!

Somehow, the plane was corrected out of the bank but now it was as if they were driving on a cobblestone road because the airplane was shaking and trembling so vigorously that Sally was certain the welds and rivets could not possibly hold and that any second now the plane would shake itself apart. Somewhere in the row behind her, she heard someone throw up. She heard children and adults crying. She heard multiple people praying.

Sally opened her eyes.

I'm going to die.

It was a certainty. She knew it.

And it became even more of a certainty when, once more, the plane dropped in freefall.

More screaming. More gut-wrenching mid-air maneuvers.

This is it!

Amy gripped her hand. Sally looked at her. Their eyes locked together. Amy's were as wide as they could possibly be and tears were streaming from them. Sally also knew she was crying.

It was so noisy in the cabin that Sally knew speaking was pointless. The whining roar of the engines combined with the various bangs and knocks combined with the screams, cries and prayers of their fellow passengers was deafening. And so Sally tried to convey with her eyes what she wanted to say.

Thank you for coming into my life.

Thank you letting me stay in yours when I told you I wasn't Jillian Ashley.

Thank you for helping me feel a special kind of joy again.

Thank you for making me feel more alive than I ever have.

We belonged together!

You were meant for me and I was meant for you.

Maybe we'll have eternity together?

And Sally was certain that Amy was receiving her messages! That perhaps, somehow, these moments of heightened and pure fear had managed to activate some dormant telepathic ability in her girlfriend's brain, giving her the ability to "hear" Sally despite no words coming from Sally's mouth.

And as Sally sat there, tears streaming down her cheeks, staring into Amy's eyes, miraculously she felt her own brain activate *its* telepathy function and—rather peacefully—Sally began listening to the messages Amy was sending her…

Chapter 35

Thank you for being with me here at the end.
You have no idea how magical I think our time together has been!
You gave me so much happiness.
You made my heart soar each time I looked at you!
I start missing you after five minutes apart.
I think you were the One.
Maybe that means we'll see each other on the other side.

Amy was straining her mind to transmit these messages to the woman sitting next to her, wanting to believe that somehow the words were really traveling through the few inches of empty space between her and Sally.

Thrillingly, she started believing that! There was understanding in Sally's eyes! And Amy noticed this just as she suddenly gained the superpower of being able to translate each tiny movement, each miniscule flicker of Sally's eyes, and turn them into words she understood!

She opened her mouth to speak, knowing she'd have to yell over the incredible noise in the cabin, but then the plane did yet another one of those rollercoaster-type dips in the sky and Amy's eyes squeezed shut and she yelped out.

Oh, fuck! It's about to happen!

What would she feel at the end? Would there be pain? Would she suffer? Or would she simply be snuffed out?

How much longer did they have? Minutes? Seconds?

Were they about to slam into a mountain or crash into the sea? Were they over a city or above farmland?

How long would it take to inform her family of her death? Her parents were also on a trip—to Wichita to visit Amy's grandmother. She had told them that she was going to San Francisco but hadn't provided much in the way of details concerning her flight information. For all they knew, she was either already back home in Carlsbad or still in Frisco. How long before they learned their only daughter was dead?

Somehow, she became aware of the fact that the plane was no longer dropping. It was flying. It still felt like being in a car on a bumpy road but at least her stomach was no longer in her throat.

She heard a *bing-bong* tone and then a voice came over the PA system.

"This is the captain. We have been cleared for an emergency landing at John Wayne International Airport. Flight attendants, emergency protocols, please. Eight minutes."

They were going to land!

Emergency land.

In eight minutes!

Eight minutes in a broken plane still high up in the sky!

Suddenly, the flight attendant in first-class was on his feet, holding onto the bulkhead to steady himself against the shaking aircraft. He looked just as pale and scared as Amy felt but she had to hand it to him, he also looked determined to do his job.

"Ladies and gentlemen," he shouted. "Listen very carefully! Make sure your seatbelts are tight across your hips and that the belt is not twisted. After you've done that, you will tuck your chin into your chest, you will lean forward and place your head against the seat in front of you and then place your hands on top of your head!"

He demonstrated by placing his hands on top of his head but almost lost his balance and fell.

"Oh my god!" Amy muttered, checking her seatbelt.

"We're going to be fine," Sally said, but Amy heard the utter fear in her voice. However, what else was Sally going to say?

In moments, Amy and Sally were ready, both of them bent forward with their heads pressed against the seats in front of them, hands in the proper position.

"I want to hold you," Amy told Sally.

"I know, baby. I want that too. So much!"

Amy made a decision.

"Fuck this!" she stated. Sitting up, she pulled down her face mask, pulled Sally out of her crash position, yanked Sally's mask down and then mashed her lips against Sally's in a bruising kiss of desperation. Their tongues met instantly and dueled as their lips slid against each other hungrily. If this was going to be their last kiss, then Amy was going to get everything out of it that she could and she knew Sally felt the same way.

When they broke, they looked at each other.

"We're going to be okay," Sally said.

"We're going to be okay," Amy repeated and then they both bent forward again and waited.

Chapter 36

"Ma'am?"

Sally blinked. Was someone talking to her? She blinked again and slowly turned her head toward the direction she thought the voice had come from.

There was a man in a uniform standing off to her side.

What kind of uniform is that?

It took her a moment to realize it was a paramedic's uniform. It took her another moment to recognize him as the paramedic who had briefly examined her after they had landed, making sure she wasn't injured.

This rang a bell in her memory.

She *was* injured. Something had hit her head during the Incident, as she now called it. Whatever it was had apparently left a slight bruise high on her right cheek. This paramedic had put something on it. Something cold. Said it was nothing to worry about; it would disappear in a day or two. Also said it might be sore for a while. Don't put pressure on it. Other than that she was fine.

So what does he want now?

She blinked again. He was holding out a paper cup. Steam was coming from the top of it.

"Coffee?" she heard him ask. "You look like you could use it."

She nodded and reached for the cup but her hand was shaking too much to take it from him.

"Here," the paramedic said. He gently lowered her hand and then placed the cup on the seat next to her. "Drink it when you're ready. I need to go help some other folks. Take care."

She nodded. Very carefully, feeling like a toddler who was just learning how to use her limbs, she reached for the coffee cup with both hands and carefully grasped it. Her hands still trembled but using both of them made it manageable.

The coffee was terrible. And it was unsweetened. She liked sweetened coffee. But how was the paramedic to know that? Anyway, it was hot and it was helping her focus again and she remembered...

The plane had landed but it had been a bumpy ride all the way to the ground. When the wheels touched down on the tarmac, people on board had screamed because they were so jittery. Sally had been one of the screamers. When you're on an obviously broken aircraft, and your body is tucked up into a ball and you can't see the ground approaching out the window, you can't help but scream when suddenly the plane makes contact with something hard and unyielding. In the split second after touchdown, her hyper-frightened mind was certain that the plane was crashing, that that was the end and so of course she screamed.

Somehow they had all gotten off the plane using that big inflatable slide. Whenever she had seen that used in movies, Sally had always thought it looked like fun but now she couldn't remember if she'd had fun using it today.

On the ground were fire trucks and ambulances. There was smoke coming from somewhere. Thick and black.

Those among the passengers who could walk were hurriedly guided to a shuttle bus; those who couldn't were put on stretchers. Her and Amy—

Amy!

Where was Amy?

"Amy!" she called out, standing and looking frantically around, not even really sure where she was. It looked like a hangar. There were scores of people around—some of them scurrying about, some of them lying on cots, some of them sitting in folding chairs, looking as dazed as Sally felt, staring off into space. Paramedics were administering oxygen and checking blood pressures; people with clipboards were sitting with passengers, asking them questions or handing them forms to be filled out. Others were pacing, talking on their phones, crying. There was a table with food and drinks. Most of the passengers, herself included, had blankets draped around their shoulders.

It was all coming back to her in fits and starts—her mind finally accepting that she was safe and allowing her memory to function again.

Her and Amy had already spoken to the airline representatives—but Sally refused to sign anything and she prevented Amy from signing anything as well. Her father was a lawyer and had taught her enough to know that when something like this happens, the last thing you do is sign any piece of paper. They had also already been seen by the paramedics and both were deemed injury-free—well, except for Sally's bruised cheek.

And then…

Sally remembered telling Amy that she needed to call her mother, but the call had gone to her hospital's answering service; her mother was in the operating room performing surgery. Sally was asked if she wanted a message to be brought to Dr. Lassiter in the O.R. No, Sally had told the operator and hung up. She was alive and for all she knew, her mother was the only thing keeping some poor guy from starring in his own funeral soon. Sally figured she could tell her mother about the Incident later. So, she had called the next person who immediately came to mind: Max.

"Fuck! I'll be right there!" he had stated. "Out the door right now!"

And then after that phone call—it was all coming back to her now—she had just slumped in her seat and stared off into space, undisturbed until that thoughtful paramedic brought her coffee.

But Amy…

She spotted Amy sitting on the ground against one of the hangar walls, sobbing, her hands covering her face, her cell phone on the floor beside her. That's right, Sally remembered…Amy had wandered off to call her mother as well.

Rushing over to her, Sally sat on the floor and pulled Amy into her arms, rocking her gently and trying to shush her.

"It's over, baby; it's over," she cooed.

Eventually, Amy calmed down.

"My mother wants to fly here to be with me," Amy said with a laugh, wiping her tear-streaked face. "I told her, 'Are you fucking kidding me? Don't get on a fucking plane! Like, ever!'"

Sally laughed.

"That's not actually going to stop her, is it?" she asked.

"I told her there's no need," Amy answered. "I'm fine. Still crying with relief, but fine."

"I think I'll be shaking all night," Sally murmured, already worried about what kind of nightmares she was in for later when (if) she fell asleep.

"I'll be there with you," Amy said, holding her tighter, making Sally feel warmth flow through her entire body.

"Yes, please don't me leave me alone tonight," she said.

"I would never," Amy assured her. "I just want to stay clinging to you for a week."

"I'd love that."

"I can't wait to get home. Can we just go straight to your place? No picking up your cat or any other stops?"

"Absolutely."

"And stay in bed?"

"Absolutely," Sally repeated.

"Wait…how *are* we getting home?" Amy asked.

"Max is picking us up," Sally told her.

"Yay!"

Amy clung tighter to her and Sally smiled to herself. She was already feeling better and she knew it was because she had Amy next to her and in her arms. A thought occurred to her: After the harrowing experience on the airplane, she felt as if she had been given a second chance at life. She still didn't know what had gone wrong with the plane and she supposed one day she'd find that out, but what she did know—as certainly as she knew her name—was that everyone on that plane had been *very* lucky and owed their lives to the vagaries of Fate and the skills of the pilots. If the pilots had made different decisions during the mid-air crisis or flipped that switch instead of this one; if a bolt on the airframe had given way instead of holding fast; if a single wire had come loose or if the plane had hit a descending pocket of cold air while they were in distress then they would have crashed and died.

Instead, they had lived. They had all been given a second chance.

And Sally knew that whatever else she did with this second chance, the most important thing she could do was make sure Amy was part of her life.

Chapter 37

By the time Max had dropped them off at Sally's condo, Amy was over the panic caused by the Event, as she referred to it. She was also past breaking into crying jags caused by it and the relief of being alive. In fact, walking into Sally's place, Amy felt like she had just chugged an Amy's Jet Fuel from La Vida Mocha, even though the only coffee she'd had recently was that awful dreck the airline representatives had served her and the other survivors back at the airport.

She felt wired! Buzzy! Energetic! Alive!

After Sally closed the front door, Amy couldn't wait any longer and pounced like a cat that had been lurking, waiting for its prey. Grabbing Sally's head between her two hands, Amy claimed her mouth in a passionate kiss, groaning at the contact, groaning louder when their tongues met.

"Hi!" Sally breathed when Amy released her.

"Hi!" Amy replied and then silenced her girlfriend with another kiss. Talking was for losers, anyway. This was a time for action.

But eventually, Sally pulled away, breathless.

"I like where this is going," she gasped, "but I could really use a shower first."

Wordlessly, Amy took Sally by the hand and led her toward the bedroom, Sally giggling as she was pulled along.

Inside the master bathroom, Amy wasted no time. Sally's cardigan sweater was pulled over her head and tossed away. The same for the vintage Pet Shop Boys T-shirt Sally had on underneath. After reaching behind her and unclasping Sally's black bra and pulling it off her shoulders, Amy started disrobing herself, while Sally shucked off her jeans.

Once they were both nude, Amy pressed herself against Sally. They were both sticky and little grimy. Amy knew that was because of the sweat caused by the terror of the flight. Running her hands up Sally's back, Amy nuzzled her face into the crook of her girlfriend's neck and inhaled deeply. A musky, sweaty aroma tinged with perfume filled her nostrils and revved Amy up even more. She brought her hands down and squeezed Sally's ass hard, possessively.

Mine!

They entered the shower. Sally had a magnificent shower! It was every woman's dream: Dark grey stone walls with a rainfall shower head and wall jets, and soon they were both enveloped by spraying water, both from above and from the sides. And now Amy's hands were all over Sally, sliding over the wet flesh, tangling in her wet hair. They kissed for who knows how long, just standing there under the sprays until Amy had enough of the kindergarten stuff. Life was too short for the kindergarten stuff. Carefully, she pressed Sally against one of the shower walls and then dropped to her knees.

Sally protested. She wanted to clean down there first. But Amy cut the discussion short by instantly locking her lips onto Sally's clit.

"Oh my fucking god!" Sally called out as she grabbed Amy's head and tilted her pelvis tighter against Amy's mouth, her protests apparently forgotten.

Amy adjusted herself so her tongue could go everywhere between Sally's legs, lapping it all. Yes, Sally's sex was more pungent than usual but it was only fueling Amy's desire. It was the pungency of *her woman* and she wanted to inhale and taste it all. Her tongue detected the tang of arousal leaking out between the pink lips and Amy darted in further, earning grunts and moans from above. After coating her tongue properly, Amy returned to the engorged clit. Sally started rocking her pelvis and instantly they had a rhythm going—a rhythm of rocking and sucking, rocking and sucking.

"Fuck, Amy!" Sally growled. "Fuck!"

They continued. Rocking and sucking. Rocking and sucking. And then…

"I'm gonna come!...Unnnggh!"

Inside her mouth, Amy felt Sally's clit jump, then she felt Sally's juices coat her chin, only to be washed away too quickly by the shower spray; then she felt Sally's fingers clutch harder at her hair as the orgasm took possession of the woman she was eating out.

When those first shudders of climax passed, Amy rose up and turned the trembling Sally around, pressing her arm against Sally's shoulder. The message was clear: *Don't fucking move!*

She ran her hand down the cleft of Sally's glistening, wet ass, found her pussy and easily slid three fingers inside.

"Oh fuck yes!" Sally grunted and pushed her ass back, driving the fingers in deeper. Amy started biting Sally's shoulders as she fucked her fingers in and out of the tight pussy. Her own center was a faucet by now; she could feel the sticky liquid dripping from her inner passage, spend the briefest of moments on her thighs and then get sprayed away by the shower.

Sally came undone a second time, a lusty yell emanating from deep inside her chest. Amy held her fingers still inside the woman as Sally's pussy spasmed around them. When it was over, Sally quick as flash lifted her pussy off Amy's hand and spun around. Amy almost came just seeing the lust in her girlfriend's eyes.

"Your turn," Sally ordered.

Amy gave a yelp of surprise when suddenly she found herself pressed against the wall, Sally behind her, the aggressor now.

"And what if I resist?" Amy teasingly asked.

Her answer came in the form of a sharp spank, the sting of it heightened because the flesh of her ass was so wet. From Sally's hand, that sting radiated right to her core and her clit pulsed three times, bringing her right to the verge.

"Still resisting…" she said through clenched teeth, earning her another spank, the pain making her gasp in pleasure, making her feel alive. A third spank quickly followed and her eyes rolled back in her head.

"For being sassy," Sally whispered in her ear before biting the lobe.

"Fuck me!" Amy begged. She couldn't wait any longer. "Please!"

And then…bliss! Fingers slid inside, stretching her, curling and flexing as they were worked in and out.

"Oh my god, baby!" Amy screeched. She brought her own hand to her clit. It was like touching a live wire but she rubbed it furiously and made incoherent sounds when she exploded with her first orgasm, feeling as if everything below her waist was going to pour right out of her. She screamed against the wet shower wall as Sally continued pistoning the fingers in and out and she continued rubbing her electric button, bringing the second climax forth.

It shattered her.

A flash of pink light burst behind her eyelids and she felt herself rise up on her toes precariously.

"BAY-*BEEEEEEEEEEEEE*!" she shouted at her maximum volume. The intense pleasure shot through every vein in her form, so strongly that even while in the throes of the orgasm, it frightened her a little because she was certain something inside her was going to disintegrate or some vital organ would burst. And it just kept going. Wave after wave after wave…pulsing through her, pure light and orgasmic joy taking possession of her, making her feel like she was going to melt and flow down the shower drain.

As it was, her legs gave out. Despite Sally pressing her against the wall, Amy could no longer remain upright and as her screams turned to moans, she started sliding down the wall, Sally following, never taking her fingers out of her pussy.

And there they lay for several minutes, on the shower's floor, the rain-like water falling on their nude forms, both of them breathing hard, recovering, seemingly content to remain there all night.

***

"I think that's a record for us," Amy gasped quite some time later. They'd been at it for hours now and she had just regained the ability to speak after coming yet again thanks to Sally's expert tongue. When they had gotten home, it had been light; now it was dark; the deep dark of deep night.

"Almost dying will do that to you," Sally said, flopping down on the mattress next to Amy.

Amy nodded. Sally wasn't wrong. Ever since they had gotten back to Sally's condo from the airport, Amy had had this insatiable desire for her girlfriend. Of course, ever since they had gotten together, Amy had always had been lustful for Sally—the woman was a sexy goddess in her eyes. But this went far beyond the norm. She wanted Sally now on a level that was akin to what a woman who hasn't eaten in two or three days feels when suddenly presented with a buffet of food. And tonight, Amy had metaphorically devoured Sally. There wasn't a part of the woman Amy's mouth hadn't touched. She had sucked on each of Sally's perfectly lacquered toes; had licked and kissed her way up each of Sally's legs—back and front; had probed Sally's navel with her tongue; had raked her teeth along Sally's arms; had bitten Sally's ass, back, shoulders, neck; had kissed her eyelids; had sucked on those gorgeous pastel pink nipples and, of course, had eaten her out God knows how many times since they'd gotten out of the shower.

Shifting on the bed now to face Sally, she winced.

"Problem?" Sally asked.

Amy smiled.

"Good problem. My nipples are sore. You really went to town on them tonight."

Sally smiled back.

"How could I not?" she asked.

"You really do like my boobs, don't you?" Amy inquired.

Biting her lip, Sally reached over and gently ran the pad of her thumb over Amy's left nipple. Her touch was magic. There was no soreness under her thumb, just tingles of excitement.

"I think they're perfect," Sally said. "Honestly."

God, this woman...

"I had a girlfriend once who suggested I get them done," Amy told her, remembering Lizette.

Sally frowned.

"Well, that's pretty selfish. And dumb. I mean, no offense, but it's pretty obvious you have small boobs; but my point is, if you're a woman who likes *big* boobs, why go out with the chick without them?"

"That's what I thought!" Amy exclaimed.

Sally scootched closer.

"When I first laid eyes on you in that coffeeshop and saw your whole body...well, let's just say that I knew one night I'd be making your nipples really sore."

Amy laughed.

"You're lying!"

"No, I'm not, I swear! I think every single fucking inch of you is sexy, babe. Especially *these*." And Sally cupped Amy's left breast, giving it a tender squeeze.

"Fuck, you're amazing!" Amy gasped.

"So are you. In fact, I think we're amazing together."

Amy let out a satisfied purr as Sally's thumb once more began stroking her nipple.

"Especially when we're in bed," she whispered. "But…I don't want you thinking that's all I think we're amazing at," she quickly added.

"I know," Sally said. "But it's a good thing for a couple to be amazing at."

Unbelievably, Amy's core was flooding again. She wouldn't have thought it was possible after all the fun they'd just had—that her body couldn't produce any more lubrication. But it was happening.

Sally must have sensed it because now her nipple was being pinched softly. Amy knew Sally was being considerate because she had told her that her nipples were sore but this was no time for consideration.

"Harder," Amy murmured, staring at Sally with lidded eyes which quickly shut when her request was granted and the pain-pleasure was felt. "Mmmmm," she hummed.

Soon they were kissing, softly at first and then with their usual hunger. Soon after that, Sally was on top of her, her thigh pressing against Amy's sex, giving Amy a surface to grind her clit against. Sally's slightly larger breasts were hanging down, her nipples grazing Amy's and every time their hard buds connected, Amy felt an electric jolt.

"I can't get enough of you!" Amy grunted, staring into the eyes of the woman above her while she rocked her hips, simultaneously coating Sally's thigh with her essence and getting closer to yet another orgasm.

"Me neither," Sally gasped. "After what happened…"

"I know! Oh my god, Sally!"

Amy felt that familiar pressure building up beneath her hairless mound.

"Eyes on me, baby," Sally whispered.

Amy nodded.

"Yes!"

It was an effort, but when she came Amy kept her eyes locked on Sally's and she could swear that something mystical happened then; that there was a transfer of spiritual energy between them as her spasming pussy again became an epicenter of ecstasy and pumped out her come onto Sally's leg. Somehow, their souls connected and entwined during this climax and Amy knew that Sally felt it as well.

She knew this would happen. That's why she told me to keep my eyes open...

Chapter 38

"Very funny," Sally said two days later, on Monday, walking into Max's house. It was just after three p.m.; Sally had left work a little early today but hadn't felt like going home to her empty condo, and because Amy was going to be at her job until a little past five and then meet with her friend Rachel for happy hour, she decided to pay Max a visit to thank him for the bouquet of flowers she was now holding.

He had sent the flowers to her office earlier, with a card reading "Glad you're not dead."

Max laughed.

"Well, I am glad you're not dead," he said. "My life would be quieter but a lot duller were you to perish."

"I love you too," Sally said after sticking out her tongue.

"Why didn't you just leave them at the office?" he asked as they headed towards the living room.

"No, I want Amy to see them," Sally said. It really was a beautiful bouquet and Sally could already imagine it on her coffee table.

Max offered to make her a drink.

"Yes, please," Sally answered. "Whatever it was that you made Amy last time."

A few minutes later, he joined her on the couch and handed her the white, creamy cocktail. For himself, he had a splash of Scotch in a glass.

"So, how are you feeling?" he asked, after clinking glasses with her. "You two didn't talk much the other day."

This was true. During the ride to Carlsbad from John Wayne International Airport, Sally and Amy had sat huddled together in the back seat of Max's Mercedes, just holding onto each other, not saying anything, both of them trying to process what they had just gone through. To his credit, Max hadn't pressed and simply played the role of chauffeur.

Sally thought about the answer to his question.

She had been right; she had had nightmares the past two nights. But each time a bad dream had woken her up and her mind finally realized that, no, she wasn't trapped inside a burning airplane or that, no, she wasn't feeling herself being torn apart as the plane smashed into the ground, Sally had looked over and seen Amy lying next to her and instantly felt better.

If it had been any other woman, Sally was certain that she would have still felt comforted knowing someone was beside her in bed at those moments. But any other woman would have been just that: any other woman. What Sally knew now was that Amy was not any other woman. After being certain at one point just two days ago that she and everyone else on the plane was about to die, Sally knew now that it was Amy she wanted as she enjoyed this second chance at life they'd been given.

"I feel a little better each day," she told Max now. "Being back at work helps. And talking to my Mom yesterday was actually helpful also."

"Talking to your mother usually gives you hives," Max pointed out.

"I know, but…it was nice hearing how concerned she was. Well, until she suggested that I go see a psychologist friend of hers who specializes in trauma survival and who just so happens to have a lesbian daughter who's single."

"Your mother knows a lot of people with unattached lesbian daughters," Max remarked.

"I know! She'd probably make more than she does as a surgeon if she created an app for meddling mothers to find dates for their gay daughters." She took a sip from the delicious drink. "Anyway…this is going to sound so cliché but I really do have a greater appreciation for life now. And for time! Like today, for instance; I could've stayed at the office longer! I have a bunch of shit to do! But I knew it could fucking wait until tomorrow."

"Good girl," Max said, tapping her knee. "Don't wait until you're my age before you stop to smell the roses."

"Definitely not," Sally agreed. Then, she decided to open up about something else. Lisa was the wrong person to have this talk with, though Sally had considered it earlier today. And her mother was certainly the wrong person. No, Max was who she needed.

"The Incident also made me realize something," she began.

"That the oxygen masks actually work in first class?" Max asked.

Sally laughed.

"No," she said. "It made me realize that Amy is the one."

Max stared intently at her as he took another sip of his Scotch.

"Well, say something!" Sally demanded. "I told you that because I want your opinion."

"Okay…" Max started. "Why would almost dying on an airplane make you realize that?"

"Because now that I'm going through all this I-really-appreciate-life stuff, I realize that one of the things I really appreciate is Amy. And I don't want to imagine her ever being out of my life."

Max didn't say anything and Sally grew exasperated.

"Max, I want you attack this! I want you to poke holes in it! Make me look at it differently!"

The truth was, that even though Sally was certain about her feelings for Amy, they frightened her. It was only a little more than three weeks ago that they went on their first date! What was happening to her? Where was Sensible Sally? Because this didn't seem sensible! Where was the Sally who had said "I love you" to only two women in her life because she always wanted to make sure a relationship was going to "stick" and had always felt justified in that approach because most of her relationships hadn't stuck.

Max sighed, but he also put an expression on his face that Sally recognized, knowing it meant he was thinking about a matter seriously.

"Okay," he began. "Well, my first thought is that it seems pretty quick."

Sally nodded.

"I already thought about that. It hasn't changed anything. I feel like I've known her half my life even though it's only been less than a month."

"Okay," Max began again. "How about this? You and her just shared a traumatic experience. Maybe that's clouding your judgement."

Sally nodded.

"Good point," she said, curling her leg under her on the couch. "But…think about this! That can go both ways, right? I could have walked away from the emergency landing looking at Amy and thinking, 'I super appreciate life so much more now! Why do I want to waste it with Amy?'"

Max furrowed his brow.

"That actually makes sense," he said.

"You always seem so surprised when I make sense," Sally responded.

"Because I often am. Anyway, what about that dry spell you kept complaining to me about? Amy is your first girlfriend in a while. Maybe you're just overly happy about that or something."

Sally nodded.

"Fine. But, Max, I've had dry spells before—not as bad, but still. And Amy…And Amy isn't just another girlfriend."

How to explain this? Especially to a man?

Sally's eyes widened. That was it! Max wasn't just another man! He was Jillian Ashley! Forget about wanting him to poke holes in what she was feeling for Amy! Right now, she wanted him to understand!

Putting her drink down on the coffee table, she took his hand.

"Max, listen…it's just like in your books! When Marisol woke up in Karen's apartment the morning after their second date and she just *knew* she'd be with her forever? Or when Jeannette introduced Ari to her parents and she felt certain she was introducing them to her future wife? You're the person who *wrote* those scenes which means you can understand what I'm feeling!"

"But those are books!" Max explained patiently. "I write what horny, lovelorn lesbians want to read! In real life, you shouldn't start getting all googly-eyed over someone until you've had your first fight, at least!"

"Ha!" Sally barked. "We had a little fight in San Francisco; but we talked about it afterwards and resolved it."

"Oh, well then! You're obviously meant for each other!"

"You're being sarcastic," Sally said, "but that's how I feel!" Sally then tried to explain to Max what went through her mind when her and Amy locked eyes during the Incident, when it felt as if the plane was about to disintegrate: that her and Amy belonged together, that they were meant for one another and that if they were going to die, that Sally was hoping she'd get to spend eternity with Amy.

When she was done, all Max could say was, "Wow!"

"Are you being sarcastic again?" Sally asked somewhat defensively.

"No, I promise! I truly mean 'Wow.' I've been around for a few of your past romances, Sally, and I've never heard you talk about any of them like this—even the ones which lasted far longer."

"But you think I should slow it down?" Sally queried.

But to her surprise, Max shook his head.

"No, Sally, I don't," he insisted. "You're right—life is something to be appreciated because—poof!—you get on the wrong plane one day and suddenly it's over. Why do you think I've still been seeing that teenager you set me up with?"

Sally blinked.

"Wait," she said. "Tiffany? You're still seeing her?" In all the excitement in her own life over the past three weeks, she had forgotten about the diner waitress.

Max nodded.

"She's actually quite wonderful," he stated. "And smart and funny too. I mean, she talks too much but I actually enjoy listening to her. I could listen to her talk for hours! And she's studying to become a teacher, did you know that? And for some reason, she's nuts about me. And you know what, I'm just going to keep on enjoying it. Life is too short to do otherwise."

Sally beamed.

Jillian understood.

Chapter 39

"And then, *boom!* The plane went like this..." Using her right hand, Amy demonstrated to Rachel how Flight 1577 out of San Francisco suddenly banked precariously. "And then the overhead bins popped open and there was luggage flying around everywhere—some of it hit Sally—and then somehow the plane got level again but it was, like, you could tell there was something horribly wrong with it. The engines didn't sound right and there were all these weird banging noises."

Her and Rachel were seated at an outdoor table at a popular Carlsbad bar, cocktails in front of them, a large bowl of nacho chips with queso dip on the side right in the middle of the table.

Amy continued telling the story of the Event, Rachel listening to her with a look of rapt attention on her face. When Amy finally reached the end—the bone-jarring landing followed by *whooshing* down that giant inflatable slide...

"Do they really make you take your shoes off before you go down that thing?" Rachel interrupted to ask.

"They do! Which, I guess make sense but I remember thinking, if this stupid rubber slide can be punctured by ballet flats, what's the point? Anyway..." And she went on to finish the tale: all of the emergency vehicles that were surrounding the plane; being shuttled to that hangar; the paramedics checking her out; talking to her mother back in Wichita and then bursting into sobs with relief at being alive, which is how Sally found her.

Rachel shook her head slowly.

"You're making me never want to fly again," she said.

"Trust me, I know," Amy replied.

"Are you doing okay, though?" Rachel now inquired. "I mean..." and she waved her hand in front of her, indicating Amy should fill in the blanks.

Amy knew what she meant. But she wasn't entirely sure of the answer. On the one hand, she wasn't cowering at home in a dark room, refusing to go outside, trying not to have flashbacks to the terrifying flight. On the other hand, she hadn't slept well the past two nights because she was plagued with nightmares about flying and crashing. And she knew Sally was having the same difficulties; they had talked about it.

On the one hand, Amy had managed to function perfectly well on this, her first day back at work since her vacation, picking up right where she had left off. On the other hand, when things at the office were quiet, she had often found herself staring off into space, seeing and hearing the Event over and over again.

And Rachel's comment right now, about how Amy's story was making her not want to fly again…Sure, Amy knew Rachel meant it tongue-in-cheek, but it did beg the question in her own mind: *When will I be ready to fly again?*

"I think I'm okay," she told Rachel, who was still waiting for an answer to her question. "But I think I'll have the heebie-jeebies for a while."

Rachel placed her hand on Amy's arm.

"Sweetie, that's fine," she said soothingly. "You went through a scary experience."

Amy nodded.

"I know." She paused because she felt the tears and sobs threatening to return and took a sip of her margarita to ward them off. "There was one good thing to come out of that experience, though."

Rachel quirked an eyebrow.

"And what was that?"

Amy held Rachel's eyes with her own.

"She's the one, Rach. Sally. She's the one."

"Wow. Really?"

Amy nodded.

Rachel bit her lip for a moment and then seemed to make a decision.

"Are you sure?" she asked. "I'm only asking because I'm your best friend and it's my job and we're not stupid teenagers anymore who think we're in love with just anyone."

Nodding again, Amy said, "I'm sure."

"Because you and her just went through something majorly scary," Rachel went on, "and that kind of thing can cloud your judgement."

"Totally get it," Amy said. "But that's not what's happening here."

She tried to come up with a way to make Rachel understand but in the end, she decided to dispense with tricks and to just to tell her the truth.

"Rach," she began, "I honestly thought I was going to die. It was *that* bad. But because I didn't die, I just feel so happy to be alive! Like, whoever thinks about being alive? Most of us just take it for granted. But now I'm happy for it! And the thing is, I want my life to have Sally in it from this point forward because her presence will make me even happier to be alive."

"Okay, fine, but—"

Amy cut her off.

"Listen," she said. And now it was her placing her hand on Rachel's arm. "This is going to sound really weird but hear me out." Amy swallowed. "There was a moment on the plane when all that shit was happening, when we were looking at each other and I swear I could read her mind, Rach. She was telling me how she feels! She was thanking me for being with her and giving her joy. She was telling me that her and I were meant for each other. She was telling me that if that was the end, we'd spend eternity together."

Rachel opened her mouth to speak but Amy quickly went on, stopping her.

"No, listen! And I was telling her the same kinds of things, just with my eyes, Rach. How she gave me so much happiness and how magical our time together was—stuff like that. And I could tell she *heard* me, Rach! Even though I never said a word." Amy stopped, making sure she had Rachel's undivided attention. "Rachel…she's the one."

Rachel was staring silently at her. Her eyes were watering slightly and Amy knew she had succeeded in making her best friend understand.

"Well!" Rachel finally exclaimed. "How can I argue against *that*?"

"You can't!" Amy told her with a smile.

"Makes me want to survive a plane crash with someone special sitting next to *me*. Brad Pitt, maybe."

Amy made a face.

"Ugh! You straight women are so weird!"

***

That night, Amy was breathing heavily and almost drooling as she watched one of her small vibrators, a smooth pink one, disappear completely into Sally's pussy, pushed in slowly by her finger. The buzzing sound of the vibrator was silenced as Sally's sex swallowed the toy whole, Sally moaning erotically.

Amy gave Sally's glistening pink folds a kiss, tasting the tang of her girlfriend's arousal, before pulling up the blue cotton panties to once more cover Sally's center.

"My turn," she said.

She heard Sally click on different vibrator from Amy's collection—another small one, this one purple. It was one of her oldest toys but it had certainly stood the test of time.

Keeping her head down by Sally's waist, Amy spread her legs and felt Sally begin to insert the toy, the tingling vibrations spreading throughout her core, making her clit pulse and swell even more.

"Oh my fuck…" Amy moaned, surrendering to it.

Deeper it went until she felt her pussy's lips close shut behind it and she felt it settle entirely inside her flooded passage, its buzzing also silenced by virtue of being completely buried in her. Then, her own panties were pulled back up, covering her sex.

It had been Sally who had suggested this. Where she had gotten the idea, Amy had no clue but she didn't care. Right now, she was beyond turned on. The tingles emanating from inside her sex pulling her closer and closer to the edge, helped along by the recent memory from just a few moments ago of seeing Sally's pussy devour that pink vibe entirely.

Managing to open her eyes, Amy saw a dark damp spot growing on Sally's blue panties. The woman must be soaked! The sight drove her crazy and she brought her face closer in order to inhale the scent of her woman. Meanwhile, she felt Sally licking one of her legs at the same time one of her hands was resting on her inner thigh just inches from her apex.

Amy brought her face even closer to Sally's panties, her tongue flicking out to run along that wet spot on the panties.

Sally purred in reaction to this. She then bit Amy's calf muscle gently and Amy's clit pulsed.

"Come up here," Sally ordered.

Amy wasn't sure she could. If she wasn't careful, the act of repositioning herself to lay face-to-face with Sally would push her over the edge she was already skating on. So, with the utmost care, making sure not to press her legs together and put pressure on her already electrified button, Amy managed to turn herself around until she was lying next to Sally and looking into her lover's eyes.

They were nude except for the panties and Amy scootched her body a skosh closer in order to feel more of Sally's form up against her.

They kissed deeply for a nice long time, tongues gently playing, hands stroking cheeks and necks.

"God, this feels so *gooooood*!" Amy grunted when their lips parted. She pressed her pelvis against Sally's.

"Doesn't it, though?" Sally responded, peppering Amy's chin with light kisses.

"So is the idea to see which one of us comes first?" Amy asked, her eyes closed. "And the loser has to do the other's laundry for a month?"

Sally chuckled.

"No," she stated. "This isn't a competition. It's not a challenge to see who can hold out the longest. No one wins; no one loses. Come as many times as you want but if you can hold out, so much the better."

Now Sally's hand was softly tweaking Amy's nipple, hardening it to stone. Amy whispered her name.

"It's about finding new levels of ecstasy by having patience," Sally went on, kissing Amy's neck. "Instead of both of us just making one another come as many times as possible, it's about slowing down and enjoying the sensations of what's happening to us. While also just enjoying *us*."

"You mean enjoying more than just the vibes inside us?" Amy asked in a murmur. That said vibe inside *her* was making her feel molten and it was taking all her willpower to keep her climax from unleashing.

"Exactly. The vibes inside us are only one sensation, baby," Sally said just before she lowered her head and sucked Amy's nipple into her mouth. "But that's another, isn't it?" she asked when she released the bud. "And this is another…" And Sally used one of her long and smooth legs to stroke Amy's, sending a thrill shooting up her spine. "And here's another…" This time, Sally reclaimed Amy's lips for another deep kiss.

As their lips and tongues moved against each other, Amy understood. The vibe in her pussy was simply the foundational sensation upon which all the other sensations—of being kissed, of having her nipple suckled, of having her skin stroked—built upon. She entangled her fingers in Sally's hair and suddenly this act—which she'd done countless times—developed new meaning and feeling. There was now an intimacy to it, along with a recognition of the trust it meant Sally had in her to let her grab her hair like this.

Meanwhile, as they continued kissing, Sally was slowly stroking Amy's back with her hand and Amy could feel each of Sally's fingers as they moved along her skin and she could visualize the pattern they were drawing. And even though Sally's touch was light, there was still a possessiveness to it, as if Sally was silently communicating to her: *You are mine and no one else's.*

That thought, along with everything else, almost made Amy come, but she didn't want to. Not yet. She was digging this and she wanted to discover how far she could go with it, and so, whimpering against Sally's mouth as they kissed, she pulled the orgasm back from the edge. And in doing so, in keeping the orgasm at bay, Amy felt her consciousness reach yet another level of awareness—a level which took her focus away from her ready-to-explode center and allowed her to feel even more of everything else.

"It sounds tantric," she whispered when their kiss broke, looking into Sally's eyes.

"That's where I got the idea from," Sally admitted. "After what we went through on the plane, I wondered if there were ways we can have our lovemaking occasionally be more than our usual assortment of activities because if this is our second chance at life, I want us to slow down every now and then so we can feel even closer to each other. Because I want to feel as close to you as possible, Amy Broadnax."

That did it.

That heartfelt statement from Sally and the sincerity with which it was delivered created such an overwhelming feeling of love and affection within Amy that it, even more than the vibe buried inside her, pushed her over the edge and made her come undone.

Arching her head back, she gripped Sally tighter against her as her eyes squeezed shut.

"Oh fuck!" she gasped. "I'm coming!"

And then it hit. Titanic waves of pleasure burst from her core, released finally to spread all through her body which jerked and spasmed in response while she held onto Sally. Her flooded and convulsing pussy with its rapidly clenching inner walls tried to expel the vibrator but the panties prevented the toy from escaping and so Amy was treated to a continuation of the buzzing tingles.

What did escape was her come. Lots of it. She was soaked outside as well as in now, her panties trapping the warm, flowing arousal, forcing it to coat her folds, her clit, her ass, spreading it around as she rocked her pelvis against Sally's.

She heard Sally moan and recognized the sound. Sally was coming now too and when Amy felt her girlfriend first seize up stiffly in her arms before her body started trembling, Amy's pussy came again and now their cries were mixing in the room.

Amy quickly brought one her hands down to between Sally's legs and pressed it against the sopping wet panties. She could feel Sally's pussy trying to push the vibrator out; she felt the end of the toy pushing against the crotch of those blue panties. But Amy kept her hand firmly in place and the vibe had nowhere to go but back inside.

She came a third time and this one shattered her. It rocked her so hard that she spasmed out of Sally's grasp, rolled onto her back, arching it to an almost impossible shape, and pinched both her nipples as she screamed unintelligible sounds, feeling her pussy explode in a sloppy, liquid mess of pure pleasure.

She felt Sally pull her panties off and even before she had gotten them past her knees, Amy's convulsing pussy squeezed out the vibrator, its buzz now joining the other noises in the room. And now Sally's mouth was on her pussy, licking, sucking, drinking and Amy got deliriously dizzy with the enjoyment of this attention on her orgasming center.

"Oh fuck, I'm coming again!" Sally grunted, ruthlessly taking her mouth away and flopping onto the mattress beside Amy as she got lost in her own throes. Amy wanted to bury her face now between Sally's legs. She wanted to watch Sally's gorgeous pussy quake with release. She wanted to drink of Sally's nectar. But she couldn't move. She had been rendered immobile by the intensity of her own releases. A couple of times, she felt her head swimming, the way it does sometimes when she hasn't eaten enough on a hot day. She needed to come down from this otherwise she was sure she'd faint.

She released her nipples and gripped the bedsheets instead. Tightly. Trying to ground herself. The orgasms were still in control, though, and continued to make her shake and shiver with sexual joy.

But finally, the ride ended. She thought she was aware of Sally coming yet again but she couldn't be sure. All she knew for certain was that she was still gasping for air and that her pussy was still pumping out her essence, making a wet spot on the sheets beneath her ass.

Chapter 40

Friday evening, Sally and Amy were driving back to Santa Ana and John Wayne International Airport. The airline had called them both separately this morning, telling each of them that they could finally return to retrieve their belongings. After getting her phone call, Sally had texted Amy and they had decided to both leave work a little early and make the drive today rather than waiting until tomorrow.

It was about time.

After the emergency landing, all the passengers had had to abandon the plane in haste, ordered by the flight crew to leave everything behind. Later, in the hangar, they had been promised that once the plane was deemed safe enough, airport personnel would find their baggage and other belongings and contact them for retrieval. Sally just hadn't expected them to take this long. Not that any hardship had been created by the delay. Despite the haste of the evacuation, both Sally and Amy—as well as pretty much every other woman on the aircraft—had had the presence of mind to grab their purses, which had been stowed under their seats, so at least neither of them had had to worry about canceling credit cards or getting new IDs. But in addition to their checked baggage, Sally's Kindle had been left behind in the cabin—who knows where after she dropped it—along with Amy's laptop. Sally had a brief flashback now of seeing the computer almost jump out of Amy's grasp just when the plane did that first gut-wrenching freefall or whatever it had done.

Driving her BMW on the I-5 as they approached Irvine, Sally said, "I bet you've been going crazy without your laptop."

Amy chuckled.

"Thank god my old one still works," she said. "But it's *soooooo* slow! I, like, try to do something on it and end up wishing I can make it drink coffee to speed it up!"

Sally laughed.

"Well, you can pour a few drops of your Amy's Jet Fuel into the circuitry," she joked. "That oughta speed it up. Anyway, I hope that they found your regular one and that it still works."

"Me too. But even if it's destroyed, everything important is backed up to the cloud. Trust me, I spend a bunch of money a year on my cloud storage."

"Oh, good. I'd hate to think the unedited, raw footage of my debut appearance on *Lesbeing* as Jillian Ashley was lost forever! That's historical, after all."

Amy nodded.

"I expect the Smithsonian to be calling me any day for it," she replied with a smirk.

Sally navigated her car around a slow-moving taxi and then sped past a dump truck. As she did so, she was smiling to herself.

She was happy.

Last night had been mind-blowingly amazing, she considered now after reading a sign stating that the airport was three miles ahead. She had always felt that so far, she had had a good sex life. Most of her past girlfriends had been good-to-great lovers, and even the handful of one-night stands she'd had pre-pandemic had been fun. But with Amy, her sex life was now pornographically good. Off-the-charts good. Stratospherically good. And with what they experienced last night…it had been everything Sally had wanted: an erotic way of opening of new doorways to each other souls.

That was unusual for her.

Usually, Sally ignored anything that had a mystical or supernatural bent to it. But after the Incident, she wasn't certain she wanted to be so close-minded anymore. So, when she started looking into tantric sex, it sounded like just what she wanted. Of course, she chose to ignore a lot of suggestions she'd read on websites about it. Eye-gazing, for one. Who wants to spend two minutes just gazing into their partner's eyes? And synchronized breathing with hands on each other hearts? Sally could do without that too. Besides, Amy's heart was under one of her gorgeous and pert breasts. Sally knew that if she placed her hand on that part of Amy's chest, it wouldn't be to feel Amy's beating heart.

And so Sally had devised her own method of tantric sex: still slow, still appreciative of her partner's presence and body…but with the added bonus of a constantly vibrating toy in her core.

In fact, she had come so hard last night that she had hurt herself, tweaking a muscle near her ribcage, close to where her Sally Brown tattoo was.

Last night's mind-blowing amazingness, however, was only one aspect of what was making Sally happy right now.

The other aspects all had to do with Amy and her Amy-ness.

Amy was meant for her, Sally was convinced now. And the thing was, she knew that she had come to that conclusion even before the Incident, even before their time in San Francisco was up. Sally had been wanting to feel the things she feels for Amy all her life. The Incident merely heightened that awareness and made her determined to keep Amy with her until…

Forever.

And okay…Amy was a bit of a workaholic; and okay, that had started to bother Sally a bit that one morning in San Francisco when they'd had that row. But Sally knew there are worse things Amy could be doing in the wee hours of the morning.

And okay…Amy drank an alarming amount of caffeine. Yesterday morning, her girlfriend had gotten up super early (no surprise) and gone to La Vida Mocha to bring back coffee for herself and Sally before they both left for work. When she returned, Sally, out of curiosity, had taken a sip of the Amy's Jet Fuel. One sip. Yet all that day, Sally had had an elevated heartrate and even wondered if she should get an EKG.

But all of these quirks, and others, were part of Amy's Amy-ness and Sally wouldn't have Amy any other way.

"Hey," Amy began, interrupting her reverie, "after we're done at the airport, can we maybe grab dinner in town?"

"Absolutely," Sally answered. "That's a great idea."

Amy reached over and laid her hand on Sally's right leg.

"God, my heart is starting to beat faster," she whispered.

Sally nodded.

"Mine too." This was true and it was because she had just steered the car onto the exit for the airport. Even though they weren't getting on an airplane—and Sally wondered when she'd be ready for *that* again—it was still a little unnerving returning to this airport. The memories of Saturday…

God, was it only Saturday?

…were rushing through her mind like one of those jump cut flashback scenes in a thriller movie.

The terror of feeling the plane freefalling.

The stomach-churning sensation of when the plane banked sharply that one time, making her feel as if the aircraft was about to do a barrel roll.

All of the noise: passengers screaming; the engines whining; sounds of metal straining and unseen things in the undercarriage banging about.

Assuming the crash position.

Feeling certain she was going to die.

The landing: successful, fine, but even Sally knew that it had not been textbook by any means. In fact, when the plane touched down, she could have sworn that she had heard even more screeching metal sounds, as if it wasn't the landing gear that was skidding along the runway.

She shook her head, trying to clear her thoughts so she could concentrate on navigating the car through the airport roads to where they had been instructed to go.

Taking her right hand off the steering wheel, she placed it atop the one Amy had on her leg.

"It'll be fine," she said.

***

Turns out, the airline people found her Kindle. And her sunglasses which she had left in the back pocket of the seat in front of hers. Her Coach carry-on bag (with the vibrator/pipe bomb inside) was intact, and remarkably unscathed. Apparently, it had fallen out when the overhead compartments had burst open and according to the customer service rep helping them now had been found all the way in the back of the economy section, so the bag must have endured some pretty severe bopping and banging around the cabin during the emergency, yet from what Sally could tell, it bore no visible signs of damage.

Always buy quality.

Amy's laptop, on the other hand, bore some new scratches. Fortunately, the damage was limited to the casing. The screen was fine and unmarred. Alas, because it had been unplugged for so long, Amy was unable to simply turn it on to determine if it still worked. However, to Sally's surprise, Amy reached into her tote bag-sized purse, pulled out the laptop's power supply cable, found a nearby outlet and plugged it in.

"Only you would have a power cable for a laptop in your purse," Sally said, shaking her head but loving the Amy-ness of it.

"Did you really think I'd be able to wait until we got home before knowing?" Amy asked, her eyes fixed on the screen. After a moment, she let out a relieved sigh. "Whew! It boots up!" She closed the cover. "I'll check it out more when we get back."

Sally was surprised. She had half-expected Amy to start writing a new blog entry, right there in the airline's customer service lounge. *The Best Laptops for Lesbians to Have in a Plane Crash*, or something like that.

Their checked baggage was all in good shape, which was a relief. Sally had had visions of being told that the plane's cargo compartment had burst into flames or disgorged its contents somewhere over Long Beach.

With their belongings returned, their work at the airport was done, which was fine by Sally. She had felt on-edge the entire time they were there. This bothered her because traveling was something she enjoyed and she didn't now want to become one of those people who was afraid of flying. There was still too much of the world she wanted to see and she sure as hell couldn't drive to it all.

This matter was still on her mind when her and Amy sat down for dinner at a Korean grill restaurant in downtown Santa Ana about twenty minutes later.

"Maybe we should take another trip soon," she said to Amy after they'd ordered.

Amy's face registered surprise but she also smiled that gorgeous smile Sally loved.

"Really?" Amy asked. "Like, how soon?"

Sally shrugged.

"I don't know, but the sooner the better, I think. I'm just hating how I felt at the airport just now and I'm worried that if I take too long to get back on an airplane, I'll end up never wanting to fly again."

Amy nodded.

"I totally get that. I feel the same. I don't want to be one of those lesbians who owns a Winnebago because that's the only way they'll travel. Ooh! Podcast episode idea! Anyway…horse…saddle…let's get back on."

Sally was liking this plan, especially the part about never seeing Amy in a Winnebago.

"Are you sure?" Sally asked. "I don't want it to be like I'm pressuring you. If you're not ready—"

"You're not traveling anywhere without me," Amy stated, looking directly into Sally's eyes.

Sally's clit actually pulsed.

"I don't want to travel anywhere without you," she said softly. "Like, ever."

She saw Amy swallow.

"*Ever* ever?" Amy asked quietly.

"*Ever* ever," Sally declared.

"Me either," Amy said. "*Ever* ever."

Sally just had the best idea.

"Let's go somewhere tonight!" she said.

Amy laughed.

"Seriously?"

"Why not?" Sally went on. "We have everything we need with us right now! Credit cards, ID, a car full of luggage…"

"Sex toys," Amy added with a wicked grin.

"Sex toys," Sally confirmed.

"My laptop," Amy said.

"Which is like a third arm for you," Sally joked.

"Where would we go?" Amy asked and Sally could tell she was just as enthused about it as she was.

Sally bit her lip, considering.

"Vegas?"

Amy made a face.

"No, too cheesy. Back to San Francisco?"

Sally shook her head.

"Nah, I want someplace different." Her face lit up as an idea came to her. "Have you ever been to Seattle?"

Sally knew by the look on Amy's face that she had picked the winner.

"I love Seattle!" Amy exclaimed. "And you can get amazing coffee, like, *anywhere* in that city!"

"Oh my god, you have a problem!" Sally teased her, rolling her eyes.

"Whatever! You love it!" Amy said, already looking at her phone and tapping the screen. In a few moments, she said, "Shit! We missed the last flight to Seattle out of John Wayne." She tapped her screen a few more times. "But there's a flight out of L.A. in three hours."

"No time to eat!" Sally declared, already gathering her purse. Amy was doing the same.

"You drive, I'll book!" she told Sally.

Their server came by, ready to take their order. "I'm sorry," Sally told the young woman. "But we have to leave." She pulled a twenty out of her wallet and hastily handed it to her. "But take this!"

In the car, before she started driving, Sally unlocked her phone and handed it along with her wallet to Amy so her girlfriend could make all the bookings.

"Ooh," Amy began when she had Sally's phone in her possession. "Now I can see what other women you've been texting."

Sally laughed.

"Go ahead," she challenged, pulling out of the restaurant's parking lot. "You'll find tons of messages from Lisa, my bestie; too many messages from my Mom; a woman from work named Sandra, who's, like, sixty-years-old and, let's see…"

"Someone named Ainsley," Amy said in a teasing voice.

Fuck!

Sally had forgotten about the handful of texts she had shared with Ainsley leading up to their one and only date.

"That's nobody!" Sally exclaimed.

"Hmm…looks like you met up for drinks with Ainsley Nobody the day after our first date…"

"Amy, seriously, she's *nobody*! It was one of my mother's stupid fix ups! And her mother's too! We agreed to meet just to get them off our backs! But I swear to you, five minutes after I met her I told her that you and I had started dating!"

"Five minutes!" Amy exclaimed, an edge to her voice. "It took *that* long?"

Christ! Why didn't I delete those messages!

"Amy…baby…" Sally began in a pleading tone. But then she stopped.

In the seat next to her, Amy was laughing.

At first, Sally was confused but then the penny dropped and she took her right hand off the steering wheel to reach over and playfully smack Amy's leg.

"So, you really believe me when I tell you Ainsley is nobody?" she asked.

"Yes, babe, I believe you," Amy said, reassuringly. She leaned over and gave Sally's cheek a quick kiss. "As if you would ever date someone named Ainsley!"

Sally nodded.

"I know, right? God, that name!"

Sally decided to leave out the fact that despite the pretentiousness of Ainsley's name, the woman herself was actually quite charming and sweet. Oh, and sexy as fuck.

"Oh, Ainsley! Oh, Ainsley!" Amy exclaimed, mimicking a woman in the throes of sexual passion. She even put her feet up on the dash with her legs spread open and thrashed about a bit in the passenger seat. "Don't stop, Ainsley! Oh, Ainsley, I'm coming!" She shuddered and put her feet back on the floor. "Brrr! It just doesn't work!"

Sally was laughing and had to slow the BMW down until she got control of herself again.

"What's her middle name?" Amy asked.

"No idea. Probably something equally pretentious, like Penelope."

"Well, anyway…you will never find out *because* I am deleting these messages from Ainsley Penelope, so say 'bye-bye.'"

"Bye-bye, Ainsley Penelope!" Sally said.

Chapter 41

This time, Amy insisted Sally take the vibrator-that-could-be-mistaken-for-a-pipe-bomb out of her carry-on bag and put it inside her checked luggage once they reached LAX.

"I know, I know," Sally said when they stopped just inside the terminal so that she could transfer the toy from one bag to another. "Season two, episode ten."

After checking their luggage and making it through security, Amy was sitting with Sally in the boarding area at the gate, her legs crossed, her hands folded in her lap, tapping her foot nervously.

This was the right decision, she considered. Getting back on a plane was the right decision but goddamn if she wasn't jittery about it. She chastised herself silently, telling herself to stop being silly. What had happened on the previous flight had been a fluke and unlikely to repeat itself.

Fine, that was true but it was doing little to help.

She took another glance over at the gate agent's station. On the wall was an LED sign displaying their flight number and destination along with a handy-dandy countdown clock showing the time left until boarding was going to start. It currently read *31 minutes*.

Amy let out a puff of breath. 31 minutes. And once more, her and Sally would be among the first passengers to board because, yet again, they had bought first-class tickets, which meant they'd be sitting on the airplane that much longer before takeoff.

Sitting. Sitting and waiting. Sitting and waiting and wondering. Sitting, waiting and wondering if the hexabolt thingamajigs which keep the wings attached to the plane had really been manufactured to the highest standards; or if the flight control software in the cockpit had been programmed by some loner dweeb who was having a bad day.

This isn't helping!

"Fuck!" she muttered.

"Hey," Sally whispered. "Why don't you work on something? You have your laptop back."

Amy shook her head, still tapping her foot.

"Good idea, but I can't concentrate on anything right now. Aren't you nervous?"

"Of course I am," Sally whispered, placing her hand on Amy's leg. That simple gesture was like a magic soothing balm which lowered Amy's heartrate instantly and sent a surge of strength through her entire body.

"Fuck, that's amazing!" Amy exclaimed, her eyes closed as she enjoyed the sudden calm.

"What is?"

"Your touch. It instantly calmed me down! You're magical…"

Sally chuckled.

"My turn," she said. "Let's see if you've got the touch too."

Amy placed her hand on Sally's leg and Sally gave her that zillion-watt smile Amy adored.

"Like Xanax," Sally said.

"Great," Amy began, "all we have to do is keep our hands on each other during the flight and we'll be fine."

"I can think of worse things," Sally replied.

"I'm crazy about you!" Amy couldn't help saying then. "Like, super, out of this world crazy about you! I just wanted you to know that before we get on another possibly defective plane in…" she glanced at the countdown clock again "…twenty-eight minutes."

"Babe, I'm crazy about you too," Sally said. "And I think this flight is going to go fine."

"If it doesn't," Amy began, "we're sticking to boats, trains and cars. Maybe the occasional bicycle."

"I can't bike all the way to Amsterdam!" Sally said.

"We will use a combination of boats, trains and cars to *get* to Amsterdam; then we'll use the bikes once we're there," Amy declared.

"I like that you said 'we will,'" Sally purred.

Amy grinned.

"I already told you: you're not traveling anywhere without me, Miss Lassiter."

"And I love that."

"Good, because it's not like you have a choice."

***

The flight went fine. The hexabolt thingamajigs kept the wings where they belonged and the loner dweeb who programmed the control software must have gotten laid because he had done a terrific job. With the exception of some minor turbulence—which Amy knew she wouldn't have noticed normally but which this time made her and Sally clutch each other's hands—the trip from Los Angeles to Seattle was smooth and uneventful.

The relief Amy had felt the instant she felt the gentle bump of touchdown and heard the rubber-burning squeak of tires on tarmac had made her incredibly horny and once they had gotten to their room at the Marriott at nearly eleven-thirty that night, she had pounced on Sally and thus started another one of their marathon sex sessions which at one point featured the vibrator-that-could-be-mistaken-for-a-pipe-bomb.

When they had finally stopped at god-knows-what-time o'clock, Amy had slept the sleep of a carnally satisfied woman who also had another great blog entry idea: *Fear and Your Libido: How Surviving Can Lead to a Night of Great Passion.*

And unlike most nights, Amy had managed to turn her brain completely off. There had been no waking up in the dark room, ideas for her blog or podcast running rampant in her skull and forcing her to toss off the covers, get out of bed and spend the pre-dawn hours tapping away on her laptop. No. This time, Amy had slept soundly until the stirring of her fabulous girlfriend next to her woke her up sometime near ten o'clock. Amy had been amazed. She couldn't remember the last time she had slept that late. On weekends, on holidays, it just didn't happen. It couldn't have just been because her and Sally had stayed up until the wee hours having sex—that happened a lot and each time it did, Amy *still* would often awaken early.

No, Amy had determined, lying there in bed, watching Sally slowly awaken. No, she had slept late because somehow during her slumber her subconscious had told her brain that when you have a second chance at life, sometimes it's okay if you just remain in bed, sleeping next to the woman you love.

Because Amy was in love with Sally. She had known it since surviving the Event, when she had felt an overwhelming relief not only at being alive but at knowing she now had a chance at a long life with one Sally Lassiter.

And she was certain Sally was in love with her as well. Amy's soul told her that. But they hadn't said the words to each other yet.

Why? Amy had wondered as she had watched Sally's eyelids begin to flutter open before deciding it didn't matter. It would happen and it would happen soon.

Now, it was late Saturday morning and her and Sally had just finished brunch at what could only be described as a *boîte*. They had had the most delicious lobster omelets ever, washed down with superb mimosas and were now walking off all the calories by strolling along the Waterfront Trail.

"Hey!" Amy said as they walked past a shop selling crystals and gems just before turning onto Alaskan Way. "We've been together a month now."

Sally smiled.

"Really?"

"Four weeks ago yesterday we had our first date," Amy informed her.

"Oh my god, you're right!" Sally said. "Fuck, we packed a lot into one month."

"Our first *and* second trips together," Amy said.

"Our first and only fight," Sally added.

"No, no, no! That was our *second* fight!"

Sally stopped and looked at Amy, frowning.

"What was our first?" she asked.

"When you told me you weren't Jillian Ashley," Amy said.

"Oh, right."

They continued walking.

"Lots of incredible sex," Sally went on.

"Oh my god, *soooooo* much incredible sex!" Amy concurred. "God, when you took me on the beach like that!"

"After our first fight, no less," Sally reminded her.

"Oh, so that means it was our first make-up sex!"

"You're right again!"

"Not going to lie," Amy began, "but when I realized that you could make me come like that when I'm fully clothed…I started getting a little obsessed with you."

She decided to leave out the fact that her clit was pulsing even now remembering that night on the beach.

Sally laughed.

"What else?" she asked.

"I got one!" Amy enthused. "We both got recognized like superstar celebrities in that bookstore."

"That's right," Sally agreed. "And let's not forget the big one, baby. Almost dying in a fiery plane crash!"

"Definitely! Ooh! If we do this eleven more times we'll have a year together." Amy put her arm around Sally's waist and rested her head against Sally's shoulder as they walked. "Imagine…a whole year."

Sally put her own arm around Amy.

"I love that idea," she said.

They walked in silence for a bit and Amy could think of no time when she was happier.

After a moment, she said, "Well, let's see…two fights a month make twenty-four for the year. I don't know if that's good or bad."

Sally scoffed.

"My parents used to fight a lot more than that in a month before they got divorced. I think we'll be okay as long as you always admit I'm right."

Amy poked her girlfriend in the ribs.

"Or," she began, "we just agree right now that I'm always right." She stopped, turned Sally to face her and gave her a quick kiss. "I won't care who's right; just as long as we promise not to sleep apart again."

"Deal," Sally said and this time it was she who claimed Amy's lips for a kiss.

They treated themselves to ice cream cones bought from a vendor with a little cart in Waterfront Park and then they walked through the park looking at the sculptures and admiring the views across the bay.

When they were done there, Sally suggested they be rebels and have cocktails, even though it had only just turned eleven a.m. Amy used her phone to find the name and location of what looked to be a hipster rum bar on Seneca Street, which was just a couple of blocks ahead. Just as they turned onto that street, something caught Amy's eye.

"Oh, look! How gorgeous!"

In the window of a jewelry store was a stunning ruby and emerald necklace on display along with several other pieces including a couple of bracelets, a handful of engagement rings and three ladies watches. But the necklace was the star of the show.

"Do you think that's real?" Amy asked, in awe.

"I bet it is. This looks like the kind of shop that sells the good stuff."

Amy nodded, wondering where she would wear such a necklace. It would have to be an amazing occasion. Lesbian Podcast of the Year Awards (once she invented that), or something similar. Or when her and Sally celebrated their 120th month together.

Ten years.

The thought made Amy smile. It also made her eyes wander down to where several engagements rings in black velvet boxes shone like stars brought down from the firmament.

Chapter 42

God, that necklace is out of this world!

Amy had good taste in jewelry, Sally considered, eyeing the ruby and emerald masterpiece in the window. She tried to imagine owning it, actually having it in her jewelry collection. Then, she tried imagining what kind of occasion would merit her taking it out of whatever biometrically-accessed, 25-digit PIN, laser-grid-protected safe she would keep the necklace in, and wear it.

She had always thought that if she ever did start her own graphic design firm, that she would host a fabulous holiday party at the end of each year. That would be a good time to break out the necklace.

Or winning an Indigo Award—that would certainly be another occasion; especially once the pandemic was good and over and things like in-person awards ceremonies became a reality again.

Or maybe an anniversary. An anniversary with Amy.

Five years. Ten...

The thought caused a warm glow to bloom in her chest and a secret smile to play on her lips.

Sally knew she was in love with Amy. Had known it for a while now. Ever since the Incident. Okay, she considered, *maybe* she had known it even before then. At the very least, she had known her feelings towards Amy were heading in that direction. But it was the Incident which really brought it home for her. Being able to walk away from the airplane on legs which had felt like jelly because she had been so scared had made Sally so appreciative of being alive and though it was now a week since that emergency landing, Sally knew she still wanted her second chance at life to be spent with this workaholic caffeine addict standing by her side now on a street in Seattle.

And she knew Amy felt the same way; that Amy was in love with her also. It was in the way Amy looked at her; in the way Amy kissed her; in the way Amy refused to go to sleep each night unless some part of her body was touching Sally. They hadn't said the words yet, though. Was Amy waiting for her to say them first? Sally had often wondered that. For her own part, Sally was waiting for the perfect moment. She had almost said it yesterday when they were in the airport waiting to board their flight here to Seattle, but who says

"I love you" for the first time to someone in an airport? Might as well say it in a post office. And she had almost screamed it last night as she orgasmed for the fourth time, but she always thought that declarations of love made mid-orgasm were not to be trusted. Besides, that was a hell of an orgasm. The truth was, Sally loved *everybody* as she was rocked with that one.

She mentally shrugged.

They'd say it when they'd say it, she figured. In the end, they were just words. What mattered was how they felt and how they treated each other. If Amy *never* said it, Sally would still be content provided Amy continued looking at her the way she did, and kissed her the way she did, and insisted on drifting off to sleep while touching her.

Sally's eyes wandered around the jewelry store's window at some of the other items. The watches caught her attention and she reminded herself that her meddling mother's birthday was coming up. A watch would do nicely, even though what her mother really wanted was a doctor's lesbian daughter as a future daughter-in-law; but Sally would insist she settle for the watch.

Oh, how beautiful!

Sally's eyes had just alighted on the cluster of engagement rings in the window. There were seven of them and what Sally liked about them all was that even though they were clearly engagement rings, none of them were very traditional-looking. The jeweler had managed to craft diamond rings that had funky, contemporary designs that were still elegant and which used a variety of metals, sometimes in the same ring.

"These are so cool!" she muttered. "I love it when jewelry designers push the envelope!"

Amy nudged her.

"Let's go in! I really like their stuff and wouldn't mind seeing more. Ooh, maybe we can try some pieces on!"

"What? Really?"

"I *love* trying on jewelry!" Amy pressed. "Come on!"

But Sally hesitated.

"I don't want to waste their time, though," she said. This place didn't look like it was part of a chain, at least a chain she had ever heard of. And the pandemic had hit independent shops hard.

Sally didn't like the idea of getting a shopkeeper's hopes up for a sale only to end up with nothing.

She explained this to Amy who responded by giving her a quick kiss.

"You are just *soooooo* fucking sweet!" she exclaimed. "So we'll each buy something! Earrings or a bracelet or something. A memento from our trip to Seattle." She cocked an eyebrow. "Don't tell me I actually have to convince a woman to buy jewelry…"

Amy's plan made Sally feel better and she smiled.

"Alright, fine."

The shop was small but well-appointed and designed in a bright, minimalist style that was simultaneously couture but welcoming. They were the only customers and were greeted by a thin and beautiful woman with exotic features—Sally guessed North African—and who was dressed entirely in black. She was even taller than Sally, a fact made even more remarkable by the fact that she was wearing flats. And as soon as this woman made eye contact with her, Sally's gaydar started pinging.

"Welcome in," the woman said. "My name is Adilah; how can I help you?"

"Oh my god, that's such a pretty name!" Amy enthused.

Adilah blushed.

"Thank you; it's Moroccan," she said. Sally felt a little proud that her secret superpower of being able to correctly guess at least the geographic region of where a person was from was still working. "By the way, I've been vaccinated and so if you're more comfortable with your masks off, feel free."

"I'm Sally and this is Amy," Sally said, taking off her mask, feeling it was only fair to introduce themselves as well. "And we've both been vaccinated as well. We *love* that necklace in the window."

Adilah thanked them again and then said, "My wife designed it."

And score one for my gaydar!

"We also love those rings in the window!" Amy said.

"And I designed those," Adilah said, with a laugh. "You two are making my day! I do all the rings and Ekaterina does most everything else. Would you care to look at some of the rings?"

The rings…?

Sally looked at Amy who smiled and shrugged playfully.

"Why not?" Amy asked. "We're here." To Adilah, she said, "Yes, please."

"Water? Coffee? Champagne?" Adilah asked.

"Ooh, I didn't expect that!" Sally exclaimed. "I'd like some Champagne." She pointed at Amy. "She, however, will probably want all of the coffee you've got, including the grounds and, if you have them, the beans too."

Laughing, Amy playfully smacked Sally's arm.

"Shut up!" she said. Looking up at Adilah, Amy then said, "But, she's not entirely wrong…I actually will have coffee, please."

When Adilah shimmered away, Amy leaned closer to Sally.

"This doesn't weird you out, does it?" she asked.

"What?"

Amy sucked her bottom lip in between her teeth and shrugged.

"That I told her we'd like to see the rings," she began.

Sally shook her head.

"No, not at all," she said, hoping she sounded nonchalant. "We were admiring them, after all. It will be cool to see them up close."

Tell her now!

She just wanted to blurt it all out. Not only that she was in love with Amy but that, no, it does not "weird her out" that they were about to look at engagement rings just for fun. In fact, Sally wanted to tell her, they might as well try on rings because…

"I have coffee and Champagne?"

This came from another woman with exotic features—Sally guessed eastern European, maybe; a former Soviet bloc country, perhaps—who emerged from a back room carrying a silver tray bearing a mug of coffee and a flute of Champagne.

"Hi, I'm Ekaterina. I don't know how you take your coffee," she said in accented English, "but we do have cream and sugar I can bring out as well."

"Black is fine," Amy insisted.

"Cream and sugar impede the delivery of caffeine to her veins," Sally quipped.

"Ignore her," Amy said.

Ekaterina laughed.

"My wife told me that you were being teased about being a coffee addict and so I brought you these as well" she said, tapping a small packet on the tray. "From my own stash."

"Oh my god, Amy!" Sally said, eyeing the packet and laughing. "Those are perfect!"

Even Amy had to laugh.

It was a small packet of dark-chocolate-covered coffee beans. Amy thanked Ekaterina, picked up the candy and stuck her tongue out at Sally.

"Just for being a smart-ass, I'm not sharing these with you," she said, tearing open the small plastic bag and popping a bean into her mouth.

"You look very familiar," Ekaterina said, after eyeing Sally for a few moments. "Have you been in here before?"

"This is Jillian Ashley, top lesbian author," Amy hurriedly supplied and then gave Sally a snarky look. "Perhaps you've seen her interview on a podcast some caffeine-addicted woman did."

Sally couldn't help but laugh at Amy's particular form of revenge. However, she also resolved that tonight, in bed, she was going to tease Amy to within an inch of her life before letting her come.

Ekaterina's eyes bulged.

"Oh my god, you're right!" she exclaimed. "I love your books!" She then turned to Amy. "And you're the one who interviewed her! I love your show!"

Adilah returned then.

"Honey," Ekaterina said, turning to her, "this is that writer I'm always reading, Jillian Ashley!"

"My real name is Sally, though," Sally added.

Adilah smiled.

"Well!" she began. "I don't read as much as my wife but let me thank you nonetheless. Whenever Ekaterina reads one of your books…let's just say I end up getting entertained as well."

All four women laughed. A few moments later, Adilah arranged a collection of engagement rings on a small table, along with a handful of bracelets which both Sally and Amy also wanted to see.

Again, going for nonchalance, Sally picked up a bracelet and tried it on, turning her wrist this way and that in order to make the piece of jewelry catch the light from various angles, but her eyes kept wandering to the array of engagement rings Adilah had brought out. In addition to the handful from the window display, there were several others Adilah had produced from one of the glass display cases in the store.

She felt Amy slip her arm around her waist and snuggle up next to her.

"So, which one do you think I would like?" Amy asked.

"Hmm?"

"The rings," Amy said. "Which one?"

That was almost too easy. Sally had known which one would catch Amy's eye the instant Adilah had set them all down.

"That one," Sally said, pointing to a platinum swirl tension ring with a dazzling pear-shaped diamond.

Amy looked up at her, beaming her megawatt smile.

"How did you know?"

"That swirl design. It's got energy and movement," Sally answered. "That's the ring of a woman whose blood is seventy-five percent caffeine and who sleep two hours a night."

Amy giggled.

"You're silly," she said.

"But right. Your turn."

Amy rolled her eyes.

"No brainer!"

"Is that right? How so?"

"Well, you're an artist, and artists typically like things that aren't traditional or expected…"

"Okaaaay…"

"And there's a lot of non-traditional and unexpected rings on the table," Amy went on.

"True," Sally agreed with a nod.

Amy then pointed to a particular ring before saying, "But you also drive a BMW and your carry-on luggage is made by Coach, and so I'm going to choose the one with the big, fat honker of a diamond."

***

In all her life, Sally had never seen such a perfect, pink, glistening and swollen pussy.

After their trip to the jewelry store—walking out with a new bracelet for Sally and a new necklace for Amy—they decided to head back to the hotel to change clothes. What had started as a gorgeous morning had turned into a gray and drizzly afternoon and like typical Southern California women, neither Sally nor Amy was dressed for it.

Of course, in the privacy of their hotel room, with clothes being taken off with the intention of changing into warmer outfits, it was perhaps inevitable that they ended up in bed, completely nude, hands and mouths all over each other.

But Sally had taken control early, subduing Amy by topping her and then binding her wrists with the tights Amy had selected to change into but hadn't gotten around to putting on.

"Complain once," Sally had whispered into Amy's ear, "and you won't get to go down on me again until we get back to Carlsbad."

That was an hour ago.

Since then, Sally had taken her time sucking and kneading Amy's breasts, leaving new bite marks on her thighs and licking very softly, very carefully, *around* Amy's pussy until Amy was now a gasping, moaning, quivering and compliant little pet, and her pussy was this perfect, pink, glistening and swollen work of art just inches from Sally's face.

Sally puckered her lips and blew a soft breath on Amy's sex.

It had the desired effect.

"Oh my fuck!" Amy shouted as her pussy, in reaction to the gust of breath, convulsed quickly three times and her clit visibly pulsed several times more. She groaned and Sally recognized it as the groan of a woman whose orgasm was *right there* but still unleashed. Amy's hips gyrated, pushing her ass further into the mattress as she obviously tried to contend with the unreleased pleasure building up inside her.

Sally's hand was under that ass, catching in her palm the tiny rivulets of clear arousal that had been streaming from Amy's pussy for quite a while now.

"Oh my god, that was a big one, baby!" Sally said as her girlfriend's center pushed out a particularly thick stream of lubrication. It was cloudier than what had come out before, a sure sign that the dam was about to burst.

"I'm so fucking close!" Amy moaned.

So was Sally. All this time teasing Amy had made her own center molten, and each time she witnessed Amy's clit jump, her own clit did so as well. Her thighs were slick and the few times she had reached between her legs to play a bit with herself, she'd had to stop because she had plans for this huge orgasm building up.

"Almost time to put you out of your misery," she told Amy.

"Oh, thank fuck!" Amy sighed.

Sally carefully slid her hand out from under Amy's ass and brought it up to her girlfriend's chest. Turning her hand over, she coated Amy right nipple with the wetness she had collected and then brought her mouth down to suck the rock-hard bud that was now flavored with Amy's inner essence, and this was making tiny fireworks explode between her legs, causing her to moan as she worked her tongue around the nipple.

When she'd had enough, she rose and quickly straddled Amy's face, slowly lowering her dripping pussy until she felt Amy's hungry lips and tongue make contact and get to work.

Gripping the headboard, Sally came almost instantly, her clit a prisoner between Amy's lips.

"A-MEEEEE! Fuuuuuuuck!" she screamed at the release, not caring if anyone outside their room heard her.

The pleasure was soul-wrenchingly immense, so much so that her hips bucked as she rode Amy's face while the come poured out of her and her entire body was shattered joyfully, the orgasm in complete control of her now.

Before the second one hit, she leaned back, holding on to the headboard with one hand and finding Amy's pussy with the other, zeroing in on Amy's clit. Then, just as that second orgasm rocketed through Sally, she heard Amy give a startled, high-pitched moan that was stifled by virtue of Sally's throbbing pussy still covering her mouth.

And then Amy was coming. Sally felt a gush of warm liquid strike her hand, felt Amy's pelvis start quaking. In throes of her own second orgasm, Sally let Amy scream into her pussy for a few seconds before she raised herself off Amy's face.

"Fuuuuuuck!" Amy yelled. "Oh, FUCK! Babe…Fuck…Babe!"

Feeling how incredibly wet things were between her girlfriend's legs, Sally now wanted her face down there. Quick as a flash, she turned herself around to sixty-nine Amy. Easily, three of her fingers slid in, squeezed instantly by Amy's tight inner walls. She kept them inside until Amy came again and then she removed the fingers. They were completely coated with sticky, ropy strands of Amy's come and she shoved them into her mouth as if she was starving.

    And that's how she came the third time: her clit once more being pulled on by Amy's lips, her mouth stuffed with three fingers covered in the tangy sweetness that came from deep within this woman she loved.

Chapter 43

Pulling on the same green tights which had recently been binding her wrists, Amy made her decision.

She only needed time to execute her plan. But she was certain she could get that time as long as she didn't act suspicious.

By now, they were both starving, even though, Amy considered with a secret smile as she stood up from the edge of the bed and finished pulling up her tights, she could still taste Sally in her mouth, her girlfriend's come still coating her throat. She had certainly gotten her fill during their sexcapades just now. But she needed real food now.

After they were both dressed more warmly, they left the hotel. The plan was to head to Pacific Place, a shopping mall here in the downtown area. There was a chowder restaurant in there they were both eager to try and then afterwards they would wander the mall a bit.

As soon as they got to the mall, Amy started looking around, trying to find the means by which she would put her plan into motion. She spotted it as they were riding the escalators up to the third floor, en route to the restaurant. Looking down to the first floor, she saw a high-end lingerie store and an idea came to her.

Perfect.

Now, she just needed to convince Sally to unwittingly be a pawn in her scheme.

"So, I was thinking," she began about fifteen minutes later in the restaurant, a delicious seafood bisque served in a bread bowl in front of her on their table. "I saw a lingerie store downstairs when we came in…"

"Ooh," Sally said, biting her lip. "I like where this is going."

Amy laughed.

"Well, I want to get something special for tonight," she said. "But I want it to be a secret until I reveal it later."

"Oh, so you want to split up after this?"

"Yeah."

"That's perfect, actually," Sally said. "I was going to suggest the same thing!"

"Really?"

"Yeah, I noticed this place has an art supply store and I thought maybe I'd wander around in it. You know, see if I can find anything worth buying. But I was worried it might be a little boring for you and so I was going to suggest we kind of do our own thing for a while and meet up afterwards."

Excellent!

"Love it!" Amy said. "Absence makes the heart grow fonder and all that."

Sally laughed.

"Well, I think they meant that for when lovers are a zillion miles apart and not away from each other for only an hour or so."

"Whatever. I know you start missing me every time I get up to go pee."

"Desperately," Sally said, smirking. "And when you're gone for the length of a shower, I actually start pulling my hair out."

Amy now had the means to execute her plan and she was suddenly super excited to start acting on it. The bisque was amazing and the bread bowl was divine but she could barely enjoy it because of how anxious she was to get this meal over with. But she forced herself to outwardly display calm. She didn't want Sally getting suspicious. After all, Sally was a clever woman and "shopping for lingerie" was hardly a reason for a person to wolf down food as if she was running late to catch an airplane.

Finally, though, they were done.

"Okay, then," Amy began, as they stood outside the restaurant. "Have fun shopping for whatever."

"You too," Sally said. "Keep in mind, I like white."

Amy frowned.

"Huh?"

"The lingerie," Sally supplied. "You know how I love white. Every time I see you in that white bralette you have we always end up having sex."

"Right! The lingerie!" Amy nodded. "And you hate red," she added, remembering Sally mentioning that to her sometime soon after they started dating.

"Can't stand it!"

Amy tapped the side of her head.

"Got it," she said. "So…meet up again in an hour?"

Sally seemed to consider that for a moment.

"Yeah, an hour sounds right," she answered. "I'll, uh, text you and find out where you are."

"Perfect!"

They kissed before parting.

"See you!" Amy said, as Sally started walking in the opposite direction.

"See you!" Sally called back.

Once she was certain that Sally wasn't going to turn around again, Amy started power-walking to the nearest down escalator while simultaneously opening the Lyft app on her phone. Once on the escalator, she walked rather than rode down it.

"Excuse me," she said, zipping past some other passengers who apparently did not have secret missions to accomplish and were just sedately riding the escalator down like morons. Even as she sped down the conveyance, Amy was still tapping away in the Lyft app and by the time she reached the first floor of the mall again she had her ride confirmed. Someone named Shirley driving a blue Sentra was going to meet her in three minutes. Amy hoped Shirley wouldn't be late.

But Shirley was there as promised.

"Short trip," the driver commented once Amy was inside.

"Yeah, well…I'm in rush," Amy told her.

"Nice day for a stroll, though," Shirley went on, and Amy rolled her eyes. A chatty driver she could do without. And was Shirley delusional? Nice day? Amy supposed. For *Seattle*, which wasn't setting the bar very high. Give her Carlsbad weather any day.

The short drive could have been shorter. But just like in the movies, when the heroine is in the back of the cab, rushing to get somewhere, a delivery truck was temporarily blocking traffic on Pike Street while it pulled out of a loading bay. Shirley would have told Amy the delay was only two minutes, but to Amy, it felt like ten. During the hold-up, Amy was only vaguely aware of Shirley telling her something about her grandkids. Or was it something about her dog? Amy didn't care either way as she sat stewing in the back seat, silently cursing the ancestors of the truck driver and wondering if—also like in the movies—she should dramatically say, "I'll walk from here!", shove some money in the driver's hand and jump out of the car in order to race down the city streets on foot to her destination. After all, she not only had her secret mission to accomplish, but she also had to get back to the mall to find and buy some sexy white lingerie. She wasn't made of time!

Finally, they resumed moving and it was only a minute after that when Shirley stopped the car again, this time at journey's end.

"Thanks.Bye.Haveaniceday." Amy uttered, opening the back door the microsecond the car ceased moving, hopping out onto the sidewalk.

As soon as Amy entered the shop, Adilah and Ekaterina both turned to her and both smiled in recognition.

"Hi! Welcome back!" Adilah greeted her.

"Hi," Amy said, feeling incredibly excited. She was finally here and ready to change her life.

"Did you forget something from earlier?" Ekaterina asked.

"Yes," Amy said. "A ring. The woman I was in here with earlier? I want to marry her."

Adilah's hands flew to her face and even from where she was standing, Amy could tell the woman's eyes were watering.

"Jillian Ashley?" Ekaterina exclaimed, her eyes wide.

Amy laughed. If they only knew, she considered. If they only knew about how she had felt the first time she saw "Jillian Ashley" on her computer monitor just prior to recording the podcast. How her stomach had flipped and how it was as if her heart had started speaking to her, telling her, "This is what I want!"

About how she knew—just *knew*—normal life had stopped for her the moment "Jillian Ashley" had walked into La Vida Mocha that Friday evening one month ago.

About how "Jillian Ashley" turned out not to be Jillian Ashley and how, even though it upset her initially, she also knew there was no way she was going to let Sally Lassiter out of her life because even after having spent only just a few hours with her that first night, she was already in too deep.

"That's amazing!" Adilah said, coming from behind the counter and rushing to embrace Amy, who felt like a munchkin in her arms because Adilah was supermodel-tall.

Just like my soon-to-be fiancée.

"Did you know which ring you want?" Adilah asked her.

"Yes, please," Amy said, wiping a stray tear which had trickled from her left eye. "That one with the princess diamond and the two tiny sapphires in the band?"

She suddenly became worried that someone else might have bought it. Was that possible? It was Saturday, after all…People shopped on Saturday. But was Saturday a big engagement ring-buying day? She had no idea.

But Adilah was nodding. "I remember you pointing that out to her. I thought you two were so funny." She hooked her arm through Amy's and led her to one of the glass display cases. "I *knew* you'd end up getting married! The way she looks at you!"

"God, yes!" Ekaterina chimed in. "You're a lucky girl!"

Amy smiled.

"I know," she said.

Adilah had the ring brought out and in front of Amy in a few moments.

Staring at the stunning piece of jewelry in its little velvet box, Amy grinned from ear to ear. This was going to look so amazing on Sally's hand! Amy's heart started fluttering as she imagined seeing Sally wearing this every day from now on, knowing what it signified, knowing what it represented.

She heard the shop's door open but didn't bother turning around. Another customer, no doubt. Probably some guy wanting to buy this very ring for his girlfriend.

Too late, loser! This ring is mine! Hope you have a second choice! I'm sure she'll still love you.

Looking back up at Adilah, Amy said, "I'll take—" but then stopped. Adilah's mouth was wide open and she was staring at a point behind Amy. Next to her, Ekaterina pretty much had the same expression on her face.

Amy turned and then yelped.

Sally was standing there, looking as shocked as someone who had just seen their eighty-year-old grandmother do a triple Lutz on an ice skating rink.

"What are you doing here?" Sally eventually asked.

"Um…" Amy said, hoping her body was effectively blocking the ring and box on the counter. "Um…Wait! What are you doing here?"

"Um…" Sally began, blushing. "Wait! I asked you first!"

Shit!

Sally had her there. That's the way the game was played.

"What are you hiding?" Sally then asked.

"Nothing!" Amy said, shifting her body a little to the left and then rolling her eyes at how ridiculous she was. She certainly did not have a future being a spy or a master criminal.

Sally slowly approached and a wave of disappointment crashed through Amy. This was so not how she wanted Sally to see the ring for the first time. Though, technically, Amy realized, it would be the *second* time.

When the taller Sally was directly in front of Amy, she peeked over Amy's shoulder.

Amy pouted.

Should have worn heels today!

That still would have left her a few inches too short, she considered, but at least it would have made her feel as if she had a fighting chance of blocking Sally's view.

"Oh my god!" Sally exclaimed, her hands flying to her face just like Adilah's had a short while ago. Sally looked at Amy and Amy could see tears welling in her eyes. "Babe…"

But Amy interrupted her.

"I wanted it to be a surprise!" she insisted. "Sorry."

Sally took hold of Amy's shoulders.

"Sorry?" she asked, chuckling. "Oh my god, don't ever say that! Well, except when you're wrong but, trust me, you are *soooooo* not wrong now! Baby, I came here to do the same thing!"

Amy blinked.

Did she just hear what she thought she just heard?

So, wait…that means…

"You came here to buy me an engagement ring?" she asked, staring up at Sally.

Sally nodded.

"I also wanted it to be a surprise," she said. "After we split up in the mall, I walked over here as fast as I could."

Amy smirked.

"Should have taken a car, like I did."

Sally laughed.

"I should have," she concurred. "Anyway…Amy…You need to be my wife! And I need to be yours! It can't be any other way!"

"Oh my god, I love you!" Amy squealed, wrapping her arms around Sally.

"I love you too!" Sally said, holding Amy tight. "You have no idea how much."

Sniffling, tears streaming down her face, Amy looked up at her. "I do know how much because I feel the exact same way."

And then they were kissing passionately and throughout it, Amy felt her soul connecting with Sally's.

"Oh my god, I can't take anymore!"

Amy and Sally both looked over at Ekaterina, who was slumped on the top of the display case, her head buried in her arms. Adilah started rubbing her back. She was sniffling also and produced a tissue from the pocket of her slacks with which she started dabbing at her eyes.

The ring Amy bought for Sally fit perfectly, but the one Sally bought for Amy needed to be sized down; however, Adilah made Hector—a middle-aged man who appeared from the back room when Adilah called out to him and who apparently took care of such things—stop whatever it was he was working on to take care of the sizing immediately.

"I want to see the two of you walk out of here with those rings on!" Adilah said.

And so, less than twenty minutes later, Amy and Sally were walking out of the jewelry shop—after tearful hugs with Adilah and Ekaterina—newly engaged and wearing the hardware to prove it.

Amy's usually bare left hand felt strange with the addition of her engagement ring…

My engagement ring!

…but she knew she'd get used to it. Besides, someday another ring would be added to that same finger.

"So…what do you want to do now, *fiancée*?" Sally asked.

"Head back to the mall," Amy answered quickly.

"Really?"

"Yes, please. I believe I promised you some sexy white lingerie…"

Epilogue
Eight months later

"Oh my god, we really have to go, baby!" Sally groaned. It was true. Malibu wasn't exactly just up the street. If traffic was bad—and this was California, after all—it could take close to three hours to drive to Max's new house.

But Amy did not seem too inclined to relinquish her current position: head between Sally's legs, using the flat of her tongue to lick the flesh around Sally's pussy, which was still recovering from another orgasm. As Amy's tongue neared Sally's buzzing clit, Sally flinched a little because the bud was so sensitive now. But Amy expertly avoided it.

"We should just…" Amy began, giving Sally's wet sex a kiss "…take a helicopter…" another kiss. "We…" another kiss, this time just missing Sally's clit "…can afford it."

And then Sally felt herself being penetrated again by that magnificent tongue and she reached down to grab fistfuls of Amy's hair, holding her fiancée's head tight against her center which was starting to tell her that it wanted another release.

Yes…a helicopter…

They could afford it; there was no doubt about that.

Shortly after returning from Seattle (thankfully without any near-death drama on the airplane) Max had called Sally and told her that Netflix had contacted him. Well, technically, Netflix had contacted *Jillian,* wanting to meet *Jillian* to discuss creating a series based on the *Gotham* books, written by *Jillian.* At least, so they thought.

"You're not about to suggest what I think you're about suggest, are you?" Sally had asked.

"It could totally work!" Max insisted, and then explained. Sally would meet with the Netflix people and simply pretend to be the author of the books, just like she was already doing.

"Already doing?" Sally had exclaimed. "Max, I get recognized *sometimes* wherever lesbians happen to shop! A grocery store or when I'm buying shoes! I sign an autograph, I pose for a selfie with the person and that's it! Now, you're talking about meeting with movie executives!"

Max had assured her it would be a piece of cake. She'd have lunch with them, they'd suck up to her a bit and in the end she'd tell them she needed to consider it.

"Besides, there could be a lot of money involved, Sally. I spoke with my lawyer and she's pretty sure that if we can get Jillian named as an executive producer on the show, the payday will easily reach seven figures. Twenty percent of which, might I remind you, would be yours."

"She wants thirty!" Amy had jumped in, taking the phone away from Sally. She had been sitting right next to Sally on the sofa and had been able to follow the conversation.

"Fine," Max had agreed. "But she signs nothing and lets me and Nora take care of all the negotiations behind the scenes."

"Fine," Amy had said, handing the phone back to Sally.

When the call eventually ended, Sally had looked over at Amy with a cocked eyebrow.

"Shall I just let the two of you plan the rest of my life?" she had asked.

"Babe, with all that money, you can open your own graphic design company just like you want!"

That was true. And, Sally had considered, it would also provide a nice financial cushion for her and Amy to start their married life with.

And Max had been right. The initial meeting with the Netflix people had been a breeze. It had taken place in Bel Air over lunch in a posh hotel's café and was, basically, just three executives—all women; all gay—treating Sally like she was a star athlete they were trying to recruit for their NCAA basketball team.

Once that was done, Max's lawyer, Nora, handled all the negotiations—ostensibly on behalf of Sally—and a deal was eventually struck. And suddenly, Sally and Amy had helicopter money.

Now, today, Sally and Amy were due at Max's place in Malibu—purchased with his Netflix money—in order to watch the premier of the first episode of the new show. They were then going to spend the weekend up there.

But first…

Sally arched her back as she came undone again, her pussy a chaotic orgy of pleasure.

"God, BABY!" she called out, the last coherent words she was able to speak during the entirety of the climax because after that it was just grunts, moans and high-pitched squeals.

This was all her fault, she realized as she flattened her back onto the mattress once the tidal wave passed. She had wanted to dress today with a bit of edgy sexiness and so had chosen a black lace bodysuit that was going to be paired with artfully torn skinny jeans and a black fitted blazer. But once Amy had gotten a look at her in the bodysuit, before she'd had a chance to put on her jeans, it was game over. Amy had pushed her back onto the bed, opened her legs, unsnapped the crotch of the bodysuit and proceeded to turn Sally into a molten puddle of womanliness.

"Now, we can leave," Amy declared, getting up.

***

"*Four* shots of espresso?" the pretty barista asked when Sally and Amy stopped for coffee in Malibu before driving the rest of the way to Max's place. Because Amy had delayed their departure from Carlsbad by eating her out twice—not that she was complaining—Sally had insisted that they hit the road without stopping at La Vida Mocha for a cup of Amy's Jet Fuel. But once in the Malibu city limits, Amy had complained of withdrawal symptoms and begged Sally to stop.

"Yes, please," Amy told the barista. "And make it really hot, too."

The barista, her mouth open in apparent disbelief, shook her head and rang up the order.

"Coffee with four shots, Troy!" she called out to the guy working the machines.

Troy looked up from what he was doing.

"*Four?*"

Sally had to laugh. But with her drink in hand a few moments later, Amy seemed perfectly content and they completed the trek to Max's house, which was only another five minutes away.

"Hiiiiii!" Tiffany greeted, opening the door of the beach house and hugging both Sally and Amy.

Sally had to marvel at this turn of events. When she had first pestered Max about calling Tiffany, she figured one or two dates, tops—if he even called. Now, Tiffany was a fixture in his life and had her own left hand hardware to prove it.

"Max!" Amy called out as soon as they entered the house. "You'd better have my special drink ready! It was a long drive!"

Max appeared from somewhere—Sally still hadn't quite mapped out in her head the layout of this new place of his. She seemed to remember, though, that the bar was somewhere in that general direction. He was carrying two margarita glasses of Amy's special drink, which he still hadn't given up the recipe for and which Sally now drank as well.

"Yeah, yeah, yeah," he said, handing the cocktails to his guests. "By the way, what took you so long?"

"She refused to call a helicopter," Amy stated.

Sally laughed.

"Oh my god, you two!"

Max stared at her.

"What is the point of having money if you don't use it for helicopters?"

"Oh, I don't know, Max…I just thought Amy and I could use it to plan our wedding, buy our first house together and, oh yeah, I forgot…I'm opening my own design firm."

Max turned to Amy.

"I hope you're more sensible with your newfound success," he said. He was referring to the fact that *Lesbeing—the Podcast* was now featured on Canada's OutTV. The network had told Amy that her personality and her quirky discussion topics about what being a lesbian in the twenty-first century is like put her show a cut above others and that it deserved a wider audience. They especially liked, for instance, the episode where she spoke with a TSA representative about the types of vibrators, dildos and other pleasure toys a woman could pack in her carry-on luggage.

"Helicopters for me all the way, babe," Amy said, raising her glass to him.

Max groaned.

"How many times do I have to ask you lesbians to stop calling me 'babe'?"

"Sorry, babe," Amy said.

Sally laughed. She loved how close Amy had become with him, teasing him the exact same way she did.

"Everything is set up, honey!" This came from Tiffany who appeared from another room. Max gestured for his guest to follow his fiancée.

"I love this outfit!" Tiffany said, taking Sally's arm as they walked.

"Thank you," Sally said. "Be warned, though, it drives women crazy!"

"And she loves it!" Amy said.

They all ended up in the living room, furnished in Max's typical mix of mid-century and art deco styles, though Sally could definitely see Tiffany's influence on the décor now in the form of some of the throw cushions on the sofa and in the choice of the lighting fixtures. There were also more houseplants than Max used to have back in Oceanside.

On a big screen TV mounted to the wall, Sally saw that Netflix was open to the start page for the first episode of the series based on Max's Jillian Ashley books. The teaser image was of the two yummy actresses playing Marisol and Karen, in bed together, facing one another as if having a heart-to-heart.

Sally felt herself getting excited. The *New York Times* had reviewed the first four episodes of the series and given it excellent marks. She had even been interviewed by the *Times* as part of that review and—entirely without Max's help—had managed to come off sounding like the top lesfic author the whole world assumed she was.

"Sweetie, I'm so proud of you," Tiffany told Max as they all sat down. She had been let in on the secret, Max deciding he trusted her enough. After all, they were sharing a life together now.

Snuggling on the sofa with Amy, Sally felt happier than she had ever been. Her and Amy had decided to wait until they received word from all their loved ones—both family and friends—that they had been vaccinated, and until the pandemic was well and truly over, or at least over enough that they could plan the wedding they really wanted, *where* they wanted it. But Sally didn't mind having a long engagement. Yes, she was anxious to marry this marvelous woman in her arms now but the only thing which mattered to her was that every day she got to wake up beside her soulmate and every night she drifted off to the uncertain dreamland of sleep knowing that her real life dream—that of having a woman in her life whom she would be rich or poor with; warm or cold with; fed or famished with;

sheltered or homeless with, was next to her on the mattress, making sure she was touching Sally in some way as she herself fell to sleep.

Sally felt Amy snuggle even closer with her.

"Comfortable?" Amy asked.

"Perfectly," Sally replied, stroking Amy's arm. "Hey."

"Mmm?"

"I love you, future wife."

Amy chuckled.

"And I love you, future wife."

THE END

Thank you so much for reading *Falling for Jillian Ashley*!
If you liked it, please consider writing a review, especially on Amazon! Reviews are super important to independent authors, and we love getting feedback from our readers.

Follow me on Twitter at *@kanelesfic* for updates on the next novel in the series, which I have already started. It's about my new favorite doctor, Ainsley *and* my new favorite realtor, Rachel.
Also follow me on Goodreads at *sabrina_kane*.

If you'd like, feel free to drop me an email at thekanemutiny@gmail.com

Made in United States
Troutdale, OR
04/27/2025